KU-604-328

Distant Images

Praise for Audrey Howard's novels

'Howard's enjoyable 19th-century historical romance of crossed love shines out.'

Daily Mail

'Her thousands of fans recognise the artistry of a true story-teller.'

Lancashire Life

'Poignant and well-plotted, this is the book to curl up with to shut out troubles.'

Woman's Realm

'This saga is, like all of Audrey Howard's books, compelling and memorable . . . a joy to read.'

Historical Novels Review

By the same author in paperback

The Mallow Years
Shining Threads
A Day Will Come
All the Dear Faces
There Is No Parting
The Woman from Browhead
Echo of Another Time
The Silence of Strangers
A World of Difference
Promises Lost
The Shadowed Hills
Strand of Dreams
Tomorrow's Memories
Not a Bird Will Sing
When Morning Comes
Beyond the Shining Water
Angel Meadow
Rivers of the Heart
The Seasons Will Pass
A Place Called Hope
Annie's Girl
Whispers on the Water
A Flower in Season
Painted Highway
Reflections from the Past

About the author

Audrey Howard was born in Liverpool in 1929 and grew up in St Anne's on Sea. Before she began to write she had a variety of jobs, among them hairdresser, model, shop assistant, cleaner and civil servant. In 1981, living in Australia, she wrote the first of more than thirty bestselling novels.

AUDREY HOWARD

Distant Images

HODDER

Copyright © 2004 by Audrey Howard

First published in Great Britain in 2004 by Hodder and Stoughton
First published in paperback in 2005 by Hodder and Stoughton
A division of Hodder Headline

The right of Audrey Howard to be identified as the Author
of the Work has been asserted by her in accordance
with the Copyright, Designs and Patents Act 1988.

6

All rights reserved. No part of this publication may be reproduced,
stored in a retrieval system, or transmitted, in any form or by any
means without the prior written permission of the publisher,
nor be otherwise circulated in any form of binding or cover other
than that in which it is published and without a similar condition
being imposed on the subsequent purchaser.

All characters in this publication are fictitious and any resemblance
to real persons, living or dead, is purely coincidental.

A CIP catalogue record for this title
is available from the British Library

ISBN 978 0 340 82406 1

Typeset in Monotype Plantin Light by
Hewer Text Ltd, Edinburgh
Printed and bound by
Mackays of Chatham Ltd, Chatham, Kent

Hodder Headline's policy is to use papers that are natural,
renewable and recyclable products and made from wood
grown in sustainable forests. The logging and manufacturing
processes are expected to conform to the environmental
regulations of the country of origin.

Hodder and Stoughton Ltd
A division of Hodder Headline
338 Euston Road
London NW1 3BH

I

She saw him the moment she entered the ballroom and her first thought as their eyes met was, it really does happen! She had read many novels, most recently *Diana of the Crossways* by Mr Meredith where the hero and heroine fell in love at first sight. Though like most young women she was a romantic at heart she had not believed it could really happen. She was wrong!

He was one of the cavalry officers leaning against the far wall. A table ran along its length, laden with bottles of champagne, Madeira, sherry, cut-crystal bowls containing punch and dozens of matching glasses waiting to be filled by uniformed flunkeys wearing white wigs and stockings. He was drinking champagne, an expression of utter boredom on his indecently handsome face, an expression that altered dramatically when his eyes met hers. He was dark, dark as the gypsies who wandered through the villages scattered about St Helens, selling pegs and sprigs of heather and offering to tell your fortune if you crossed their palms with silver. His hair was almost black, like the smooth wing of a blackbird, but it was his eyes that held her attention. They were a vivid, startling blue, heavily fringed with thick black lashes above which his eyebrows swooped fiercely. The shade of blue was one she had never before seen, at least in a man's eyes. It was the colour of the speedwell that grew in the wall at home, or was it the cornflowers that carpeted the meadows surrounding the park in which Lantern Hill stood? She didn't know, nor did she care, for he was the most beautiful young man she had ever seen.

As was always the case when the family entered the ball-room, or indeed *any* room, the two young daughters became the focus of everyone's scrutiny, male or female. They walked a little way ahead of their parents, though walking hardly described the way they moved, for they seemed to glide effortlessly, their expensively shod feet barely touching the polished ballroom floor.

"Great God, Dicky," drawled the tall, immaculately turned-out cavalry officer whose glance had captured one of them, "who is that glorious creature?"

"Which one?"

"Well, either would do but I must admit to being rather smitten with the one in the pink dress."

"My dear chap, you have as much chance of dancing with Mrs Langtry as you have of getting one of those two beauties on the floor. Their father is like a dragon and well known for his animosity to any man who shows an interest in them. Their would-be suitors are legion."

"I saw her once, you know, when she was in her prime."

"Who?"

"The Jersey Lily. God, she was sublime, but these two compare very favourably, particularly the one in pink." The officer drew deeply on his cigar and his eyes narrowed spec-ulatively but Dicky laid a cautionary hand on his arm.

"Hugh, I'm warning you, don't go charging in there in your usual high-handed fashion. Not unless you want a bloody nose from their father. He has a fiendish temper. Find someone who knows them and ask to be properly introduced."

"Who are they? Their names, man?"

"They're the Goodwin twins, Beth and Milly. The most popular and eligible young women in Lancashire. Not only are they lovely but they will be very wealthy, for their father owns God knows how many factories, glass works, brick works and other business concerns too numerous to mention."

"Of the manufacturing class then?"

"Yes, and he's aiming for a member of the peerage at the very least for both of them. Come to think of it you might have a chance. But you'd have to mind your manners."

"Would I, by jove! Well, I can be very charming when I choose, Dicky, old boy and—"

"Here's a chap who might be able to help you," Dicky interrupted as a third officer joined them, as tall as they were and, like them, wearing the full dress uniform of their regiment, the 3rd Battalion of the King's Regiment (St Helens), which was stationed near Longworth. His scarlet jacket had a high collar cut square in front and hooked closely beneath his proudly lifted chin. Gold braid adorned it and the blue facing of the cuffs. A blue sash was draped over his left shoulder, ending in a fringe level with the bottom of his tunic. His trousers were dark blue with a gold stripe down the outside of each leg and a red leather belt was strapped to his lean waist. His buttons gleamed, as did his eyes, and his teeth shone white in his brown face, for the regiment had only recently returned from Egypt to where the army had retreated after the fall of Khartoum two years ago. His brother officers, many of whom were dancing, were just as colourfully and magnificently turned out, surpassing even the fashionable and expensively dressed ladies. He was attractive, his hair the colour of dark chocolate, straight and heavy and, since he despised the pomade most of the gentlemen of the day used, was always falling over his brow. He was tall, wide-shouldered, his waist and hips slender and his long legs were in perfect proportion to the rest of his body.

"Help you with what, Hugh?" he enquired languidly, for it was the fashion among the officers to be languid.

"You know the Goodwin family, don't you, Todd? Aren't you connected with them in some way?"

Lieutenant Todd Woodruff smiled as he reached for a glass

of champagne, taking a sip before he answered. "I am. My mother is their housekeeper and has been for many years. I was brought up with Beth and Milly and it's thanks to Noah Goodwin I was able to buy my commission."

"You don't say, old boy. How very intriguing," drawled Captain Hugh Charles Thornley, sixteenth baron in a line that stretched back into the dim and distant days of Henry VII and who to his knowledge had never had anything to do with the son of a housekeeper. Each baron had married money and once there had been land in Cheshire, Yorkshire and Scotland, but all that had gone, along with their great wealth, gambled away by this man's father. All they owned now was their ancestral home at Thornley Green and the rents that the land provided. Hugh, Lord Thornley had chosen the army as his career. Generations of Thornleys had been distinguished for their military prowess. Indeed he himself had fought courageously in the Boer War six years ago. He was recklessly daring, wild and dashing, seemingly unaware of danger to himself and the men he led, and his mother repeatedly begged him to come home and look after his inheritance but so far he had resisted. Though it caused great hardship Lady Thornley managed to supply him with a small allowance just big enough to pay his mess bills. He was a gambler, like his father, but, unlike his father, a lucky one and so far what he won kept him in the style expected of a captain in a cavalry regiment. Since he had reached the age of eighteen his mother had been on the lookout for a suitable, *wealthy* young bride for him. Of his own class, naturally, which was well bred, well polished, privileged and cultured. None she had presented for his inspection had yet met his high standards!

"Perhaps you could present me to them," he drawled, helping himself to another glass of champagne. He had been aware that Todd Woodruff came from a less privileged background than his own, but then didn't all his brother officers? He was not at all sure he cared to be associated with a man whose mother was a mere housekeeper. Still, if it got him into the group of laughing, chattering guests, one of whose daughters he had taken a fancy to he knew he must remain civil. Once he had her on the ballroom floor he would have no need to remain with them. He would whisk her off to some quiet corner with a bottle of champagne and two glasses and engage in the dalliance that was the stuff of life to him!

The party of five that had entered the room was soon surrounded by a dozen people, most of them elderly, for Abby and Noah Goodwin, Abby forty and Noah approaching fifty, had a great many friends. Besides the two exquisite girls and their parents there was a man who seemed to be in his late twenties or early thirties. He was tall, lean, with an athlete's build, and those who had visited the great seaport of Liverpool and seen the diverse nationalities that passed through it would not have been mistaken in thinking that he had a Nordic background. His thick, curling hair was so fair as to be almost silver and his eyes were the deep, dark aquamarine of a Norwegian fjord. He was not handsome in the accepted sense, but his face was pleasantly good-humoured with a wide, mobile mouth that appeared to be always on the verge of a smile.

The party gathered round a table where a white-haired gentleman and a pretty, elderly lady smiled up at them, the lady putting an affectionate hand on Abby Goodwin's arm. Abby, who herself was still very lovely at the age of forty, sat down on a velvet and gilt chair beside her, and after nodding and smiling at several other ladies who were also seated, was soon engaged in earnest conversation with her.

"Are you well, Laura?" she was heard to say. "You look very smart in that gown; the colour suits you. And John? Has he recovered from his cold?"

"Oh, yes, but I still had a great deal of trouble getting him here. You know what he's like about these kinds of functions. The girls look very smart, but should that surprise me?"

The gentleman, Noah Goodwin, the fair young man and three other striplings who obviously thought they might have a chance with one of the Goodwin twins, stood beside them. Champagne was offered and though Noah Goodwin frowned slightly when his daughters took a glass each, he allowed it.

"Who's the fair chappie?" Captain Hugh Thornley asked his companion. His eyes were still narrowed and there was a hard twist to his well-cut mouth. He had straightened up, lifting his chin with the inbred arrogance and pride of a man who is not accustomed to being denied, which of course he did not expect to be.

"Now look, Hugh, it's no good—"

"I only asked who the fellow was, Todd." Hugh's voice was deceptively mild. "There's no harm in that, surely." He emptied his champagne glass and reached for another.

"His name's Archie Goodwin. He's some sort of relative of Noah Goodwin. He helps him to run his businesses and lives in the old family home at Edge Bottom by the glass works. There's some mystery about the time he came to live with them twenty years ago, but like me he was educated at the local grammar school. I always wanted the army and won a place at Sandhurst but Archie went to university and has a degree in engineering. He's a nice chap and is well thought of. I think . . . perhaps I shouldn't say it, but I believe he has a soft spot for Beth."

"Has he indeed? She's the one in the pink dress?"

"Yes, but listen to me, Hugh, if you have designs on her—"

"*Designs on her!* What a terribly dramatic fellow you are, Todd. Isn't he, Dicky? Did you ever hear such a thing?"

"Well, you do have a certain reputation with the ladies, Hugh, and this one is a decent girl from a decent family so if I were you I'd look elsewhere."

"But you're not me, Dicky, old boy. And if I'm not mistaken, and I seldom am when it comes to the ladies, *she* has an eye for *me*."

He was right, for Beth Goodwin's eyes, a gleaming silvery grey, turned constantly in his direction and she was aware that if she didn't stop it and take more of an interest in the general conversation her mother would notice. She thought Milly already had because she kept turning to look where Beth did. Todd was there with two other officers and when he caught their glances he bowed in their direction and raised his glass.

"What does that young fool think he's up to?" Noah Goodwin growled, scowling at Todd. "Bowing and scraping like a damn fop and who are the two other grinning jackanapes with him? They need to mind their manners or I'll have something to say to their commanding officer."

"Oh, Father, for goodness sake. They are only being polite. Can't a man bow in our direction without you taking umbrage?"

There was a sudden rush of young officers and gentlemen in the formal black and white of evening dress begging to be allowed to put their names in Beth and Milly's dance cards and within minutes both girls were on the floor dipping and swaying to the lilting music of a waltz. Beth, whose gown Hugh Thornley had described as pink, was in a soft ivory rose, so pale there was scarcely any colour in it at all. It was low-cut, revealing the top curve of her small breasts and the satin smoothness of her shoulders, with short puffed sleeves. Though the fashion was for lavish trimming none of the Goodwin women, including their mother, cared for it. It was said in the fashion magazines that it was "impossible to put too many flounces, puffings and flowers on the tarlatan, gauze, grenadine or tulle skirts of ball dresses" but the Goodwin women were satisfied with an overskirt edged in narrow pleated ruching which draped over the small crinoline at the back. Against her mother's wishes Milly was in a vivid turquoise blue silk. Abby Goodwin thought it too striking for a young unmarried woman but as usual Milly had her way. It was much the same design as her sister's and both sported an enormous silk rose, matching the colour of their gowns, in the centre of the coil of their upswept glossy copper hair. Many of the other ladies were in the startling, bold colours that were coming in to vogue, maroon, mustard yellow and emerald green being prominent, sometimes with a mixture of three or four colours and materials so that the swirling mass of dancers might have been allied to peacocks or parrots from the jungle.

The ball had been advertised as a "Masque of flowers" and the entire Town Hall, from the steps at the entrance to the ballroom itself was decorated profusely with every flower in season. Great arrangements of roses mixed with Canterbury bells, gypsophilia, carnations of every colour, sweet william, pom-pom dahlias and hothouse magnolias filled the air with their fragrance. The ballroom was packed with the influential, the wealthy, the prominent, the élite of St Helens, those who could afford the price of the very expensive tickets to this ball, which was being held in honour of their Queen. It was 1887, Her Majesty's Golden Jubilee, fifty glorious years on the throne. Yesterday had been a triumph as the nation had been wholly given over to the thanksgiving celebrations that had taken place the length and breadth of the land. There had been a great Jubilee procession from Buckingham Palace to Westminster Abbey in London, the route decked with flowers and flags and edged with cheering crowds of Her Majesty's loyal subjects, many of them come from the provinces to see their Queen on this special day. Triumphal arches decorated every street corner under which the procession passed. There were guards of honour formed by the Grenadiers, the First Life Guards, the Indian Cavalry, cadets from Woolwich and Sandhurst and many others. A fanfare of trumpets heralded Indian princes, a maharajah ablaze with jewels that outdid those worn by Her Majesty, and royalty from many great countries. From open barouches the royal family waved and smiled graciously, Her Majesty seated with her eldest daughter, the Princess Imperial of Germany, and the Princess of Wales. Their barouche was surrounded by a brilliant cavalcade of horsemen composed of her sons, sons-in-law, grandsons and grandsons-in-law. She was greeted rapturously by the crowd. The description of the ceremonial had been read out that morning at the breakfast table by Noah Goodwin and now they were here to celebrate the historic occasion with a ball whose splendour had never before been seen at the Town Hall.

Noah Goodwin, the inevitable cigar clenched between his white teeth, glanced round him appreciatively, bowing to acquaintances, but his hand was inclined to hover at his seated wife's shoulder, for it was well known in St Helens that he doted on her and could not bear to be parted from her for longer than was necessary. Many of the gentlemen, having deposited wives and daughters among the other ladies in a safe, well-chaperoned position at the edge of the ballroom, were making their way to the gaming-room where card tables were set up but Noah remained beside his beautiful wife and daughters.

Hugh Thornley ground out his cigar, placed his emptied glass on the table, lifted his imperious head and, ignoring the open-mouthed stares of Todd Woodruff and Dicky Bentham, strode arrogantly around the edge of the floor, not in the least surprised when the crowd parted before him like the Red Sea before Moses. He meant to bow courteously to the manufacturer and his wife, for though they were socially far beneath him they had what he wanted, which was one of their lovely daughters who had been returned to them by their last partners. Already two officers were hanging about waiting to claim them for the next dance. He meant to introduce himself, his name and title, naturally, overwhelming them into allowing him to scribble his name in their dance cards, both of them, for he, a practised seducer, had noticed that the sister in the turquoise gown was looking at him from under her dark lashes, the corners of her mouth lifting in the beginnings of a flirtatious smile. If he could manage it, and he usually could, either with his good looks, his charm or his title, he meant to take one of them into supper.

"Good evening, sir." He smiled boldly into the astonished face of Noah Goodwin. "May I introduce myself. My name is Thornley. Captain Hugh Thornley. I have a place at Thornley Green." He bowed to the equally astonished ladies, knowing he had no need to mention his title, since everyone knew of Thornley Green and the rank of the gentleman who lived there. But he had not reckoned on the pride, the temper and the arrogance, matching his own, of Noah Goodwin, who cared nought for titles and even less for a cocky young fool who thought he could get round him with smooth words.

"Oh yes?" he asked menacingly. He was seriously displeased and those who knew him shrank a little. Did this handsome young captain know what peril he was putting himself into by casually approaching the wealthiest, most powerful man in St Helens? Noah Goodwin was obsessive about his wife and his daughters and though he was well aware he had nothing to fear where his wife was concerned, for they were devoted to one another, his daughters needed watching every minute of the day and night. Particularly Milly!

Hugh Thornley straightened his tall frame and at the same time did his best to curb his inclination to tell this manufacturer to go to hell! He would have one of these young women on the ballroom floor as soon as possible and the fool must be made to see it, but he knew he would do his cause no good if he did what he longed to do and that was ignore the father and sweep one of his daughters into his arms.

Noah glared at Beth and Milly as though they had caused

this incident, which of course they had, but could he blame them when they were so incredibly pretty that every insolent pup in the room wanted to dance with them. They were so perfect, his daughters, so exactly as his wife had been at the same age, but they both had spirit, a strength of spirit come from their mother and from him, especially Milly who was eyeing this young lordling with an appreciative eye. He could not tell what the expression was on Beth's face as her eyes were cast down as though she had something to hide.

"I would be honoured if I might claim a dance, sir, from one of your lovely daughters. Todd Woodruff is a friend of mine—"

"Is he indeed and why should you think that makes a difference?" Noah's face was thunderous and his wife laid a hand on his sleeve.

"Darling, don't you think—"

He threw it off. "No, I don't, Abby, and I'll thank you not to interfere. I will not have every Tom, Dick and Harry sniffing around our girls. Tricky young fools believe—"

"Sir, I object to that and I must ask you to apologise for the insult you have offered my family name. I have introduced myself in a perfectly gentlemanly way, asking politely if I might lead one of your daughters into a dance—"

"Well, let's get the thing over and done with, shall we? No, you may not lead one of my daughters into a dance. Good God, man, we don't know you and as for—"

Hugh Thornley's face became alarmingly shuttered and without expression and his eyes darkened until they were almost black. That this man who came from what he considered to be no better than the working classes should have the effrontery to question him, to stand in his way, to thwart him who had been indulged all his life, by his mother and by his nanny, was insupportable and by God he'd make him sorry for it.

"I am Hugh Charles Thornley, sixteenth baron of Thornley Green, sir. My father was—"

"Aye, lad, we all know who your father was and what happened to him so don't come here with your dandified ways—"

"Father, please, Captain Thornley is doing no more than asking for a dance. Anybody would think he had offered you some appalling insult the way you are behaving. I for one will dance with him. You don't mind, do you?" Milly turned and smiled brilliantly at the young second lieutenant who was hovering at her elbow and whose name was scribbled in her dance card.

"No . . . er, no," the young officer stammered, backing away from the frozen face and threatening figure of Captain Hugh Thornley, for the captain's reputation, not just as a gambler, a womaniser but the best swordsman in the regiment, was well documented.

"Milly," her father thundered and this time his wife hastily stood up and began to urge him towards the floor, for the commotion about them was beginning to excite attention. An officer in the full fig of a lieutenant-colonel was making his way towards them, since it seemed that one of his officers was the cause of it.

Abby was eager to get one of her daughters into the arms of the alarming Captain Thornley and on to the floor before a worse situation blew up. "Come, darling, do dance with me. Milly will be quite safe with the captain, I'm sure. She can come to no harm with the whole of St Helens watching."

Noah Goodwin reluctantly allowed himself to be led on to the dance floor. As soon as he had his arms about his wife he could feel the calm of her relaxing him. He did not like to be bested, especially by an insolent young dog like Thornley. The bloody gentry thought they owned the town and everybody in it and once upon a time they had but not any more and Captain bloody Thornley should have been made aware of it. And Milly hadn't helped! Just wait until he had her home: he'd give her what for. She'd be the talk of the town the way she carried on, the little devil, but then wasn't she a female version of himself with a wicked need, since she had been a toddler, to have her own way.

"I don't like it, Abby, and I don't like him. His father was a bad lot and came to a bad end. You remember him, don't you? He came to some function here years ago with his toadies. He asked you to dance but you refused him which didn't please him and now his bloody son's doing the same with our daughter."

"Noah, there's no harm in it. He is dancing with her in a ballroom full of our friends and no harm can come to her."

The future is hidden and it was a mercy that Abby and Noah Goodwin could not see into it!

2

She arched her back and lifted her eyes to look into his face. He was smiling down at her, the brilliant blueness of his eyes catching her breath and clenching a fist round her heart. She had noticed him the moment they had entered the ballroom, probably at the very same time Beth had, for she had seen where her sister's glance lingered, but in Milly's world it was the brave, the one not afraid to take chances, who won the day, and the only way to win it was by going after it! She was used to the admiration of young men and though she liked it well enough – what girl doesn't? – this one was the first to stir her senses and capture her imagination. Not that she'd let him see it, for that was not Milly Goodwin's way, but she had never reacted like this before to any man and she was not aware that what she felt was revealed in her face nor that as a man of the world he recognised it.

He was a good dancer and so was she. They made a striking couple, he so handsome, she so lovely even her parents, circling the floor with a sedate glide, watched bemusedly as their daughter, their wilful, headstrong daughter, skimmed the ballroom floor, dipping and swaying in the arms of, and in perfect unison with, the dashing cavalry officer. Even the other dancers waltzing decorously, correctly as propriety demanded, turned their heads to watch, making way for them as they circled the room. Guests who had been chatting, laughing, drinking champagne, greeting friends and acquaintances, ladies gossiping, gentlemen taking the chance to do a little business, grew watchful and quiet, glancing curiously now and then at

Abby and Noah Goodwin to see what they would do, particularly Noah who was known for his short temper. It seemed to them that only the fact that his wife held him close to her in the waltz kept him from striding across the floor and wrenching his beloved daughter from the man who had her in his arms!

"You dance very well, Miss Goodwin," were the first words he spoke to her. "I have seldom had a partner to equal your grace."

"Nor I, Captain Thornley, or should I address you as Lord Thornley, or even my lord? I'm not quite sure of the niceties in such a situation, never before having danced with a . . . a baron, is it?"

"It is, but perhaps . . . Hugh?" He grinned down at her and the thumb on his hand in the small of her back moved slightly, caressingly.

"Oh, hardly on such short acquaintance, Captain. We have not even been properly introduced."

"There was hardly time. I think we were both . . . eager to be on the floor, Miss Goodwin."

She smiled up at him boldly from beneath her long fluttering eyelashes, her lips parted, her little tongue visible between the perfect white of her teeth.

"I do love to waltz," she murmured.

"May I ask what else you love to do?"

"Captain, I do believe you are teasing me."

"Never! I would not dare."

For several minutes they did not speak, both enjoying the wonderful sensation of floating around the floor as though they had wings, their bodies moving in perfect rhythm. The room was well lighted with a hundred candelabra whose glow caught in the deep brown of Milly's eyes and placed a diamond in those of Hugh Thornley who was gazing not at her but over her head at her sister who was also on the floor. Milly was so enchanted with the moment she failed to notice.

"And does your father allow you to ride up on the moor, Miss Goodwin? Alone, I mean?"

"Far from it, sir. He cannot bear us out of his sight, for in his opinion every man in the room has designs on one or the other of us. He has his eye on us this very minute. One on myself and the other on Beth. Well, perhaps not quite so forcibly on Beth because she's dancing with Archie."

"And Archie is . . .?

"A sort of brother, I suppose. My parents adopted him years ago and my father took him into the business. He's sweet on Beth but . . ."

"She's not sweet on him?"

"I shouldn't think so."

"She's . . . interested in someone else, perhaps?" It was as well to be aware of any opposition.

"She'd tell me if she was. We are twins, you know."

Milly's mind raced in headlong turbulence and she wondered on the strangeness of it. She knew quite well, for as she had just told Hugh Thornley she and Beth were twins, that Beth was as interested in this man as she was herself. She had been intrigued by the way Beth's glance kept wandering towards the group of officers by the refreshment table, thinking at first that it was Todd Woodruff who had captured her sister's attention, then the image of the godlike man lounging against the wall had swum, in perfect detail, into her vision and she had been . . . what? Lost? Exalted? Transported? Dear God, what was the matter with her? She, who had been moved to no more than a faint amusement by the antics of the gentlemen who, despite her father, had done their best to court her, was now ready to hang on every word that fell from this man's lips. His well-shaped, smiling lips which, at this very moment, she was wondering how they would feel against hers. She had been kissed before by inexperienced young men and, of course, by Todd, who was always ready for a bit of fun, using any excuse to kiss any pretty girl and whose kisses had been more expert. She had enjoyed it but then Todd, like Archie, was almost her brother so it didn't count. But this man whose body was no more than an inch or two from hers was neither Todd nor Archie. He swung her expertly round and round until her skirt belled out in the most immodest way, showing more than was decent of her pale cream silk stockings and she was well aware that her father would have something to say the moment the dance was over but she didn't care.

Hugh Thornley held the girl in his arms even closer. He still had the image of the surprised silvery grey eyes in the rosy-tinted face of this girl's sister on the edge of his mind and at the first opportunity he meant to get closer to her in some way, perhaps not here but in the immediate future. There was a sweetness about her, an innocence, an air of waiting, which intrigued him and also surprised him, for he was not ordinarily attracted to that sort of thing. He liked his women to be experienced, experienced in the ways of pleasing his own sexually mature body, but there was no doubt she would make a splendid wife, one even his mother would approve of, and at the same time she was very rich and extremely lovely. Where had she and her sister got that air of polished graciousness, that lift to the head, that straight and elegant back, the delicate oval-faced beauty, for her people were hardly from the top drawer? But though she was looking at him gravely as she danced by in the arms of the man called Archie, there was a certain provocative curl to her lip which titillated his senses. Yes, as innocent as a newborn lamb, as was the one in his arms, for the daughters of their class were guarded like the crown jewels. Yet at the same time the one in his arms had a golden brown glow in her eyes, a thrusting of her small breasts, which told him she was not unaware of the effect she had on a man.

The music ended and couples smiled at each other, their breath quickened, as it seemed the dip and sway and twirl of

Milly Goodwin and Hugh Thornley had put life in them all. They parted, the young ladies returning to their mamas and the gentlemen preparing themselves for their next partner. For a moment Hugh hesitated but he was well aware that if he was to ingratiate himself with this girl's very wealthy father he must be circumspect and do as the other gentlemen were doing. He knew that Miss Milly Goodwin, in her belief that she could do whatever she fancied, was prepared to defy all the rules of etiquette. She would allow him to sweep her off in another dance if he so wished, but Hugh Thornley knew full well that though it was not his nature to be humble, he must, for the moment, do the correct thing and return this lovely baggage to her parents. Besides, he had a fancy to dance with the other one, the one with the incredible silver eyes, and to be accepted as a partner for her he must curb his pride and his temper, which grew irritable under constraint, and do the *correct* thing.

He could see Milly Goodwin was ready to argue with him, to state plainly that she was not yet ready to be taken back to her mama and papa who were waiting for her on the edge of the floor, for she was a young woman who knew what she wanted and would fight like a tiger to get it. But she must be shown that it was Hugh Thornley, sixteenth baron of the line, who called the tune. She might, in the end, be the piper who paid for it, or at least her father would, but it was himself who would eventually call the tune. He always did and he always would.

He placed her hand on his arm and led her across the shining floor to where her mother had perched herself anxiously on the edge of her chair and her father stood threateningly beside her. Hugh bowed to them both, his smile charming, courteous.

"Your daughter dances divinely, Mrs Goodwin," he said to her mother, "so I hope you will forgive me for stealing her from you for so long a time. I'm afraid I was somewhat precipitate in rushing her on to the floor as I did but—"

"For God's sake, man," Noah Goodwin snarled, "d'you

think I don't know my own daughter by now? She's the one who dragged you on to the—"

"Father, please," Milly hissed, "there is no need to make a scene. Everyone is watching."

"And if they are, my lass, it's you who made them."

"Noah . . ."

"No, Abby, this girl of ours needs—"

"Sir, I beg you, don't blame your . . ."

All the while this polite absurdity was taking place Beth Goodwin studied Hugh Thornley's face with the concentrated gaze of someone imprinting on her mind every shade and tone and hue of his skin, every flat plane of his well-shaved cheeks, the curving line of his mouth, which she did not recognise as sensual and which held more than a hint of cruelty. She could feel the pulse beneath her jaw throbbing and hoped no one noticed it.

Archie said something to her, she didn't know what, but she tore her eyes away from the masculine beauty of Hugh Thornley and turned to him.

"What?"

"Will you honour me again with a dance? Unless you are otherwise engaged." He smiled whimsically at his own formal question.

"I beg your pardon?" She stared at him uncomprehendingly.

"Your father and Milly are about to start one of their infernally boring arguments and your mother is becoming upset but I'm sure the charming captain will smooth everyone's feathers. After all he is the sixteenth baron . . ."

"Archie, you are not a bit amusing."

"I wasn't trying to be amusing, Beth. The man is an arrogant bastard who believes he can talk his way into, or out of, any situation and I have no wish to watch him do so now. If you won't dance come with me to the refreshment table for a glass of champagne. This could go on for ever." He took her hand

and, though he had no idea he was doing it, his thumb rubbed gently, lovingly across the back of hers.

Beth looked into the deep blue-green eyes of the man who had been in her life for as long as she could remember and therefore was, so to speak, part of the scenery. He had always been there, loved as a brother and like a brother taken for granted. For a second she caught a strange expression in those eyes, equally as brilliant as Hugh Thornley's but familiarity had blinded her to their beauty. The expression fled at once and, since she had not recognised what it was, she forgot it. She shook her head, still hoping in her fast-beating heart that Hugh Thornley might ask a dance of her but her sister's defiance and her father's intransigence were making that impossible, yet she could not bear to tear herself away. She smiled vaguely at Archie and turned back to the family group.

Archie Goodwin, as he had been called ever since he had been brought to Edge Bottom twenty years ago, for he had not known his own surname, was in love with this beautiful daughter of Noah and Abby Goodwin, though he was careful not to allow anyone, particularly her, to know of it. She was as vital as her sister but in her were a sweetness, a goodness that Milly did not possess and Archie was waiting for the moment, the hour, the day, when he could tell her of his feelings. She loved him too, he knew it, but she was not as yet *in love* with him. The family lived at Lantern Hill, which Noah had had built fifteen years ago, a lovely house to the east of St Helens on a splendid ten-acre slope surrounded by forty acres of parkland, saying he no longer cared to live so close to the glass works. He wanted to look out of his front windows and see not the rooftops of his brick works but open fields and a stretch of blue sky above them unblemished by smoke. There was a thick hedge of rhododendrons, sweet-scented shrubs and an acre of rose beds, a paddock for the children to race their ponies in – Archie being one of those fortunate children – massive gates, a gatekeeper and trees to

ensure Noah's privacy. Archie owed his very life to Abby and
Noah Goodwin who had brought him up and given him the
chance to become the man he was, but he was not convinced
they, or at least Noah, would give one of his precious daughters
to a man who had no idea where he came from. Liverpool was all
he knew, and his forebears probably from Scandinavia if his
looks were anything to go by. He only knew he loved Beth
Goodwin and he meant to marry her. But he did not care for the
way she was gazing, stars in her eyes, at Hugh Thornley who was
at this moment bending over her mother's hand and, by the look
of it, mesmerising her as he had mesmerised her daughters.

Noah still frowned and drew deeply on his cigar but Hugh
Thornley was clever, smooth-talking, with an inborn knack of
knowing when to press his case and, more importantly, when
not to. And he had that authoritative air of breeding which
spoke of generations of influence, superiority and advantage
which allowed him to rise above the wishes of those he
considered beneath him. He had the accents of privilege
and the complex charm that thrives in the families of those
born to govern. He was, in fact, a gentleman, come from
generations of gentlemen, which these people were not. Nevertheless he did not allow his contempt for them to show. He
kissed the air above Abby's hand, then did the same with Milly
and Beth, gazing perhaps for a shade too long into Beth's eyes,
a look Archie did not like, for it seemed to be conveying
something to her that he wanted no one else to see.

He bowed again, then, smiling, sauntered back to his brother
officers who were still gathered about the refreshment table. He
spoke to them, glancing back towards the Goodwins party and
several of them laughed, though Archie noticed that Todd
Woodruff did not join in.

"Well, I fancy a ride out," Milly announced casually the next
morning at breakfast, so casually that everyone at the table

turned to look at her suspiciously. "I think I'll take Flame up on
to the moorland and give her a good gallop. She hasn't been out
for a week."

"Harry has her out every day so I don't see how you can say
that," Beth remarked quietly. "I saw him come in with her this
morning as I was getting dressed."

The two sisters eyed one another warily. They both knew full
well what was in the other's mind, for the moment Hugh
Thornley had burst like a shooting star into their lives at the
Jubilee Ball the night before had been a significant one for them
both. Neither of them had been in love or found any particular
man of much importance and it was said that if they didn't look
sharp they would be left on the shelf, but a look that had passed
between them the night before had been recognised for what it
was. Their shared interest in the dashing captain could prove to
be a disaster for one of them and an antagonism was already
beginning to reveal itself. The pair of them, apart from the
childish spats that had bubbled up in their childhood and
girlhood, got on well together but this morning something
was taking place between them that, remembering the ball, was
not hard to understand, at least to them. Hugh Thornley, as
though he sat at the breakfast table between them, divided
them. They had both been attracted to him, that seemed
obvious, and now, though nothing had been spoken of last
night, Milly was filled with the excited belief that he would be
up on the moors waiting for her.

"Well, exercise your animal by all means, my lass," her
father said equably, reaching for another piece of toast, "but in
the park. There are plenty of open spaces to give you a good
gallop."

"But, Father," Milly wailed. "It's not the same as being on
the open moor. No sooner have you got up a good speed than
you come to some obstruction and you are forced to turn and
make your way back. It's just not the same."

"No, I'm sure it isn't, but you'll do as you're told." He fixed her with a fond, fierce eye, speaking plainly as he had done all his life and not just with his children. "D'you think I'm half-witted, girl? I know what you're up to after the tarradiddle at the ball last night. Your route to the open moor will take you past the garrison and who might come galloping out of there on his no doubt expensive thoroughbred but Captain bloody Thornley and I'll not have it, d'you hear. The man's a scoundrel, from what I've heard, as was his father before him." He scowled at something, some memory that he didn't find pleasant, then turned irritably to the maidservant who hovered at the sideboard waiting to serve the family. "Is there any chance of some *hot* coffee, Nessie, or must I go out to the kitchen and make it myself?"

"Noah, leave poor Nessie alone," his wife said placidly as the maid scurried frantically from the room to inform the kitchen servants that the master was in one of his "paddies".

Nessie had been a scullery-maid fifteen years ago when the household had left Edge Bottom House and moved to Lantern Hill. At first the servants had been overawed by the magnificence of the newly built house, swearing to one another that they'd get lost in its maze of rooms, that they'd never get used to the absolute luxury, the proliferation of bedrooms – though they did not use those exact words – the vast spaces that surrounded the house which was reached by a long tree-lined drive. But it seemed Edge Bottom House, where the family had lived for generations, had not been grand enough for the master whose growing wealth had made it possible for him to have whatever he fancied. And he had fancied this grand house! It was set on a slight rise of the land, hence Lantern Hill, the ornamental ground falling away from it like a wide, tiered skirt. Smooth lawns and flowerbeds and immaculately clipped box hedges bordered the house. There were statues of white marble, many of them indecently clothed in the servants' opinion, a conservatory crammed with flowers, singing birds and fragile white cane furniture which was a favourite place with the mistress. A summerhouse sat beside a small lake with a covered, trellised walk from the house, all draped about with hanging baskets of ferns and blossoms. There was a carpet of daffodils in the spring, forsythia and lilac and the massed heads of rhododendron shading from the palest pink to deep and royal purple; roses and carnations, vivid marigolds and zinnias in summer, massed oak and fragile willow by the lake. And all surrounded by parkland and woodland. It had been said in Edge Bottom that Noah Goodwin would be bound to have deer drifting about in it, which he did!

The breakfast-room where the family ate the first meal of the day was the smallest of the downstairs rooms, freshly painted in the palest yellow with white lace curtains at the window so that the sun could flood in from the east. It was, by the standard of the rest of the house, simply but lovingly furnished in glowing satinwood, an oval table with six velvet-covered chairs, a couple of sideboards, a picture on the wall over the white marble fireplace of Abby, Beth and Milly when the girls were about ten years old. The room was placed back to back with the kitchen so that Noah's breakfast, which he liked to be freshly cooked and plentiful before he went to the glass works or the brick works or any of the many businesses he was concerned with, would arrive hot from the oven. The sun streamed in through the long windows, promising a hot day and in the oblongs of sunshine two golden Labradors lay, ears twitching, tails slowly moving, eyes open and fixed on the company, for sometimes there might be titbits available.

"Well, I think that's the end, really I do, Father. I never heard such nonsense in my life. I dance once with Hugh Thornley and now you are accusing me of . . . of . . . well, I don't know what." Milly knew she was being over-argumentative, acting the part of an innocent when she was guilty. She did not believe that her father seriously imagined she was desperate to get out on to the moor and search for Hugh Thornley, which was the case, but it meant that it would make finding him more difficult. She had no idea what the daily duties of an officer were nor how easy or problematical it would be for him to avoid them and ride out to meet her but she was absolutely certain he would.

"Lass, I'm accusing you of nothing but I saw the way he was with you and I don't trust him, nor you, come to that." He shovelled bacon and eggs into his mouth with the same determined force he had been known to use to feed the furnace in his own glasshouse. "Give you an inch and you take a bloody mile and you're known for liking your own way and—"

"Like you, Father. I *am* your daughter after all." She grinned shamelessly and was relieved to see her father relax.

"Aye, that's the truth but nevertheless I'd be obliged if you'd do as you're told. Keep in the grounds until that scoundrel has forgotten you, which won't be long knowing his reputation for fancy women and . . . other things, and then you can ride the moor, perhaps with Harry, or even Beth, if she's willing."

"I'm too busy for riding at the moment. I shall be at Claughton Street all morning—" Beth began but was allowed to say no more.

"What! On a Sunday?" her father interrupted. "And I suppose you'll be going with her," turning on his wife.

"Laura has arranged a meeting—"

"On a bloody Sunday?"

"Darling, it's the only day some of the women can manage." Abby Goodwin stood up and moved to where her husband sat at the head of the table. She put her arms about his shoulders and rested her cheek on the top of his head. His hand went up to her at once and stroked her arm.

Nessie, who had returned with fresh coffee, took no notice of this display of the affection that existed between her master and mistress. She was used to it, as they all were.

"But I promise as soon as the meeting is finished we'll come straight back." When he smiled and turned to whisper in her ear she smiled too.

She returned to her seat and shook out her napkin. "I'll have another cup of coffee, please, Nessie, and some more toast."

"You don't eat enough, my darling, that's your problem," her husband said fondly, while the rest of the family placidly continued to tuck in to bacon and eggs and all the good things Cook turned out each morning. "And what's on the agenda today?" he continued, not because he wanted to know but because he loved her and wanted to please her.

"Laura has managed to get Josephine Butler to come and talk to the members. About the fight she has had to get the Contagious Diseases Acts repealed and the passage of the Criminal Law Amendment Act. Not that it seems to be doing much good. Some of those children they bring in are certainly not sixteen. Nevertheless Mrs Butler has shattered the secrecy and silence with her campaign and I for one agree with her that we must fight for enfranchisement which will bring about the total transformation of the lives of women . . ." She paused and laughed softly. "I'm sorry, I'm getting on my soap box again, aren't I, but you know how strongly I feel. How Beth and I feel."

"Oh, Mother." Milly sighed with boredom and at once her mother turned on her, her normally serene face rosy with anger.

"Don't you Mother me, my girl. You haven't talked to some of these women as I have. Oh yes, I know they are prostitutes but they *are* the same sex as yourself and they are subjected to the appalling double standards that exist today. Men use them and to keep them clean, the women, I mean, so that these same men would not be contaminated, the police authorities are allowed to arrest any women they suspect of being a prostitute and compel them to submit to an examination by speculum.

Do you know what that is, Milly? They are taken to prison and held down while—"

"Abby, my darling, not at the breakfast table. Besides which, Milly is well aware of what the Contagious Diseases—"

"I should hope she would, brought up in a household where universal franchise is believed in. Women must stop being regarded as sexual objects, Noah. There are so many respectable ladies who knew nothing about such evils but who have listened to Josephine and are now flocking to join the movement. Believe me—"

"We do, my darling, we do, but shall we . . ."

"Have you seen a speculum, Father?" Beth asked him quietly. "Do you understand the workings of it and the way it can injure—"

"That's enough, Beth." Her father's voice was sharp and he rose to his feet. "Go to your meeting, which I allow though I do not agree with many of things your mother and you are fighting for. But I love you both and know that short of locking you up I cannot stop you. At least your sister is not interested in such wild ideas."

They had been driven away in the splendid satin-lined carriage that was to take them to Laura Bennett's home where the meeting was to take place, while at the front steps Noah waved them off. And from the stable yard at the back of the house Milly set her chestnut mare, Flame, towards the gate that led out into the parkland. She urged her horse into a gallop directly across the park and into the woodland at the far side of the property where she disappeared.

3

"It's been nearly a year since the Act was repealed and still they're being dragged in. It's an absolute disgrace, Beth. You should see the state of the lass they brought from the police station in Longworth last night. She lives . . . lived near the garrison. Torn about by that damned instrument and it turns out she was not a prostitute at all but a decent serving girl. A virgin, she was, but not any more. Come, I'll show you."

John Bennett, a man as old as her father who had been their family doctor for over twenty years, led Beth along the bare ward that was devoid of anything that might be described as frivolous. It was achingly clean, scoured and polished, even the beds in which the women lay neat, white and firmly tucked in so that she wondered how the occupants managed to move. Women of all ages, though she suspected that most of them were young and only gave the appearance of age because of the suffering, the injuries and torments brought on by the cruelty of the men who treated them as nothing more than sexual objects. Because of overbearing husbands, because of too many pregnancies and their poor diet which did not allow them to recover quickly they had come to this pitiable state. This was a ward in an obstetrical clinic at the Providence Free Hospital run by Doctor Bennett and helped by his wife Laura, who was an old and trusted friend of her mother and was a sister in the cause that they had supported for the past twenty-odd years. Next door to the obstetric clinic was a lying-in ward from where could be faintly heard the cry of a newborn. Any complications on this ward could be instantly transferred to the obstetrics ward where a competent nurse would take over from the equally competent midwife, all the women trained by Doctor Bennett himself. Though she might have suffered before she arrived, perhaps at the hands of a brutal husband, or a sadistic client, lucky was the woman who found her way to this haven of peace and healing.

It was Laura who had introduced Abby – who had gone to the meeting without Beth – as a young woman, to the cause that had become her passion, a passion that she had passed on to her daughter Beth. In the 1860s women of the middle classes who could articulate such ideas had begun to feel that they had rights that needed to be addressed. One of their aims was the right to vote as many men did and so the women's suffrage movement was born. Their second goal was social reform. They declared vehemently that charity was not enough and that the power of the state was needed to bring about social progress. Third, they believed staunchly that only education could help to bring about this revolution. In 1832 the great Reform Bill had enfranchised "male persons" and it was this that had provided the focus of attack and was a source of resentment from which grew the women's suffrage movement. The women's fight continued, though the meetings, the protests, the petitions, the voices of men in government who supported their cause, the articles written, many of them by Beth herself, had so far had little influence on the progress of the National Union of Women's Suffrage Society of which Beth and her mother were both members.

Most of the women who lay in the clean beds, probably the first they had ever known, smiled up at Doctor Bennett and he stopped now and again to lay a hand on a forehead or speak a word or two of comfort. It was a long ward with a table at the far end where a starched, forbidding person, but who proved when she glanced up to have kind, twinkling eyes, sat writing.

On the table was a vase jammed with a mass of gaily coloured antirrhinum, crimson, yellow, white and pink, brought by Beth herself from the gardens of Lantern Hill, their brilliance contrasting with the drab utilitarianism of the room.

"Here she is," the doctor said, stopping just before the nurse's table at the bed of a young woman who appeared to be sleeping. Her face was the colour of tallow on the pillow, her dark hair lank with sweat and her hands, which were as thin and tiny as a sparrow's claw, were clasped across her flat chest.

"Mary," the doctor whispered, unwilling to wake her should she be sleeping, but her weary eyelashes lifted and her clouded eyes looked up into his face then drifted over to Beth, widening as though she were gazing at an angel from heaven. He put a strong, warm hand on hers and leaned over her.

"How are you feeling, my dear? A little better, I hope?"

A smile tugged at the corner of her soft mouth but she seemed unable to speak.

"I've brought someone to see you, my dear. A friend. She would like to hear your story, for in retelling it she might help others who may suffer what has been done to you. Now, I know you are not strong enough to speak for yourself" – he turned for a moment to Beth who had crept to her knees beside the bed so that the young woman could see her – "she lost so much blood," he murmured, "but I will tell it for you and if I make a mistake press my hand. Is that all right with you?"

The girl managed to nod her head but Beth thought there was deep apprehension in her eyes.

"Very well. Now this is Mary Smith, Beth. She is eighteen years old and has been in domestic service for the past twelve months and her employer was well pleased with her. Mary met a young man, respectable, she thought, but he wanted her to leave her situation and go and live with him. She refused so the vile fellow avenged himself by denouncing her to the special police. These men went to the house, found Mary at her dinner, and her mistress, a respectable tradesman's wife, out for the day. To Mary's bewilderment they ordered her to go to the hospital at once to see the doctor. She informed her mistress on her return, who, feeling perfectly certain of Mary's good behaviour, told her not to go. The police came again, insisted on her going and threatened her with imprisonment if she did not appear. I am correct up to now, am I, Mary?" Doctor Bennett smiled down kindly into Mary's blanched face. She nodded, though Beth could have wept herself for the despairing tears that oozed from Mary's eyes.

"Mary's employer thought she had better go, for as she said she could not have the police continuing to call at her house. Mary went and as she was at the time menstruating could not be examined. She was detained and her mistress, beginning to think that perhaps there was no smoke without fire, as the saying goes, began to believe the police and employed another servant to take Mary's place. Mary was put among prostitutes and when she was able was examined by the doctors, several persons holding her down while the speculum was inserted into her vagina, breaking the hymen, for she was a virgin, and causing her to bleed profusely. The loss of blood necessitated her being sent here. She has lost not only her job, but her virginity, her dignity and her young belief that if a girl works hard and behaves herself she will get on in life. There is a garrison nearby, Beth, and the men, soldiers, who use women as they do, must, so the authorities say, be protected against the diseases that these poor creatures can give them and which they probably gave the women in the first place. If a woman is found to have a venereal disease she is treated, 'publicly cleansed' as Mrs Butler calls it, and then allowed back on the streets. This poor lass will recover but this still goes on despite the repeal of the Contagious Diseases Act. I cannot believe what this society does to our women . . ." He sighed gustily. "But then you know as well as I, which is why we and you and Abby work as we do to try and redress the terrible wrongs perpetrated by men against women." He shook his head sadly. "Will you listen to me ranting on, silly old man that I am, but really, I despair sometimes."

The doctor rose stiffly to his feet, putting a polite hand beneath Beth's elbow, though it was himself who could have done with a lift. He patted Mary's frail hands. "Miss Goodwin will help you, Mary, have no fear. Rest and eat the good food and get better and then, when you are feeling more yourself, you will be found decent employment."

Beth bent again over the painfully thin form of the girl in the bed. She smiled. "Don't worry, Mary. You have no need of worry. There are many women eager to help you, and others who are exploited by men. I'll come again to see you." Surprising herself, she bent her head and dropped a kiss on Mary's pale cheek then stroked a tear away with gentle fingers. "Don't cry, Mary, you are not to blame."

The sun was hot on her head, even through her bonnet, as she sat in her father's luxurious carriage and stared unseeingly at the broad back of Clem Woodruff, her father's elderly coachman. Mary's desolate face was still imprinted on her brain and her mind was busy with the many ways she could help her. She and her mother with the assistance of Laura had formed a branch group of the NUWSS which gave more practical help to those who had been brought to the pit of despair by the evils not only of prostitution but of the sickening taste some men had for children. Mothers sold their girl children for as little as £5, for some men, those with the means to purchase it, demanded a virgin, since a virgin, having known no man's touch, could not pass on a venereal disease.

She was still appalled by the image of the poor, torn-about figure of the girl in the hospital bed. She had not seen her injuries, of course, but she could imagine them for was she not a woman too whose own female body could be just as mutilated by a man, a thought that made her cringe.

Opening her dainty, ivory-handled parasol, which was really nothing more than a froth of white tulle ribbons and rosettes supported by a scrap of organdie to match her gown, she raised it over her head, for the sun beat down fiercely from a deep blue sky clear of all cloud. She had not passed through the town of St Helens itself, as Claughton Street and the hospital were on the outskirts, but behind her a great yellow pall hung over the hundreds of chimneys that belched filthy smoke and soot. St Helens was an industrial town crammed with factories that made soap, vitriol, alkali, smelting copper and was concerned with the manufacture of nails and bolts and, what had made her own family wealthy, making glass. Foundries and refining plants added their filth and around the town were the collieries which provided the coal to feed the furnaces that kept it all going. It was a thriving, growing town, filled with hard-headed businessmen like her father, men with sharp minds and the ability to make a profit and not caring how they did it!

Her gown of apricot organdie was light and pretty but the half bustle at her back and the petticoats she wore did nothing to help her keep cool. The meeting at Laura Bennett's house had gone well: at least three dozen of the leading ladies of the town, all keen advocates of the equality of women, had crammed into Laura's drawing-room and hallway and had even stood in the doorway that opened into her dining-room. Mrs Butler had spoken well and feelingly on her crusade, sixteen years of it, to have the Contagious Diseases Act repealed, in which she had at last succeeded. But there was still much to be done, she said on behalf of women and girl children everywhere. "This very night in London, and every night, year in and year out, not seven maidens only, but many times seven, selected almost as much by chance as those in the Athenian market-place drew lots as to which should be flung in to the Cretan labyrinth, will be offered up as the maiden tribute to modern Babylon," she had cried. She had brought tears to many eyes as she described what she, and others, had suffered at the hands of men at their meetings, the obscene verbal abuse, and even physical abuse, but nevertheless they had to carry on.

The meeting almost over, Doctor Bennett, who, with other enlightened gentlemen, supported the women's cause and who had stood to listen to Mrs Butler, drew Beth aside with the request that she accompany him to the Providence Free Hospital on the edge of town where a young woman needed help. Perhaps Beth's own particular help in the near future.

The carriage rolled eastwards towards Lantern Hill along a lane deep in the colour and scents of summer. Bracken grew a vivid green on the slopes of the gentle moorland that surrounded the town, patched with the dense purple of heather. Dry-stone walls edged the dusty lane and were submerged with hedge parsley, dock, nettle, meadow cranesbill, ragwort and foxglove, the plants somehow finding sustenance between the stones and in the dry ditches. The tantalising smell of sweet cecily, which grew a foot high, mixed fragrantly with the rest. A chiff-chaff was perched on the delicate branch of a hornbeam, pecking at the catkins but it winged away as the carriage approached. A linnet sang sweetly and, on the far side of the wall, standing belly-deep in the meadow grass and scarlet of poppies, a cow lowed plaintively. A sad sound which aroused melancholy in Beth's breast. She felt no inclination to return to Lantern Hill where she knew Milly would be full of her morning's ride, no doubt boasting of her conquest of Hugh Thornley, for Milly had a way of making things happen and if Hugh was about in the area near the garrison, her sister would find him. Father would be in a mood of outrage caused by Milly's wilful flightiness, not helped by his wife's continued absence and all Beth wanted, needed was, at this moment, peace and quiet to contemplate the pitiful state of Mary Smith and women like her and how to alleviate their condition.

There was only one place where she would find such tranquillity.

"Take me to Edge Bottom, Clem," she told the broad back of the coachman. "I think I'll beg lunch from Archie."

"Edge Bottom, Miss Beth," Clem answered in horror, as though she had stated her intention of travelling to London for an hour or two. "Nay, tha' pa will be waitin' on yer at Lantern Hill. Yer know what he's like." With the familiarity of an old servant the coachman was prepared to argue. They all knew how their master fretted when the mistress was at one of her meetings and with Miss Milly galloping all over the place, as Seth had described it this morning when he had seen her take off towards the woodland, the master would be in a right state. Besides, Clem had been hanging about all morning, first at Claughton Street and then at the hospital, and he was eager to get home to his wife and the good dinner she would have ready for him on the table. He'd have to get back to Claughton Street as soon as may be to fetch the mistress and the detour to Edge Bottom, where Archie Goodwin resided, was not something he relished.

"Never you mind, Clem. My father can manage without me for once and anyway surely Milly will be back to eat lunch with him by now."

"Well, I dunno . . ." Shaking his head, ready to give her further argument.

Her voice was sharp. "Clem, will you just drop me off at Edge Bottom and Archie will bring me home in the gig."

"I'd rather tekk yer directly home, Miss Beth. Tha' pa'll—"

"Clem, must I argue with you?"

"Now, Miss Beth, yer know I'm responsible—"

"Clem, will you do as you're told. I shall be perfectly safe with Archie. If you don't turn round now I shall get out and walk and then my father really will be angry."

Clem sighed dramatically but, doing as he was told, he clucked to the horses and at a handy farm gate turned the carriage in the direction of Edge Bottom.

Archie Goodwin's face lit up when Beth came round the corner of the house and began to walk across the stable yard towards the paddock. He and Clancy had a pretty little grey mare on a lunge rein and the animal was walking neatly round and round the perimeter of the paddock before being urged into a trot. Archie held a whip, not to beat but to guide her, for Archie Goodwin, second only to his feelings for Beth Goodwin, loved horses. He had four, and it was his plan to breed from them, to fill the two paddocks with foals from Molly, a chestnut mare of impeccable lineage, and from the well-bred grey mare named Genette when they were old enough. He had a black and white Welsh cob, a sturdy, frisky little mount he had called Firefly, which he knew would make a good mount for a child, for the children he hoped to have one day, and a black hunter who, because of his inclination to leap at anything to which he was put without fear, he called Plunger.

It was Genette who was being trained on the lunge rein and it was Archie's fierce and determined hope that one day she would be ridden by Beth Goodwin, though, naturally, nobody knew of it.

Archie was careful to hide the joy that ran through him as Beth approached. A small, rough-haired terrier with a torn ear, which flapped comically as he ran, and which had been dozing in the rough grass on this side of the paddock fence leaped to his feet and began to bark, at the same time wagging his tail furiously in welcome.

"Be quiet, Boy," Archie told him, quiet himself as was his way, then, handing the rein to the groom, climbed the fence and jumped down nimbly. Striding towards her, doing his best not to appear too eager, he smiled the slow, deep smile that was peculiarly his. His lean body was taut and graceful and the sun turned his thick, fair hair to a golden halo. His teeth were firm and white in his sun-browned face, for Archie, when he was not at the glass works in his role of manager, spent all his time out of doors. He played football for the Edge Bottom Wanderers, cricket in season in the works team, enjoyed the foot races which were popular in the area and hunted with the Edge Bottom Hunt.

He had begun at the Edge Bottom Glass Works and its companion the Edge Bottom Brick Works when he was twenty-one years old or thereabouts, for none of them knew his exact age, when he had obtained his engineering degree, and for the last seven years had run the business for Noah Goodwin, at the same time waiting patiently for Beth Goodwin to grow up. He had stood it well for a man who had never laboured in a factory, especially at another's beck and call. Noah was a man who believed that unless his hand was on the tiller the ship would run aground and was therefore inclined to interfere. But Archie had not only kept the vessel on a steady course but had doubled its profits and was himself fast becoming a wealthy and very eligible young man.

When he returned from university Noah had suggested to him, not because he wanted to be rid of him, he was assured, but because a man of his age could hardly relish living at home with his family, that he take over Edge Bottom House, the Goodwin family home which had been empty except for a caretaker since the Goodwins had moved to Lantern Hill. Last year he had been able to ask Noah to name his price and had bought the place for, as he said to his employer and patron, he would need a home to which to bring the bride he meant to have. Noah had agreed but could not draw Archie out on who that bride might be.

Though his hair had the pure fairness of a Scandinavian heritage and his eyes were an incredible blue he was not what might be called a handsome man. Quite plain, in fact, the kind of man who had a face which, when he was absent, was soon forgotten. A medium sort of a man Milly had once spitefully described him as, finely built, his face thin with an air of great quietness about him. A man who, apart from his love of sport, observed life more readily than he participated in it. When he spoke his voice was low so that one had to listen in order to hear him, not hesitant as the men at the works could have told you, but perfectly in keeping with the first impression of inner quietness he offered new acquaintances.

"Beth," he said with great good humour, his eyes intent on hers. "This is a nice surprise. I thought you were to go to Claughton Street to listen to Mrs Butler." He took her arm protectively and began to lead her back towards the paddock, his head bent to hers. "Does this mean you are to lunch with me?" He was dressed in buff-coloured cord breeches, knee-high riding boots and a white shirt, the collar undone and the sleeves rolled up to reveal his lean brown forearms.

"Yes, I'd like to and yes, I did go to Claughton Street but Doctor Bennett took me to the hospital to see a young girl who had been . . . Oh, Archie, she had been examined, dragged to the police station unjustly; a decent girl who was wrongly accused of being a prostitute. Despite the repeal of the Act they forced her . . . Dear God, raped her with that cruel instrument, Archie."

"Beth, I'm so sorry. Let me—" Whatever it was he meant to say or do was interrupted as Beth burst into tears, turning to him like a child who has been unjustly chastised. His arms rose at once to hold her to him and for several joyful minutes, joyful to him at least, she wept into his shirt front, wetting it through. Her slender frame shook and Archie's arms tightened about her. He put his lips to the brim of her small bonnet, wishing he could remove it so that he could kiss her shining, fragrant hair, but she stepped away, sighing deeply, sniffing dolefully. At once his arms dropped to his sides.

"Better?" he asked smilingly.

"Yes, but I must do something for her. The trouble is we are overrun with maidservants at home. I don't suppose . . ." She looked up at him eagerly, teardrops still quivering on the ends of her lashes.

He laughed and shook his head. "Dear God, your waifs and strays come dear, Beth Goodwin. That lad Tucker has taken on in the garden shies away from me every time I speak to him."

"You know he was beaten black and blue by his stepfather, Archie. Can you blame him for being afraid? His mother was so thankful a good place was found for him, though I believe she is paying for it herself since that man is a brute."

"Please, dear Beth, don't ask me to take in his mother as well."

"No, but what about Mary?"

"Mary?"

"Mmm, from the hospital."

"Well, I'll have to consult with Mrs Kyle, of course, but I suppose . . ."

"D'you want me to have a word with her? She's kind-hearted and I'm sure—"

"No, no, I'll do it."

"Oh, Archie, what would I do without you?" She stood on tiptoe and planted a warm kiss on his brown cheek. "Thank you, thank you. That's why I come here so often, you realise that, don't you? I find such peace here with you, peace I can't find at home with Milly forever—" She bit off her words, then, taking his arm, began to lead him towards the paddock where the pretty grey mare was now ready to be led back to the second paddock where the other horses waited for her. The black and white cob whinnied a welcome and he and the mare galloped madly about the grass as though they had been parted for days.

Beth leaned companionably against Archie, dropping her cheek to rest on his shoulder.

"You have some lovely animals, Archie. Is that grey mare a recent purchase?"

"Genette, yes, I saw her at a sale last week and took a fancy to her."

"Isn't she a bit small for you?"

"Yes, she is but I thought—" It was his turn to cut short his sentence.

Beth turned to look curiously into his face. "What?"

"Oh, nothing really, only I suppose one day I might have a wife to ride her."

"*A wife!*" Beth was clearly astonished. Not just at his words but at the sudden dart of something that pierced her chest, then the image of an audaciously grinning face, the deep blue eyes set in it wickedly twinkling, swam into her vision. Black tumbling hair, glossy as a blackbird's wing, a proud lift to a proud head and she was immediately dry-mouthed and breathless, her heart, which had faltered for a moment at the idea of Archie with a wife, quickening its beat for Hugh Thornley.

The man who had affected her so bewilderingly was at that moment kissing with great expertise the full, inviting lips of her sister. Though he had been vastly intrigued by the luscious country bloom of Beth Goodwin, comparing her to a delicious apple waiting to be bitten into, he was never a man to pass up a chance of a dalliance with a willing woman and Milly Goodwin was very willing!

4

It was the following Sunday, another warm and sunny day, when Captain Hugh Thornley, accompanied by Lieutenant Todd Woodruff and Lieutenant Dicky Bentham, galloped wildly up the smoothly raked, tree-lined drive of Lantern Hill, coming to a slithering stop at the foot of the steps that led up to the front door. The gravel scattered across the closely shaved lawns with the force of their horses' hooves, incensing Jack Martin, who, with his undergardener had just spent three hours raking it to perfection and would now have to pick it all out of the grass to avoid damaging the mowing machine. Deer, which had been grazing peacefully, fled in terror as the drive erupted with hoof-beats, a wild-riding, hell-raking sound, which for some reason brought Milly to her feet and held her in an appalled and astonishing rigidity.

They had just finished lunch, Abby and Noah Goodwin, their daughters, Archie Goodwin and Laura and John Bennett, a splendid meal of Chantilly soup, mixed salads and fresh-caught lobster fetched at an exorbitant cost from the fishing village of Lytham. It was followed by compote of apples in syrup with whipped cream, all the preparation supervised by the Goodwins' excellent housekeeper, Harriet Woodruff, mother of Lieutenant Todd Woodruff.

The three gentlemen, Noah, Archie and John Bennett, having smoked their cigars and drunk a glass of brandy in the masculine comfort of Noah's billiard-room, had just re-joined the ladies in Abby's drawing-room, the Bennetts saying they must be off since John had a call to make at the hospital, their ancient carriage and equally ancient carriage horses ready to be brought round to the front of the house when the racket was heard.

"Who the devil's that?" Noah asked ominously, for Sunday, being the only day when his furnaces were not at work, he liked to spend in the peace and quiet of his family and friends. The doorbell rang; in fact it went on and on ringing as though whoever was at the door was actually leaning on it and Ruby could be heard remarking plaintively as she hurried across the wide hallway, "I'm coming. I'm coming."

"It seems the cavalry has arrived," Archie said mildly from the tall French windows that led out on to the terrace. The windows stood open to allow in the soft summer breeze and the fragrance of the flowers planted in Jack Martin's extensive, colourful borders and the big Grecian urns that lined the terrace. Three horses, good mounts too, which one would expect from cavalry officers, were being led away by Harry and Reuben, two of the Goodwin grooms. "I believe one of them is Todd Woodruff."

"And the others?" Milly asked breathlessly.

"Now then, miss, what's all this then?" her father asked suspiciously. "Why should Todd Woodruff come knocking on our front door when his mother and father live in one of our cottages at the back? Answer me that, for it seems to me you were expecting company and what I'd like to know is—"

"Oh, hush, Father."

A very flustered Ruby, who had been employed by the Goodwins for over twenty years and was an experienced parlour-maid and had never been known to be flustered, had flung open the door. "Are you at home, ma'am," she twittered, bobbing a curtsey in her mistress's direction.

"At home! On a bloody Sunday—" Noah began.

"Oh, sir," she interrupted, "there's three soldiers here . . .

well, one's young Todd" – as though he didn't count – "and they beg to be received. That's what one of them said, any-road."

"Dear God Almighty, what next?" Noah roared, but his wife, who had stood up ready to see Laura and John off, put a soothing hand on his arm. Of course she was well aware who had set this tempest to blowing, for wasn't the culprit fidgeting guiltily in the background, her face flushed, her eyes snapping with feverish excitement.

"It's all right, dearest," she said quietly, then, turning to the maid, told her to show the gentlemen in.

They stood to attention just inside the doorway as though they were on parade, and for a moment Beth was convinced they were about to salute. Lieutenant Woodruff, looking somewhat sheepish, for though he had been brought up and educated with the Goodwins and by the patronage of Noah Goodwin, his parents were servants in their employ; Lieute-nant Dicky somebody-or-other – she had seen him at the ball but had not been introduced and she couldn't remember his name, but evidently a gentleman of good family; and Captain Hugh Thornley. Ruby announced them correctly, being well trained, before closing the door on the stunned company and squeaking back to the kitchen to inform the others.

". . . an' one of 'em's young Todd," she finished trium-phantly into Harriet Woodruff's startled face. "So what d'you mekk o' that then? After our young ladies, I'll be bound, though what Todd Woodruff's up to is anybody's guess." What the dickens did the lad think he was doing calling on the young ladies of the house where his mother and father were servants?

There was a certain amount of jealousy on Ruby's part, for her Harry, not much younger than Todd, and who had shared the lessons he and the others had learned, had climbed no higher than a groom, like his father, while Harriet's Todd was now an officer in a cavalry regiment.

"Todd does serve with gentlemen of good family, Ruby," Harriet told her icily, "and he is therefore included in their social life."

"Is he indeed!" Ruby sniffed disdainfully. "Well, what I'd like to know is—"

"It is nothing to do with you, me, or any servant in this house, so I suggest we get on with our work, as we are paid to do."

"I were only sayin'—"

"That will do, Ruby." And since all the women servants were under Harriet Woodruff's command they reluctantly moved back to their allotted tasks.

In the drawing-room Hugh Thornley, as was his well-bred right, spoke first. "Mrs Goodwin, forgive our calling on you unannounced and not at the correct calling hour but I felt it would be good manners on our part to further our acquaintance at the ball last week. But first let me introduce you to my friends. I believe you know Lieutenant Woodruff . . ."

"Aye, we should do, lad," Noah sighed.

"And this is Lieutenant Dicky Bentham."

"We've met."

"But I failed to introduce you which was most remiss of me."

"Those spurs are doing my carpet no good, young man," Noah interrupted him, taking no notice of his lordship's sudden baleful glare, his eyes on the deep-pile floor covering which had cost a fortune.

Abby moved forward, her hand again going out to her husband's arm, saying smoothly, "How very nice of you to call, gentlemen. Won't you sit down?" Which they did. Laura Bennett, with a nod at her John, returned to the chair from which she had just risen, indicating that he must do the same because she was not about to miss whatever was to happen.

"Is it not a glorious day?" his lordship asked them in the long vowel sounds of privilege. "We could not resist the temptation to ride over and enquire after your family's health, could we, chaps?"

The chaps agreed that they could not.

His lordship – for that was who he was this afternoon, not merely Captain Thornley – cast his disarmingly wide smile about the company, inclining his head courteously in the direction of the daughters of the house, making a show of being polite but no more. He ignored Archie as though his own breeding told him instinctively that here was a man of no consequence.

Beth sat carefully in her chair, which was a strange way to describe it but she had a horrid feeling she might just topple out of it. She smoothed the tawny silk of her skirts about her, her back ruler straight and at least four inches from the chair back, her rounded breasts rising and falling rapidly, which undoubtedly caught the eyes of the four young men in the room. Her breath was trapped in her throat and she prayed that no one would speak to her, for she knew she would be unable to answer. Her heart, which she was certain had stopped as Hugh Thornley entered the room, was beating again rapidly and she could feel the flush rise from beneath her bodice and up to her hairline.

Tea was brought by an overwrought Ruby, helped by Sarah, an under-parlour-maid, both immaculate in their black afternoon uniforms, icy-white aprons and fluted caps. Lord Thornley remarked on how unusual it was to be served by maidservants, saying that it was a custom at Thornley Green to have footmen, except in the kitchens, of course, to which his host "hmmphed" sourly. Lieutenant Woodruff said nothing and Lieutenant Bentham, who had advised strongly against calling at Lantern Hill, advice that was, naturally, ignored, laughed nervously at any witticism that came from Hugh's lips.

Noah glowered at the company, determined to show his displeasure to these impudent young pups who had come uninvited to his home and vowed to have a word with Todd Woodruff, for though he might have done well in his chosen career, thanks to himself, he might add, that did not give him the right to make free with Noah Goodwin's hospitality.

Laura and John drank their tea and did their best to keep the polite drawing-room conversation moving pleasantly along, though John did look pointedly at his watch several times while Hugh Thornley, perfectly at his ease, chatted amiably about this and that and the other, enquiring how many acres Lantern Hill might have, proclaiming on the beauty of the garden and the view from the window and the graceful herd of deer which had resumed their grazing. Noah remarked later to his wife he would not have been surprised if the damned insolent fellow had demanded to know the size of his bank balance.

They took their leave half an hour later. The three officers bowed politely over each lady's hand, clicking their heels and standing to attention at the door before being shown out by an entranced Ruby, who could not get over having a real live lord in the house.

"Well," said Laura, "what can we gather from that, I wonder?" keeping her eyes from straying too obviously in Milly's direction. The girl had sat decorously beside her mother, her eyes lowered, her mouth smiling innocently but saying not a word which, in Laura and Abby's opinion, who both knew her wilful, ebullient nature, spoke volumes! She had danced only one dance with the dashing captain at the ball last week but it had not been what might be described as seemly. They had held one another far too closely for society's liking; they had laughed and flirted and though the fellow had left Milly alone afterwards, to her obvious chagrin, here he was calling on the family. What could it mean?

"There is nothing to be gathered from their visit, Laura," Noah proclaimed coldly, "and I would be obliged if you would not imply there might be. I know nothing of Dicky what's-his-name but Todd Woodruff has always been a scamp."

"Oh, Noah, you cannot say that. He is a charming young man," Abby murmured but Noah was not to be put off.

"He is a scamp and I had hopes that when he went into the army we might see little of him. Clem and Harriet are such steady, reliable folk one wonders how they bred a lad such as him."

"Really, Noah . . ."

"No, Abby, he has been indulged from birth and the result is as you see and in a way I blame myself. As for that insolent rogue Lord bloody Thornley he can go to hell on a handcart. Worming his way into my house, admiring the bloody view and hoping, no doubt, to get one of my girls. I heard he has made it clear he intends to revive the Thornley Hunt which means dozens of hounds, whippers-in, earth-stoppers, not to mention the price of a decent hunter. A wealthy wife would not go amiss, I'm thinking, but if he hopes he can come sniffing round here, then he's got another bloody think coming. Oh, John, Laura, you off then? Yes, I agree, it's been a damned queer afternoon, and Laura, you know I meant no offence. Well, you know what I mean."

"My dear Noah, think no more of it. I realise you were . . . well, come along John," beckoning to her husband, giving the impression that it was he who had held up their departure.

Nobody but Archie, who saw all but said little, noticed the jubilant smile on Milly's face as she followed her parents to the front door where the Bennetts' carriage waited, nor the rigidly held, slightly trembling figure of Beth at her back. The ladies kissed warmly, the gentlemen shook hands. Archie said he must be off as he had accounts to go over, which was not true. He needed to hide himself away from public gaze while he faced the appalling truth that Beth, *his* Beth, along with her sister, had feelings for Lord Thornley.

Beth had called at the hospital to check on the progress of Mary Smith, taking more flowers and a basket of fruit. Apples from the orchard, Early Harvest which had just ripened, plums and damsons, peaches and pears and even a pineapple cultivated in the greenhouse, which aroused great interest since none of the women, nurses or patients, had ever seen one. Mary was still weak from loss of blood but her wounds, which Doctor Bennett had been forced to stitch, were healing well, the nurse told her. Mary had smiled shyly at Beth, nodding her head on the pillow in lieu of the customary curtsey.

"I have found you a post, Mary," Beth began, crouching at the girl's bedside.

Mary's face lit up and a touch of colour tinted her cheek. "With you, miss? Oh, I should like to work for you. I don't want ter have anything to do with men, not after . . . you know . . ." Her eyes beseeched Beth to understand.

"Well, no, it's not at my house, Mary, but in the kitchen of a very good friend of my family. A relative, in a way. He even has the same surname. Mr Goodwin, he's called, kind and respectable. He is a bachelor but his housekeeper is a good woman who will allow you to work as your health demands. Doctor Bennett has assured me—"

"Oh please, miss, let me come ter you." Mary was so agitated her work-roughened hands scrabbled in the air, doing their best to reach up to Beth's face. "I don't care what I do . . . scrubbin', anythin'." She began to cough, her fiercely drawn breath rasping in her throat. The nurse looked up anxiously from the table where she was writing something and half rose from her seat.

Beth patted Mary's hands and murmured soothingly but it was very evident that Mary's fear and horror of the male sex would not allow her to take employment in a house where there was no mistress to turn to. The images of what had been done to her, first by a man who she believed loved her and whom she had trusted, then by doctors at the prison, were as vivid in her mind as though it had happened this morning. Even Doctor Bennett, who had administered a drop or two of chloroform to render her passive while he sewed her up, was regarded suspiciously and it had been left to the nurse to examine her injuries since and report to the doctor. It had been partly Mary's own fault that she had been so mutilated, for had she not struggled so violently – and could you blame her? Doctor Bennett asked – she might have sustained less tearing.

But that was not the problem now. The damage was done and Beth had made a promise to the girl and she meant to keep it. She would have to prevail on her mother, who at least was aware of the dreadful evil that was done to women, to take Mary on in the kitchen. Harriet might declare that she had no need of another maidservant but surely in the circumstances she would understand.

"Now you must not worry, Mary. I promise you will be found work in my own home. Doctor Bennett will get you well and then . . . I'll come and see you and when you are better you shall come home with me. Sleep now . . ." For the girl was drained by even this short conversation.

When she reached home there was no one to greet her except Sarah who opened the front door as the carriage drew up.

"Yer mam's out callin', miss," Sarah told her cheerfully, "an' Miss Milly's gone with 'er. Not that she were best pleased about it, I can tell yer. She wanted ter go ridin' but yer mam weren't havin' that. 'Yer ter come wi' me, lass,' she told her. Now, will I fetch yer a nice cuppa tea, Miss Beth, or 'appen hot chocolate?"

Beth reflected on the difference between this girl, who must be about the same age, and the one she had left lying hollow-eyed and haunted with nightmares in her bed at the hospital. But then Sarah, who, she supposed, worked hard in her capacity as parlour-maid, had known nothing but kindness in the Goodwin household. Harriet was a strict disciplinarian but she was fair with the maidservants and thoughtful of their welfare.

"No, thank you, Sarah, but I think I might have a walk across the park. It's such a lovely day and I've been cooped up in the hospital all morning." Where the smells were not at all fragrant, she might have added.

"Eeh, Miss Beth," the maid said, taking Beth's bonnet, her gloves and parasol. "Yer shouldn't be goin' ter such places. Not a well-brought-up young lady like you. Yer never know what yer might pick up. Me mam'd have a fit if I were ter go, I can tell yer." She tossed her head as though she were the lady and Beth the housemaid!

"Some of the patients have no choice, Sarah. It's that or the workhouse."

"Aye, I suppose so," Sarah said sadly, then brightened, for it was nothing to do with a respectable girl like herself. Prostitutes, she had heard, and here was Miss Beth mixing with them. It was quite shocking, really it was. She sighed then smiled her apple-cheeked smile. "Now you go and get a breath of fresh air an' I'll tell Mrs Ellman ter cook yer summat nice fer yer lunch," just as though young Sarah Sidebottom had the ordering of the kitchen! "But won't yer tekk yer parasol?" For Sarah, having worked in a gentleman's residence for six years, had become accustomed to the general notion that a young lady's complexion should be protected from the rays of the sun which did not affect the ordinary working woman.

"No, I won't be long, Sarah."

The parkland stretched out on four sides of the house and cultivated gardens, rolling green hillocks and hollows dotted with great oak trees, which had been left in place when the land was cleared to build Noah Goodwin's house, and all leading to the woodland that lay at the far side. The rough grass, which was grazed by the small herd of deer who wandered un-hindered within the property walls, was sparse and brown in a circle beneath each tree which were all in full summer leaf and, sheltering from the heat of the midday sun, the deer themselves lay dozing in the shade.

She had passed the paddocks where the horses, despite the warmth, at the sight of her began to trot and canter as though showing off, arching their necks, kicking and strutting as they broke into a mad gallop, tails streaming. Flame was Milly's sorrel and her own Rosy, a smaller chestnut, the two coal-black carriage horses, Piper and Major, and her father's tall bay whom he had named Albert in memory of their Queen's dead husband.

She wished she had taken Sarah's advice and brought her parasol, for the sun beat down on her unprotected head, turning its rich russet to flame and putting a silver glint in her eyes.

There was a wooden fence dividing the parkland from the wood to keep the deer from straying and she approached it with some dismay. The woodland on the far side looked cool, the leaves of beech and hornbeam overlapping to cast a pleasant shade. There was a particular glade that was a favourite of hers, calm and restful with only holly bushes able to grow in the limited light and the trunk of a fallen tree on which to sit. But first she must get herself over the fence, which was not easy in her fashionable, sheath-like gown with its modest bustle and small train. It was white, a light leno which was a transparent, muslin-like textile of linen thread. The sleeves were short and puffed, the bodice well fitted and the skirt straight in front with a small "apron" edged with pink roses and silver ribbon. Her boots were of white kid but already they were grass-stained and she wished she had changed into something more suitable for walking. She had not meant to come so far but the clear cool depths of the wood drew her on.

Well, there was nothing else for it but to tackle the fence in the only way possible and that was to hitch up her skirts and petticoat and, revealing her frilled drawers which, after all, only the deer would see, throw first one leg over the fence, then the other, and jump down.

"That was well done," a voice said laughingly and her heart tripped and began to hammer as her wide eyes took in the ebony hunter, a star blaze between its eyes, which was tethered to a stunted hawthorn and the restless hound dog which sniffed at the ditch at the edge of the track. She hardly dared move though she knew full well who the voice belonged to. Her hands went to her breast when he stepped out from behind the gnarled and twisted trunk of an oak tree and there he was, the man who had occupied so much of her thoughts since the Jubilee Ball. He had not danced with her though their eyes had met and exchanged some message as she entered the ballroom, but here he was after that astonishing visit to her home, apparently waiting for her beneath the trees.

"I wasn't . . . I didn't . . ." she stammered, a bright blush pinking her cheeks, and Hugh Thornley was enchanted.

It was not actually her he had been waiting for, though he was overjoyed that she was the one to turn up. It would not be at all like the delicious hour he had spent with her sister last week, for this one was as innocent and pure as a snowdrop, the thought surprising him as he was not usually of a romantic or sentimental turn of mind. Milly had allowed him several small intimacies as well as responding most satisfactorily to his kisses, all promising a great deal of entertainment in the future, but this one was different, and in the arrogant and unequivocal belief that his name and breeding would allow nothing to stand in his way he decided right there and then that Beth Goodwin would be his future wife, which was not to say that in the meanwhile he would not continue to dally with her sister. It had been something of a challenge to him, for both of them were lovely and would be very, very wealthy. Milly was spirited, self-willed, with a quick temper and he would have enjoyed breaking her in. But this one had something for which he could find no name. She stood with her back to the fence, her eyes a deep and velvety grey, huge in her rosy face, her lips parted a little and as he watched she moistened them with her little pink tongue. He felt the heat of his desire gather in the pit of his belly and his eyes narrowed speculatively, but she was shy, wide-eyed, perhaps a little afraid, like a young doe caught in a beam of sunlight. Dear God, he must be careful. Dear sweet Christ, he must not alarm her in any way.

He smiled gently. "You were to take a walk in the wood-land?" he questioned and when she nodded speechlessly he offered her his arm. "May I go a little way with you?" he asked gravely and was elated when she took it and allowed him to lead her across the mossy woodland floor where violets and wood sorrel grew.

thin, plain, awkward, shy and twenty years old when she met

5

"Have you a moment to spare, Mama?" Hugh asked silkily as he opened the dining-room door to allow his mother to pass through on her way to her drawing-room.

Startled, she looked up into his face, hesitating for a moment before continuing across the hall. It was not often her son sought her company, in fact she had been surprised when he suggested he dine with her this evening. He was still in his uniform since he had come straight from the barracks, outrageously attractive and charming, and she wondered now as she so often wondered in the dark, troubled hours of the night whether she could go through again with her son what she had suffered with his father. He was so like Miles to look at. Incredibly handsome but with that mocking smile that was so confusing even to her who had given birth to him. It promised so much and yet meant so little, for like his father he was quite without a heart.

She had been Lady Caroline Woodward, daughter of Sir Ernest and Lady Felicia Woodward. She had been rich, tall, thin, plain, awkward, shy and twenty years old when she met the then Honourable Miles Thornley, son and heir to Lord Thornley of Thornley Green, fourteenth baron of the line. That had been over thirty years ago and now, in her fifties, she was the same as she had been then, apart from the fact that she was no longer rich. She had hair of no particular colour with perhaps a shade more grey in it, a face sallow and heavily lined, for one does not retain one's youth when forced to live as wife to a roué, a gambler, a libertine, an adulterer, a rakehell and, worse still, to give birth to a boy who grew into his father. And yet she could not help but love him as she had loved his father. She was a lady with pedigree bred in her bones, from the same privileged class as her dead husband and she had convinced herself that if some young lady of quality could be found, a young lady with a decent dowry, one who would equal her son's lineage, it would steady him. Settle him to the life he should be leading as one of the county's great landowners. With a wife and children and the financial means to do so he might be persuaded to resign his commission and become as his grandfather had been, the grandfather after whom he had been named.

They had dined, one at each end of the table which glowed like silk in the candlelight. Rich silver, though slightly tarnished, gleamed alongside delicate crystal glassware. They had partaken of a clear soup, turbot *à la crème*, lamb cutlets, finishing with cheese and grapes. Caroline Thornley had expected to drink her coffee alone beside her small drawing-room fire, for every night that he was home, which wasn't often, her son made his polite excuses – he was always unfailingly polite – and, leaping into the saddle, galloped off to whatever diversion he had chosen for himself. He had drunk a great deal of wine, of which a few good bottles remained, put down years ago by his grandfather. The cellar at Thornley Green had been famous for its wines, for though Hugh Charles, the fourteenth Lord Thornley was a moral, God-fearing man he had liked the good things in life. In moderation, of course, and how he had ever sired a son such as Miles was a puzzle that had mystified his friends for years. Some throwback to a past generation perhaps, and now that son had sired a son who, if his mother could not get him to settle to a decent life soon, would end up like his father.

"Of course, Hugh. Perhaps you would care to take coffee with me?"

"Thank you, Mama. That would be very pleasant."

"Coffee in here then, Jackson." She nodded graciously at the hovering footman who hurried away to pass on the amazing news that his lordship was to take coffee in his mama's drawing-room.

"Well, I'll be blowed," said the cook, not caring really, for it was not her job to make or serve the coffee. It had already been laid out on a tray by Polly and was, by now, barely warm, since Polly, like the rest of the servants in the carelessly run house which had long been without a housekeeper, had her feet up for the evening.

"What's he up to then?" Barker, the under-footman asked. "He must want summat."

"Don't he always," Jackson remarked laconically, hefting the tray up and making for the door that led into the enormous hall and which even now in the late summer was as cold as a tomb. Once, of course, when there had been money, a great fire would have roared halfway up the chimney, which was at least six feet wide, but those days had long gone.

Jackson placed the tray on the table close to her ladyship, bowed, and hurried back to the only room in the house to be warm. Lady Thornley poured the coffee, handing a cup to her son who leaned indolently against the marble fireplace, one arm resting on the mantelpiece. He appeared to glance about him as though noticing for the first time the neglect and decay of the once beautiful room. It was twenty years almost since his father had died in mysterious circumstances, something to do with a woman, it was whispered, and in that time, and even before, there had been a gradual running down of the standards that had once prevailed. In fact he really had no idea how his mother managed, for there must be at least ten servants' wages to be found. The carpets were frayed and the brocade of the handsome sofa on which his mother sat was faded, worn, its stuffing ready to escape. Cobwebs hung high in the ceiling from the dimmed crystal droplets of the chandelier. The tabletops had a fine film of dust on them and he had acknowledged as he cantered up the drive that led to the house that the grounds had been seriously neglected.

"How many gardeners do we have, Mama?" he asked abruptly, reaching into his pocket for his cigars, then lighting one without asking her permission.

She blinked in surprise. "Two, I believe."

"You believe! Don't you know?"

"My dear, have you not recognised that I can't get about as much as I would like? I have . . . well, let us just say I suffer a great deal of pain when walking and with only the gig and the cob to pull it, it is very difficult to—"

"That will all change very soon, Mama, which is why I asked to talk to you. To tell you that I am to be married and to a young lady with a splendid dowry."

"Oh, Hugh, my dear Hugh." His mama's face lit up and she struggled to rise from the sofa and embrace him.

He allowed her to put her arms decorously about his shoulders, then, smiling, stepped away and moved across the room to the window that overlooked a park which made the one at Lantern Hill look like a small garden set about a semi-detached villa.

"Who is she, dearest? I can hardly believe it. I don't think I have ever been so happy, but why have you been so secretive? I didn't even know you had an interest in any young lady. Do I know her, or her family? And where is their place? My dear, I am so excited. Oh, please, do come over here and sit down. I want to know every detail."

He did as she asked, returning to the sofa opposite the one on which she sat. He lounged in it, his head on the high back, his legs stretched out and crossed at the ankle. Throwing the stub of his cigar into the heart of the small fire, he immediately lit another. His coffee stood untouched on the mantelpiece.

"No, Mama, you don't know her, or her family. Their name is Goodwin and her father is reported to be the wealthiest man in St Helens, perhaps even Lancashire. They have a place between here and St Helens. Newly built." Which it was to Hugh whose ancestral home had stood for hundreds of years. "He owns many businesses and—"

"*Businesses?*" Caroline Thornley's voice rose an octave and her hand went to her mouth in consternation. So great was her horror he might have stated his intention to marry one of her scullery-maids. Her already sallow face drained of what colour it had.

"Yes, he is a businessman. Glass works, brick works, that sort of thing, shares in any venture that makes money and, Mama, he has a lot of it. Miss Goodwin is a lovely girl, well brought up—"

"But who are her people—"

"I've just told you. I believe her grandmother was married to an Irish labourer. She had an illegitimate daughter, Miss Goodwin's mother, and still lives in a cottage in—"

"*Hugh!*" The shriek that skirled from Lady Thornley's mouth could be heard in the kitchen and the servants all lifted their heads to listen, looking at one another in amazement.

"Now what's up?" Cook quavered but none could give her an answer.

In the drawing-room the cause of the shriek spoke quietly. "It's no good, Mama. I have made up my mind. I knew you would not be pleased . . ."

"*Pleased!* Dear God in heaven!"

". . . would not approve but I'm afraid the decision has been made."

He stood up impatiently and pulled the bell to summon a servant and when Jackson hastily entered the room told him to fetch him a whisky.

"A whisky, m'lord," the footman repeated unwisely.

"A whisky, man. You have such a thing in the butler's pantry, I believe. In fact bring the bottle and then clear off."

Her ladyship sat as though poleaxed, her hands gripping one another fiercely, the knuckles white, her eyes staring at some ghastly picture which included illegitimate children, Irish labourers, sod cottages and factories. Her quiet dignity, part of her breeding, the lineage from which she had come, was ready to be shattered. She was of the ruling class, stiff-backed, stiff-necked, unbending in her self-belief, with a high-bred endurance that had got her through the years of her marriage and the cruelties she had suffered at her husband's hands. She had lived in genteel poverty for many years and would go on doing so for the remainder of her life rather than have her son marry into a family of the manufacturing class.

"I forbid it, Hugh. No manufacturer has ever crossed the threshold of this house, and never will. We will be shunned by good society and—"

"May I remind you, Mama, that though you are the mistress – for the time being – this is *my* house and I will bring whoever I like into it. I have been reluctant to invite my friends here since the delapidation has become so pronounced and the roof and windows are . . . well, that will all be put in the hands of a capable steward when I am married and have the wherewithal to do so. I mean to revive the Thornley Green Hunt, restock the stables and begin preserving game birds on the moorland as was done in my grandfather's day."

"Hugh, please," his mother said faintly. "This girl will never fit in among . . . among our friends. She will be an outsider."

"*Our friends!* What friends? How much entertaining has gone on lately, tell me that, Mama? When did we last have a dinner party, a ball? Well, I mean to rectify that with Goodwin's money. And you will find Miss Goodwin well-mannered and submissive. She will not shame you or our family. She is shy, very pretty and is madly in love with me."

He smiled his devilish smile and for a moment Lady Caroline felt a dart of pity pierce her for this unknown girl Hugh had chosen for a wife. She was to marry him not because he loved her but because she could bring him the life he thought himself entitled to. In fact for the exact reasons Miles had married her.

"I am telling you this, Mama, because I wish you to invite her family to a dinner party at Thornley Green. Some of our old friends would be glad to come, I'm sure. What about old Lady Hawthornthwaite from the Hall and Lady Faulkner would be glad to renew her friendship."

"We were never close friends," Lady Caroline said hollowly.

"Then look through your guest book and find someone who is. I will go over the guest list with you and the invitations. You will have to smarten the servants up and tell that cook to buck up her ideas, for the Goodwins, I have been told, have the finest cook in the county. Now, Mama, I must be off."

"Hugh, I beg you to reconsider. There are many eligible young ladies who would jump at the chance of marriage to an old family like ours. Selina Morton-Hamilton for one. Her family has no title but comes from a long line descended from some of the greatest names in the country. Her grandmother was the daughter of a viscount. They have no money but immense prestige—"

"There you have it, Mama. No money! Miss Goodwin has everything I need. Looks and money and comes from good stock, working class, of course, but she will have strong children. She will fit perfectly into her role as mistress of this house and mother of my children so you had best start inspecting the dower house. Now, I must be off. I have an urgent appointment and I'm late already. Shall we say by the end of the month then?"

"Hugh." The whisper of despair followed him as he strode

from the room but he merely smiled as he called for his horse to be brought round to the front of the house.

She was waiting for him in the tiny clearing they had found in the woodland at the edge of the park. It was September and for the past three months he had been coming here, leading his animal through the small arched gateway which she had unbolted, and looping the reins on the branch of a holly bush. There was an enormous hornbeam, the roots of which formed a deep nest, rising to hide them from prying eyes, though there were none, of course, and mosses that created a soft velvet bed on which they lay.

It was not yet quite dark and he could see her leaning against the trunk of the tree. He knew she would be furious at being kept waiting but he didn't much care, for within thirty seconds he would have that sulky mouth beneath his own, silenced, opening, biting, caressing, her tongue reaching for his as he had taught her to do.

Within minutes he had her naked in his hands, then himself, laying her back, her legs spread. She had tiny pointed breasts, like her sister's his heated mind had time to reflect, though he had not, of course, seen Beth's, the nipples hard and thrusting into the palms of his hands. After three months of making love to her he really had not the time, nor the inclination, to bother with the preliminaries so after running his hands casually over her, his manhood surging demandingly against her belly, he penetrated her at once as he had done many times. He cried out in orgasm, as she did, and all about them the small night animals were still and quiet.

He lay for several minutes, heavy and inert across her body, both of them breathing harshly, then she pushed him off and sat up, her pert breasts falling forward in the most delightful way. Her hair, so gloriously a shade of copper in the sunlight, fell in a tumbled cape to her naked buttocks, dark now as night fell. For a moment he was tempted to begin again but her words, sharp and sibilant as the hiss of a snake, drove all such thoughts from his mind. Indeed *every* thought from his mind, for this was not what he had planned. This was not the sister he meant to marry and for several seconds as her words echoed frighteningly in his head he was speechless, his quick wit and tongue paralysed.

"Hugh, I believe I am with child," were the words she spoke.

At first they made no sense, which was mad really for had he not been making love to her for the past three months? In a daze he wondered why it had not occurred to him that he might make her pregnant, then as his brain cleared he realised that he had never before had intercourse with a woman of good family. Those he had lain with had either been farm girls, dairymaids, actresses, shop girls or older women, married women who knew how to look after themselves. It had not concerned him if he had got a child on a girl from the lower classes, for a guinea or two would shut them up. But this one was from a decent family whose father, surely the most powerful man in St Helens, would not take kindly to his unmarried daughter being with child. His brain was still stupefied, unable to think this out, for while he had been making love to this one he had at the same time been gently leading Beth Goodwin along the innocent and proper path towards marriage. It had titillated his perverted senses to be the gentleman in the afternoon and the rampant lover in the evening, since he had been unable to resist the sensuous advances of her twin sister. He had never known a woman with such fire, passion, a seemingly unending, un-slaked sexual urge as Milly Goodwin. Her hunger, her lust was almost masculine in its ferocity and he had quite simply been carried along with it. Marriage had never been mentioned between them and that very fact had lulled him into believing that, like him, she wanted nothing more than what they took from each other.

But her female biology had caught them out just when he had begun to put into action his plans for Beth Goodwin. This very evening he had set in motion through his own mother the means to pave the way to marriage with Beth.

"Are you sure?" The standard question put by all males in the ageless quandary their lust had got them into.

"Of course I'm sure. I'm three weeks late and I'm punctual to the hour."

"Jesus wept!" He wrapped his arms about his bent knees and bowed his head on them.

"And what's that supposed to mean?" Milly snapped, for though she had come to the conclusion in the last three months that she really did not love Hugh Thornley, not in a romantic sense, that is, his body set hers on fire and it had been hard to resist.

"I don't know, for God's sake. An abortion, I suppose. I could ask Dicky. He got a girl into trouble last year and took her to Liverpool where this doctor did the job. I'd pay for it, naturally."

He raised his head hopefully and none of his friends would have recognised him at this precise moment. Not exactly hangdog, but worried about how this was to affect his plans for Beth. Even if Milly was willing, could he arrange for her to have the child got rid of and then turn round and ask her sister to be his wife?

"You bastard! If you think I'm going to some back-street quack and have my inside ripped out, you can think again. This baby is yours, a Thornley, and I want it born legitimately. My father will try to kill you but he won't allow me to be shamed, nor his family name dishonoured."

"God in heaven! Anyone would think his family name meant something." But even as he cursed her and himself a face drifted across his vision. A face the smooth creamy white of a camellia, fine, transparent skin, eyes wide and a pale silvery grey set in long, dark lashes. A mouth the colour and sweetness of a ripe apricot stretched over white, even teeth when she smiled. Beauty and grace. Beth Goodwin, who he had meant to make his wife. She would have made a splendid Lady Thornley. And now this bitch had, through her own bloody carelessness, ruined everything. All the careful plans he had made would be swept aside and, by God, if he could have killed her and got away with it he would have done.

She had reached for her clothing and was shrugging herself into them, arranging her lace petticoats and silken skirts, buttoning up her bodice and tossing back her hair with a calmness that infuriated him. She was confident, smug even, firm in the belief that she had caught herself the most handsome, eligible bachelor – apart from his lack of money, and her father would take care of that – in the county. He did not believe she had deliberately set out to trap him with the oldest trick in the world, for what woman of good family wants her reputation ruined, but she was not displeased with the results.

She pulled on her stockings, adjusted her garters above her knees, then her boots, and when she was once more decent, turned to him expectantly. "Well," she said, "are you to get dressed or are you to see my father as you are?" Her eyes travelled smilingly across his nakedness.

"I'm not sure I understand you, my pet," he drawled, for little by little he was recovering and becoming more the Hugh Thornley he had been since his young manhood. He had always managed to avoid – or smash right through – anything that might get in his way. His mother had indulged him and any boy, or, as he grew, young man, or woman who challenged him was swiftly and ruthlessly dealt with. His magnificent, deep blue smile bewitched and if that didn't work he tried persuasion. Just a quiet word at first, spoken good-naturedly, to let whoever it was opposed to him know that it really would be best to reconsider. But it was the next stage in his determination to get the better of a man, or a woman, that was the most frightening. He became so violent he sometimes alarmed himself when the episode was over, for the menace within him was a living, vital thing. He could feel himself begin to snarl like a beast as something inside him fought to escape the gentlemanly chains that had been bred in him. He had never known fear. He had never known any soft feeling such as the love other chaps spoke of. At twenty-seven he was really no more than a scraped-out void, a man so emotionally laid waste there was nothing to him but the masculine beauty he showed the world. He was a mixture of avarice, pitilessness, self-interest and contempt for those whom he considered his inferiors. He was bored so he searched for relief in any way he could and his boredom had led to this moment, this woman who was telling him that she expected him to get into his uniform and cross the park with her to Lantern Hill where he was to confess to her family that he had got her with child and was prepared to marry her.

He reached into the pocket of the high-necked frock-coat which, along with a waistcoat and tight, high-waisted overalls, was the uniform of duty officer and which he had worn to dine with his mother. He took out his cigar case. Smilingly he lit a cigar then, with a swift, vicious movement, hit her across her face with the back of his hand, stunning her. She fell backwards into the deep roots of the tree where she lay still. Rising gracefully to his feet, he put on his uniform, pulling on his highly polished boots, then, with an ease and casualness which said he had all the time in the world, he strolled to where he had left his horse. He was about to mount the animal when from somewhere came the thought that he had just chucked away, as though it were the farthing one might throw at a beggar, a great deal of money: the life he was to lead, the hunt, the thoroughbred hunters, the free hand at the gambling table, a bottomless pocket which held the wherewithal to pay his tailor, the wine merchant, the restoration of Thornley Green. All had been put at great risk because of the vicious rage that had coursed through him at what he had believed was the ruination of his plans.

He leaned his forehead on the gelding's glossy neck, standing for several long seconds allowing his clever, dangerous mind to consider what he must do, then he began to smile. Hell's teeth, what was he thinking of? They were all the same with their drawers off and their legs spread, when all was said and done. Females with the same female equipment, the same capacity to breed sons, so what did it really matter which one he married? Both would bring him the income he required, so why should he care whether it was Beth or Milly Goodwin who became Lady Thornley? The one he had just smacked in the face had already proved she was fertile and, as he had once imagined with a passing thought, she would be a joy to tame. She was as sexually greedy as himself; as active and lusty in her needs as any full-blooded man could wish for and it might be amusing to humiliate her. He knew of many ways!

He sighed, since the other one, the quiet one, had quite caught his fancy as a novelty to his jaded sexual appetite, but thank God he had gone no further with her than a stroll through the woodland. They had sat talking on the fallen trunk of a tree in a small clearing which she had shyly admitted was her favourite place to which she liked to escape. He had made her laugh and prompted her to reveal her dreams for the betterment of women, which, naturally, he would soon knock on the head, and had never been so bored in his life, but not once had he laid a hand on her, let alone tried to kiss her.

He patted the gelding's arched neck, for strangely he was never cruel to animals, then made his way back to where Milly was trying to sit up. She was crying and for a moment she shrank back as he approached, then like a shrieking fury she launched herself to her feet and straight at him, her nails reaching for his face.

"You devil . . . you beast. I'll kill you for this. I hate you . . . just wait until my father hears of this."

"Don't, my darling, don't." It was the first time he had called her his darling and it caught her attention. "Don't you see, I was confounded, taken by surprise, though why I should be I don't know for there's been nothing but this for the past three months. I lost my temper and I'm sorry. I'm a bit inclined to lash out when . . . well, you'll find out when we're married. You'll have to be patient with me, sweetheart, for the role of husband will be new to me."

He put his arms about her and drew her tenderly to him. "Let me see . . ." framing her face with gentle hands, then bending to place a soft kiss on her cheekbone which was already beginning to swell. "Say you forgive me, my dearest love, and then come and sit down again beside me while we make our plans."

"Plans?" she whispered, her head still ringing from his blow, allowing him to lead her back to the sheltered spot in the roots of the tree.

"Naturally we must make plans, my love, the first being how we are to tackle your papa who has made it quite clear he despises me and all my class."

"We . . . you want to marry me?" For once Milly was almost speechless.

"Of course, haven't I said so? As a matter of fact I have just dined with my mother and told her all about you. Well, not quite . . ." He laughed, glancing about him. "She wants to meet you and is to send out invitations to your family to a dinner party."

"Lady Thornley?"

"Indeed."

"I mean, I will be Lady Thornley."

"If you accept my proposal."

"I can't believe it."

"This is what I have had in mind since we met, didn't you know? Mind you, I had hoped to go about it in a more conventional way but . . . well, the wedding must be arranged at once. No, not tonight, my love. Tomorrow I will call formally on your father but, darling, I think it would be unwise to mention the child at this juncture. Wait until we are married, but it must be soon."

"Of course, but what about my face? There's bound to be a bruise. I can hardly say my future husband did it, can I? God, you're a brute, Hugh Thornley. I've a good mind to smack you back."

She was regaining her confidence, the lofty arrogance that matched his own, glaring into his dark face, but he could see she was triumphant. Well, let her have her moment of power, as she thought it, for it wouldn't last long.

"Tell them you fell or something. Knowing you, my darling, you'll soon think of a plausible lie. Now, one more kiss, then I'll be off. Until tomorrow then."

6

Her mind slipped a shade or two away from reality, leaving her with the odd sensation that she had known this was coming, coming from a long way off, slowly and inexorably, but coming just the same, for she had been aware all along how her sister felt about the man Beth loved. Though she had not prepared for it, the part of her brain that produced anguish did so now and she thought she might faint, or scream, or laugh hysterically, any one of which might break her. She wished she could die of it.

"But we scarcely know him," she heard her mother say uncertainly. "He has been here only once, then he was a guest at a couple of garden parties in aid of the NUWSS . . ."

"And the Jubilee Ball, Mother, don't forget that."

"Hold still, Milly, while I put this compress to your face. How you came to fall, indeed what you were doing in the garden at this time of night when we thought you were in your bed . . . it's a good job your father's in his study."

"He's coming tomorrow, Mother, to speak to Father."

"*Sit still*, child," her mother begged her, turning distractedly to the woman who stood beside her holding a bowl. "Is there more ice, Harriet? Send Tim to the ice-house, will you?" The woman moved to the fireplace and rang the bell and when Nessie entered gave her instructions for another bowl of ice.

"I shall be Lady Thornley, Mother, think of that." Milly preened but as Hugh had cautioned her, made no mention of the child in her belly. Would you call it a child at three weeks?

she wondered, then turned to beam at them all. Time enough for confessions *after* the wedding and perhaps, if they got a move on, there might be no need at all. Plenty of women had babies at seven or eight months, premature babies and she would be one of them.

Her mother reached into the bowl Harriet was holding and took another handful of melting ice. She wrapped it in a clean cloth and applied it to Milly's face. As she did so she exchanged a look with the housekeeper, who raised her eyebrows. Neither of them was as gullible as Milly imagined and it was very strange that, having drifted about Emmeline Tyson's garden at the last party she gave to raise funds for the cause – which was the last time Milly and Lord Thornley had met and when, presumably, he had proposed – it was hardly likely that it had taken until this evening for Milly to tell them about it!

So where had she been for the past two hours?

There was a polite knock at the door and Nessie entered, her eyes bright with speculation, for all of them in the kitchen had been transfixed fifteen minutes ago when Miss Milly had stumbled through the back door, bringing them all to their feet, clutching at her face and crying that she had fallen. Everyone had spoken at once, asking what was to do, telling her to sit down, to put her head between her knees, for surely the lass was going to faint, and it was not until Nessie had been sent running to fetch the mistress that order had been restored.

"Here's the ice yer sent for, ma'am," Nessie said, venturing a peep at Miss Milly who, despite her swollen face, seemed to be in the best of spirits.

"Thank you, Nessie," Mrs Goodwin said. "That will be all."

Nessie left reluctantly, for something was going on but whatever it was, it was not about to be disclosed. Mrs Woodruff who, despite the lateness of the hour, had still been working on her accounts in her housekeeper's sitting-room, had taken over with calm efficiency. She had immediately sent Tim for ice and had accompanied Mrs Goodwin and Miss Milly to the drawing-room. The others were not surprised, for Mrs Woodruff was more than housekeeper. She and the mistress had been close for years, so perhaps she might have something to tell them when she returned to the kitchen. Mrs Woodruff was getting on a bit – she must be in her sixties – but she was spry and had all her wits about her and though Nessie knew that Ruby had hopes of taking her place one day, Nessie could not see it happening soon! And where was the master in the midst of all this commotion? Nessie wondered as she scurried back to the kitchen. He must be deaf not to have heard it. She'd not like to be present when he saw the state of his daughter!

"Hold this compress to your face, Milly," her mother said sharply, "and then perhaps you would like to tell us where you have been this evening. And while we're on the subject explain to us when it was that Captain Thornley proposed to you. You said nothing last week."

"No. Oh, Mother, I suppose it was wrong of me but, well, Hugh and I have been meeting secretly. I'm sorry, I'm sorry, but there was no other way. We're in love, you see, but he realises, as a gentleman, that it could not go on so – tonight – he asked me to be his wife. I know Father doesn't care for him and it will cause a row of gigantic proportions—"

"I suspect he will knock Captain Thornley's teeth down his throat," her mother said calmly.

"*Mother!*"

"He has not acted as a gentleman should with a lady and I fear your father will never forgive him. I shouldn't wonder if he forbids him the house. He is not a fit husband for you, Milly. Your father will believe that Captain Thornley is trying to get his hands on his money."

"No, Mother, he loves me, he really does." Milly's voice suddenly turned cold. "I will marry him with or without Father's blessing. We shall elope."

"No, my girl, you will not. And from now on you will only leave this house in the company of your sister or myself. Is that clear?"

"Mother, Hugh is calling on Father tomorrow, a formal call to ask for my hand in marriage." She giggled. "Doesn't that sound stuffy, but Hugh wants to do things properly. He has told his mother—"

"Even before he has spoken to your father?" Her mother was aghast.

Milly ignored the interruption. "She wants to meet me and is to give a dinner party to which, naturally, we are all invited. Mother, there really is nothing more to be said. I will marry Hugh and that is the end of it." She lifted her head and her firm little jaw stuck out at a belligerent angle, a sign they all dreaded, for it meant a battle of wills until she got her own way.

"Well, we'll see about that, my girl."

"See about what?" a voice from the doorway asked and as one they turned to look at the figure who stood there. Noah Goodwin was an imposing man, tall and putting on a little weight in his middle years but still handsome, his shoulders broad and powerful. His daughter quailed at the storm that she knew was coming.

"Dearest . . ." his wife began but he put out a hand to silence her, for he knew that whatever she said to defend what was going on here he would not like it. It was always the same with Milly. She was like him in her determination to get her own way in everything and had been the same since she was a baby struggling to assert herself, against her sister, her mother, Harriet and the other servants, but she had never, to his knowledge, got the better of himself.

He advanced into the room, moving to stand before his daughter, his expression turning to stone as he saw for the first time the state of her face. His eyes narrowed dangerously, for it seemed to him that his daughter had a bruise on the left side of her face that would certainly turn into a black eye by morning and how had she come by it, that was what he wanted to know. Her golden brown eyes, so like his own, were fearful and yet at the same time her face wore a familiar expression of defiance.

"Well?" His voice was as cold as his face.

"Darling, can we not—"

Noah turned, took his wife's hand and gently led her to the sofa where he sat her down with the gallantry of a knight of old, for he loved her as much, if not more, than he had when he first realised his true feelings for her. They had known great troubles together and had overcome them and she was the most precious thing in his life. He often told her when they were alone that without her he would be nothing and if he had to choose between "all this" as he called what he had, and her, then he'd throw the whole bloody lot away.

"Sit there, my darling, and let me get to the bottom of whatever is happening here." She submitted passively. He swung round to his daughter. "Now then, miss, would you care to tell me who gave you that 'shiner'?"

"No one, Father. I fell on the path and—"

"Fell? What path? When did this happen? You did not have it at the dinner table."

"No . . . no, I was out walking and . . . oh, Father, please, let me tell you the wonderful news. I have been seeing Hugh Thornley—"

"Seeing?" His voice was dangerously calm.

Milly repeated almost word for word what she had told her mother, babbling about garden parties and . . . er, little walks in the park, and all the while her sister sat like a figure carved in marble, for her face was just as white. Her eyes stared into nothingness and she was calm, her numbed mind praying that the calmness would last long enough to get her to her room and the privacy she needed. She could hear her father's voice rising to a bellow of rage when, presumably, Milly informed him that he was to have Hugh Thornley for a son-in-law. In her place by the fire her mother wept quietly, becoming so distressed her father turned to her, sitting down beside her and cradling her to him and Beth knew that Milly had won, for no matter what happened her father would not have her mother unhappy. Should he refuse his permission Milly would run away, she was shrieking, and surely it was what he wanted, a title in the family and anyway, Hugh was coming tomorrow and if Father refused to see him she would simply go with him to wherever he had in mind. Gretna Green, probably. Her father did not voice his opinion that if there was no money coming with Milly, there would be no marriage for Milly. But Milly was adamant and besides that, she hissed, she would not tolerate delay.

At last it was over. Noah Goodwin led his wife to their bedroom where, Beth presumed, they would comfort one another in the certain belief that their daughter's marriage would be a disaster, but since they did not want to lose her they must agree to it. Harriet took Milly to her room where she would be cosseted as she thought was her due, not just because of her bruised face but because she was to be Lady Thornley and Beth, her voice quiet, said goodnight and slipped into her own room where Mary had lit a fire. Despite it, as she crouched down before it, she was shivering. Her detachment was complete, at least the part of her brain that controlled it, and she knew she must keep it about her like a cloak to protect her from the cold, the frozen, icy sureness that though Hugh Thornley had begun to court *her*, he had asked Milly to marry him. The truth of the matter was very simple and yet very complicated. He had liked her and had seemed to like her better at every meeting. He had not said he loved her and though it had been on her own lips a dozen times, she had not said she loved him, but she had. She knew there were rumours that he was wild but then so had been her own father in his youth. It had not stopped her from loving Hugh, just as it had not stopped her mother from loving her father and look how their marriage had turned out; if she, Beth, had married Hugh she was certain it would have been a successful match. But he was to marry Milly.

The thought sliced through all her defences and she knew she could not cope with it. How could she stand – probably as bridesmaid – in a church and see Hugh and Milly married? A vicious hammer-blow struck her, battering away the merciful numbness and she thanked God that she was alone, but there were days, weeks, probably months before the wedding took place and in all those days, weeks, months she must keep faith. Not with Milly, or even her family, but with herself. No one must know that her heart was broken. She wished in a way that Mary had stayed to help her undress and brush her hair, which, since she was training to be Beth's maid, she did most nights. It would have been a great easement to her desolate heart to unburden herself to the young woman, who had been a servant at Lantern Hill for two months now, ever since Doctor Bennett had released her from hospital. She had, when she had recovered somewhat from her ordeal and been fed on Cook's nourishing meals, put on weight and had proved to be a pretty girl, though very quiet. The other servants did their best to draw her out and join in the kitchen conversation and, at the end of their day, have a bit of a laugh, but something had been taken from her in her young womanhood and she found it difficult to respond. They did not know, of course, why she had been in hospital, only that their Miss Beth had taken pity on her and given her a job. Sally Preston, Ruby's daughter, had been maiding all three ladies but it had been decided that Mary should work just for Beth. She was devoted to her and they had become friends somewhat in the strange way that Harriet Woodruff and Abby Goodwin had become friends in earlier years. She was shy, withdrawn, but intelligent and was eager to show her gratitude to the girl who had rescued her from what might have been a perilous life. She had even taken to going to the suffragist meetings with her young mistress, despite, or perhaps because of what had happened to her and would one day make a useful worker for the cause.

As though her thoughts had winged their way down to the kitchen where the servants were getting ready to make their way to their own beds, there was a light tap on the door and with barely a pause for her to answer Mary slipped inside, closing it behind her. Before Beth could arrange her face into an expression that gave away none of her thoughts, not a happy face exactly, for how could she manage that, but something approaching normal, Mary moved quietly across the room and sat down on the low velvet pouffe at Beth's feet. She had a steaming cup of chocolate in her hand and carefully, as though Beth were a small child, she placed it between her cupped hands, clasping her fingers about it, keeping her own fingers about Beth's. She said nothing but her eyes, a plain hazel in colour, neither brown nor green, gazed up into Beth's face, filled with sad sympathy. She herself had once been in love and deserted and the horror that had followed still lingered in her dreams. Her smile was warmly affectionate and still she said nothing, waiting for Beth to speak, or not. Then, "Drink this, Miss Beth. I put cinnamon on top the way you like it. It will help you to sleep."

Obediently Beth sipped at the hot drink and slowly she felt the merciful and yet terrible numbness creep back and she allowed Mary to hold her hands round the cup and when it was empty to take it from her.

"Come," the maid said, helping her to her feet. "I'll help you get undressed and into bed," which she did, sitting by the bedside in the low velvet chair as Beth began to fall uneasily into a light doze.

"How did you know?" Beth murmured, her eyelids beginning to droop, glad of the hand that held hers.

"I watched you go out and set off across the park in an

afternoon. I knew you must be meeting someone. And your face, at that last garden party, d'you remember, when he was there: it gave it away, Miss Beth. I had a face like that once. I saw it in my mirror and so I knew what it meant."

"Oh, Mary. Mary, what am I to do?"

"Nothing, not now, just sleep and in the morning we'll get through it together. One day at a time, Miss Beth. That's how I did it, with your help, and you shall have mine."

The interview with Hugh Thornley took place the next morning. He arrived on a magnificent charger, one of those used for ceremonial parades and displays. He was quite splendid in his uniform, from the high, gold-braided collar of his scarlet tunic to the toes of his highly polished boots. Epaulettes, insignia, buttons, all gleamed in the pale sunlight and Nessie was quite overcome, her eyes wide with wonder as she showed him into the master's study. They all knew why he was here, of course, for such a thing could not be kept secret, and she ran back to the kitchen to describe the marvel of the soldier their Miss Milly was to marry. All a bit sudden, of course, for not one of them had had any inkling that a marriage proposal was in the air. In fact, since that first time his lordship, the captain – dear God what were they to call him – had never once been in the house!

No one knew what was said between Hugh, Lord Thornley and Noah Goodwin, only that it took a long time. The ladies sat in the drawing-room, listening to the tick of the French gilt clock which had an exquisite, hand-painted, porcelain dial and with terrible regularity struck the half-hour, each time making them jump. Three times they heard it and though Beth sat with a face as expressionless as a death mask, Milly chewed her lip, sighed, got up and wandered to the window, peering out as though she expected a visitor. She picked up a book from a low table and flipped through it, then dropped it with a small clatter which made her mother sigh with her.

"Oh, do sit down, Milly. You know your father. He'll not be satisfied until he's wormed every part of Captain Thornley's past from him and what he intends for the future. As any father would do. He is concerned that you will be well looked after when he passes you into another man's hands and then there is his family, his mother—"

"Oh, for goodness sake, Mother, what is she to do with me?"

"Is she to live with you?"

"I don't know. Hugh and I haven't discussed it."

"It seems to me there is a lot that you and the captain have not discussed, Milly, and that is why your father is taking his time in deciding whether this young man will be a suitable husband. He is probably, and I agree with him, telling Captain Thornley that should he give his permission to an engagement between you, it should be of at least a year and then—"

Milly, who had sat down again, jumped to her feet and was just about to explode into instant disagreement when the door opened and her father and Hugh came into the room, the captain standing politely to one side to allow Noah Goodwin to enter first. The captain was smiling but somehow Beth could see it went against his upbringing to stand aside for anyone. He was of the aristocracy and his future father-in-law was nothing but a money-grubbing member of the millocracy, but for the moment he was prepared to back down to a man he considered his inferior. He stood just inside the door, looking at no one, certainly not at Beth, but Milly could contain herself no longer.

"Well?" she said, her voice rising in excitement or was there a touch of hysteria there? If her father should refuse his permission for her to marry Hugh, which in law he was entitled to do, she would be forced to elope, which would be very romantic but she was not absolutely sure her father would have anything to do with her if she did. And at the back of her mind, where she had carefully hidden it, was a certain something, she could put no name to it, that Hugh would not be best pleased if she did not bring a decent dowry with her.

"Father?" she demanded.

"Be quiet, child," her father told her, "and sit down, for God's sake," seating himself beside his wife on the sofa.

In her chair by the window where she had placed herself so that her back was to the light, Beth felt her heart freeze and for a panic-stricken moment thought she might simply stop breathing. The dread of what her father was to say crept through her veins as though her blood had turned to ice, she didn't know why really, for whatever his decision it would make no difference to her. Hugh Thornley loved Milly and would marry her, with or without her father's permission. Hugh had done *her* no wrong. He had made her no promises, merely been kind to her on a few short walks. He had not jilted her and she would give no one cause to think he had. Thank God, no one except Mary knew of it and though she was heartbroken and quite desperate she must make sure the interlude was never discovered.

"Lord Thornley has asked for your hand in marriage, Milly." And with those words, the use of his title, they were all made aware of what Noah Goodwin was about to say. "Now I have discussed the terms of the marriage contract with him and we have reached an agreement—"

"Does that mean you agree, Father?" Milly had never looked so radiant as she stood, poised like a bird about to take flight towards her future husband.

"I have, but there is still—"

"Oh, never mind that. As long as you agree—"

"I didn't say that, lass. What I said was—"

"Please, Father. May we announce our engagement at once?" She had taken Hugh Thornley's arm and though her heart was like a lump of lead in her breast, Beth had to admit that they made a handsome couple and though they were not alike in colouring their way of standing, head high, back straight, arrogant and strong-willed, was identical. Milly was tall for a woman and slender, but her head barely reached the ear of the handsome head of Lord Thornley. He put a strong, horseman's hand over hers where it rested in the crook of his arm and smiled down at her and Beth wondered if any of the others had noticed the quick, darting expression that flickered momentarily in the depthless blue of his eyes. She did not exactly recognise it but she had a feeling that her sister would not rule this man as she had the others in her life.

"Now then, my dear," he said wryly, "let your family get used to the idea that we wish to be married before you start naming dates. My mother is anxious to meet you all and I think it would be better if you dined with us at Thornley Green and then we could begin making plans. I know we are both eager to be man and wife but we must consider our families in this."

"But Hugh . . ." Milly began, but with a charming smile her betrothed took her hand and led her back to her mother.

"May I suggest Saturday, Mrs Goodwin, if you are free. That gives my mother four days to arrange it all."

"But, Captain," Abby Goodwin protested, "surely that is not enough time for your mother to prepare a—"

"She is well used to such things, Mrs Goodwin," smiling urbanely, putting her mother in her place, Beth thought, for was not his mother a lady, the widow of a baron, and accustomed to entertaining the best in the land. A dinner party for the likes of the Goodwins would present no problem at all.

Beth thought it more than likely that when Milly became his wife they would see little of him, for which she would be truly thankful. It was bad enough that he was to marry another woman but that that woman should be her own sister was heartbreaking. And she knew Milly so well. She would be giving herself airs, preening and letting them all see how well she had done for herself. At her mother's tea-time she would condescend to her mother's callers with tales of the background of the Thornley family who had viscounts and dukes among their forebears and though the St Helens matrons knew there was no money there, not what they would call money, they would be impressed nevertheless.

She rose with the others when Lord Thornley declared he must be off, for there was so much to be arranged for the weekend. He bowed over the ladies' hands, even hers, but his eyes slid somewhere over her head, she noticed, for she looked directly at him.

"Until Saturday, then." He smiled, and it was not until he had gone, dashing off up the drive on his wild charger, knowing, of course, that they all watched him, that her father gave vent to his true feelings.

"Slippery blighter," he stormed. "I've a good mind to cut the lass off without a penny—"

"Father . . ." Milly wailed.

"Noah, darling . . ." his wife faltered, for she knew as well as he did that should he do so there would be only disaster. Her mother's instinct told her there was more to this engagement than met the eye. She knew her daughter and though she had barely spoken two words to Lord Thornley, she had known his father!

7

Archie Goodwin sat in the front pew of the church beside Abby. He had escorted her from Lantern Hill in the glossy black carriage pulled by four equally glossy black horses and after leading her up the aisle had seated her at the end of the pew, somewhat tearful, for her daughter was to be married today. She was dressed in a gown of shimmering sky-blue satin, the skirt drawn up into a small bustle at the back with a rich fall of frills to her ankles. The bodice was separate, tight into her slender waist but flaring out into a peplum. The neck was high, edged with cream lace, and on her breast was pinned a spray of creamy roses which was echoed in those under the brim of her cream straw hat. The hat was tied beneath her chin with wide blue satin ribbons and if she had not been the mother of the bride one might have mistaken her for a woman of no more than twenty-five.

Archie himself was immaculate in a grey frock-coat and waistcoat, his stock snowy, his thick crop of fair hair unusually neat, his grey top hat on his knee. Next to him were Laura and John Bennett, their finances not allowing for new finery but both smart and neat, their hands clasped as though this happy occasion brought back memories of their own wedding day.

In rows of descending importance from the front were the many friends of the Goodwin family, or, to be more precise, friends and fellow-members of Abby Goodwin's in the NUWSS: Miss Emmeline Tyson who was herself a wealthy woman since her father died. Miss Jane Bowman, Mr and Mrs

Jack Arbuthnot, Jack a business acquaintance of Noah, their son Philip and Philip's wife, Maud, Mr and Mrs Arnold Earnshaw among others of the millocracy, the ladies dressed as was the fashion in rich shades of plum, a variety of dark greens, midnight blue and magenta. There were diamonds catching fire in the dimness of the church, all a bit ostentatious, the gentry thought, but then new money was known to be showy. And a feather in the cap of Noah's wife, who was, of course, a hard worker in the cause for the betterment of women, was the presence of Mrs Josephine Butler who had done so much towards the repeal of the Contagious Diseases Act.

Behind the main guests were the servants from Lantern Hill, among them Harriet Woodruff and her husband Clem, who, having just driven his mistress to the church, had breathlessly inserted himself, with many apologies for treading on feet, in the pew beside his wife. Abby had argued fiercely with Noah that Harriet was her friend and should be with the family but as Noah patiently pointed out they could hardly place Harriet without Clem, who was, after all, merely a coachman, among the family guests. It was all a bit awkward but Harriet understood and sat quite regally among the maids in their best Sunday dresses and flowered hats, the men in their sober Sunday suits reverently clasping their bowler hats to their chests.

On the other side, the groom's side, sat the landed interest, family and friends of Hugh, Lord Thornley, the ladies and gentlemen who had come to see one of their own joined in matrimony to the daughter of the manufacturing classes. There were dozens of scarlet dress tunics from the rank of lieutenant to a full brigadier come on their dashing horses from the barracks at Longworth where the garrison was stationed to view this well-dowered young woman married not only to an officer but a baron, and what must this paragon be like, apart from very rich, to have captured the dangerously wild Hugh Thornley. Surprisingly, one of them was Lieutenant Todd Woodruff whose mother, housekeeper to the Goodwins, was only a foot or so away from him across the aisle. The division of class was conspicuous, the Faulkners of Primrose Bank gravitating naturally towards the Woodwards of Cheshire from where Lady Caroline herself had come, the Rawstrones, the Benthams of Leicester who were kin to Hugh's friend and drinking partner, Dicky.

If any of them wondered at the suddenness of the marriage, a mere month after the engagement was announced, none of them was ill-mannered enough to mention it, though naturally they all glanced at the bride's waistline. Hugh was known for his promiscuity with women and this one was very rich, so the question of whether they had anticipated their wedding night was in every guest's mind.

Milly had determined that this would be the most splendid wedding that St Helens had ever seen. White roses were heavily massed at the altar and baskets of white petals had been strewn along the path that led up to the church porch, a carpet of beauty for her satin-shod feet to walk on as she would, she was quite certain, walk for the rest of her life. She was dressed in white satin and Honiton lace and her six bridesmaids, of which her sister was one, were in a delicate peach with dainty coronets and bouquets of peach roses. Her groom, in full dress uniform and incredibly handsome was, for that half-hour in the church, quite superfluous to requirements as Milly Goodwin became Lady Thornley.

Beth heard little of the service. She had begun to smile as she rose from her bed that morning, blankly and brilliantly with nothing in her mind but the necessity to impress on her sister's wedding guests that she could not be happier for her sister. She watched her father place her sister's hand in Hugh Thornley's, who smiled with what seemed to be triumph as he took it, then her father sat down beside her mother, taking her hand, for comfort, frowning, perhaps wondering if, after all, he had done the right thing.

Milly looked radiantly beautiful, magnificent in her own triumph and as the Faulkners and Woodwards, swallowing their pride and displeasure, came to congratulate her, Beth found herself for a moment standing beside Hugh Thornley, who glanced indifferently at her then away as though she were nothing, had been nothing to him and she knew she could not endure it. It was as simple as that and as she began to cry, which did not matter, for all the other manufacturing ladies were also filled with the emotion appropriate on such an occasion, a hand was slipped into hers and standing beside her was Archie who, smiling gently, passed her his clean handkerchief.

"Don't cry, sweetheart, it will be your turn next," he whispered, in his voice something she had not heard before, though she could not have said what it was and she felt his breath sweet for a moment on her cheek as her heart cracked with pain. If they had been alone she felt she might have flung herself into his arms, but there was a pealing of bells and Milly and her bridegroom, he looking very autocratic, were driven away in a carriage lined with white silk and drawn by four high-stepping white horses to a wedding breakfast that would be the talk of the town for many weeks. There was a marquee on the round lawn at the front of Lantern Hill, an endless flow of champagne passed round on silver trays, mountains of confectionery and a cake which Beth knew weighed a full two hundred pounds, for she had seen it made, decorated with sprays of white roses and white satin ribbons with two figures on the top, one purporting to be Milly, the other Lord Thornley attired in the scarlet jacket of his captain's uniform.

Again there was a gulf between the classes, the "county" set keeping to itself while the manufacturers did the same, the languid elegant young ladies and gentlemen from one side viewing the other, the millmasters, the ironmasters, the cotton spinners, as though they were some species they had never before come across.

There was Milly, Lady Thornley, with a plain gold band on her finger, circling among the guests with great composure, even going so far as to embrace her mother-in-law who was dressed in black as she had been since the death of her husband. The dowager Lady Thornley was seen to recoil somewhat, for she was not accustomed to public – or even private – demonstrations of affection and since she felt none for this girl whose money was to restore Thornley Green to its former glory, she merely smiled frostily as her cheek was kissed, then she turned away to speak to Lady Faulkner, her disapproval of her son's bride very evident.

They left, the happy couple, the new Lady Thornley quite glorious in a rose-coloured gown embellished with white swansdown, on their way to London, which would be the first step on their wedding journey. Knowing she must release the iron grip that she had imposed upon herself, or be crushed by it, Beth wandered through the ornamental gardens, along neat pathways between flowerbeds vivid with colour. She took a route that led to a small lake at the side of the house where a summerhouse sat drowsing in the unusually warm October air. She was taking flight, she knew, alone and bowed down with misery, and for some reason when he appeared at the entrance to the summerhouse she was not surprised to see him, for had he not always been there when she needed him. Even as a small girl he had rescued her from trees, from nettle beds, from the skittish frolicking of her new mare, from the unwanted attentions of young men at her first ball. He stood for a moment in the wide-arched entrance-way, looking down at her where she slumped, his expression curiously serious and she wondered vaguely in the midst of her despair what it meant. He had been part of her life since she was born, ever since her mother had taken pity on him as a ragged street urchin and offered him a home. Here was a man who was the brother she had never had, who was offering her his affection at a time when she was bruised and lonely and needed desperately to be loved. Through the tears that poured from her eyes she watched him walk towards her and when he took her hand she clung to his.

He made no mention of her tears, thinking perhaps she already missed her sister. "You looked quite lovely in the church, Beth."

"Did I?" she sniffed. "I can't think why."

"What makes you say that?" He was clearly puzzled.

"No woman looks at her best when she is crying."

"You do."

She bent her head and looked down at her hand in his. Besides successfully running the business he was a man who did hard physical labour at the Edge Bottom Glass Works, for it was his belief that a man should be able to do what his employees did. If I can do it, so can you, was a saying well known to the men at the works. He could take off his expensive, well-cut coat and work with the best of them, even in the glasshouse where the temperature was fierce and his hands were proof of it. Hard, strong, brown with small half-healed burns, and yet slender with well-kept fingernails.

He turned towards her so that he could hold both her hands, his blue eyes, not the brilliant blue of Hugh Thornley's but soft, almost clouded with some deep-felt emotion.

"Have you the slightest idea how much I love you?"

She looked up at him, totally astonished, her mouth open for a moment, then the simple, basic need to be warm again, to bask in the love he appeared to be offering, *was* offering drew her towards him, the terrible rigidity of her spirit easing as his arms came round her. She felt a childlike, trusting need to nestle against him, to relax her tired body and drop into a healing sleep.

"My love, my little love," he murmured into her coronet of roses, "I can't tell you . . . for so long." And closing her eyes against the familiarity of his face she lifted her own to be kissed. His mouth rested very carefully on hers and then, when he met with no resistance, parted his lips and then hers. His whole body was still gentle but trembling with a need that thawed her own, not to passion but to relief and gratitude. Hugh was still engraved on her heart but she sensed in this dear man, for he was dear to her, a quiet dignity, a quiet endurance, something fragile in him to which she responded. He loved her and that was enough. She would never hurt him. She would be the wife he wanted and deserved, for though he had not mentioned marriage, not yet, this moment in the summerhouse had been an unmistakable gesture of proposal and acceptance.

They were married on a grey-gold November morning, the sun spread low across a hazy sky, not the fashionable wedding that Milly and Hugh had had but quiet, small, no one of great importance there but her family, Laura and John Bennett, Todd Woodruff and the servants from Lantern Hill. Her father gave her away and she walked with him up the aisle, no bridesmaids following her, for Milly, it seemed, was with child and though it barely showed she did not feel up to being peered at, she said. She clung to Hugh's arm, dashing in a tawny-gold gown of silk that had been made for her in Paris, an Empire dress, a high-waisted style disguised by a very broad sash swathed low and sewn into place and with no bustle at all. The bustle was completely out, she told them, as were bonnets and her hat had a high crown with bird's wings of the same colour about the brim. She looked quite magnificent but no more so than Beth whose simple gown was quite exquisite. The material was of stamped velvet, bearing in mind the time of the year, high to the throat with long sleeves and a short train. She wore a veil, which fell to her waist at the back and front, and to keep it in place a small circlet of white rosebuds that Mr Jones, head gardener at Lantern Hill, had grown for her in his hot-house. She carried a small posy of the same flowers tied up with white satin ribbon. Mary had dressed her hair in a neat chignon at the back of her head but, eager to show how her maiding skills had improved, had allowed small tendrils to escape above her ears. The bridegroom, when he lifted his wife's veil at the altar to give her the traditional kiss, tucked a curl tenderly behind her ear, to Mary's chagrin!

The reception at Lantern Hill was again a simple affair. Champagne, of course, and a wedding cake that was not on the same scale as the one at Milly's wedding. This time Harriet was included, not as a servant but as Abby's friend, and beside her was Clem who had taken Miss Beth and the master to the church and brought back Mr and Mrs Archie Goodwin. It had been odd in church when the vicar had asked *Archie* if he would take the pale girl at his side as his wife, for the reverend gentleman seemed to think that Archie could only be a shor-tened version of Archibald but Archie had insisted on *Archie* since it was the only name he had ever known. What was wrong with Archie, he asked, comically, and as none of them could give him an answer Archie it was!

They took the train from St Helens to Windermere and then a carriage along winding lanes to Grasmere where a small, low-beamed, slate-roofed cottage overlooking the lake was to be their home for the next two weeks. They had wanted to be alone on their honeymoon night, no grand hotels such as those Milly had stayed in, no complicated menus, no after-dinner conversations with perfect strangers, and the cottage at Gras-mere, a book-lined, leafy retreat, a cottage garden and a discreet housekeeper, offered perfect solitude. There were a couple of cats of no particular pedigree which sat on the dry-stone wall overlooking the pale silk water of the lake and its hazy green island in the centre. The weather had turned sharp-textured with what seemed to be a feeling of frost in the air, but inside the cottage it was warm and fragrant with pot-pourri and beeswax. The wooden floor was black with age and gleaming with polish, covered with rugs and plump armchairs and footstools were drawn up to a log fire, while a huge bunch of chrysanthemums in a vast copper jug stood on a gate-legged table.

"There's herb pudding an' grilled trout fer supper, ma'am," the housekeeper told them, "but if tha' fancy a walk it'll be half an hour."

They walked the lake path for half an hour and watched the sun set in a blaze of gold, apricot and rosy pink over the far mountain, the name of which they did not know at that moment but which they learned later was called Silver How, then made their way back, hands clasped, to the cottage where Mrs Gunson scolded them gently, for another minute and her trout would have spoiled. She sat them before the fire at the gate-legged table, the chrysanthemums having been removed to the window bottom, and waited on them before telling them she was off now, and would be back in the morning to make the fire and see to breakfast, and at last they were alone.

She had promised to honour and obey him, which seemed inadequate in the depth of her feelings for him which already included love though not the sort a woman feels for a man. It didn't matter. Whatever he asked of her she would give him. Her willing body this very night. She respected him, trusted him implicitly, admired what he had made of his life, for he had been nothing but an illiterate, barefoot lad sweeping horse manure from street crossings in Liverpool when her mother found him. He was clever, more so than she was, and well educated, her superior in so many ways and he had offered her something that would be very precious to her. She would love him, adore him. She would not let him down.

He undressed her with unsteady hands beside the deep,

lavender-scented bed, glad that she had not insisted on undressing herself as many brides did, or so he had heard, and when she was naked, without taking his eyes from her, he removed his own clothes and lay down carefully beside her.

"You must be tired. Do you want to sleep?"

"Do I, Archie? Is it customary?" She was genuinely puzzled.

"I believe so . . ."

"Then I shall be different. Please, put your arms about me, for I need you to hold me." For the first time she held a naked man in her arms, amazed at the change in his body and when he groaned and turned towards her, his hands still gentle, his embrace retaining a wondering apologetic quality as if some wrong was being done her, it did not displease her. She was innocent, but his stroking caresses were pleasant, releasing in her an unfamiliar languor which made her stretch and sigh.

Then it was over. A sharp pain but not excessively so and he gave a long shuddering cry. For a moment her bemused mind thought, So that is all it is, but she smiled at him in the candlelight and smoothed his cheek, her own fingers gentle and loving.

"I love you, Beth."

"Yes, please love me," and she leaned forward so that her hair fell about him in a cloud, suddenly feeling very strong and sure of her ability to please him. "Archie, I shall not break, you know. You have not hurt me and you have not shocked me and perhaps, when we have slept a little, we may do it again."

He laughed joyously and drew her against his chest on which the fine blond hair tickled her cheek. His warmth, his strength, his arms, soothed her and at once she fell asleep.

She was the first to wake, watching their first morning together come slowly through the window, his arms still about her. She studied his sleeping face, his eyelashes long, fine and golden, the sweet-tempered humour of his wide mouth, the flat planes of his cheeks, his strong jaw and neck, pushing down the covers to caress his chest and when he woke, his eyes still filled with dreams, he grasped her strongly, wrapped her legs about him and took her fiercely so that it was her turn to cry out.

They lay afterwards, drowsing and murmuring, while downstairs Mrs Gunson could be heard raking out the fire. Pressed together they laughed, doing their best to be quiet, wondering how long she had been in the cottage and if she had heard the noises they had both made, but not really concerned for they had the feeling that Mrs Gunson was not a woman easily shocked.

The days slipped easily by, fine and cold and dry, the hint of frost in the air creeping over the garden and the roofs and the mountains each night. They climbed through great wooded areas up into the dying bracken to the summit of Silver How, leaning against a rocky cairn to gaze out over the magnificence around them, pausing every few moments to touch a hand to cheek or exchange a lingering kiss. It seemed Archie could not get enough of the feel of her and at night, now that he knew she was delightfully, surprisingly responsive to him, he brought the candle to their soft, deep bed and turned her naked body this way and that, touching the curve of her eyebrow, her breasts, the hollow behind her knees, her ankles, sighing his delight when she returned his caresses. She smoothed his fair skin, the lean length of his body, the strong slenderness of his legs and even the strange organ that grew between his legs and as he reached that peak of desire when he could hold back no longer, arched her back to receive him. He slept then, his head on her breast, his body sinking into satiated sleep.

"I don't want to go home," she said, sounding so much like a child at the end of a party that he kissed her laughingly.

"We shall do this at home, you know. Every night and probably in the morning too."

"Promise."

"I promise, cross my heart and hope to die."

And so at the end of the fortnight they said goodbye to Mrs Gunson and the cats and returned to St Helens and Edge Bottom House which was to be her home again.

It was many years since she had lived at Edge Bottom House, as child and young girl, but Archie had changed nothing when he had taken over residence. He was probably twenty-nine or thirty, it was thought and, apart from the servants, had been the sole occupant of the house since Noah Goodwin had built Lantern Hill. It was a small house compared with Lantern Hill but set in pretty gardens and with open fields about it. One of the reasons, apart from needing to show off his success, that Noah had moved was because he had believed building would take place around the house but it had not happened. There were paddocks for Archie's horses, among them Beth's mare Rosie who had been brought over while she had been away, orchards loaded with apples and pears and a vegetable garden which provided all the family's needs. Beth, in the month before her wedding, had supervised the redecoration of the main bedroom, Archie obligingly moving to another while she prepared what would be their room. It was done in the shades she loved, pale peach and apple green with a carpet the colour of sand. The half-tester bed had been draped with white lace and on the bed lay a patchwork quilt worked, she had been told, by her paternal grandmother. The curtains were silk as were the walls, all in the palest peach, and the woodwork was white. Archie said he hardly dared walk on the carpet and was he to take his boots off every time he entered and was surprised and delighted by his wife's impertinent rejoinder regarding the rest of his clothing! Her father had put in a modern bathroom and had been toying with the idea of gaslight when he had moved his family to Lantern Hill. But she and Archie had decided against it, preferring the intimacy and softness of candles and lamps. Beth had found that she and Archie agreed on almost everything which was a delightful surprise, for though they had been brought up together for several years he was ten years her senior and had lived a separate life for a long time. Of course, the truth was, she soon realised, that what pleased her pleased Archie and the only arguments they had were over who should make the final decision over something or other, he wanting to please her, she wanting to please him.

They arrived in the dark, since the days were shortening rapidly, but the house was a soft blaze of lights, lamps lit in every room, the front door opened wide to receive them. Harry Preston was there to help with their luggage, and Mary Smith hovered in the doorway beside Mrs Kyle who was Archie's cook/housekeeper. At their back was Ruth, the parlour-maid, all of them beaming, for they had taken a great fancy to their new young mistress.

"Welcome home, madam, sir." Mrs Kyle radiated goodwill. "Your room is ready and it goes without saying there is a fire lit. You'll be wanting a hot drink, I'll be bound, so I'll have something sent up at once. Did you have a good journey, Mrs Goodwin, and how was the weather?" All the while Mary did her best to get at Beth, not to hug her which she would have liked to do, but to let her see how glad she was that her mistress was home.

That night Beth lay in her husband's arms while he slept peacefully and for a moment allowed an image of Hugh Thornley to enter her mind, then Archie stirred and murmured her name and at once she held him closer, ashamed of herself for thinking of another man when she was with the husband who loved her so much he sighed her name in his sleep.

8

The note was delivered by Lord Thornley's coachman and addressed to Mrs Archie Goodwin. She and Archie had finished breakfast in their bedroom and Beth was brushing her hair before her bedroom mirror. Last week they had arranged to have dinner guests, the first since their marriage. Todd Woodruff was to be one, which had surprised Beth since she had come to think of him as in Hugh Thornley's camp, so to speak, but it seemed Archie found him a decent fellow when he was pried away from Hugh's influence.

"Don't forget he had a sound education and was brought up in your family, which must have left some impression on him. He's easily led but he's not a bad sort and it might be worth while cultivating him. I've been to the music hall with him and some of the officers and for a bite to eat afterwards on several occasions and found him good company. He has a kind heart, Beth, and with the right company is really quite a decent chap."

"You never mentioned it."

"What?"

"That you were friendly with Todd."

"Well, not exactly friendly but having known him all his life I have a . . . well, I suppose you would call it a brotherly affection for him. Ask him, my darling, and that other chap, what's he called, Dicky Bentham and perhaps that friend of yours from the NUWSS, Philip Arbuthnot's wife. And Philip, of course."

"Do you mean Maud?"

"Do I? You've spoken of her and seem to admire her work

for your cause. She's a pretty little thing and Philip's good-natured. It's time we started to entertain a bit."

Now he was eyeing her with a look with which she had become increasingly familiar. "You look very fetching, my love, and instead of going to the works I must admit I would far rather remove that bit of a thing you call a negligee – is that the right word? – and take you to bed for the rest of the week!"

"But we've only just got out of it."

"So?"

Archie was at the mirror arranging his cravat, but with a wicked gleam in his eye he began to untie it again.

"Now stop it, husband. I've to see Mrs Kyle about tonight and Mary will be up—"

"Damn Mrs Kyle and damn Mary. Slip off that bit of nonsense – though why you should need to take it off I don't know since I can see you clearly through it. Dear God, Beth, does this need ever lessen?"

"Darling, I would love to oblige you—"

"Oblige me! Aren't you yourself obliged every time we make love?"

"Yes, but . . ." And in her need never, ever to fail this good man who had rescued her from what she had thought to be her purpose in life, that of loving Hugh Thornley, giving her another, which was the happiness of her husband, she allowed him to kiss her bare breasts, her throat, his hands holding her fiercely to him by her buttocks. Her arms wound round his neck and she kissed him warmly in return.

For several minutes they were locked in an embrace, her negligee slipping off her shoulders, her naked breast pressed against his shirt front which he was endeavouring to remove, but a loud knock at the door flung them apart. Mary always knocked loudly and waited, for she had once found them in a very intimate situation on the bed and since then she had been very careful to announce herself with as much noise as possible.

They were so in love it was the talk of the kitchen, not in a crude or offensive way, of course, but with fond smiles and the hopes that soon there would be a child of their happiness.

Reluctantly, Archie had gone to the works, Mary had dressed her and brushed her luxuriant auburn hair into a shining coil and she had hurried down to the morning-room where Mrs Kyle waited.

"The fish-man's at the back door, madam, and I must say the turbot looks lovely. Fresh from Fleetwood this very morning, he said, and it would be my first choice. I could do a nice lobster sauce with it. With some of Tucker's new potatoes and green beans, a clear vermicelli soup to start with and perhaps as dessert a really good rich *crème* Chantilly, with pears marinated in brandy? Or would you prefer *millefeuilles* with strawberries? I'm sure Tucker can find us some in the hothouse."

Mrs Kyle raised her eyebrows questioningly. She knew her own worth and her own talent. She was a superb cook and had worked in several great houses, but she was getting on a bit and the small household at Edge Bottom suited her admirably. She had the run of the kitchen and the ordering of the food. She was her own boss and she was content. And the young Mrs Archie was easy to work for and to lead in the way Mrs Kyle wished to go. This small dinner party was as nothing to a woman who had been arranging and cooking for dinner parties for fifty guests or more.

The note was brought in by Ruth who had been parlour-maid at Edge Bottom for five years. She was a bonny, apple-cheeked country girl come from a farm at Primrose Bank and though she had been apprehensive at the thought of having not only a master but a *mistress*, young Mrs Archie had, in the three months since Mr Archie had brought her home as his wife, proved to be no trouble at all!

"This just come from Thornley Green, madam," she said, bobbing a neat curtsey and looking suitably impressed as she

handed over an envelope on the back of which was the
Thornley crest. They all knew that their mistress was sister
to a baroness whose husband was a member of the peerage and
lived at a grand place called Thornley Green. "Shall I ask
coachman ter wait, case there's an answer?"

"Yes please, Ruth. I'll ring the bell when I'm ready."

Ruth sketched another curtsey and scurried from the room.
Going to the front door of the house, she crossed the lawn to the
wall that divided the garden from the lane that led to the stable
yard. The Thornley carriage in all its splendour looked totally
out of place in the narrow country lane and Ruth wondered
how the thing was to turn round. In the yard, she supposed.
There was the crest on the door of the carriage and Ruth almost
bobbed a curtsey to the high and mighty being who was
perched on the coachman's seat, but after all he was only a
servant like herself.

"Mistress will let yer know," she said, to which the coachman inclined his grand head.

The note was brief and plaintive:

*Beth, will you come and rescue me from this appalling
boredom? Hugh won't let me ride or even go out in the
carriage lest I damage his precious son. Oh, yes, it is to be a
son. Nobody has been near me for a week and I shall go out
of my mind if I'm forced to bear the company of my mother-
in-law for another hour. Please come and cheer me up. The
carriage will bring you and take you home.*
    Milly

Beth sighed. Wasn't that just like her sister. Whatever Beth had
planned for the day was to be cancelled while Beth entertained
her sister, who was quite enormous though her baby was not
due until June. So Milly told them! She could hardly have
climbed into her carriage, never mind on to the back of a horse
and you could not blame Hugh for refusing her permission to

do either. Well, at least the arrangements for the dinner party were well in hand. Mrs Kyle could be trusted to get on with things for an hour or two and then, after perhaps an early lunch with Milly, Beth could get home and see to the table and the flowers.

Beth was shocked when she was shown into her sister's sitting-room. It was two weeks since she had last called with her mother and Milly had been bloated then, so much so that her mother had begged to be allowed to send at once for John Bennett, who was an expert on pregnancy, on childbirth and the health of mothers-to-be. The dowager Lady Thornley had, unfortunately, been present and had said stiffly that her own doctor was looking after her daughter-in-law and there was absolutely no need to seek further medical advice. Her mother had given in.

But today, her ladyship being absent, Beth could give way to her dismay. Not only was Milly floundering like a landed fish, breathless and swollen with her pregnancy, but around her mouth was a rash of small ulcers and cracked sores. She could not heave herself from her deep chair by the fire and she waved her hands helplessly, her face a shade somewhere between magenta and plum.

"Dear God, Milly, what on earth . . .?"

"Now don't start, Beth. I feel bad enough without you telling me what a sight I look. Dear heaven, if I'd known having a baby was as appalling as this I would have stayed celibate for the rest of my life. Well, I'll tell you something, as I told Hugh, this will be the last. I know there is something you can use to prevent pregnancy and I shall find out what it is before I let him come within a mile of me. Ring for Jackson, will you, and sit down before you fall down. And close your mouth." She smiled somewhat sulkily and went on, "I must say you look exceedingly smart in that outfit and I'm exceedingly jealous."

Beth lowered herself into the armchair opposite her sister,

her mind quite unable to form the words she wished to say and yet at the same time looking for words of comfort. Her lovely, vital sister who was the real beauty of the family, despite what Archie said, was like a spotted toad and Beth wondered if the sores around her mouth extended to any other part of her body, for Milly's hand wandered here and there, scratching and scratching, particularly at the base of her enormous stomach.

"Darling, what on earth is wrong? You are only five months pregnant and yet you are—"

Milly laughed harshly. "Oh, don't be such a prude, Beth. Surely you knew that Hugh and I were intimate before we were married. I daren't tell the old hag downstairs, or even Mother, but the baby will be here before June, thank God. I couldn't stand it otherwise."

Beth found she was not surprised, knowing as she did now Hugh's reputation with women. "But should you have such a . . . a sore mouth? What does the doctor say?"

"The old goat that treats the old hag! God, he must be a hundred if he's a day and I'm sure his practice doesn't include pregnant women. Anyway, it's not just my mouth. It's on my body as well and he would have a fit if I suggested he examine *under* my clothes."

"But what does he recommend?"

"I'm to moderate my diet and drink porter! Porter, I ask you . . . ah, Jackson, I wondered where you had got to," as the liveried footman, complete with white wig, entered the room. "What d'you fancy, Beth? Chocolate?"

"That would be nice."

The footman left, bowing deferentially, but Beth noticed that the sitting-room, which she had seen only once when old Lady Thornley had invited them to dine with her last September, was still somewhat untidy, a layer of dust clinging to every surface, the rugs unbrushed and a vase of daffodils, long past their best, needed removing. It seemed that Milly, for all her grand talk, was not particularly domesticated and cared little for this side of her new life. In the first weeks of their marriage she and Hugh had given several balls and dinner parties but that was all gone now as she advanced into her pregnancy.

They drank their chocolate, which was not particularly hot, while Milly kept up a constant flow of chatter, wailing on about her lack of companionship since Hugh was always away on manoeuvres, musketry practice, parade-ground drill, training recruits, exercising his horses and since the season started rode to hounds two or three days a week. He had, of course, bought two expensive hunters, and had employed a huntsman, whippers-in and earth-stoppers and purchased fifty couple of hounds. Stable expenses were exorbitant; there were private kennels and in addition there was the expense of preserving game birds on his land, for which a gamekeeper had been taken on. Oh, yes, he was having a fine time of it. He even slept in the spare room and could you blame him, for who would want to lie beside her in her present state? She and the old hag hated the sight of each other and on and on and on until Beth halted the flow sharply.

"You cannot go on like this, sweetheart. You are not getting proper care."

"Oh, don't fuss, Beth. As soon as this baby comes—"

"No, Milly, no. I have some small knowledge of pregnant women, having worked beside Doctor Bennett at the hospital and it's my belief you should—"

"Beth, I will not be told what to do."

"How are you to prevent it? I shall fetch Doctor Bennett and no matter what . . . what the old hag says" – she tried a ripple of laughter – "I shall insist that he looks at you. No, it's no good arguing. If you wish to present Hugh with a healthy son you will do as you're told. I'm amazed that Lady Thornley—"

"Beth, oh Beth," and with a suddenness that alarmed her sister, Milly began to weep. Milly had always been the strong tomboy of the family. Nothing was beyond her. Nothing ever got her down. She could do anything the boys did and if she fell out of a tree or scraped her knees on the gravel she would not cry. If it killed her she would not cry. And now she was crying as though her heart were broken.

Beth flew to her side and drew her into her compassionate arms. "What . . . what is it, darling? Tell me, what frightens you?" For it was clear Milly was very frightened.

"Oh, Beth," she wept, "I'm so scared . . . mumble . . . mumble . . . down there."

"Dearest, I can't hear you. What are you trying to tell me? Down where?"

"It hurts so much, and itches."

"What does?"

"Dear God, here . . . here between my legs and there is nasty-smelling stuff. I don't even know what to call it and I feel so exhausted."

"But surely that is the baby."

"Do all women have what I have?"

Beth stood up and reached for her fur-lined pelisse which she had thrown on to the back of a chair. "I don't know but I intend to find out. I'm going directly to Doctor Bennett's and your coachman can take me." Her voice was soft and she leaned over her sister's distraught figure and softly kissed her cheek. "We'll get you better, darling. Just stay exactly where you are and within an hour help will be here, I promise you."

Milly had syphilis! When John Bennett gently broke the news to Beth she sat down heavily in the chair by the window and began to lose her senses, and had it not been for the smelling salts he thrust under her nose would have fainted.

"Don't go delicate on me now, Beth," he said sternly. "I'm going to need you to help, so pull yourself together and listen to what I have to say."

Old Lady Thornley had been outraged when the Thornley carriage containing Beth and Doctor Bennett had drawn up at the steps that led to the front door of her beautiful home, demanding to know who had given them the right to enter uninvited. And what's more she could not credit that Mrs Goodwin had been ill-mannered enough to get out *her* carriage and *her* coachman to go on some private errand of her own.

"Your home, Lady Thornley? This is my sister's home and I would be obliged if you would stand aside and let Doctor Bennett examine her." For her ladyship had taken the unprecedented step of moving into the hallway from her drawing-room to see what the commotion was at her door.

"How dare you address me in that way, young lady. Your sister may have married my son but this is still—"

"Milly is my sister and I am worried about her. Please don't stand in my way. I demand that the doctor and I be allowed access."

"My family already retains the services of Doctor Newland and the last time he called he seemed perfectly satisfied with . . . with my daughter-in-law's condition." She spoke the word *daughter-in-law* as though it were some foul obscenity she had been forced to utter. The footman stood impassively by the opened door but his eyes darted excitedly from one face to another, ready, should her old ladyship, as they had begun to call her, give him the order, to run for Barker the under-footman to help him deal with these intruders.

But with an impatient lift of his hand John Bennett pushed past him and her ladyship, eager to get to Milly whose symptoms Beth had described and which he didn't at all like the sound of. They were familiar to him, for he had treated women, *decent* women who had shown the same signs. The medical profession's handling of venereal diseases was a disgrace, in his opinion, for it seemed many doctors were in a conspiracy of silence. Male physicians had been accused by feminists and members of various women's movements, the suffragists included, of helping their male patients, particularly if they were about to marry, to cover up venereal disease, advising them as to how they might camouflage their gonorrhoeal discharge and therefore cohabit with their brides. The suffragists had demanded women's entry into medicine and recently the number of women who had obtained registration had risen to fifty-four. A hospital for women only had been opened in London where women were treated by female doctors, for it seemed most women did not wish to trust themselves to male physicians. Evidence had been produced of a particularly gruesome nature to support their fears that doctors performed clitoridectomies for no other reason than it was their opinion the operation was necessary and the patients did well on it. It certainly made them more passive, which was what a decent husband wanted!

Milly was still sprawled where Beth had left her and she felt Doctor Bennett recoil when he saw her. "Oh, dear sweet Jesus," she heard him whisper, then he was kneeling at Milly's feet and speaking to her in that soothing, comforting way he had, calming her fears as Beth had seen him do so often in the hospital. Between them they had lifted her from her chair and shuffled her along the landing to her bedroom where they had got her into a loose wrapper and on to her bed.

"Sit down on the sofa by the window, my dear," he said gently to Beth, for what he was about to do would certainly embarrass her. Milly was moaning in some sort of pain, though Beth did not know where it was. She scratched at the lesions that were on her chest, back, arms, hands, legs and even on the soles of her feet, complaining that her throat was sore and when Doctor Bennett with a nod of his head indicated that Beth should remain where she was Milly writhed painfully as he examined that private core of her womanhood, which seemed to be agony to her.

"I want my nurse sent for at once," he told Beth abruptly.

"Tell that coachman to go immediately to my house. Laura will know what to do and if the old lady gets in your way tell her not to interfere if she wants his lordship's heir to live. That should shut her up. I'm going to give Milly a draught. She needs sleep. I will stay with her until the nurse comes, my dear. See, she is falling asleep already. Now don't worry, for I promise you I will cure this appalling thing. Off you go. There are several treatments and between us you and I will see she recovers. Dear Lord knows what Abby and Noah are going to say but . . ." He smiled and pushed his hand through his white hair. "We'll deal with that when the time comes."

"Can she not be brought home to Lantern Hill, Doctor Bennett?"

"Beth, my dear. You must know we cannot remove a man's wife, especially his pregnant wife, from the marital home without his permission. Now, off you go."

She stalked past Lady Thornley who came to her drawing-room door and demanded to know what was happening but Beth did not answer. The carriage had gone, presumably back to the stable yard, but pulling on the bell beside the fireplace in the hall Beth waited until the footman came running.

"I need the carriage again," Beth told him shortly, hearing Lady Thornley's gasp of outrage.

"Mrs Goodwin, I demand—"

"My sister has syphilis, Lady Thornley, and she could only have caught it from your son. The matter is somewhat urgent so I'd be obliged if you would tell this man to send for your carriage." The footman's face was a picture of vicarious excitement and stunned astonishment as he glanced at his mistress, not only for her reaction but her permission to order up the carriage. She had sat down abruptly in the nearest chair, her face turning to bone white, but her upbringing came to her rescue and with a barely perceptible movement of her head she nodded.

Beth sat upright in the centre of the carriage seat, her back like a ramrod, her face rigid, for only as such could she keep her mind from flying away in a dozen different directions, the most keenly felt being horror. She could see his face as though he sat in the seat opposite, handsome, laughing, a charming tilt to his eyebrows, his eyes so blue, so filled with an expression that said he was the best fellow in the world and she was the woman he wanted. It had been a death blow when he had married her sister, flung her, Beth, indifferently aside, for she supposed it was all the same to him which sister he married since they would both bring money. But Milly had been the chosen one, presumably because she had become pregnant and look at her now. The winner! The chosen one. The victor and look where she had ended up. The diseased cast-off of an uncaring husband. She might lose her baby and her own life if Doctor Bennett could not find a cure.

She felt frozen inside and yet at the centre of the ice that filled her heart and blocked her veins was a core of something so twisted with rage, with hatred, with loathing for the man she had once loved and who had done this appalling thing, first to her and now to Milly, she could feel the need to hurt him fill her to the brim and overflow.

She drew up outside Doctor Bennett's house in Claughton Street and the carriage had hardly stopped before she flung herself out and up the steps of the house. The door was opened by a red-faced Biddy, ready to give what for to whoever was ringing the doorbell so violently but Biddy fell back, her hand to her mouth as Beth pushed past her. Her face lost its high colour in fear, for surely something must have happened to the doctor as Miss Beth was usually so calm, and as Beth flung open the door of Laura's parlour she was close on her heels. There were women in the room, members of the NUWSS who all sprang to their feet as Beth entered but it was to Laura she spoke.

"It's Milly . . ."

"Dear Lord, not the baby already."

"No, but the doctor . . ." She gulped and could not get the words out. "He wants a nurse, he said you would know of one."

"Of course, sweetheart. Now, won't you sit down and let Miss Bowman pour you a cup of—"

"No, no. I must go."

"But where, dear?" The ladies, who all knew her, gathered about her, urging her to sit down and drink a cup of tea, but she held out her hand to hold them off, for nothing was to stop her in what she meant to do.

"Thank you, thank you, but no."

She had delivered her message. There was nothing, for the moment, that she must do until she returned to Thornley Green. Only one thing and she meant to do it immediately.

The coachman looked at her enquiringly as he helped her into the carriage.

"Where to, ma'am," he asked respectfully.

"To the barracks at Longworth."

had been told of the communion in the hall by Jackson, who in

9

It was as though the weather was doing its best to distract Beth from the task she had set herself. A lark was singing, the first to be heard that year but she didn't hear it. It was mild and sunny, the sky the pale, innocent blue of early spring. Snowdrops and winter aconites and primroses were in blossom in the gardens she passed on the edge of town and, in the edges of the lane, peeping modestly from beneath the greening hedges, were crocus. Young nettle leaves were sprouting in the ditch and birch catkins were in bud. She didn't see them. A chaffinch, its breast a pretty pink, flew across the lane, disappearing into a goat willow bush from which catkins hung, evidently making for its nest. She didn't see it. She stared impassively at the back of the coachman, her explosive, maddened thoughts well hidden.

The coachman, whose name she did not know, sat stolidly on his seat, glancing back now and again at his silent passenger, wondering what the devil he was doing taking her young lady-ship's sister to the barracks where his lordship was stationed. He had been told of the commotion in the hall, for Jackson, who in his opinion was a half-witted fool, had been bursting with it in the kitchen. The dread word had been spoken and some of the kitchen-maids had been ready to faint, for though they were good girls and knew next to nothing of such things, they were shocked to hear it spoken in the house and in the presence of her ladyship. They knew that his lordship's new wife was expecting a baby, of course, but it seemed things were not as they should be, her maid, Sally Preston, who had come with her on her marriage, had reported to them, and Margaret, who cleaned her ladyship's rooms, had told them that she looked awful, whatever that meant.

The carriage drove through Longworth at a smart pace and out on to the road that led to the barracks where the garrison was quartered. The wide, wrought-iron gates stood open and a sentry with a rifle at his shoulder stood to attention, his eyes fixed on the opposite side of the road. The Thornley coachman was about to rein in the horses, not knowing what else to do, but his passenger told him curtly to drive on, which he did. The sentry went so far as to step away from his post and stare after the carriage in which sat a pretty young woman, unsure what to do. He was not exactly *guarding* the barracks, his post was for show really, but this had never happened before, an unescorted young lady driving as calm as you please on to the parade-ground. He watched as the carriage continued along the paved road until it reached the parade-ground from where, his mouth open, an officer ran forward and signalled for the carriage to stop. The coachman drew it to a halt and waited. What a tale he would have had to tell when he got back to the servants hall, that's if he had been a gossiping sort of man, which he wasn't.

"Can I help you, miss?" the young officer asked, his tone respectful, for this was a lady he addressed, he knew that.

"I'm looking for Captain Hugh Thornley. Can you direct me to where he might be found?"

"I believe he is on parade drill, miss, but if I can be of any assistance? It is not customary, you see, for ladies to enter the barrack." He smiled winningly. He was longing to be told he might do instead of Captain Thornley but the young lady interrupted him.

"And where is that?"

"Miss?"

"Where is the parade-ground?"

"Well, right here, miss," turning to look behind him where dozens of lines of soldiers marched and wheeled and came to a crashing stop when ordered, the sound of their boots echoing across the ground. "He's just there, miss, but as you can see he is involved—"

"Thank you," the young lady said, and to the young second lieutenant's consternation she got down from her carriage and began to walk towards where Captain Hugh Thornley elegantly sat on his horse, one first curled on his thigh, his eyes on the men before them. They were, of course, cavalry soldiers but they must still learn to march in step, to wheel and halt, to carry heavy packs on their backs, to present arms and to stand to attention.

They did not notice her for a few moments, the briskly marching soldiers in their vivid scarlet jackets, their spiked helmets, their shining boots, their white belts, stamping in unison on the concrete surface of the parade-ground. The sergeant-majors, several of them, shouted their incomprehensible commands, which were instantly obeyed with the precision the army expected, but as she walked towards the still figure on his magnificent charger, her buttercup-yellow gown, her fur-lined pelisse, her pretty hat with a mass of silk buttercups on the brim began to catch the soldiers' eyes. She did not wait for each column to pass but walked briskly forward as though they did not exist and, without waiting for the command to halt, they halted, for they did not wish to mow down the slender figure of the young woman who was purposefully walking across their lines. Soldiers bumped into one another, cursing quietly, for there was a lady on parade, but cursing just the same. Their bayonets were in danger of stabbing in the back the soldier who marched in front and the chaos began to accumulate.

Beth Goodwin was aware of the great many soldiers about her but since they seemed to hang back to let her pass she did

not hesitate and continued to march, as they were trying to
do, in a direct line from the carriage to the mounted figure of
Captain Hugh Thornley. He had by now become aware of the
confusion in the ranks and had turned in surprise, a surprise
that changed to amazement as he saw the small figure of his
sister-in-law striding towards him. His mouth fell open and for
a moment Hugh Thornley did not know what the devil to do.
Sit where he was on the back of his horse, or dismount, as a
gentleman should, when approached by a lady? He was on
duty on the barracks square and the proper action to take in the
circumstances had not been written since it was not expected to
happen. She was upon him before he could decide.

Considering the great number of men on the parade-ground
it had become very quiet as though the soldiers, officers and
other ranks, brought to a shambling standstill, were all aware
that some critical situation was upon them, or, more to the
point, upon Captain Thornley before whom the young lady
stopped. The captain was well known, despite his newly
married state, to be a one for the ladies and perhaps this
was one of them come to berate him. Those nearest to him
hardly dared breathe lest they miss a word of what was to be
said and those further away strained their ears for the same
reason. It had become so quiet birds could be heard trilling and
twittering in the trees that surrounded the ground. When one
soldier cleared his throat those in his vicinity hastily shushed
him.

"Captain Thornley," she said, her voice clear, and it seemed
to Dicky Bentham who was not far away that she was making a
great effort to enunciate clearly so that none should miss her
words.

"Beth, for God's sake," Hugh hissed, clearly thunderstruck.
"What the bloody hell—"

"I wish to speak to you . . . no, *accuse* you of such a
horrendous crime it can hardly be talked of without—"

"A crime, God's teeth. Beth, what on earth are you saying?" He had no idea what she was about to reveal but it was clear his consternation was turning to anger. He was conscious that every pair of eyes on the parade-ground was directed at him and his sister-in-law and he did not care for it. "I cannot imagine what could have possibly brought you here in such a way."

"Can you not, then let me enlighten you."

"Don't be so bloody ridiculous. If you have something to say, then say it, but not here. I cannot conceive what could have made you forget yourself but if you must speak, and it had better be something of vital importance to interrupt me in my duties, then follow me to—"

"No, Captain, or should I call you my lord? It *is* of vital importance and I will not keep this thing secret for it is something the world, or at least *your* world should know about. I have just come from Thornley Green—"

"Stop it, Beth. Get a hold of yourself and try to act in a ladylike manner. I appreciate that you are not—"

"A ladylike manner. And what of you? You call yourself a gentleman and dare to insult me but that is of no consequence. It is my sister who I have come to tell you about. Your mother is fainting away at the scandal that will ensue, for make no mistake I shall spread it all over Lancashire."

"What the hell are you going on about, woman?" he snarled. His famous temper was beginning to rise and in the ranks the men were as still as statues and just as silent.

"I am talking about your wife, Captain. The doctor is with her as I speak."

"The child?"

"No, not the child, though its life lies in the balance. I am talking about the evil disease you have given my sister. She has syphilis, Captain, and you gave it to her. You are a disgrace not only to your name, your rank and your regiment, but to the male race, though I must admit I have known some appalling deeds done by men in my work for the cause of women. She is rotting away, so Doctor Bennett tells me, and if she lives, and the child lives, it might be blind, or even born with the disease you gave to Milly. It could have a heart defect or deformity of the joints, be deaf or mentally retarded and you have caused this. I don't know whether you had this . . . this foul thing before you married her, or whether you picked it up from some whore since and passed it on casually to my sister. But whichever it is I shall make sure your name stinks to high heaven in St Helens. And God knows what my father will do when he hears of it."

Hugh Thornley dismounted slowly and several of the men who were closest moved forward, for it seemed he was about to strike the woman who had just totally destroyed his reputation. It would be recovered because he was an aristocrat, an officer and a gentleman and they had a habit of overcoming this sort of thing, but he had been humiliated in the most terrible way in front of every soldier in the garrison. The brigadier could be seen coming hurriedly from the officers' mess, his face a picture, for it seemed some damn woman had thrown his whole parade-ground into chaos, but before he reached Captain Thornley the young woman turned on her heel and walked towards her carriage.

"I won't forget this, you bitch," the captain shrieked after her, his face purple with rage, almost stamping his feet in temper as he used to do as a small boy.

"And neither will I, Captain," she shouted over her shoulder, and as the soldiers said afterwards to one another, they felt like bloody cheering, for had you ever seen such a plucky little thing stand up to a bastard like Captain bloody Thornley.

The coachman said, "Very well, ma'am," when she told him to drive her directly to Edge Bottom Glass Works, his face expressionless as though he were quite accustomed to being given orders by a woman not his mistress. He had watched her as she marched across the parade-ground, wondering what the hell she was up to, but like all the other silent men he heard every word she spoke to his lordship. He had been shocked but at the same time could understand how she must feel about the man who had done such a dreadful thing to her sister, to his own wife. God knows what the old lady felt but then that was none of his business. His lordship had always been a bugger, like his father, he had heard. He did not look round at his passenger until they entered the gates of the glass works and then it was only to see if there were any particular building to which she wished to be taken.

"The office, please. I'm sorry I don't know your name . . ."

"Archer, ma'am."

"Thank you, Archer, you have been most kind." Which surprised him as he was only doing his job. "Just there, by the steps will do."

The yard was busy, as always, with wagons delivering sand, coal, saltcake, and taking away enormous crates of finished glass for delivery to the railway. Men were everywhere like ants, hot and sweating despite the coldness of the day, brawny muscled arms rippling in the pale sunshine as they unloaded the makings of glass and loaded the finished product. Horses' hooves clashed mightily on the cobbles as great shire horses moved off and others tossed their heads, their harness jingling, but Beth, so used to the scene from childhood when she would come to see her father, noticed none of it.

Archie raised his head enquiringly as she burst into his office, leaping to his feet and coming round his desk to sweep her into his arms, alarmed at the paleness of her face.

"What is it? Darling, what's happened?" He waved away the old clerk who had been there since her grandfather's day, then led her to a chair. "Tell me." He knelt down at her feet and rubbed her cold hands, peering up anxiously into her face. "Is it Milly? The child?"

"Yes, but there is worse."

"What?" He could not bear to see her troubled and he frowned as though in anger at whoever it was who had brought about this state.

"She is . . . ill. Dear God, Archie, I hardly know how to tell you and what I shall say to Mother and Father . . . Oh, dear heaven."

"Tell me."

"She has a disease."

"A disease: what sort of a disease?"

"Syphilis," she whispered.

Archie sat back on his heels and the expression on his face was one of bewilderment which, as he took in her words, changed to horror. "*Syphilis!* Oh, sweet Jesus, do you mean . . .?"

"Yes."

"But how?"

"The usual way, I suppose, and there are no prizes for guessing who gave it to her."

"The unspeakable . . ."

"So I told him."

"He was there?"

"No, I've just come from the barracks, the parade-ground actually, where he was drilling his men. I told him what I thought of him and believe me when I say you could have heard a pin drop. Every man in the regiment heard me, as I intended."

"Bloody hell!" Archie's voice was no more than an appalled murmur. From the yard came a shout and someone was whistling "It was a lover and his lass . . ." A woman's laugh rang out, followed by another and in the office one of the brand-new telephones that Archie had had installed rang out then was silent as it was answered.

"What are you to do?" Archie asked, for he knew his wife would be doing something.

"I'm going back to Thornley Green to help Doctor Bennett but I want you to go over to Lantern Hill – not yet, not until the news is better . . ." Her voice petered out but she lifted her head bravely. "Which it will be, and tell them. Oh, Archie, I'm so sorry to give you this dreadful task but there is no one else. You can imagine what Father will do . . ."

"Jesus . . ."

"But you will?"

"You know I will, but I shall be over to Thornley Green later to make sure that you are safe." Who knew what that evil bastard might do and he meant to be there to defend his wife.

"I will not be shipped off to some God-forsaken spot just because of whispers that are going about, whispers spread by some malicious woman who herself had hopes of becoming my wife. This is a female way of getting revenge, sir, and I object to being made to pay for it by being sent to the bloody Indian frontier. My wife is expecting our first child and I naturally wish to be with her when it is born."

"That may be so, Thornley, but I cannot ignore the rumours that are circulating, not just about the barracks but in the town. This happened the day before yesterday but already it has reached the ears of the general and he has given me instructions to sort it out. Now, I realise that a man, when his wife is with child, if he is a gentleman, that is, must find a solution to . . . to his needs, but it seems you have gone to the wrong sort of woman and infected your wife, a lady, with this terrible thing and until it blows over the general suggests you spend some time in India. They need officers. The Black Mountain tribes have been troublesome for some time and only last month they attacked a British party on a route march and killed two British officers. It would be—"

"Thank you, sir, but you have no need to worry yourself, or the general, any further. I intend to resign my commission. I would be grateful if you would put it in hand."

The brigadier looked surprised, yet he could not help but think what a relief it would be to get rid of this arrogant lordling who thought himself to be above the accepted rules of their class and, worse still, of the army. This was not the first time Captain Thornley, or Lord Thornley as he supposed he should call him now, had been in trouble with women, with gambling debts which he had somehow managed to pay, with mess debts and disquieting reports regarding his treatment of the men under his command.

His face was cold, stiff with displeasure. "Very well, that will be all, Thornley."

"Thank you, sir." With an insolent grin on his face, Hugh Thornley turned on his heels and without the customary salute which was recognised as directed to the rank, not the man, lounged from the office.

Doctor Bennett had scarcely left Milly's bedside and when he did, for there were other calls on his time, Beth huddled in the chair by the fire, frequently moving to put her hand on Milly's forehead, though she was aware that the nurse disapproved. If she had her way Nurse Corbett, who was a trusted member of Doctor Bennett's staff at the hospital, would have barred her ladyship's sister from the room, but the doctor was of the opinion that anything, no matter what, that eased a patient's suffering should be allowed. He even admitted husbands, for God's sake, to a wife's room at her lying-in, cluttering it up with anxiety and nerves when the mother needed peace and calm.

The patient was being treated with potassium iodide which Doctor Bennett had much faith in since it had proved effective in other cases and already there was a slight improvement. Her ladyship's temperature had gone down and she had slept peacefully, which was all that could be hoped for in the circumstances. So far the husband, his lordship, had not put in an appearance at his wife's bedside, which was a good job, nor her ladyship's parents, which surprised her but at the same time was a great relief. Neither had her ladyship's mother-in-law who, living in the same house, would have been expected at least to ask after the patient. But then, the ways of the gentry were a mystery to Nurse Corbett and at least the sister seemed to have a good heart.

Beth had not been home for three days, sleeping on a cot in the dressing-room despite the disapproval of the nurse. Archie came each evening after work, admitted grudgingly by the footman who, on the first occasion, had kept him waiting on the doorstep while he asked permission of his mistress.

"You've not told Mother and Father?" Beth asked, clinging to him, for this man was her rock, her one steady and utterly reliable foundation in the mad shaking world in which she had become enmeshed. She longed to let him lift her into his arms and put her in the carriage, taking her to Edge Bottom House where she could sleep in his arms until the exhaustion she suffered had been eased. She had dozed fitfully in the chair, or in the little bed in the dressing-room adjoining Milly's, urging the nurse to rest herself while she watched her sister.

Archie had brought her a change of clothing, packed by Mary who, Archie said, had begged to come with him, but until she knew Milly was well on the road to recovery she would not leave her, Beth told him, and there were plenty of servants here to see to Milly's needs. In fact, the nurse being such a tartar, they leaped to do her bidding in the shortest possible time.

"No, my darling, I've said nothing but your mother sent a note asking why you hadn't been to see them and saying she intended driving over to Thornley Green to visit Milly. Would you like to go with her, she says. I'm doing my best to put her off but you must send her an answer or she'll suspect something is wrong and demand to know what it is. Is Milly not up to having visitors?"

"It's only been three days, Archie. Doctor Bennett is pleased with her but she is far from recovery. She . . . she confided to me that she and Hugh had made love before their marriage and she was pregnant, about two months, she thought, when they married, so the baby is due sooner than we believed. And this disease is likely to bring on an early labour, so Doctor Bennett told me. I can only be glad Hugh has chosen not to come home."

Archie's mouth thinned to a grim line and he held her in a firmer grip as though the very fierceness of his protective instincts would keep her safe, for there was no doubt that Hugh Thornley would never forgive the humiliation he had suffered at her hands. They were huddled together in the dowager Lady Thornley's conservatory, sadly neglected for years, the plants still wildly overgrown, for Hugh had more pressing needs on which to spend his wife's money than the resurrection of his mother's conservatory. It was dusk beyond the filmy windows and cold, since no fire had been lit in the drawing-room. Her old ladyship was in her own private sitting-room where she kept to herself, having no wish to come across her daughter-in-law's sister roaming about *her* house. For five months she had been forced to endure that middle-class woman her son had married, that woman who was said to have a dreadful disease, a disease that she refused to believe her son had given her. The other way round more likely, she was inclined to think, for she had seen her at the parties and balls Hugh had given at Christmas time, cavorting, flirting, laughing, ogling men and it was clear to her what sort of woman she was!

"Come home with me, my love," Archie begged his wife. "Milly's in good hands and if you are needed I'm sure John Bennett would send for you. You say that she's improving so why don't we go together to Lantern Hill and tell your mother and father?"

"Oh, God, Archie, I dread the very thought," Beth moaned, burying herself deeper against his chest.

"Well, just one more night, then I insist you come home with me. We will go and tell your mother and father when you have had a decent night's sleep at home. I mean it, Beth. Tomorrow you come home with me and the following day we go to Lantern Hill."

IO

Archie thought his father-in-law was about to have an apo-
plectic fit as he hesitantly told him of his daughter's condition
and so, apparently, did his mother-in-law, for though she was
as deeply shocked as Noah Goodwin she rose to her feet and
staggered towards him where he stood by the fireplace, prepared to hold him steady. Beth also rose to her feet, moving
swiftly to her mother's side, putting an arm about her father in
case he fell. Archie was already on his feet, unable to sit in one
of the comfortable chairs in Abby's drawing-room as he broke
the appalling news.

Archie could see that Abby had been surprised when he and
Beth, after being shown in by Ruby, had refused tea or coffee,
though he had been tempted to ask for a brandy to get himself
through this critical situation. Milly was showing signs of
responding slowly to the treatment John Bennett had advised
so at least he would be able to tell her parents that to comfort
them. But the actual disease, a horror in itself, would surely
drive them out of their minds, as it would any decent mother or
father when told their child suffered it. And to have to inform
them that the man who had given it to her was her own husband
appalled him.

Noah was clinging to the mantelpiece, his hand white-
knuckled and his face, from being an attractive shade of amber
then a vivid puce, slowly lost all colour and he was heard to
moan softly deep in his throat. His other hand reached out to
his wife's arm, gripping it so fiercely that she winced. Her own

face was a putty colour and her eyes closed as though to shut out some dreadful sight.

"She's going to be all right, Father, Mother. Doctor Bennett says he has caught it in time, though the baby . . ." Beth cried, ready to weep for the hell her parents were suffering, stroking her father's arm.

Still Milly Thornley's parents seemed unable to speak, to force words, any words, from between their rigidly clamped lips, and with a swift movement Archie moved across the room to the small cabinet where he knew Noah kept his brandy. Taking out two glasses he poured a decent measure in each and passed them to Abby and Noah who, still in a state of tranced shock, took them, looking at them as though they were not sure what they should do with them.

"Drink," Archie said gently. "It will pull you round, put strength—"

Noah Goodwin came to savage, frightening life. With an oath so obscene his wife and daughter gasped, he flung the glass across the room, straightened his shoulders, lifted his arms, curving his hands into claws and roared. In the kitchen the maids exchanged terrified glances, for the sound of the shattering glass and their master's raised voice, though they could not make out what he said, turned them to stone. Ruby had told them she thought something was wrong when she returned to the kitchen after showing Mr Archie and Miss Beth into the drawing-room and the following sound of the master's maddened voice confirmed it.

The expression on Noah's face was so menacing Archie moved forward as though afraid that, unaware of his own strength, in his rage his father-in-law might do damage to the women.

"She's to come home," Noah roared, "where she belongs and if that—" – here again he used foul language heard only in the gutters – "thinks he can prevent it I'll kill him. In fact I'll find him and kill him anyway. Where is he?" He turned on Archie and grasped him by the lapels of his jacket, hauling him up until he was no more than an inch from his own incensed, wild-eyed face. "Tell me where he is and then get my shotgun from my study, though shooting's too good for the bastard. I knew, I bloody knew he was no good, the silken-tongued bastard, talking my little girl into marriage while all the time he was consorting with the dregs, whores. Dear God, I can't stand it. Abby, Abby, where are you? I can't bear the thought of him putting his filthy rotting hands on my girl. Oh, Jesus . . ."

Only Abby Goodwin, the wife he loved more than life itself, more than his own girls, could handle him now, Archie knew that, for she was the only voice he listened to. She might be as distraught as he was but she was at least in command of her actions which, left to himself, Noah wouldn't be. He was doing his best to wrench himself from the grasp of his son-in-law, his daughter, even his wife, mindless in his agony, but Abby had her arms about him, hanging on to him as he attempted to throw her off, to reach the door, to charge up the hallway to his study where his guns were kept.

"Noah . . . Noah . . . Noah," she was shrieking in his ear and again the maids in the kitchen exchanged glances and cowered against the table and the dresser. Harriet Woodruff made a move towards the back door as though she were about to fetch her husband, for surely murder was being done in the drawing-room; then she halted, since there was only the family there and it was hardly likely they would be attacking one another, was it?

Suddenly Noah calmed and though he was still trembling he lifted his dark head, now with more than a few grey hairs, and spoke to his wife.

"Ring the bell and tell Clem to bring the carriage round to the door. Get Harriet to fetch your wrap, for it's cold out and wait for me at the front door."

"Noah, what are you to do?" Abby asked fearfully.

"I cannot kill the bugger as I would like to but I shall take my whip and have the hide off him. Then we shall bring our daughter home where she will get the best care and if he comes within a bloody mile of my house I shall kill him."

"Noah, you cannot take a man's wife from his home," Archie began, but Noah held up his hand, walking towards the drawing-room door.

"Can I not? Not even if she is my daughter who has been . . . been abused? I have a lot of influence in this town, Archie, and there are not many who would stand against me. She is carrying my grandchild and I mean to protect her and the child from that beast. Now then, Abby, are you coming or not? I would be glad to have you, for God only knows what I would do without you by my side."

Ruby's frightened face appeared timidly at the door but the master spoke gently to her, bidding her send for Clem and the carriage. "We are to go to Thornley Green, tell him, to bring my daughter home."

"Yes, sir," Ruby breathed, hurrying away in the direction of the kitchen with the news that Miss Milly was to be brought home but for what reason she or the others could not say. She was pregnant, they knew that, but none of them had seen her since her marriage. Something dreadful was happening, that was for sure. Did that arrogant man she had married have anything to do with it? A real toff he was, who thought himself way above the Goodwin family, and on the few occasions he had been to Lantern Hill before the marriage he had treated the Goodwin servants no better than the muck beneath his feet!

Though Noah brandished his whip in the face of the astonished footman it failed to produce the arrogant figure of his master who had not been home for some days, he quavered. No, he couldn't say where his lordship was but perhaps Lady Thornley might be able to help him. He stayed well out of reach of the whip that Noah held dangling from his hand. Now and again he allowed it to curl about the footman's feet like a snake and Jackson was relieved when her ladyship appeared at her drawing-room door, drawn there by the compelling tones of her son's ill-bred father-in-law.

"May I ask what you are doing?" she began in her authoritarian, yet ladylike way, but Noah was not concerned with the mother, only the son.

"Where's that bastard who has abused my daughter?" he asked her, his tone of voice more frightening than any bluff or bluster might have been. "He deserves to be horse-whipped and that is precisely what I mean to do. Take the bloody skin off him, the filthy sod."

"You will watch your language in my house, if you please, Mr Goodwin. We are not accustomed to such talk," her ladyship began just as icily, but she did not dismay Noah Goodwin.

His wife, who held his arm in a vice-like grip, though it would have taken at least a couple of heavyweights to hold him back should Hugh Thornley have appeared, interrupted them both. "My daughter is . . . is ill, we have been told."

"*Ill*," Noah exploded. "That son of yours, who it seems keeps company with whores, diseased whores, has brought back what they gave him to my lass and if it's the last thing I do I shall punish him."

"*How dare you?* How dare you blacken my son's name," her ladyship said in a tone of icy contempt. "If your daughter has this disease which, since that doctor of yours will not allow *my* doctor to examine her, has not been confirmed, I believe she brought it herself into my son's home."

Noah surged forward in outrage but his wife held him firmly, for he could hardly strike a lady, could he?

"Might I ask where your son is, Lady Thornley?" Abby asked her quietly, still hanging on to Noah's arm, the one holding the whip.

"No, you may not. He . . . he is hunting somewhere, I believe but—"

"Bloody hunting, while his wife could be dying," Noah snarled, but Abby tightened her grip on him.

"I would like to see my daughter, Lady Thornley, if you please, and if I consider it necessary I shall take her home with us where I can nurse her and make sure she is—"

"Are you implying she is not getting the care she needs for . . . for whatever it is that ails her?" her ladyship asked haughtily.

"Syphilis is what ails her, so if you would show us the way I will see for myself. There is no better doctor than John Bennett and that is what he has diagnosed. He has had a great deal of experience of—"

"Yes, so I heard," her ladyship sneered. "Even in his own home he consorts with the dregs—"

"My daughter's room, if you please, Lady Thornley."

"You will not interfere with my son's wife, Mrs Goodwin."

"*My daughter*, Lady Thornley. Now my husband and I will see her if I have to roam your house shouting her name."

The expression on her face was inscrutable but with a slight nod her ladyship turned on her heel and moved back into her drawing-room. She did not like her daughter-in-law but privately she admitted that her home had been a great deal more comfortable since she wed Hugh. She had an enormous fire crackling in her drawing-room fireplace and hot chocolate or tea whenever she cared for it. She was warm and well fed and was in no hurry to move to the dower house as her son had suggested and, as for the girl, she hadn't seen her for several weeks, nor did she care overmuch. A child would be born, a Thornley, an heir, and that was all that mattered. This talk of . . . of a nasty disease was probably exaggerated by that high-handed doctor the other daughter had brought, but until Hugh came home there was little she could do against this low-bred family. It went against all the standards of the mannered class to which she belonged even to stand here defending her son. Hugh would see to it when he returned from wherever he was. She closed the drawing-room door quietly.

They took her home in the carriage, wrapped in somewhat threadbare blankets, accompanied by the nurse Doctor Bennett had employed. She was not happy about moving her patient, she told them worriedly, but she could not stand against the distraught parents who, she was sadly aware, were deeply shocked by their daughter's appearance. Lady Thornley was heavily sedated and Doctor Bennett was keeping her that way despite the danger to the child in her womb. He had been sent for, or at least a message had been delivered telling him of his patient's move to her parents' home and she really had to admit that the standard of comfort and cleanliness she found at Lantern Hill far outweighed that at Thornley Green. A sadly disorganised group of servants were employed there but then what else could you expect when they had no housekeeper to guide them and no mistress with the strength or interest to see that her home was well run.

With the help of what seemed to be a dozen willing maidservants to run to do her bidding she soon had her ladyship tucked up clean and comfortable in a lovely room which, she had been told, had been her ladyship's before her marriage. A fire leaping in the grate, constant hot water and soft white towels, maids eager to help her, to fetch her tea or anything else she fancied and the special diet Doctor Bennett had arranged for her patient. Mrs Goodwin sat by her daughter's bedside, holding her hand and weeping silently, while in the hallway her deranged father strode up and down waiting while Doctor Bennett, who had come at once, examined his patient.

"She will recover, Abby," the doctor told Mrs Goodwin gently, taking her hand from her daughter's and leading her to the window. "She is young and healthy and with proper care and nursing she will soon be herself again. Tell Noah—"

"And the baby?"

"Ah . . ."

"You are saying it might not survive?"

"It could be . . . damaged."

"Damaged?"

"I will be truthful but for God's sake don't tell Noah or he . . . well, God knows what he might do."

"Please." Abby clung to this man's hand, this doctor who had known her since she herself was younger than her daughter. He had seen her and those she loved through illness and injury, through desolate sadness, he and his wife standing staunchly beside her until she had at last come out into the sunlit peace of her marriage to Noah.

"The child could be born with the disease."

"Dear God." Abby reeled, her hand to her mouth, wishing she had the strong arm of her husband about her, but in this it must be she who was the strong one.

"It . . . might be blind, or have a heart defect, or . . . or mental retardation."

"John, what are we to do? How are we to get through this? You know how Noah feels about Milly. He might do—"

"Don't tell him, Abby. I know it's a lot to keep to yourself but Beth will help you. She knows what you know and perhaps Harriet. She will stand by you. The baby is due soon."

Abby looked startled. "Soon? June, we were told."

"No, my dear, probably April, or it might be sooner in the circumstances. But will you promise me that until the baby comes you will say nothing of this to Noah? He is—"

"I know, I know." Abby's tears slid across her grey cheeks

and the nurse watched sympathetically, for what mother could stand the horror of what was happening to her child.

Beth and Archie, doing their best to pretend that this was a normal family meal, stayed to dine at Lantern Hill but, with Noah glowering at the end of the table and her poor mother scarcely able to speak, it was almost impossible. What was there to talk about when all their minds were fastened on the woman who lay half-comatose upstairs? And though they had been told only that afternoon by his mother that Hugh Thornley was elsewhere, the women at least had half an ear cocked for the front doorbell. When it did ring all four of them jumped to their feet, badly startling Ruby and Nessie who were serving them. And the meal wasn't one of Cook's best, she had grumbled as she thrust it on to the tray, for how could she concentrate on cooking when they were all thinking on poor Miss Milly who lay so ill in her old bedroom.

It was John Bennett who had arrived to check on his patient accompanied by Laura who came to be with Abby and Noah, she said, and if there was anything she could do they had only to ask. They were all aware by now that John had a slender but definite belief that Milly would recover; nevertheless the thought of the child she carried and its chances of survival, or, worse, to live as an invalid, was not far from their minds. She embraced them both, then sat with them in the drawing-room drinking coffee and watching Noah toss back brandy after brandy, none of them having the slightest effect on him. Stone-cold sober, he was, but when Archie and Beth declared they had best get home he uncharacteristically dragged Beth into his arms and held her without a word.

"I'll be here first thing, Father," she whispered into his neck.

"Aye, my lass. Now sleep well, d'you hear. Why don't you ask John to give you something?"

"I *have* something, Father," she replied, taking her husband's arm.

Her father bowed his head as though in thanks that one of his lasses was well cared for, protected and loved by her husband, blessing the day his wife had brought this man, then a skinny urchin, into their home. He remembered how incensed he had been at the time, saying he was not prepared to take in every waif and stray she found, but a thousand times he had thanked the fates, for Archie Goodwin had brought a wonderful calming love to his daughter, to his wife and a great respect to himself. His businesses were safe in Archie's hands and though many thought him a sombre, unobtrusive sort of a man he had a great deal of quiet charm and humour. At least Beth was safe with him, which could not be said for the bastard who had married Milly.

A week went by and Milly continued to improve though the disease was far from gone. In the old days, John explained, mercury would have been used, either in ointment form, orally or with vapour baths, but twenty or more years ago potassium iodide had been found to be more beneficial, especially in the tertiary stage which was usually fatal. No, no, they must not be frightened, Milly was far from the tertiary stage but she was in what was called the secondary stage. She must have gone through the primary stage that usually cleared up after a week or two, leaving the patient to believe he or she was cured. Milly, after several weeks, had moved into the secondary phase and with the potassium iodide, rest, good nursing and diet, should be better by the time her child was due.

"That's in June, John," Noah began hesitantly but John shook his head.

"Sooner than that, Noah," leaving Milly's father to work out for himself what he meant.

Beth went each day to sit with her sister who was no longer under sedation, though it seemed she was somewhat confused as to why she was here in the bedroom of her girlhood home instead of the one she now shared with her husband.

"Where's Hugh?" she asked fretfully. She had not been told what was wrong with her and Doctor Bennett had advised them to keep it from her. The terrible chances had almost gone and Milly was more comfortable but amazingly – at least Beth found it so – she fretted for Hugh and asked almost hourly why he wasn't here with her and, what's more, why she was here. As she improved she became increasingly impatient, swearing she must get back to him, demanding that Beth call Clem to bring the carriage to take her home.

"God knows what Hugh's got up to," she declared impatiently, evidently not trusting him out of her sight, doing her best to fling back the bedclothes and lever her ballooning figure off the bed. The nurse, taking advantage of Miss Beth's presence, had gone to her own room and rung the bell for a teatray which she found immensely satisfying. While she wished no further ill on poor Lady Thornley she half hoped this job would last for many weeks to come, for she had never known such comfort, waited on hand and foot by Mrs Goodwin's servants and, now that Lady Thornley was improving, getting a decent night's sleep in a warm and comfortable bedroom.

"Milly, you can't go back to Thornley Green yet, darling. There really was no one to look after you there. The old lady . . . well, you know what she thinks of the family her son married into, was quite prepared to leave you to the servants."

"Dear Lord, don't I know it, the old cow, but I'm not bothered about her. That nurse can come home with me until the child is born and with Doctor Bennett—"

"Milly, Lady Thornley does not approve of Doctor Bennett and the moment you got back to Thornley Green she would bar him from the house and bring in that old fuddy-duddy who had you in his care and let you get into such a state."

"Well, I'm better now and it's time I went home to my husband. I'm surprised he allowed you to bring me back to Lantern Hill in the first place. Why hasn't he been over to see me?"

"Well . . ."

"Yes?" Milly struggled to sit up, indicating to Beth that she was to pile some more pillows at her back. "Has he been?"

"Well, no. I believe . . . Lady Thornley believes he is hunting somewhere."

"Hunting somewhere. What does that mean? He's a soldier. He can't just go gallivanting off whenever he chooses."

"I know nothing about that, Milly. He wasn't there when we brought you home and . . . well, it was Father, really. You were so ill and needed special nursing . . ." Beth knew she was babbling, filling the strange silences with words so that Milly wouldn't ask the questions to which Beth could give no answers. It seemed Milly was anxious about her husband, and was it any wonder. He had been a womaniser before they were married and her own upbringing must have told her that no decent man, gentleman or no, would make love to an unmarried woman, even if he did intend to wed her. He had proved himself a blackguard, not only by his treatment of Milly but the way he had led her, Beth, to believe he was interested in herself. She was not slow to realise, or so she believed, that if he had not got Milly pregnant it would have been herself who would have become Lady Thornley. The thought made her go cold, for though she was aware that Archie loved her more than she loved him she could not bear to think of having another man for a husband. She could not always attain the physical pleasure he did, that climax that came only infrequently, but the rich love he wrapped her in, his need of her, that expression that crossed his face when she met him at the door was more than enough for her.

"I love you, Beth," he would murmur into her hair.

"Oh yes, love me, love me. You make me so happy I want to give you everything. I must make you happy, as you make me." She knew she was not in love with him in the piercing, consuming love she thought she had felt for Hugh, and sometimes her fear of failing this beloved man created a tension in her. But he was unfailingly gentle with her and in all other ways she knew they were happy.

Milly appeared to have dozed off, slipping cumbersomely down the mountain of pillows, her head lolling to one side, when the commotion began at the front door and at once she raised herself, reaching for the hairbrush with which Beth had brushed her hair, just as though she knew who was shouting at the front door.

There was a cry, Ruby's voice, then a man shouting, though she could not recognise the voice, nor what it said, for the bedroom door was closed.

But she knew who it was, of course. What they had all dreaded, at least she and her mother, was about to happen.

I I

Hugh Thornley had spent the last three weeks in Leicester-shire, staying with an old school friend whose nature was very much like his own or he would not have palled up with him. Johnny Cassell was himself a baronet, his mother the daughter of a marquis, and was as wild and excitable as an unbroken colt despite being twenty-seven years old, the same age as Hugh. They had created havoc at their well-known public school, learning nothing that could be called remotely academic, avoiding expulsion only because their families were of ancient lineage and all the sons had been pupils there ever since it opened. His family, unlike Hugh's, was fabulously wealthy and Johnny spent his days drifting from one sybaritic pleasure to another. His father was dead and his fond and indulgent mother could see no harm in her son enjoying himself, since money was no object. Hunting, naturally, in the winter, the London season, Cowes, Henley, shooting and deer-stalking in Scotland and gambling in Biarritz. Indeed all the appropriate, upper-class activities that were expected of a young gentleman with the means to indulge himself. He and Hugh did not see a great deal of one another, since poor old Hugh had been forced to pick some profession, the army being his choice, but when he turned up at Cassell House in a cab hired at Leicester railway station, saying airily that he felt the need for one of his and Johnny's "junkets", Johnny was delighted. It was a weekend and the house was filled with two dozen ladies and gentlemen who were regular "Friday to Monday" visitors. Hugh, known to them all, was welcomed with open arms.

"My wife . . ." he began, but was greeted by shrieks of dismay from the ladies and hoots of derision from the gentlemen and it was not until he persisted that they fell silent, for good old Hugh was the last person to get himself entangled with a woman. At least a *good* woman.

"I was forced to it, Johnny," he said, smiling wryly. "A rich wife was needed, I'm afraid."

And they all nodded understandingly, for was that not what all chaps needed, those who were not as lucky as Johnny. There were several couples among them who had married, not for love, but for monetary reasons, which, of course, did not prevent them from enjoying themselves hugely at weekends such as this. The ladies, once they had provided the necessary heir, were free to do as they pleased, since their husbands did the same and Hugh meant to have a bloody good time. He had thought it expedient to leave the vicinity of the barracks and his home for a few weeks until the incident on the parade-ground had been forgotten and the acceptance of his resignation become official.

"My wife is with child so . . ." He shrugged his shoulders, his meaning clear. What could a chap do with a pregnant wife but keep out of her way until the child was born? They all understood.

He had enjoyed himself immensely, riding to hounds on one of Johnny's expensive hunters, attending the races, dancing, playing cards, drinking fine champagne, shooting over Johnny's grouse moor, giving syphilis to three unsuspecting young wives, until at last he supposed he had better go home and see how Milly was. He had left Thornley Green without a word and had sent none.

It was almost the end of March as he drove in a hired cab from St Helens railway station, his luggage stacked on top, for he had had the foresight to take the necessary clothing with him. A hunting costume of scarlet frock-coat, breeches, top boots and hat, an evening suit in the latest fashion of dress jacket and narrow trousers, a morning coat, a tweed suit in which to shoot, as a gentleman was expected to wear the correct attire for every occasion. He had smiled to himself as he had packed his gear in the middle of the night at Thornley Green, waking the boot boy who slept in the pantry and sending him for a cab. He had given him sixpence and scared the living daylights out of him as he threatened what he would do if the lad breathed a word. Like a ghost he had slipped out and now, no longer needing to hide his activities, he rode up the long gravelled drive to the wide steps and front door of his home.

"Afternoon, Jackson," he said to the astonished footman who opened the door to him. "See to my luggage, there's a good fellow, then fetch me a brandy to my study."

"Very good, m'lord," Jackson quavered, longing to be present when it was divulged to his master that his wife was not under his roof and at the same time hoping to God he was nowhere near when it happened. To get in the way of his lordship, even as an innocent bystander, was tantamount to being put in a cage of wild animals!

"Where is Lady Thornley?" his lordship asked casually, making his way towards his study.

"Er . . . which one, m'lord?"

"My wife, of course, you fool. Has she dropped her little bundle yet, Jackson, or am I to be present when the happy event occurs?"

Jackson dithered at the front door, wishing he'd let Barker answer the bell as he had wanted to but sometimes Jackson liked to show his authority and this afternoon had been one of those times.

"Er . . . well, I'm not sure, m'lord, you see . . . well . . ."

Hugh Thornley stopped, then turned slowly and Jackson cowered back against the door, while at his back the driver of the cab struggled and grumbled as he did his best to get his lordship's trunk up the steps.

"Give us a bloody 'and, mate," he begged and was somewhat startled when the poncy flunkey almost fell down the steps.

"Come here, Jackson," Hugh Thornley told him, his voice soft and yet very dangerous.

"M'lord," Jackson gulped. They were all terrified of the master. There were only three women employed at Thornley Green: the cook, Mrs Newby, who was fifty if she was a day, an elderly parlour-maid and an extremely plain, dim-witted kitchen-maid called Polly of whom it was said a man would have to be blind and half-witted himself to fancy. No girl with a claim to looks would work at Thornley Green. It had been hoped that when his lordship married and a mistress properly installed maidservants would be safe from his attentions, but so far her ladyship, her *young* ladyship, had remained indifferent to the state of the house and its servants, keeping to her room after the initial round of parties and balls had been curtailed because of her advanced condition.

"Yes, Jackson?" his master asked smoothly. "You have something to tell me?"

"Her ladyship's . . . well, when that doctor came—"

"Doctor? My wife is ill?"

"Please, m'lord, I really know nothing. Perhaps her ladyship . . . your mother can explain."

"Where is she?"

"Your . . . your wife or your mother?"

"Either."

"Your mother's out calling and . . . and your wife's . . ."

"Yes, Jackson?"

"Her pa came an' took her home. In his carriage, sir. She was that poorly and the doctor said—"

"She has gone back to her father's house?"

"Yes, m'lord."

"When was this, Jackson?" Lord Thornley's voice had that silky tone the servants recognised and for some reason he put out his hand placatingly.

Jackson gulped and the cab driver stared into the hall with his mouth open.

"About three weeks ago, m'lord."

"Three weeks. I see. Well, run to the stables and have Jack Fell bring round my horse at once."

"Yes, m'lord." Jackson began to gallop towards the back kitchen, his training that said he must be calm and dignified at all times if he wished to become a butler vanishing from his mind, but an irate voice from the doorway stopped him for a moment.

" 'Ere, wharrabout me fare? I've carted this bloody trunk up them steps an'—"

As the toff began to move towards him slowly something in his face made the cabbie shrink back. He didn't know why, he said afterwards to one of the other cabbies on the station rank. He'd dealt with some tough customers in his business and never been bested but something in that gent's face, in his eyes, made him turn tail, leap on to the seat of his cab and whip the old horse down the drive as fast as the thing could go.

It was Ruby who answered the door to the frantic hammering, but before she did she insisted that Tim, the boy who cleaned the boots and cutlery, come with her. She wished later that she had waited for her Olly, or even Clem, though the coachman was getting a bit past it now.

Before she had the door properly opened Miss Milly's husband had flung it back so that it hit her in the face, breaking her nose. Tim, a brave lad usually, began to shout but he backed off from the positively terrifying figure of the man who had just knocked Mrs Preston to the floor. There was blood on her face and she was crying and he didn't know what to do, for he was only the boot boy and this man was gentry.

"Where's my wife?" the man snarled, beside himself with rage and then, thankfully, the hallway was full of people, brought there by Ruby's shriek of pain, all shouting, the women crying, the gardener, who had been peacefully weeding his beds in readiness for the show of spring flowers that were beginning to break through the rich, well-fed soil, wielding his hoe with an excited Billy at his back. Billy was his lad and, until he saw poor Mrs Preston laid out on the floor, had been thrilled to bits with the excitement of the moment.

At that moment Miss Beth came down the stairs. She walked calmly, straight-backed and square-shouldered, her head high as though to say she was not frightened of this powerful man who seemed to be threatening her mother's servants, but when she saw Ruby lying on the floor her face, which was pale, lost all its colour and she picked up her wide skirts and began to run. The silence was palpable, so dense it could almost be seen. The servants stood back as Beth flung herself to the floor beside the prone figure of the maidservant.

"Ruby, dear, what happened? Did this man hit you?"

"No, Miss Beth," Ruby mumbled, holding her white apron to her bloody nose, "I walked inter't door." Which was true in a fashion but she dared not tell the truth for fear of further trouble. Her Olly pushed his way through the group of frightened servants, his face a picture of disbelief and concern, going to his knees beside his wife, followed by their son, Harry, and a few moments later by Clem who was not as spry as he once had been. Harriet took his arm, for surely there were enough of them to deal with this visibly menacing man. He seemed to have lost his mind, his face a mask of insane rage, his small riding crop slashing against his booted leg.

"Where is my wife, madam?" he hissed at Beth. "I have come to take her home where she belongs and if anyone tries to stop me they will pay for it, I promise you. I will have words with your father later, unless he is hiding somewhere in the house and if so, bring him out."

"My father is at his business, Hugh, but can be fetched in half an hour. In the meanwhile, my sister will remain where she is. She is seriously ill with the disease you gave her and may go into labour at any moment. Doctor Bennett will not allow her to be moved." She stood up and motioned to Harriet to help Ruby, who by this time had been lifted to her feet by her solicitous husband. With a glance Ruby had conveyed to her young mistress that she must not tell him that it was Lord Thornley's violent action that had smashed her nose or Olly would go for him, sure as eggs is eggs!

"Harry, saddle a horse and go at once for Doctor Bennett. He will see to Ruby." She turned to the trembling maid: "Go with Harriet, Ruby, and rest in her sitting-room until the doctor comes. The rest of you go about your work, and tell Reuben to go for Mr Goodwin. This needs a—"

"Nay, I'm not leaving yer alone wi' this . . . this madman, Miss Beth," Clem said stoutly.

"Me neither," said Mr Jones, the head gardener at Lantern Hill. He brandished his hoe in the direction of Lord Thornley, and at his side young Billy bristled bravely, though that riding crop looked lethal.

Hugh Thornley laughed in what seemed to be great amusement. "Really, Beth, if you think you can stop me from taking my wife home you are in for a rude awakening. She is Lady Thornley, for God's sake and the son she carries is the heir and must be born at Thornley Green where the eldest son is always born. It is imperative for him to know his heritage from the moment he comes into the world, to become part of the chain that binds us from the past and into the future."

"As you were and look how you turned out."

"You're an interfering bitch, Beth Goodwin, who would do well to stay out of my affairs. You have damaged me once before and I swear you will pay for it and for this insolence you offer me. Now then, tell me where my wife is and ask your coachman to be at the door with the carriage in five minutes. I will send for her things later."

"I will not and you would be advised to stay where you are until my father and probably my husband arrive."

"And who is to stop me, my pet? These clods you have around you?" smiling at Mr Jones, Billy and Clem, who had slipped out to fetch the pitchfork he used in the stables and was brandishing it courageously.

"I forbid you to enter my father's house and remove my sister."

"Like your father entered *my* house and removed my wife. I have the law on my side, sister-in-law, you should know that. A man's wife is his property as are any children of her body he gets on her. Now, I have had enough of arguing and insist on being taken at once to my wife."

The two men and the boy moved unhesitatingly towards the foot of the stairs, Clem motioning to Miss Beth that she was to get behind them. "Leave this to us, Miss Beth," he said confidently, for surely the two of them could handle this bugger and they had only to shout to fetch Olly from his wife's side. "Nathan" – who was the second gardener's lad – "has run ter fetch Frank" – who was assistant to Mr Jones – "and fer Tommy who's in't paddock so us'll see this gentleman don't get no further. Mr Goodwin'll no doubt send for the constable when he arrives."

"I don't think so, fellow, for I shall be long gone by then." And with a melodramatic flourish Lord Thornley produced an elegantly engraved revolver from his pocket and pointed it directly at Beth. "It would give me the greatest pleasure to put one of these bullets into you, Beth, and then the rest into these dolts about you, but that would not suit my purpose, not at the moment. But I will if I am challenged."

Beth felt the breath which she had been holding leave her in a rush as though someone had punched her in the stomach. He was insane, this man her sister had innocently married, or if not insane his temper was so great he could not control it. If she had been alone she would have stood up to him in defence of her sister, for surely no man, even one as unbalanced as Hugh Thornley, would shoot an unarmed woman. But she could not take the chance that he might wound, or even kill, these men who were so bravely defending her. He was the kind of man who held the lives of those he considered beneath him to be totally worthless, except in the capacity of the service they gave him. Should he wound one he, being of the upper class, would certainly not be prosecuted for it in the courts, or so he would believe. Milly, spoiled and wayward Milly had brought this into their home. With her usual hot-headed determination to have what she wanted, which happened to be Hugh Thornley, she had brought this on them and on herself, but that did not give him the right to treat her as he had. She had not been aware that Hugh had syphilis, true, and was a victim of his ruthlessness but was she, Beth, prepared to defy this deranged man for the sake of her twin, gamble her own life and that of these faithful servants on his backing down?

At the sight of the gun the men had begun to move awkwardly from foot to foot. With their hoes and pitchforks they were no match for a speeding bullet. There were five shots in the revolver, Clem knew. He was interested in guns of all sorts and was a loader at many of Mr Goodwin's shoots, and he was aware of the firepower of the small revolver.

"Stand aside, Beth, if you please, and remove your watchdogs or I will shoot them. Not to kill, but to maim. Quickly, if you please, for I believe someone is arriving."

There was the crunch of carriage wheels on the gravel outside the front door which still stood open and a red-faced Doctor Bennett flung himself up the step with an equally red-faced Harry at his heels.

"What the devil is going on here?" he began angrily, but at the sight of the revolver in Hugh Thornley's hand and the small group of people he held at bay with it they both came to an abrupt halt.

"I presume you are Doctor Bennett, the same chappie who had the effrontery to remove my wife from her home?" Hugh said pleasantly, motioning with the revolver for Doctor Bennett and Harry to stand beside the others, which they did. They formed a semicircle about Beth, but Beth Goodwin had had enough. Throwing caution to the wind, her face a mask of fury as great as that of Hugh Thornley's, she stepped forward, ignoring the revolver pointing directly at her breast, and lifting her arm slapped her brother-in-law full in the face, making him reel back in surprise. Hugh was not accustomed to having anyone, let alone a woman, stand up to him.

"Miss Beth . . . Dear God." The men were appalled but Beth Goodwin was too incensed to listen. She came from a line of men and women who had the red blood of courage and endurance in their veins. Her own mother had risen above illegitimacy to become the lady she was. Her father, her great-grandfather had built up the great empire that Noah Goodwin ruled and nothing had been allowed to stand in their way and certainly not this bastard who was the epitome of all that Beth, as an ardent suffragist, deplored. She, her mother and their group of socially minded women were fighting men like this on behalf of their sisters, fighting to balance the equality which women of all classes were denied. She had been to dozens of rallies, meetings, and had listened to Barbara Bodichon, Emily

Davies, Elizabeth Garrett and many others speak passionately about the wrongs done to women in this man's world, and had now seen it at close range with her own sister. And here was one of those monsters who treated women as though they were not worth considering as human beings. Was she going to allow him to defeat her and all that she believed in? The answer was no!

As he recovered his equilibrium he might have shot her, for his senses reeled away in a mist of fury, but a bellow from the kitchen doorway paralysed them all.

"Stand away, Beth," Noah roared at her, "stand away for I don't want to hurt you." All of them, including the man with the revolver, looked automatically towards him and taking advantage of the moment, as Noah Goodwin had done all his life, he raised his arm. There was the whistle of a lash and like a snake the whip that Noah carried struck Hugh Thornley across the hand that held the gun and with a cry he dropped it. Noah had disarmed him and the men all breathed a sigh of relief, beginning to move towards Miss Beth who seemed ready to fall now it was all over, but Noah Goodwin was not done with this man who had almost killed not one of his daughters but both of them. He had been waiting for three weeks for his son-in-law to reappear from wherever it was he had gone and now he was here and though he would not kill him as he had threatened, he meant to punish him.

Archie was behind him and for a moment it looked as though Hugh might dart away down the front steps to his horse as Beth was dragged away by her husband and into his arms, distracting Noah who didn't want to strike either of them, but then the lash hissed through the heavy air again and a stripe of scarlet appeared across Hugh's chest, shrivelling away the fine cambric of his shirt. Beth, peeping from the shelter of Archie's arms, watched as the whip hissed and whined, a whole cobweb of crimson patterning Hugh's chest, then as the man seemed about to fall, the last one opening his cheek from eyebrow to chin.

"Father, that's enough," she cried out, for though she loathed the man who swayed before her she knew that if her father was not stopped, in his mindlessness he might simply have whipped him to death. The men, those who had stood to defend her, who had been as horrified as the family at what had been done to her sister, were standing, white-faced with shock. Billy ran suddenly for the front door from where he could be heard vomiting into the flowerbeds.

"Get out of my house." Her father's voice rasped with the sound splintered bone might make, harsh and whistling in his throat and though Doctor Bennett, his instinct to minister to the sick and wounded, sprang forward to go to Hugh's aid, Hugh waved him away. He held his right arm across his bloody chest while from his face the blood ran fast and thick.

"Leave me alone," he whispered, turning towards the door and through the hatred and outrage they all felt there was a thread of admiration for this man's courage. He walked steadily to the front steps, passing Billy who was wiping his mouth at the bottom of the steps. He reached for the reins of his horse which he had flung carelessly over the balustrade at the side of the steps when he arrived and fumbled his way into the saddle without a sound, though he must have been in agony. Doctor Bennett made another move to go to him, turning to Noah, about to ask that the carriage might be brought to take him home but Hugh Thornley seemed to read his mind.

"Don't bother, old man," he rasped. "I'll get myself home. I usually do. But let me say this will not be forgotten, Goodwin. You and yours will be sorry for this, I promise you. Nobody gets the better of Hugh Thornley so I advise you all to watch your backs. That includes these oafs who you employ. Dear God, you have no idea what you have unleashed here. And tell my wife she is to be home by the end of the week. My son is to be born at Thornley Green."

Spurring his horse, he set off at a wild gallop down the drive. Crowding to the door, they watched him go and not one of them, except perhaps Noah Goodwin who still had the heat of fury in him, did not fail to shiver as he disappeared round the curve of the drive.

12

Milly Thornley gave birth to a daughter that evening. Her labour began as her husband galloped wildly down the drive of her father's house, brought on, John Bennett thought, by the stress of the commotion downstairs in which her husband's shouting could plainly be heard in every room from the attic to the cellar. She had been alone for, knowing that Beth was with her, her mother had taken the carriage to visit Laura Bennett but Beth had gone downstairs to find out what all the noise was about.

She had called out, she told them. She had even tried to get to the slightly opened door but it had been beyond her. The voices downstairs, those of the servants, her husband, who was to be sent up at once, her father and even Beth's raised tones had alarmed her and if someone didn't tell her what was going on she'd scream the damn place down. It was no good Doctor Bennett telling her to calm down, how could she calm down when she knew Hugh had been here and now they were telling her he had gone. Why hadn't he come up to see her? And where was her mother? She wanted her mother and if this bloody baby didn't come soon and release her from its bondage she'd go stark, staring mad. She was sick of it. Sick of looking like the fat sow in the pen at Updale Farm. For God's sake, she shrieked, would Doctor Bennett do something, anything to take away this niggling pain in the small of her back, and please, please would Beth send Olly to fetch Hugh to come back and take her home. The terror, the horror she had known when she was told that Hugh had passed some dreadful disease on to her had slowly receded as Doctor Bennett had made the dreadful thing go away. She was almost free of the sores and the itching and Hugh's part in it had been forgotten, at least, if not forgotten, then pushed to the back of her mind and she wanted nothing more than to get rid of her burden and return to her life as Lady Thornley. For a brief time she had been enchanted with her new position, the balls they had given, the parties, the fun, that is until she had become ill and bloated with her pregnancy. She meant it when she said she would have no more children, for she was well aware that Beth had the knowledge, gleaned from her "sisters" in the cause, to make sure she would not get with child again. This one would be a boy and Hugh would be pleased and Milly Thornley could get on with the life she had chosen for herself.

"Milly, my dear, you are not fit to go home yet," Doctor Bennett told her soothingly, while motioning to the nurse hovering at the bedside to get ready the paraphernalia needed for childbirth: hot water to be kept simmering, towels, bowls and the tiny garments that Beth and her mother, knowing that Milly had made no preparations, had stitched.

Beth wanted a child of her own. She was consumed with longing to hold her own child in her arms, to feel it tugging at her hand, needing her, but she was reminded by her mother's anxious face as she hurried into the bedroom that at this moment Milly needed her more. Milly had been married in October, only a few weeks before Beth and Archie and had given them all to understand that the child would be born in the summer, deliberately vague, for she had privately told Beth that she and Hugh had been intimate almost from the day they first met. June or July, so the child could be due in April. But Doctor Bennett had intimated that the syphilis Milly had caught from Hugh could bring on a premature birth. They had all – not just Milly – longed for the baby to be born, for how was the poor little thing to turn out? With an eye infection that could cause blindness, a heart defect or a joint deformity? Or perhaps with nothing, which was what they had prayed for: a healthy child. As Milly became aware that the pain in her back was something more than the result of lying in bed for weeks on end, she began, amazingly, to scream for her husband. Doctor Bennett gave her something to quieten her and then sent them all from the room, all except the nurse, telling them that the birth was imminent.

"The child will be small, I think," he said in an aside to Abby and Noah, who had hung about on the landing ever since Hugh Thornley had been despatched.

"But . . . perfect, John. Please let it be healthy," Abby pleaded, then turned to throw herself into her husband's waiting arms.

"It's in God's hands," John Bennett murmured, then, with a quick smile at Beth, he hurried back into the bedroom.

Beth leaned against the wall, wondering why she felt so tired. She was totally drained. She supposed it was the terrible events of the morning, of Hugh Thornley's threatening menace then her father's wild fury and his attack on the man who had infected his daughter.

"Beth." A quiet voice came from the top of the stairs and when she turned Archie stood there.

"Oh, Archie . . ." was all she could manage then his arms came round her and he held her firmly, lovingly, steadfast as he had always been. He had been at her father's back while he had whipped Hugh, doing nothing but being there should he be needed. As he had always been. No fuss, very few words but as strong as a rock in the centre of a mad whirling river. A rock to cling to, then a hand to draw her to the river bank before she was engulfed. This man loved her, quietly and staunchly, enveloped her in a peace and quiet no other person had ever given her. He told her he loved her so she felt loved. He told her she was beautiful so she felt beautiful and what he gave her refreshed her spirit. If only she could do the same for him.

"Come and rest for half an hour, my dearest," he murmured into her tumbled hair. Her old room was next door to Milly's from where came sounds of combat, for Milly was not going to suffer this without making a great deal of fuss about it. "Doctor Bennett will let us know when—"

"Archie, I can't leave them . . ." indicating her mother and father who clung together at the door to Milly's bedroom, their faces chalk white and desperate. They were well aware that their daughter, who was a strong and healthy woman recovering slowly, but recovering all the same, from the venereal disease under John Bennett's experienced hand, would be well again, but the child, their first grandchild, in what condition would it be born?

"Come, darling, lie down with me for a little while. I'll have a word with Abby. She'll let us know when."

Beth allowed herself to be led to her room where Mary Smith was seated by the fire, in her hands an item of underwear on which she was sewing. Mary had insisted on coming to Lantern Hill with Miss Beth whenever she drove over from Edge Bottom, just in case she was needed. Mary Smith would die for Beth Goodwin, if asked, for she would never forget the plight she had been in and how Miss Beth had rescued her. Where would she have been without her? she often asked herself, since a girl who had been in the hands of the police for prostitution, even if she didn't happen to be one and had proved to be free of disease, would find it hard to get employment of a decent sort.

"I'm sorry, Miss Beth, I needed something ter do so—"

"Of course you did, Mary, but your mistress and I—"

"Yes, sir, I'll go and . . . and . . ."

"Perhaps Mr and Mrs Goodwin would be glad of a cup of tea." Though he was well aware that Abby and Noah

Goodwin's servants would be hanging about longing to be of service.

Mary's face cleared and, dipping him a curstey, she hurried from the room.

They lay on the bed facing one another, fully clothed, their arms about one another, their faces almost touching, his deep blue, love-filled eyes steady on hers, conveying the message that no matter what was to happen here today, or indeed on any day until the day she died, he would be here to love and protect her. From anything!

She stretched out her right hand and placed it on his cheek. "I love you, Archie," she said. She had not realised until the moment she said it just how much she meant it. Always it had been, "Yes, please love me, Archie," but something had happened today that had made her realise his true worth. Perhaps it was in contrast to the jagged relationship shared by her sister with Hugh Thornley. A trust that did not exist, nor ever would, between Milly and Hugh.

"I love you," she said again, just for the joy of it. She leaned forward and with a delicate concentration placed her lips on his. They had made love many times since their wedding night and it had been sweet, joyous, pleasing her, but she had been aware that it had been, for want of a better expression, somewhat one-sided. She had enjoyed Archie's embraces, his tender, gentle love-making and had been aroused by his touch, but he had never brought her to the peak of sexuality which he himself reached. But she loved him. She knew that. He had given her a sense of homecoming, of reaching a blissful and longed-for haven after a long journey. She loved him. He was her resting place when she was tired, her shelter from a storm, the sun that warmed her, the rain that refreshed her.

"I love you, Archie," she murmured against his lips and as she spoke there came a sound, the thin wail of a newborn from the room next door. They both sat up abruptly, their faces turning to the wall that divided the two bedrooms. At last the child was here and the dread, the anguish, the state of fear and trepidation was soon to be replaced – please, God, *please*, God – by the delight of a baby, a whole and healthy baby. Milly could rest and be pampered as she loved to be. She could be spoiled, surrounded by chocolates and flowers and gifts and told how clever she was and how brave and the past would be wiped out and the future, whatever it might contain, be looked forward to.

Simultaneously she and Archie both leaped to their feet and dashed across the bedroom, flinging open the door into the hallway.

"It's a girl," her mother said, staggering against the doorway like an old woman while beside her her husband bent his face into his hands. "Milly's fine; she's come through well, John said."

Beth saw something in her mother's weeping face that she was not quite sure of. A certain doubt, not exactly fear but an expression that crumpled it and dragged at her mouth as though it were not sure whether to cry with relief or fear.

"The baby?"

"Come and see, darling. The nurse is just cleaning her up; she's a bit . . . a bit small . . . and . . ."

"What, Mother? What is it?" Beth's hand fluttered anxiously towards her mother and Archie placed his arm about her shoulders.

"Come and see, dearest. She is the prettiest little thing you ever saw, despite . . ."

The two men stayed in the hallway, Archie standing close to his father-in-law, for though Beth might tiptoe hopefully into Milly's bedroom to see the infant girl just born he had a feeling that all was not right and Noah knew it.

The baby had been washed hastily and placed in her crib beside Milly's bed. A wet nurse was waiting upstairs in the room designated as a nursery, for when Lantern Hill had been built there had been no thought of other children and therefore nurseries had not been included in the plans. Milly lay back on her pillows, her hair brushed, the crumpled detritus of birth removed, dressed in a clean and pretty nightdress and was demanding already that she was hungry and would be glad of a cup of hot chocolate. The servants, Beth knew, were hovering in the downstairs hallway, longing for news, longing to be told the sex of the newborn, longing to help in some way, and within seconds Nessie was at the door, a message having been passed down of Lady Thornley's needs, with a tray bearing the chocolate.

But it was to the cradle that Beth was fearfully drawn.

"Look, dear," her mother said and Beth knew she was crying. Beth obeyed, looking down into the nest of pretty, frilled pillows on which a tiny, dark head lay. Long eyelashes rested peacefully on her cheek, her breathing was shallow but even and the fingers of one hand lay curled delicately in perfect innocence.

"Is she to go up to the nursery?" Milly asked fretfully as though already the bother of being a mother was too much for her. Abby bent her head for a moment since her daughter had not yet seen the child.

"Are you not to . . . to nurse her for a moment, Milly?" she asked.

"Mother, I'm exhausted and wish to do nothing but sleep. I'll see her presently. Oh, and send Olly with a message for Hugh, will you? Tell him he has a daughter and his wife would like to see him at once."

Doctor Bennett was still attending to something with the nurse and he turned his head at Milly's words, for he knew, as they all did, that there was no possible way that Lord Thornley could make the trip to see his newly delivered wife and daughter, not after the flogging he had received at Noah's hands. Besides which, it was unlikely that he would be eager to see the first *legitimate* child of his loins, since she happened to be a girl. A son might have made all the difference to the unhappy plight of Milly Thornley.

"I don't think that's a good idea, Milly, not just yet. I'm going to give you something to help with your continued progress and to make you sleep so drink your chocolate, then lie back and have a rest."

"Oh, for goodness sake, Doctor Bennett, surely I can see my own husband. After all he is the child's father," came the irritable reply and Beth was made aware that the family and servants of Lantern Hill were in for a hard time with Lady Thornley!

The cradle was carried up the stairs to the room where the nursemaid and the wet nurse sat in readiness for the new arrival, springing to their feet as Mr and Mrs Goodwin, their daughter and their son-in-law entered the room, the baby's grandfather carrying her crib.

"Mother . . ." Beth said hesitantly as her father rested the cradle on the bed. This was the moment she had dreaded, the moment they had all looked forward to with great trepidation, and yet with hope that the child, the beautiful little girl in the cradle, would be whole and perfect.

"Yes, darling, but you must come and look at—"

"Oh, Mother, I can't bear it if she is . . . damaged."

"You must, darling. She is part of our family and, though Hugh is bound to come and take her and Milly from us since they are his family, we must be here for her should . . ."

"Mother . . ." Beth could feel herself beginning to tremble. It took her a long time to cross the room, a dreadful time to cross that room to look at what her mother was determined for her to see and when she did reach the cradle she could not bring herself to look down but bent her head with closed eyes.

"Look, dear," her mother said for the second time, pulling

back the soft fleecy blanket in which the child was wrapped. She was still naked, for she had not been properly bathed and in every aspect of her tiny baby proportions she was perfect. Except one.

Her left leg was deformed, being an inch shorter than the right, the foot curving inwards, the toes completely missing.

Beth could hear her father breathing heavily behind her and she knew he was weeping hot, angry tears, for they were all cruelly aware that the baby's deformity could be placed at no other door than Hugh Thornley's.

As she looked down at her niece Beth felt something enter her heart, a warmth, a melting, a complete and unquestioning love that she supposed most new mothers felt when they first looked into the face of their newly born child and yet this was not her child! Her little body was pink and smooth despite the remains of the birth battle. She was frail-looking, fine and delicately put together, weighing, her mother whispered, a mere four and a half pounds but John had assured them that apart from . . . from the leg, she was as healthy as any premature baby could expect to be. With careful nursing and feeding she would grow to be a fine child, not perhaps as robust as others, but bonny.

Beth leaned forward with no particular plan in mind but without thought, just acting purely on instinct, she put her arms under the child's back and lifted her into the crook of her arm. The child stirred and her long eyelashes lifted to reveal eyes as brilliant a blue as her father's. They looked at one another, she and her aunt, and Beth wondered how much the infant could see, then, with a small sigh of what seemed to be perfect content, the baby turned her head into Beth's breast and settled back to sleep.

With a tightening of her lips that was a prelude to a display of pigheadedness, Milly absolutely refused to see her daughter.

No, not until Hugh had come would she even consider having her in her bedroom, for it was something that should be shared with the baby's father, she said mutinously. She had been told that the baby had a slight shortening of her leg, news she had received with white-faced horror and a flash of temper that told them that Milly Thornley could not possibly have produced something that was not perfect, and which had them all scurrying to do her bidding. The nursemaid, who had just carried the "poor little mite" down from the nursery for her mam to see, was hurried out again. Beth, who had accompanied the nursemaid down the stairs, could feel the explosive anger and resentment grow inside her and she wanted to go over to Milly's bed and slap her. It was not the child's fault that she would assuredly have a limp, and when she thought about it, it was probably not Milly's either, for she had not asked to become infected with syphilis. This could all be laid at Hugh Thornley's door. At least the child was not blind or deaf and, so Doctor Bennett told them after exhaustive private tests of his own, she did not appear to be damaged in her brain. Nor could he see any signs of the congenital syphilis he had feared. She knew enough to make the most of the plump, bounteous breast of the wet nurse, who, feeding her own healthy boy, had enough milk for a dozen, she said cheerfully. She was already beginning to thrive, though that could not be said of Milly.

"Where's Hugh?" she whined a dozen times a day. "Are you sure Olly gave him my message? Why hasn't he come?"

"He will, darling," her patient mother told her. "He . . . he has had a fall from his horse and is somewhat bruised," which was the only lie they could think of to calm the fragmented and distraught anxiety of the new mother.

And Milly refused absolutely to consider a name for the child, as, again, she and Hugh must decide this together. Perhaps the Thornleys had a family name they might want to give this baby. Beth, who drove or rode over from Edge

Bottom every day, not specifically to see her sister but to gloat over the progress of her baby niece, had privately decided she liked Alexandra but then she would not have the choosing of a name, would she?

It was three weeks later when Lady Thornley declared herself to be quite recovered from the birth of her daughter and if Mother would fetch up the carriage she intended going home. They were all there in the drawing-room where Doctor Bennett had allowed her to be carried in a chair, the first time she had been downstairs since she had been brought back to Lantern Hill and the silence that followed her announcement could only be called stunned.

"Well, if I am to be allowed out of bed and sit in the drawing-room it might as well be my own," she asserted. "Doctor Bennett can continue his treatment at Thornley Green and, besides, I miss Hugh and if he can't come to me then I must go to him." She glanced round imperiously, that tell-tale tightening of her lips letting them know she would have her own way on this.

The silence lasted no more than thirty seconds, then her father roared out of his chair and began to pace the room in what they all knew presaged a storm of gigantic proportions. This girl of his was very dear to him. She was the one most like him in temperament and looks and he could obviously not bear the thought of letting her go back to her brutish husband and perhaps becoming reinfected with the disease she had caught from him. But though he strode round the room barely holding in his ferocious fear and anger he knew that there was nothing he could do to stop her. She had always been self-willed, self-centred, but her charm, her wit, her good looks had more than made up for the deficiencies in her character. She was not a bad girl, just proud and spirited, as he was, so determined to have her own way that she had always been prepared to barge straight through any hurdle that stood in her path, as he was!

"No, Milly, no, please, darling, you're not ready yet," her mother moaned, rising from her chair and instinctively moving towards Noah, not just for support but to prevent him doing anything or saying anything that might upset the already unbalanced state of her daughter's wilfulness.

"Of course, I'm ready, Mother. The child is born and Doctor Bennett has cured me of . . . of my complaint." *Complaint!* It was as though Milly was resolute in her belief that the infection she had suffered was really nothing at all and certainly had had nothing to do with Hugh. He was her husband. She was Lady Thornley with a position to keep up and she could hardly do it lolling about at Lantern Hill, which was no longer her home.

It was a Sunday and the family, including Beth and Archie, had just had luncheon, a delicious meal as usual from the clever hands and brain of Mrs Ellman. It was mid-April and a cold day so a good vegetable soup to begin, hearty and nourishing, for Lady Thornley needed feeding up, boiled salmon and dressed cucumber with Mr Jones's mouth-watering new potatoes, followed by her own rhubarb tart with cream thick enough to stand a spoon up in. All aimed at bringing back their Miss Milly, as they called her privately, to full health. As it happened Miss Milly declined to eat with the family and had a tray sent up to her room and Mrs Woodruff, who was very close to Mrs Goodwin and therefore more outspoken, was heard to mutter to herself that some folk were getting above themselves! Still she was Lady Thornley now, and had gone through a rough time, all in all, so perhaps Mrs Woodruff was being a bit harsh.

Now, according to Nessie, who had served them their coffee in the drawing-room, Ruby keeping to the kitchen on account of her still swollen nose, she, Miss Milly, was set on going back to Thornley Green. What would she do there with that little mite who had as yet never clapped eyes on her own mother? Would the poor lamb be as well looked after in the Thornley

Green nursery as she was at Lantern Hill? All of them, including the men in the stable yard and the gardens, were willing to die for the still un-named infant, and the fuss that Mrs Goodwin and Miss Beth made, well, no child could be more loved or cared for.

Nessie did not hear the rest of the conversation since she could hardly hang about by the door, could she, so she was not privy to the bombshell that exploded in the drawing-room at Lantern Hill.

Milly stood up and began to make her way towards the door that led into the hall. She was still plump and Beth noticed her glance down at herself with what was clearly disgust. She walked quite steadily though, watched by her distraught family. Beth thought she could not bear it. She loved the baby unreservedly, and so did her grandparents. Doctor Bennett had told them that there was a lot that could be done for the child when she was older and they had felt somewhat more optimistic, but how would she fare with a cruel and disinterested father, a callous and indifferent mother and a grandmother who would probably be as unmoved by the child's plight as Milly and Hugh? They had all wanted a healthy son not a crippled daughter and the neglect the child would suffer did not bear thinking about.

"Milly," her mother pleaded, "you're not ready yet. Give it another couple of weeks and then perhaps Hugh will be over and—"

"I'm tired of waiting for Hugh to come, Mother, so I am going to find out for myself what is happening. Besides, I am Lady Thornley of Thornley Green and my place is with him." She lifted her head regally as her hand reached for the door handle.

"My grandchild is not to be removed from Lantern Hill until you can prove to me that you are capable of caring for her," Noah thundered. "She needs to be with—"

"Oh, don't worry, Father. I'm not taking her, for as you say I cannot look after her and I'm sure Hugh is not the kind of man to engage himself with a daughter who may never walk. No, I shall leave her here for the present and then, well, we will see. Now, if someone would summon the carriage I'll be off."

13

Hugh Thornley studied his face in the cheval glass, his brilliantly blue eyes on the scar that ran from the outer edge of his left eyebrow to his chin. It was thin and had healed well without stitches but the line was plain to see, fading over the past few weeks from an angry red to a silvery white. It stood out plainly against the amber brown of his suntanned skin, which, as he was a man of the outdoors, never lost its attractive colour. Thank God the whip had not touched his eyes and, though he loathed the man who had given it to him and indeed his whole family, he thought quite complacently the scar gave him a look of distinction. Devilish, and it did not at all deter from his good looks. His speculative glance dropped down to the criss-cross webbing of scars across his chest which had taken longer to heal and still had a tendency to scab, but old Doctor Newland, who had once been a ship's surgeon when he was younger and knew all there was to know about flogging and how to heal the torn flesh, had done a damn fine job of it. He was also privately treating him for the "clap" which, naturally, he did not criticise Hugh for catching since many young men of good family were afflicted with the disease. A man must have his easement somehow and it was not always possible to find a clean woman.

Hugh stood back and admired himself, for all in all that bastard at Lantern Hill had not ruined his good looks as he had first thought. That did not mean, of course, that Hugh would let him off lightly and for the past few weeks, while he had been healing, he had been keeping to his own home and the surrounding parkland, his sharp brain devising a plan for his revenge which would devastate them all. As he rode his acres he had been fully occupied with thoughts on how he was to repay not only Goodwin but that bitch of a daughter of his. Both had publicly humiliated him and both must be taught that nobody, *nobody* crossed swords with Hugh Thornley and got away with it.

But he didn't look at all bad and he thought he might ride into St Helens this evening and show himself off to the ladies at the club. See what their reaction was, try his hand at the tables and then end the evening in the arms of a suitably attractive young female. The old doctor had warned him not to go near a woman just yet for fear of passing on the disease as he had done to Milly, but, what the hell, they were only whores after all, one of those who had given it to him in the first place. Besides, he was nearly cured and he was filled with a lusty need that must be satisfied.

As he pulled on his shirt he was disturbed by the sound of carriage wheels on the gravel drive below his window and when he sauntered across the bedroom to find out who was disturbing the peace of the afternoon he was amazed to see that lout of Goodwin's, the one who had threatened him with a pitchfork, jump down from the coachman's seat, open the carriage door and hand out none other than his own wife. Milly, for God's sake, and there was he thinking he had seen the last of her for a long time. The message he had received to tell him he was the father of a girl had filled him with such fury one would have believed that a woman could decide on the gender of the child she was to bear and that Milly had deliberately chosen a daughter just to cross him. A puling girl and what the devil was he to do with one of those since it seemed, from the doctor's letter he had received, she was not even sound of limb! She would need a great deal of care, the doctor had told him, as if it were anything to do with him, and to show his contempt for the man, and for his wife, he had thrown the letter disdainfully into the fire.

It was one of those cold, blustery days which come sometime in April. There was no sunshine to light up the ruddy blossom on the elm and alder trees that stood to the side of the house. The sky was heavy and low as though it might snow and the wind raced the clouds from one horizon to another. Daffodils were just breaking into yellow, masses of them beside the drive, but his wife had no eyes for them as she hurried across the drive and up the steps, her face buried in the glossy fur cape that was wrapped about her. Jackson was there, and Barker, ready to help her indoors and carry her luggage, but it seemed she had none and he remembered she had gone from the house barely conscious, or so he had been told, and had certainly not had time to pack.

And she had not, it appeared, brought back the child, which was a relief, for the last thing he needed was to be asked to coo over a daughter he did not want! Perhaps she was as uninterested as himself in being a parent, at least of a daughter, though he had been led to believe that a woman changed when she became a mother. But apparently Milly was one of those who were prepared to be separated from her offspring. Dear God, he did hope so, for the thought of a grizzling baby, probably a smelly baby, though the child would be in the charge of a nurse in the old nurseries, was not one he fancied.

He sighed and grimaced at himself in the mirror: was he to be deprived of the evening's entertainment he had promised himself? He supposed he could avail himself of Milly's charming body but then would it be charming after the birth of a child? The very idea was distasteful to him at the thought of what had come out of the place that he had been so keen to enter.

The bedroom door opened and there she stood, the woman he had married for her money, plump, whey-faced, half-healed sores about her mouth, hesitant for the moment and certainly not the beautiful girl he had married such a short time ago. True, she had been ill and had given birth, but would she ever regain her looks, he brooded, be the lovely, vivacious young woman who had never turned away from a bit of fun, a laugh, a flirtation, a giddy dance with his brother officers? Dear God, the prospect was appalling and he must make it clear from the very beginning that there was no way he proposed to resume relations with a woman he did not find sexually attractive even if she was his wife. Mind you, he did need a son, a *legitimate* son, so he supposed he had better not be too hasty. She might improve; in fact from what that damned doctor had told him she would if she continued the treatment he had prescribed for her, so perhaps it would not be such a chore to get her with child again. Later on, when she had regained her looks, of course.

He watched the expressions on her face change. First there was a sort of hesitancy which was unlike her, as though she did not know where to begin, then bewilderment obviously at the sight of the healing scar on his face, then a sudden outrage which he knew heralded a storm. She held her fur cape firmly about her as though for protection and took a determined step into the room.

"And where the hell have you been?" she shrieked.

Down in her drawing-room where she was just enjoying a cup of tea the dowager Lady Thornley almost dropped it into her lap. She had heard Jackson go to the front door and since he did not come to the drawing-room had presumed it must be someone for Hugh who had not been at all well these last few weeks. Some ruffian had slashed at him with a whip across his cheek and it had taken a while for the scar to heal and he had remained near the house during that time. Doctor Newland had attended him and still was and Hugh seemed to be on the road to recovery. There really were some dreadful people about, violent people, not as they had been in her day, and by the sound of it the one she disliked more than any other was upstairs this minute acting like a harridan and not the lady her ladyship would have chosen for her son. So, she had come back, and had the daughter she had borne come with her? The one Hugh had described as "not in the best of health". Dear sweet heaven, at her time of life she could do without this chaos the woman had brought to her home. It was delightful to have some money after the frugal years and Hugh was very generous, giving her an ample allowance to run the house but perhaps now that her shrew of a daughter-in-law was back she would take it over. Caroline Thornley didn't care as long as she had her carriage and the comfort the woman's money had brought her. She lifted her cup to her lips and purposefully deafened her ears to what was going on upstairs.

"Milly, my pet, so you're back," Hugh drawled, "but still not fully recovered, it seems, by the state of your face and the . . . er, shape of you. I suppose that doctor fellow is going to be attending you."

Incensed by his remarks about her appearance, which she knew was not as she would have liked it to be, she continued to scream her fury. "Never mind that. Why haven't you been to see me and your daughter? I've been lying in my bed at Lantern Hill, waiting for my husband at least to visit me, if not to *stay* with me but did you come, no, you damn well didn't and I'd like to know why. And what the devil have you done to your face?"

Hugh stepped into the pale spring light that struggled to get through the window. It was getting dimmer and dimmer outside, as it was April and the days were still short; besides which it was a grey day. When Milly saw the full extent of his injuries she gasped. He had opened his shirt and the criss-cross welts put there by Noah Goodwin showed up clearly among the fine, dark hairs that were scattered across his chest.

She gasped and put her hand to her mouth. "Dear God!"

"Aye, dear God indeed. And shall I tell you who did this to me when I *did* come to Lantern Hill in order to return you to your home where I wished our child to be born? Your swine of a father. Oh, yes, he took a whip to me and with the help of several burly men from his stables drove me from his home and from my wife who was pregnant with my child. He seemed to think he still had the right to dictate your life, but believe me when I have recovered I shall let him see that he is wrong."

Hugh's eyes were wild and for a moment Milly felt a spark of fear, not for herself but for her father of whom she was very fond. She of all people knew what savagery Hugh was capable of, for since they had married he had shown that side of himself when he took her to bed. It was not that she resisted his advances but if she showed the smallest amount of reluctance he . . . well, she could only say he raped her despite the fact she was carrying his child. He had wanted a son and yet he had still put the unborn child's life in jeopardy in his lust.

But Milly had a hard streak in her and a will of iron and what she had survived in the past nine months had hardened her even further. She was Lady Thornley of Thornley Green, wife to a baron, a member of the peerage and no matter what Hugh did to her she meant to keep her position in society. She meant to turn this gloomy mausoleum into a place fit for a queen. It was a lovely house but she could do so much with it. The staircase out of the great hall led to an enormous room that would make a splendid ballroom, a proper ballroom instead of the drawing-room they had had to make do with in the past. And the hall itself, with some decent floor covering, expensive carpets which she was accustomed to at Lantern Hill, some deep armchairs and a fire in the huge fireplace, would be ideal for house parties. There were dozens of bedrooms that needed refurbishing and she supposed the kitchen, what she had seen of it, was less than adequate but she would soon rectify that. A decent housekeeper, a butler, a good chef would attract the best people and if the dowager Lady Thornley pulled a face then let her. It was Milly's father who was paying for what she meant to have.

But Hugh must be made to see that Noah Goodwin held the purse strings and at any time he chose he could pull those purse strings tight.

"I heard the commotion from my bedroom and I'm sorry that my father was so . . . brutal but you had passed on the disease from which I'm only just recovering. He had a right to be furious, and so did I, although I suppose you must have had it when we married." She was resolute in her belief that Hugh had been faithful to her since their marriage. "We shall keep away from Lantern Hill."

"Ha, d'you think I'd set foot in that bloody place again after what he did to me?"

"But promise me you'll go no further with . . . with . . ." She was not sure how to word her fears in case she should further enrage Hugh, but what she would have liked to say was *revenge*. "Father is a powerful man in these parts with a great deal of influence and money so it really would be in our best interests to stay away from him." She herself could go whenever she wanted to visit her family but it would be advisable to leave Hugh at Thornley Green for a while. Then there was the problem of the baby! She was well aware that Hugh wanted nothing to do with a child who was not perfect. He might have accepted their daughter had she been whole and pretty but, because of what he had given to her, his wife, the baby was deformed in one leg, Doctor Bennett had told her gently, and would never be as other little girls were.

"Then there is the child."

"Don't think you're going to bring that . . . thing into my house, Milly. I won't have it, d'you hear? There has never been a Thornley who has been less than straight-limbed, healthy and attractive. Male or female and I refuse to allow my friends to feel sorry for me because the child *you* bore is none of these things. Let your bloody family look after it. They were ferocious in their attempts to keep me from you when you bore the child so let them keep it. D'you hear?"

Milly took a deep breath, moving further into the room. She shrugged off her cloak, for the room was warm. It was still shabby because as yet no money had been spent on it but at least there was now a plentiful supply of coal. It was the room where she and Hugh had started their married life and though she knew she did not attract him in the slightest at the moment she meant to change that as soon as possible. Doctor Bennett was making her well and when she had regained her figure and her looks she would take Hugh to bed, which she knew quite easily how to do now, and conceive another child, a son. She would ensure first that Hugh was also free of the malignant disease that had caused their first child to be so damaged and then, when she had given him an heir, her position as Lady Thornley would be assured. The daughter to whom she had given birth and whom she had never seen could stay with her grandparents until her state of health was more clear. Doctor Bennett had murmured of exercises and surgery, a thought that made her shudder, for, like Hugh, she could not bear the idea of a deformed child. Her parents would dote on her, her mother would make sure that she had the best of care and the baby would have a good start in life. She knew herself not to be a maternal woman, for even had the little girl been perfect she would have had little to do with her. A nanny and nursery-maid and then a governess, which was the way the aristocracy brought up their children, and when the time came and her *son* arrived, although he would be reared the same way, at least she would be proud of him, as Hugh would be.

Hugh stirred, sighed, then turned and moved to the window where he peered out as though looking for something or someone. "It looks as though it might snow," he remarked absently, pausing for a moment, then, "I presume the absence of the child means that you are as unenthusiastic as I to bring it home?"

"I thought it best. She is well taken care of at Lantern Hill. A wet nurse—"

"For God's sake, Milly." An expression of deep distaste was on his face as he half turned towards her.

"Oh, don't worry, Hugh, I shall not brood over her. I intend to concentrate on getting well and then perhaps . . . a son. A healthy son." She moved a couple of more steps into the room as though she would reach out to him but he slipped away and walked purposefully towards his dressing-room.

"I was just on my way out when you arrived. I thought I might call on Dicky, see how the old regiment's getting on without me, then I have some business to attend to. Don't wait up for me, my pet. I shall sleep in my old room for the time being. I'm sure you understand and will agree that you need all the rest and peace a bedroom to yourself will bring."

"Of course, but Hugh . . ."

"Yes?" He smiled a cold, icily polite smile, turning for a moment.

"I must just say this." She reached for the bell to summon one of the servants and when it jangled those in the kitchen jumped guiltily as though they had been committing some crime. In fact they had all been nervously awaiting a call, for now that her young ladyship was home, perhaps for good, they would have to jump to it every time she rang the bell.

"Yes?"

"Until we are both free of this loathsome disease you are not welcome in my bed. I want a healthy child, a son, as you do, and we won't get one unless—"

He began to laugh. "Sweet Jesus, have you looked in the mirror lately, Milly, my dear? I have no intention of coming near you ever unless there is a dramatic improvement in your looks."

"Then you'll never have a legitimate heir, Hugh Thornley." Her laughter was as broad as his.

The three men were so deep in conversation they did not notice the hubbub, the laughter, the loud voices that swirled about the bar in the Cock and Feathers Inn which was situated handily for the ranks at the barracks close by to frequent. There were only two public houses in Longworth and the Cock and Feathers was the nearest so it was usually filled with noisy soldiers of an evening. Though they knew him well none of them recognised the tallest man at the table for he wore a wideawake hat of soft felt with a low crown and brim, the sort used by country gentlemen, and a concealing cloak and a muffler. The other two were the sort of men who, having once been seen would be quickly forgotten, strangely alike in their height, their girth, which was not great, and their neat but nondescript clothing. Snatches of their conversation, which mostly took place in low murmurs, could be heard from time to time.

". . . take no notice of what she . . ."

". . . a struggle?"

"A couple of strong men like you . . ."

"Aye, sir, but she's . . ."

". . . the first one is nobody . . ."

". . . what money are we . . ."

". . . trust me?"

"Aye, sir, but what you're asking is . . ."

". . . want to do it or not because there are others . . ."

"Nay, sir, me an' . . ."

"No names, yer fool . . ." One man grasped the other forcefully by the arm, looking about him to see if they had been overheard, but the men, common soldiers, farm labourers, colliers from the mines, factory workers, were all too absorbed with their own affairs. One of them had begun to sing and others took up the tune, "Cockles and Mussels", for the singer was an Irishman. They banged their pots on the bar top in time to the song and the commotion grew. The three men's conversation was carried on with no fear of eavesdroppers and the company was so carried away with itself none saw the packet pass from the man in the wideawake hat to one of the others. Their business transacted, the man in the hat stood up and, nodding to the other two, left the bar, striding out into the yard and across it to the stable. He untied his horse, a fine ebony gelding with a distinctive white star between his eyes, mounted and then picked his way carefully out of the yard and turned into the road that led north.

The man who knocked on the kitchen door of Edge Bottom House was decently dressed and the horse from which he had just dismounted, though poorly bred, was in a good condition. When the door was opened by Morna, the kitchen-maid, he at once doffed his cap and smiled politely.

"Good morning," he said, "would you be Mary Smith?" He raised his eyebrows enquiringly.

"No, I wouldn't," Morna told him, "and what would you be wanting with Mary Smith?" She was suspicious, for Mary was such a quiet, unassuming young woman it was unlikely this chap was what was known as a "follower", which Mrs Kyle wouldn't have under any circumstances. Besides, if he was he'd hardly come knocking as bold as brass at the kitchen door, would he? So what did he want?

"I'm sorry to disturb you, miss, for I'm sure you're busy but I have an urgent message for Mary Smith from her mother."

"Her mother!" It was the first she, or any of them, had been aware that Mary had a mother. Miss Beth had brought her home from the hospital where Mary had been a patient of

Doctor Bennett's, though it was not clear to them why she had been in hospital in the first place. She had been ill, that was all they were told and of course, being such a good-hearted soul, the mistress had found her a job with them. A nice little thing, without a word for the cat, willing to do anything to help out, not afraid of hard work and Miss Beth had promoted her to lady's maid. She was, in fact, at this moment giving Ruth a hand with the drawing-room since the mistress, as she was most days, was over at Lantern Hill with the new baby, poor little soul!

"Yes, I'm afraid she's not at all well and the doctor has advised that her daughter come right away."

"What doctor?" By this time Mrs Kyle was at Morna's back, a spoon in her hand because she had been basting the nice bit of pork she had in the oven for Mr and Mrs Goodwin's dinner.

"I believe he said he was called Doctor Bennett," the man said solemnly, for surely this was a solemn moment.

The faces of Morna and Mrs Kyle cleared instantly, since if Doctor Bennett was involved what the man said must be true.

"Is she about?" he said again.

Mary was sent for and at once became agitated, for Mary's experiences had taught her to trust no one, but as soon as Doctor Bennett's name was mentioned she ran at once to collect a few things. She and her mam had not been in one another's company much in the last few years as Mary had been in domestic service since she was twelve years old but still, she could hardly refuse to go and see her if Doctor Bennett thought it necessary.

"But how am I to get there?" she asked the man. "It's a bit of a walk to Longworth."

"Now don't you fret, lass. I can give you a lift – that's if you don't mind climbing up behind me – as far as the edge of the village then you can run down to your mam's and be there in an hour."

They all fussed over her and she was made to realise how lucky she was to have such a good place as this. Cook insisted she take some of her freshly baked jam tarts just in case her mam fancied something tasty and she was to make a broth out of these bones which Cook herself was saving for that very purpose. Now if she waited a minute she was sure Tucker would let her have some grapes, but the man outside was showing signs of impatience, glancing at the side gate as though expecting someone.

"I must go, Cook, but tell Miss Beth I'll let her know how things are and I'll be back as soon as I can."

"Miss, we must hasten," the man said rather sharply, surprising them all, but they watched her clatter off, bumping up and down on the rump of the man's horse, Cook shaking her head sadly, for it seemed to her it might be bad news for poor little Mary.

14

Beth tiptoed across the makeshift nursery, her face soft with anticipation, but from her rocking-chair by the good fire the wet nurse laughed. Beside her, the girl who had been employed as nursemaid stood by the fender folding tiny garments which had been airing and her apple-cheeked face creased into a smile.

"Nay, Mrs Goodwin, there's no need to tiptoe. She's awake an' if I didn't know better I'd say she was waiting for you. She's ready for a sleep but will she go off? Not on your life, not until she's seen her Auntie Beth. Five weeks old and as lively as a basket of kittings."

"Really, Jane, do you mean to tell me she already knows me?" A huge grin crossed Beth's face as she peeped into the cradle and the baby, who had not yet been named, let alone christened, seemed to grin back. Beth felt the love swell in her heart for this tiny scrap who seemed to her to be doing her best to be what they all wanted her to be, as though to make up for the deficiency of her deformed leg. Not that the baby knew anything about that, of course, but she appeared to be always smiling, eager to respond to every face that looked down at her. The nursemaid, who had come from a large family and knew about such things, said it was only wind, for a five-week-old baby did not smile but Beth knew better. This child was special and Beth loved her passionately and lived in dread that a summons would come from Thornley Green demanding she be sent home at once.

Two weeks Milly had been gone and though Mother had been over to see how she was progressing it seemed the baby was barely mentioned unless it was Abby herself who spoke of her. Mother gave Milly an updated report on the baby's health, which was good, Milly was told, the weight she had put on, which Milly treated with indifference, her hearty appetite, her beauty, for she was beautiful. She had grown a dark, curling fluff on her head which was the exact colour of Hugh Thornley's but her eyes had lightened to what could only be called lavender, surrounded by long dark lashes. She had a small pouting mouth, a golden, honey-tinted skin, warm and rosy on her cheekbones, and plump starfish hands, one of which Beth kissed with a passion of love. The child was thriving and she had overheard Jane, the nursemaid, telling Alice, the wet nurse, that despite being a premature baby she was a good weight. Jane, of course, did not know that Beth was just outside the bedroom door and showed a certain amount of confusion, blushing to the roots of her hair when the young Mrs Beth entered the room. The two of them called her Mrs Beth so as not to confuse her with the baby's grandmother who had again gone over to Thornley Green to see the baby's mother. It was very awkward, this business of names, not just for the aunt and grandmother of the baby, but for the baby herself. Whoever heard of a child of five weeks having no name? They called her "lovey" and "lamb" and "dearie" and Mrs Beth called her "darling" but a name must be found for her or the child would have no proper identity in the house.

"Can I pick her up, seeing that she's awake?" Mrs Beth asked Jane. Always polite was Mrs Beth, taking nothing for granted, bowing to Jane's experience with infants.

"O' course, madam, she do love a cuddle, that's for sure."

Beth picked her up and lifted her to her shoulder where she turned her head and rested her cheek, her eyes beginning to droop as Beth walked across the room to the window. It was early May and beyond the window spring was exploding in an ecstasy of colour. Frank and Jack were kneeling side by side carefully weeding the wide flowerbeds that surrounded the round, central lawn, and trundling a roller across it, pulled by Mouse, the gardening donkey, was Billy, the lad. Nathan, the second lad, was leading Mouse, doing his best to keep the stubborn donkey in the straight line Mr Frank and Mr Jack demanded.

"Look, darling," Beth murmured to the baby, who was almost asleep and in any case could not have focused properly on the movement in the garden. "The wild daffodils are a picture under the trees and will you look at the periwinkle. Isn't it a lovely blue against the pink of the aubretia? And the wallflowers are beginning to flower. I think we should order a perambulator soon so that I can take you out to see it all. Wouldn't that be lovely?"

The two women by the fireside exchanged glances, for what good would a perambulator be if the poor little mite was to go to Thornley Green where she belonged. They couldn't see that mardy woman, the child's mother, condescending to push a perambulator about the grounds. Dear sweet Lord, she hadn't once clapped eyes on her daughter and her five weeks old!

The door opened and Mrs Goodwin entered and at once Jane and Alice stood up. They were both quite relaxed with Mrs Beth but though Mrs Goodwin was perfectly pleasant she was more formal in her treatment of the baby, leaving the actual care of the child in their capable hands. Naturally she came up with her husband, who was rather fierce, to inspect their granddaughter and you could see they were fond of her, but not like Mrs Beth who couldn't keep away and when she was here couldn't keep her hands off the baby.

Mrs Beth smiled at her mother then moved to the cradle where she gently placed her niece in her nest of warm blankets. "See, Mother, she's settled now," just as though the baby had been making a blistering row before. "Isn't she lovely?" She continued to gaze down at the sleeping child and Abby Goodwin did the same but not with the same intensity.

They turned to smile at one another then Abby took her daughter's arm and led her towards the door. "Let's go down to the drawing-room, darling, and have some tea. Your father and I want to talk to you."

"Is it about the baby?" Beth looked quite stricken, for surely this was the moment that she had been dreading for the past two weeks. Mother had just come back from Thornley Green with a serious look about her which did not bode well for her granddaughter, or so Beth decided. She felt the blood in her veins chill and a shiver passed through her and she knew it was caused by fear for her niece.

"What is it, Mother? For God's sake tell me. I don't believe I can stand it if . . . if Milly wants to take her to . . ."

Her father stood up as they entered the drawing-room, taking her mother by the hand and leading her to the sofa where he had been sitting. He was approaching fifty now but still strong and healthy and could quite easily have continued to work in his many businesses had he chosen to, but it seemed he preferred to be with his beloved wife, leaving the running of his companies to Archie whom he trusted implicitly, riding over about once a week to have a look at his glass works and brick works. He and Abby had got into the habit of travelling to the Lake District where he had bought a house on Lake Ullswater and they had, until this emergency with his daughter broke out, spent many weeks there during spring, summer and autumn. He also knew that Archie, being a sensible chap, was aware that it would all belong one day to him and Beth, and Milly, who would have her share, of course, and it was to his own advantage to keep Noah's business concerns running smoothly.

He began to speak as soon as they were all seated. "I don't like it, and she knows I don't like it but I know your mother wouldn't settle unless she looked in on Milly as often as possible. I've told her that if that bastard's there she's to come straight home but so far she's managed to avoid him. God knows where he gets to, off spending my money, I've no doubt." He sighed heavily. "And if it didn't affect my daughter I'd cut the man off without a shilling but I know it will be Milly who suffers. At least he's leaving her alone and allowing John to attend her. She's improving, John told me this morning when I went round to see him—"

"Father, please, can we not get round to what is to be done with the baby? Is she to stay with you or—"

Noah Goodwin held up his hand and Beth subsided, ready to weep with the uncertainty of it all. The idea that the child she loved so devotedly might be taken away from those who also loved her and put in that great house with three uncaring adults and indifferent servants to look after her was more than she could bear, but suddenly she noticed her mother was beginning to smile and her father was patting his wife's hand, smiling too, as though he were the happiest man alive to be giving her a prize of great worth.

"First of all we now have a name for our granddaughter which I think will please you since you mentioned that—"

"Not Alexandra!"

"Yes, indeed. Your mother persuaded her, Alexandra Caroline Thornley. I believe Caroline is . . . is her grandmother's name and she is to be christened as soon as it can be arranged. Milly thought you and Archie might care to be godparents."

"Oh, Father, I cannot begin to tell you—"

"There is more, my darling."

Noah Goodwin was not what might be called an emotional man, except where his wife was concerned and that was not seen except by her, but it seemed as though his eyes were moistening with something that might have been vulnerability, a softness, and yet at the same time there was another expression in his eyes which could have been anger.

"Father, please."

His voice was hard now. "It seems her parents have no interest in Alexandra." He used his granddaughter's name for the first time and his wife smiled mistily. "Milly claims she is not well enough to care for her and, of course, one presumes his lordship is of the same opinion. I am trying to be charitable here, Beth" – which was hard for him, his manner said – "but that a daughter of mine, and that swine . . ."

Beth jumped to her feet, on her face a look of such shining joy the mouths of both her parents fell open, then they began to smile with her, kissing one another and then her as she fell on them, her arms outstretched, her eyes wet with tears.

"Alexandra, Alexandra!"

"Does that please you, darling?" her mother asked tremulously.

Beth held out both her arms and began to waltz about the room, her wide skirts swinging like the bell in the tower at St Mary's Church where the family occasionally attended a service, particularly at Easter and Christmas. The gown was a lovely silvery grey silk with gleams of pale blue. There was a touch of white lace at the neckline and cuffs and her hair, as she passed the window and the shaft of sunlight falling through it, turned to the colour of dark molten gold. The copper in it flamed and her shining silver eyes, almost the colour of her dress, were brilliant with ecstatic tears.

"Please me, *please me*! I don't think I have been so happy since the day . . . the day I married Archie. I couldn't bear to think . . . well, you know my thoughts . . . and dreams."

"Beth, don't get too excited, darling. She is still Milly and Hugh's child, you know, and if they should decide they want her back—"

Beth stood still abruptly. "Want her back! Do you seriously believe they will ever want her back? She is nothing to either of them. Nothing! Hugh wants a son and it's my opinion Milly wants no child at all. She is only interested in being Lady Thornley of Thornley Green and all that goes with it." Her voice was as cold as chipped ice and her father, who knew her to be an intelligent, compassionate and generous young woman, was startled by the look of contempt on her face. But she was also uncompromising and direct, both characters tempered with humour, which made her forgiving. "Besides," she went on, "I don't believe Hugh will let her alone until she gives him an heir and then perhaps they will forget about the little one upstairs. Let's hope so. Now, I must go and see Archie. I have an idea I want to put to him and later discuss with you."

She kissed her parents fondly and with a light step left the drawing-room, almost running in her eagerness to be off home on whatever mission she had in her head. Both of them thought they knew what it might be!

It was Sunday and when the carriage turned into the stable yard she could see him down by the paddocks exercising Genette, the grey mare he had purchased. She was a lovely animal, her coat shining in the spring sunlight, the colour, Archie said, reminding him of his wife's eyes, which was why he had bought her. Beth knew he was not speaking the exact truth, for though she did have a lovely silvery grey coat, she also had an excellent pedigree and he hoped that she and Plunger, his own black stallion, might produce a good colt or two.

She watched him fondly for a moment then ran through the back door into the kitchen, startling Mrs Kyle who was just putting a nice piece of beef sirloin in the oven for what she called "Sunday dinner". She had all her fresh-picked vegetables about her and would make Yorkshire pudding, for that was where she came from and this was a traditional dish of that county. She had already made the horseradish sauce, now stored in the pantry. Ruth was polishing the silver ready to set the table in the dining-room and Morna was rolling up her sleeves ready to tackle the veg once Mrs Kyle had decided which she would have on the menu. There were Brussels sprouts, cauliflower, spring cabbage, parsnips, carrots and swedes, for Mrs Kyle was very partial to mashed carrots and swedes and they could eat those in the kitchen.

They all stopped what they were doing to watch Mrs Beth rush headlong through their domain, their eyes wide, their mouths open.

"It's to be Alexandra, Alexandra! Don't you think that's the loveliest name?" she gasped as she sped towards the door that led into the main part of the house. "It was the name I chose and I've no idea how Mother got her to agree but agree she did and . . . Oh, Lord, I can't believe it: they don't want her. Well, I can believe it, I'd believe anything of those two and to think—"

She stopped speaking suddenly, realising she was about to say too much, and to servants, but then they were all decent women and were as concerned as she was about the "poor little mite" after whom they asked every day. She smiled.

"Alexandra," she murmured, her eyes bright with unshed tears.

"That's a right pretty name, madam," Mrs Kyle offered, putting the heavy roasting pan containing the beef on the table, waiting politely until Mrs Beth had finished.

"Isn't it? Now I must go and change. I fancy a ride out before luncheon. Will you tell Mary I need her?"

She looked round at the now smiling faces of the maids, even the skivvy who was Morna's sister and had just begun her new job by scrubbing out the scullery, still inclined to snivel for her mam since she was only twelve.

"Mary's not back yet, Mrs Beth."

Beth frowned. It was not that she couldn't manage to change into her riding habit on her own but a slight twinge of uneasiness ran through her. She knew Mary wasn't far away, within walking distance really, and that if her mother was ill she would be forced to stay with her until she was recovered. Doctor Bennett was attending and would soon have Mrs Smith back on her feet but Mary could read and write and she was surprised not to have had a note from her to say what was happening at home. She might just ride over to Longworth later, perhaps she and Archie, and enquire after Mrs Smith's health, take her some fruit and eggs, but first she must speak to Archie, tell him the news about Alexandra!

"Well, I suppose since she only went yesterday . . ." Her voice trailed off and with a bright smile she swept from the kitchen, reappearing ten minutes later wearing her riding habit though without her hat. The latest fashion in riding habits had a shorter train with as little width in it as possible and had vents in the skirts which were about two inches deep at the sides to allow for easier walking and mounting. Under the skirt was worn a pair of kid trousers, fitting tight to the leg so that when riding, should the skirt fly back all was decent beneath. Beth's was a lovely shade of russet that matched her hair, not the customary black or navy, and at her throat she wore a white frilled jabot. In her hand she held a small crop, though she would not have dared strike her mare with it had she wanted to, for Archie and his stable lads and grooms, all picked for their love and experience of horses, would have turned it on her!

Archie saw her coming and raised his own crop in greeting but continued his patient schooling of Genette. Harry Preston was there, the son of Olly and Ruby Preston who still worked for her parents at Lantern Hill, Clancy Morris, a gnome of a man who had once been a jockey but was now Archie's groom, Alfie and Arthur, stable lads, all watching with the fascination of true horse-lovers as the master put the handsome animal through her paces. In the next paddock, Plunger, Firefly, Molly and Rosy, her own chestnut mare, all had their heads over the fence, their necks arched, their lovely eyes watching, it seemed, with keen interest what was going on. Boy, Archie's rough-haired terrier, lay with his nose just beneath the fence waiting patiently for his master. His tail waved gently in greeting but he kept his eyes on Archie.

"I won't be long, darling," Archie shouted, while the men all studiously avoided one another's glance, slightly embarrassed by the master's use of the endearment which none of them, even in the privacy of their marriage bed, would have dreamed of using. "Me old dear" perhaps when they were feeling particularly amorous and they had just had a pint at the local pub, and Harry could remember his pa calling his ma "sweetheart" when he was younger.

She watched, leaning her arms on the top bar of the fence until, with a last delicate movement, Archie brought Genette to a standstill, threw his leg over her shoulder and slid gracefully to the ground.

"Put her back in the paddock, will you, Harry, and then fetch out Plunger. I want to have a look at that hock of his."

"Aye, sir," said Harry, the past when they had been boys and larked about together in these very fields and paddocks, Archie a few years older, long gone if not forgotten. Their lives had taken a different turning, for Archie had been educated to become Mr Goodwin's heir, and Harry, though he could read and write thanks to Mrs Goodwin, was a servant and wanted nothing more than to work with the horses.

Archie climbed the fence and before the disconcerted gaze of the men, who all looked away hastily, he put an arm round his wife's shoulder and, turning her face up to his, kissed her on the lips.

"And how is she today?" he asked good-humouredly, for he of all people knew of Beth's devotion to the Thornley infant.

"Oh, Archie, you'll never guess," they all heard her say, looking about them for somewhere to go, something to do so as not to intrude.

"Tell me." But his eyes were watching Genette walk gracefully towards the gate in the next paddock, whickering in welcome to Plunger who was waiting his turn.

"Take him for a ride, Harry," he shouted to the groom, "and Molly might as well go, too. Clancy, saddle her up and give them both a good stretch."

It was a particularly lovely day. Winter had gone and the sudden mildness had taken them all by surprise. The uplands to the north-east of St Helens, stretching towards the Pennines, were rich in forest and farmland beyond the industries of coal-mining and glass-making and all the other commercial activities that made up the town and surrounding area. They were a patchwork of multicoloured fields varying from many different shades of brown where already planting had taken place. There was green where sheep and new lambs and cattle grazed. Drystone walls divided them, not only serving as boundaries but, like the hedgerows in the lower lands, a focus for wildlife, for the green mosses and lichens to mark the end of winter.

The stream that ran at the back of Edge Bottom House was full and placid, the reeds standing sentinel on its far side reflected mirror-like in its calm surface. Trees crowded close, pussy-willow bending their newly forming golden catkins to the water. There was shade and warm sunlight, a soft drowsing day and the two horses, put to the gallop, cleared the stream in one easy leap, eager to be off. Archie watched them go, smiling his content, then, conscious that his wife was chafing at his side, he looked down at her. The other men had moved off and they were alone.

"I'm sorry, my darling, what were you saying?"

"I should think so too. Here am I wanting to tell you something of great importance and talk to you of something of even greater importance and all you are concerned with is your horses, your damned horses."

He was immediately contrite. "My dearest, I'm sorry. Forgive me but you know what I'm like when . . . now then, tell me. What is Miss Thornley up to today? Is she walking yet?"

"Archie, she may never walk, so please, don't joke."

He put his arms round her and tucked her head under his chin, kissing her bright hair with great tenderness, his eyes sad for her and for the family. He was not as involved as she was in the tragedy of Milly and her baby, for he was a man with a man's tendency to become absorbed with men's affairs. The glass works, the brick works, all the many fields of business with which Noah Goodwin had made his fortune and which he now ran. The small empire that was now almost totally under his control.

"Forgive me, love. Come, come and sit by the fence, yes, you too, Boy, and tell me your great news."

He settled her in the crook of his arm, his head bent to hers, his lips on her brow, his hand smoothing her cheek, which he was surprised to find wet with tears.

"She is to be called Alexandra, Archie. She will be the Honourable Alexandra Thornley and . . ." She paused and there was a wobble in her voice.

"Yes?" For he knew there was more to come.

"And they don't want her."

"I'm not sure . . ."

"Mother was at Thornley Green this morning and Milly was totally indifferent to what her child was named or even when she was to be christened. She agreed to Alexandra but asked Mother to keep her because she wasn't well enough and from the way Mother spoke, never would be. And, of course, Hugh couldn't be less interested. He doesn't want a crippled daughter. He wants a strong, healthy son and I suppose that is what Milly is going to try and give him."

"And Alexandra?"

"Is anybody's who cares to take her, like some puppy who doesn't quite come up to scratch."

"So your mother and father are to—"

"No, I want her."

15

It had been arranged that Alexandra was to move to Edge Bottom House in the next couple of days, for no matter how keen Beth was to have her with them there were certain things to be done before she was brought over. There were, of course, nurseries and even a schoolroom at the top of the house, for hadn't there been five children brought up there, but the rooms needed a coat of paint, the curtains and carpets renewing, fresh pictures on the wall, a night cot, a day cot to be bought, toys to be inspected and a hundred and one baby items to be ordered, including the perambulator. Holdy, Beth's old governess, was to be moved eventually to live in the small suite of rooms next door to the schoolroom and she was eager to meet her new pupil, though it would be a few years before Alexandra was of an age for lessons.

The christening would take place in two weeks' time and though there was so much to be done, to be planned, to be arranged, not just at the house but at the church and Beth was frantically busy preparing for the baby, she found she was restless, wandering from room to room to make sure everything was being done that should be done, driving the maids mad, they told one another smilingly, though they really didn't mind since they were as excited as she was.

She was so happy and not just because of the coming of the child but because she held to herself a small secret that she had shared with no one, not even with Archie. They noticed her smiling when she thought herself to be alone, her silvery eyes gleaming in her honey-tinted face as though she had just been advised of some coming occurrence that pleased her enormously. She was dreamy and inclined to drift from window to window and, when she had informed them that she was going to do this or that, she was often found sitting on a window seat gazing into the garden, watching Tucker turning over the rich soil ready for summer planting.

Archie had been somewhat nonplussed with her enchanted declaration by the paddock fence that Alexandra was moving to Edge Bottom House and though his wife was the centre of his life, his world, his reason for living, he was not awfully sure that this passing of an infant from one sister to another was the right way to go about it, nor that he wanted to do it. The baby was another man's child and the man and his wife lived only a few miles away. Now if the child's mother had died and there had been no suitable member of the father's family to care for her, that would have been a different matter altogether since it would have been perfectly natural for an aunt to take in a motherless infant. Besides which, Hugh Thornley was a tricky bastard and God alone knew what he might be driven to if he felt something to his advantage might come of it. Archie's kind heart had been stricken by the child's plight, but he was afraid that his beloved wife might be hurt in some way should the plan she was so excitedly putting together come to nothing, or, worse, that the baby might settle in, not only into the nursery but into Beth's heart, and then be torn away again on the whim of her sister who was known to be unreliable.

"Darling, you know I have the greatest sympathy for . . . Alexandra, is that it? But are you sure this is wise? You will become very attached to—"

"I'm already attached, as you call it, Archie. I love her and I feel that nobody else does. Oh, I know Mother and Father are very fond of her since she is their granddaughter but they are too old and she needs something special, being the way she is, and I want to try to give it to her. I don't want her to be brought up by servants. Please, don't stop me. I promise she won't interfere with our life together. Jane and Alice will come with her and . . ." She clung to his hands as though to force her own intensity of purpose into him, her face turned up to look into his, her eyes great shining pools of silver, like the lake at Lantern Hill when the reflection from the moon lay across its surface. "I . . . I love her, you see, and she knows me already. That poor little leg will need attention, probably some sort of surgery, and do you honestly believe that Milly and Hugh are going to take the trouble to supervise the care Doctor Bennett says she will need? She must have special boots as she grows so that she can walk."

"Whoa, whoa." Archie laughed, drawing her into the sheltering care of his own arms. "I can't believe you think me capable of turning my back on the little girl. If this is what you want and believe is best for her then it shall be done. I just wanted to point out to you that—"

"Milly and Hugh might turn nasty."

"Yes, my darling, and I can't bear to think it might break your heart, and the child's who will come to love and rely on you."

"Am I being incredibly selfish, Archie?"

"No, you are just being you. I love you so much that being without you is an agony I couldn't bear. I want nothing more than your happiness and your love."

For a dreadful moment, though she told herself a dozen times a day that she loved Archie in the way a woman loves her man, her special man, she wondered if he sensed that though she *did* love him and would die to save him a moment's hurt, sometimes what she offered him was not quite enough. That she was not giving him what he really deserved: her total devotion. Oh, Archie, I do love you, I do.

She was so absorbed with this wondrous event that it was not until Wednesday that she gave a thought to Mary who had been gone since Saturday, with no word, no note, nothing to indicate the state of her mother's health or its improvement. How could she have been so thoughtless? With the slight worry in mind that she had felt at the beginning of the week growing to a deeper concern, she resolved to go over to Longworth and visit Mary's home.

In answer to Beth's enquiry Mrs Kyle wrote down Mary's address from a notebook she kept in her apron pocket, one in which she wrote odds and ends of information that might come in handy some time. She was surprised that Mrs Beth didn't have it herself since she and her maid were close but Mrs Beth said she did somewhere but hadn't the time to lay her hands on it.

"I might just walk over there this morning. It's a pleasant day and the exercise will do me good," Mrs Beth told her, though why she should say such a thing about exercise was a bit of a mystery. Mind, she had been a bit odd ever since the decision to bring Miss Milly's baby to stay with them had been aired. And the girls said she was ever so forgetful, dream-like, not quite focused on what she was doing. Anyway, it was nothing to do with her, for she'd scones in the oven and the salmon to see to for luncheon. She thought she might cook it *à la Genevese*, with shallots, parsley, bay leaves and carrots, with the addition of Madeira and white stock.

"Take care, lass," she heard herself saying with great surprise. "Them soldiers at the barracks can be a bit of a nuisance at times. Who don't you let Harry drive you?" But no, Mrs Beth felt like a walk and off she set in what she called her walking outfit, which was so plain and simple she might have been a maidservant off to the shops, a basket on her arm with a few bits and pieces for Mrs Smith. Mrs Kyle forgot her as she shrilled out for the new skivvy, Dottie, to come and scrape the carrots and prepare the shallots. The girl was never where she should be, drat her, snivelling in some corner and Mrs Kyle rued the day she had allowed Morna to talk her into introducing her young sister into Mrs Kyle's kitchen.

Beth dawdled a bit on the walk over the fields, for it was another nice day, stopping to admire a great bunch of Jack-by-the-hedge which grew along the wall that divided the lane from the field. Brimstone butterflies hovered on the mild air and a chiffchaff swung on the branch of a hornbeam. Rabbits nibbled among a clump of primroses, freezing as she moved past them and in the fields ewes with their newborn lambs reached for a patch of gorse, which they appeared to savour.

But as she approached the small garrison town of Longworth she was surprised when the sun suddenly slid behind a cloud and the sky darkened. There was a pall of smoke hanging over St Helens and a strange mist obscured the rooftops of Longworth as though the smoke were drifting from west to east. She asked a woman who passed her by where Balaclava Street might be, and was directed hesitantly, for the woman seemed astonished that any decent female should be going there.

"It's not a nice place, miss," she said. "There's bully-boys and . . . well, bad women down them streets. Worst part of the town, it be, an' I'd be careful if I was you."

"Thank you, I will," she promised the woman, who was only trying to be kind, but her heart sank as she turned the corner from the main thoroughfare and into what was no more than a narrow alleyway. Every other building seemed to be a public house and even at this hour of the morning men were hanging about in groups by doorways, their eyes following her, watching every hesitation in her step. There were soldiers: what were they doing hanging about here when she would have thought they would have duties at the barracks? She began to despair of ever finding Balaclava Street, not knowing on which side of the alleyway it was, nor how far it might be into the maze of courts and passages beyond. She dared not ask the men nor even the women who also appeared to be hanging about with nothing to do, for none of them was approachable.

She had just spotted what looked to be a wider street than the others, more respectable somehow, hurrying forward to read the flaked sign on the side of a tumbledown house, when a soldier lurched up to her, grasping her forearm in an iron grip.

"'Ow much?" he asked.

"I beg your pardon?" she gasped, doing her best to pull away from him but he held her firmly and though her heart had been bucking and plunging ever since she had entered the alleyways, now it felt as though it might explode from her chest in terror.

"'Ow much, chuck? Surely that's plain enough. I don't want owt fancy. Just a quick fuck in't doorway will do." And he began to pull her towards the handiest one. She was so stunned and horrified that for a moment or two she allowed it, tripping on the hem of her skirt, then she began to struggle, to jerk her arm away from him, but he was tall, broad-shouldered, strong and she felt her feet beginning to drag on the cobbles.

"Let me go at once," she shrieked, looking about her despairingly for someone to come to her aid, but those who leaned against walls and in doorways watched indifferently. For a moment she knew a great sense of relief when two decently dressed men challenged her, and the soldier slunk off without another word. She turned to them thankfully, her mouth trembling, tears in her eyes, her back pressed against the wall, her face, bleached of all colour, a white blob against the crumbling brickwork. She had dropped her basket and the eggs she had brought had smashed on the cobbles. Two cats slunk from a dark corner and, hardly able to believe their luck, began to lap at the broken eggs.

"Oh, thank you, thank you," she gabbled to the men. "I can't imagine what the soldier wanted or why he should think . . . well, I suppose because . . . but thank you. Now if you could

direct me to Balaclava Street I would be so grateful. I am to visit
a friend whose mother is sick and perhaps you might know
where there is a cab rank, close by," looking about her as if
it were hard to believe that such a thing might exist in this
dreadful place.

"Never mind that, miss. Just come with us, if you please and
let's get this over and done with. It's no good arguing so save
your breath for the Justice of the Peace who will probably order
a medical examination at the lock hospital where they treat
venereal disease. We don't allow this sort of thing in our town,
you should know that, and you've been pointed out as a known
prostitute. All women picking up customers on the streets
are detained, for we can't have our soldiers contaminated
with—"

"*Contaminated!* What? I don't understand and please take
your hand off my arm or I shall call a policeman."

"We *are* policemen, lass. Special police with the authority to
pick up prostitutes, so you'd best come with us unless you want
to be carried, or dragged, through the streets to the magistrates
court where you will be . . ."

Her heart, which had quietened somewhat when the two
men came to her rescue, jolted and then stopped, then made
some wild irregular rapid movements. She was breathless,
dizzy, unable to see and her mind would just not function,
then, from nowhere came the dreaded phrase that had haunted
so many women for so many years but which Josephine Butler
had fought for sixteen long years to have repealed. *And
succeeded.*

The Contagious Diseases Act! They thought her to be a
prostitute, she supposed because the soldier had been handling
her, and were doing to her what had been done to women for
years in garrison towns, seaports, anywhere soldiers or sailors
might be congregated. What had been done to Mary and
hundreds of thousands of others, but surely these men knew

that the Act had been repealed and it was no longer legal simply to haul off any woman they found in the streets and take them before a magistrate. To the special hospital where, having been given permission to do so, they would be compulsorily, cursorily examined by a careless doctor and, if found to have a contagion, would be kept there and treated until they were deemed to be healthy.

"Don't be ridiculous," she said sternly, as though talking to a pair of schoolboys. "You know this is illegal. The Contagious Diseases Act was repealed two years ago. You have heard of Mrs Josephine Butler, I presume. Now, if you will allow me to be on my way I shall say no more about the affair. You have made a mistake but if you continue in this manner I shall be forced to send for my husband, Mr Archie Goodwin, of Edge Bottom Glass Works, and believe me you will be in the most serious trouble when he hears—"

They simply took hold of her, one to each arm and dragged her, resisting and beginning to scream, along the street towards a horse-drawn van parked discreetly at the corner. They knew who she was and they had been well paid by someone of far more importance than her husband to take this action. They would quietly slip away when they had delivered her to the hospital, since they had no intention of bringing in the law, and the doctor, who was also in the pay of the important man, would do the rest. No one was taking the slightest interest in her screaming protest, for it did not pay to cross the police, especially these special police in this part of town where prostitution flourished.

They did not miss her until her husband came home at the end of the day, though Mrs Kyle had been most put out that the salmon she had prepared had been taken to the table and then brought back uneaten. Well, it was an ill wind, she said petulantly, so she and the rest of them had a lovely meal, she grumbling that she did think Mrs Beth might have sent a note to say she was having luncheon at Mary Smith's place.

At the end of the day Archie delivered his Molly into the hands of the groom then wandered over to the paddock to watch the animals, smiling at the strange friendship which his handsome black hunter had formed with the mowing pony! They stood nose to tail beneath the oak tree at the far side of the paddock then Plunger saw him and began to wander over, followed by the pony. They both nuzzled his shoulder for a moment, then, finding nothing to eat, strolled off again.

He entered the house by the side door and went upstairs immediately, expecting his wife to be there dressing for dinner, which she usually was but the room was empty. Surprised, and yet should he be for she spent so much time now at Lantern Hill, he rang the bell and when Morna knocked and entered, demanded to know where his wife was. It was almost six thirty and she should be at home by now, he said, frowning. He did like her to be here to greet him, though he didn't say this to Morna, but she had spent so much time with Alexandra, as he supposed he would have to get used to calling her, over the past five weeks he did think she might have been here when he came home, then was sorry to be so petulant. He sympathised with her and understood that she loved the child but he was hoping they might have had a child of their own on the way by now.

"Where is my wife, Morna? Has she gone over to Lantern Hill? The carriage was in the coach house when I came by so perhaps her mother came over and . . ."

He was alarmed by the sudden look of unease that crossed Morna's face, his own beginning to darken, for though Archie Goodwin was a mild-mannered man who was not easily aroused to wrath, where his wife was concerned he was not quite stable. His imagination was ready to run riot if she could not be easily found and it seemed that Morna, from the expression on her face, was not awfully sure where her mistress was.

"Well, sir, Mrs Kyle did say . . ."

"Yes, confound it, woman, what did Mrs Kyle say, and when?" He took a step forward and Morna took one back.

"She – Mrs Beth – was worried about Mary."

"Mary, what the devil has Mary got to do with it?"

"Her mam's poorly, sir, and Mary went over to see her. Doctor Bennett sent for her and that was on Saturday and we'd had no word so Mrs Beth—"

"What the devil are you trying to say?"

"It was this morning, sir. Mrs Kyle had done salmon *à la Genevese* for lunch but when Mrs Beth didn't come home we . . . well, sir, we ate it and—"

"Where the bloody hell was she going, damn you?"

Archie roared like a wounded lion, or so Morna said tearfully to the terrified servants afterwards and she had thought he was going to hit her but instead he took her by the forearms and shook her until her cap fell off.

"Longworth, sir. Mrs Kyle has the address. She give Mrs Beth a basket of food, eggs an' such and Mrs Beth said she'd walk over."

"I'll kill that bloody Harry Preston, allowing her to go to a garrison town on her own."

"He didn't know, sir."

"Where's Mrs Kyle?" As though everyone in the house wouldn't know where Mrs Kyle should be at this time of evening.

"In the kitchen."

He was down the stairs three at a time, bursting into the warm kitchen like a stampeding bull, flinging back the door and making Ruth drop the gravy boat which smashed into a dozen pieces and Mrs Kyle burn herself seriously on the hot fat in the pan. Dottie squeaked and cowered back into the scullery, for not one of them had ever seen Mr Archie in such a towering rage.

"The address, Mrs Kyle and you" – pointing at Ruth – "run to the stable, run, woman, and get that good-for-nothing Harry to saddle Plunger."

She lay in the none too clean bed at the lock hospital and stared at the ceiling, which was cracked and stained with the mildew gathered there in the damp air, her eyes unseeing, her lips bitten through, the blood congealing around her mouth and chin. There were other women in the ward, all quiet and pale, one row on either side, and in the bed opposite was Mary Smith. There were three slatternly women in soiled aprons sitting at a table drinking tea, taking no notice of their patients and no one called for attention, knowing they would get none if they did. They would be chucked out as soon as they could get out of bed. They knew that and some of them, older and worn down, were quite glad of the rest.

They had held her down on a wooden table, a formidable woman on each arm and another at her ankles holding her legs wide apart and though she had struggled violently and screamed her horror it had only made it worse, as they kept telling her it would. Her dainty drawers were stripped from her and thrown to one side. They had ripped into her with that dreaded "instrument from hell" as she had heard it called, the speculum its correct name, tearing that soft, secret, tender part of her body where nothing had gone before but the loving fingers and male organ of her husband. It had torn the tissue, ripped it viciously and the more she struggled the worse had been the damage until something ran from her and she knew it was her own blood and that precious burden she had begun to believe she carried. She had heard a muffled curse from a man – she never saw his face – and then, stuffing some rags between her legs they had half dragged, half carried her to this ward and laid her in the bed.

The disjointed words still echoed in her head.

". . . careful . . . a lot of blood . . . wasn't aware she was pregnant . . ."

"Some of them are . . ."

"Probably glad to get rid . . ."

"But she was clear from . . ."

"We weren't to know that. Information was laid . . ."

"What did the magistrate . . ."

"God knows . . ."

They had gone away then and left her to her agony.

A hand was laid gently on her shoulder and when she turned a painful head, for every part of her hurt, hovering over her was the weeping figure of Mary, her dear Mary who had gone through this twice now and whose face she had vaguely noticed on the soiled pillow of the bed opposite.

"I'm that sorry," she was moaning. "They took me on Saturday. They took me before I even got to her."

"They said I was a prostitute, Mary." Weak tears slipped down her cheeks.

"I know, lass, and it's all my fault. They used me to get to you."

"Who?"

"Nay, love, I don't know." Mary fell to her knees, too weak, it seemed, to stand up and one of the nurses shouted at her to get back to her bloody bed, but Mary laid her face next to Beth's on the pillow. Her bed *was* bloody, literally, but her young mistress appeared to have lost consciousness though her eyes remained open. Mary was aware, for she had suffered this before, that, as she had done, Mrs Beth was hiding from what she couldn't bear. Her eyes were unfocused, for her mind had gone to some shelter where the horror of what had been done to her could not reach and Mary hoped she would stay there until she was able to bear it.

Beth could feel the bloody rags between her legs choked with her own blood and whatever other matter it was she had lost and then her senses fell thankfully away.

In the Cock and Feathers the same three men sat in the corner at a secluded table, drinking the brandy one of them had shouted for. Several of the drinkers noticed that he was a cut above the rest of them, his voice containing the cultured and arrogant tones of the upper classes. He passed a packet to one of the other men who slipped it into his pocket. When they had finished their brandy the two men stood up and quietly left the bar but the third gentleman shouted for another brandy.

"Drinks all round," he bellowed, evidently in high good humour and the men about the bar needed no second invitation.

"A good day's work," he kept repeating, and though they had no idea what the hell he was on about they agreed with him, for free drinks were not often come by. He continued to drink steadily though he was none the worse for it and when he climbed on to his horse, a well-bred beast, several noticed, he was sure and unwavering in the saddle, setting off in a northerly direction.

16

The whole of Balaclava Street was awakened by the thunderous knocking on the door of number four, the home of Thirza Smith, a widow with one daughter. Wives clutched at husbands and husbands cursed, for who the bloody hell was knocking the shite out of Thirza Smith's door at this time of night? Balaclava Street, though it was in the centre of what was a poor, rather notorious part of Longworth, was where decent, hardworking families lived, the husbands in full employment at the various glass works, alkali works, collieries in the district, their wives thrifty and as clean as the shortage of water allowed, and they had been in their beds ready for the next day's labour. They sat up, their children called out in terror, for surely the "bogey-man" had come for them, lighting candles and peering from the windows to see who was hammering at Thirza's door.

It was opened reluctantly and Thirza Smith fell back in alarm, clutching at the loose wrapper she had hastily thrown on as the gentleman pushed past her and glared round her tiny hallway, while behind him another man stood ready to murder her in her bed, she was certain, though she was not actually in her bed.

"Wha' . . . what?" She trembled, holding her candle before her like a shield.

"Where's my wife?" the gentleman bellowed. "What have you done to her? And where's that daughter of yours? Where are they? Come on, woman, speak up before I fetch the constables. She left home this morning to enquire after your health and find out where Mary had got to and no one's seen her since. Now get out of my way because I'm not leaving until I've searched this house from top to bottom." But it was clear to Archie, even as he ranted and raved at the poor woman, that she had no idea what he was talking about. She kept falling further and further back down the narrow hallway before his advance, her face like a sheet, her eyes wide and terrified and Archie felt the terror fill his own mind, for if Beth wasn't here where was she?

Nevertheless he persisted as though the more he pounded on her the more likely he was to find the truth. "Your daughter, Mary, works at my house and last weekend you sent for her to come; you were sick, the note said. It mentioned Doctor Bennett and a chap . . . a chap came, I was told, to take Mary. Dear sweet Lord, tell me, please tell me they are both here." He passed a trembling hand over his sweated face, putting the other against the wall to stop himself from falling and behind him Harry got ready to hold him steady. Harry had never loved a woman. He had tumbled one or two in the fields but he had never known what it was to *love*, not like Mr Archie loved Mrs Beth. He had been brought up with the pair of them, to a certain degree, sharing the schoolroom, and getting a bit of education, but he could not be said to share their lives now, except as their groom. The master was absolutely mad about her and God alone knew what he would do if anything happened to her, which it seemed it had.

"Go with him, Harry," Mrs Kyle had told him as he saddled up Plunger. "And you, Clancy, ride over to Lantern Hill and fetch Mr Noah and perhaps it might be as well to send for Doctor Bennett." Mrs Kyle was a great one in an emergency, and this seemed to be one to her, herding the swirling servants into some semblance of order, telling Morna, who was weeping, to make a pot of tea, and Ruth was to give the fire, which had been damped down for the night, a stir with the poker, and fresh coals would be needed, she told Dottie, who dithered and babbled in a positive lather of terror. She wasn't even sure what was up but they all seemed so upset it must be something awful.

"Come inter't kitchen, lad," Thirza said unnecessarily to the white-faced, trembling gentleman, knowing who he was now and beginning to feel the first splinter of ice pierce her, fear, not for herself but for her daughter and this poor chap's wife. It was a bad area with bully-boys and whores skulking on every corner, drunkards floundering out of the pubs and even young lads ready to terrorise anyone they thought might easily be picked on. This was where the soldiers, the rank and file came when they wanted a woman, wandering around, picking up whores, making a nuisance of themselves. She herself had lived here since her marriage twenty years ago and they all knew her and left her alone, besides which she was too old to be of interest to any man, but she wouldn't give much of a chance to a woman, her own daughter included, who wandered into these maze of streets by mistake.

"Are they here, Mrs Smith?" he asked desolately.

"No, lad, they're not."

"And you . . . you are not and have not been ill?"

"No."

"So you didn't send for Mary?"

"No." She put her hand to her mouth and sat down heavily in a chair, for this was not the first time their Mary had been in trouble, not of her own making, of course, and it had been this man's wife who had restored her to health and the acceptance that life went on. Good to her, Mrs Goodwin had been. Put her back on the right road, so what the devil was going on that two decent girls, women, should be . . . no, it couldn't happen again, surely not.

Mr Goodwin startled her by leaping towards the door, shoving the other poor chap out of the way.

"We'll start searching the streets, Harry. She might be hurt, lying somewhere."

Harry, who wasn't so involved as Archie and could think more clearly, though he was fond of Beth, shook his head. "We can't just go blundering about these parts at this time of night, Archie," calling him by the name he had used as a child. "There's some bad devils hanging about here who would think nothing of bashing you over the head for the shoes on your feet. Let's wait until morning and then—"

"Bugger you, Harry Preston, if you think I'm going to sit about and wait for daylight when my wife might be . . . be . . ." He gulped as the pictures that filled his mind reached his heart where they nearly felled him. "If you haven't the nerve to come with me I'll go alone."

"I was going to suggest that we go to the police station and report Beth's disappearance. And Mary's of course," he added hastily, for the poor girl's mother was sitting there looking like death. "And then there are the hospitals. If there's been an accident . . ."

"There's more to it than that, Harry. Two women, and don't forget Mary hasn't been seen since Saturday when she rode off with a perfect stranger—"

A strangled sound from Thirza stopped his flow and he turned to her apologetically. "Mrs Smith, I'm sorry, I shouldn't have. But, Christ, I don't know what I'm saying."

Harry took his arm and began to lead him towards the front door, glad that Mrs Kyle had had the foresight to send him along with Archie, for the poor chap didn't know what the hell he was doing, his usually sharp mind totally clouded by fear for his wife. He was about to put his hand on the latch, doing his best to look hopeful for Mrs Smith's benefit when the door nearly flew in on him, its hinges bending under the strain of its second pounding in an hour.

"Dear God in heaven," Thirza moaned from her chair by the fireplace.

Harry lifted the latch and the door surged open and for a

moment he thought they were being attacked by a gang of thugs as Noah Goodwin, his face the colour of a ripe damson but with a white line about his mouth, fell into the passageway, nearly knocking down Harry, Archie and Thirza, who had come to stand behind Archie, like a row of skittles. Clancy was behind him and behind Clancy was John Bennett. Clancy was doing his best to hold the three horses who were lathered and inclined to be nervous.

"Where is she?" Noah thundered. "Where's my lass? What's been done with her? Where is she?"

John Bennett stepped forward and took Noah's arm while Clancy backed off with the horses. Up and down the street doors were opening and anxious faces peered out, for what the hell was going on at Thirza Smith's house? Men all over the place and horses stamping and rearing and neighing. This was not the sort of area where horses were seen, not unless it was the rag-and-bone man or the milk dray, but they were all crowding into Thirza's, the door shutting behind them, only the chap with the horses remaining outside the house.

"D'yer think I should go over an' see if Thirza's all right, our Jack," Madge Pendlebury asked her husband worriedly, but Jack had been in the middle of his weekly conjugals when the commotion had occurred and he was fretful about being interrupted.

"No, lass, come back ter bed. Time enough in't mornin'," so Madge reluctantly climbed into bed and lifted her nightie.

Had it not been for Doctor Bennett, who simply marched into every hospital and infirmary in Longworth and the surrounding area, demanding admittance, even the lock hospital where he had no influence whatsoever, since, as it implied, it was a prison hospital of sorts, it might have taken days to find her. They all, even Clancy who had tied up the horses, marched in through the front entrance, seriously affronting those in charge, and demanded to be given access to every ward in the place.

"You'll stand out of my way or by God I'll shut the bloody place down," Noah snarled to the officious doctor who seemed to be in charge. "Who the hell d'you think pays for it in the first place, tell me that? Me and a lot of other gentlemen who give to charities and if I ask them to withdraw, they will. I have influence in Lancashire you can't begin to imagine." And so on at every hospital but it was Doctor Bennett's quiet authority that opened the doors and had doctors and nurses running all over the wards looking for the grand and outraged Mr Goodwin's daughter. Up and down stairs and in every corner of every ward they looked, but it was not until they got to the lock hospital, the five men and their tired animals, that they met resistance.

"These women are infectious and I will not be held responsible should they contaminate—"

"Get out of my way, you sod," Noah told the frock-coated doctor. "This gentleman is Doctor Bennett. I suppose you will have heard of him?" For who had not heard of the illustrious doctor who with his wife had done so much for the poor and down-trodden men and women of the parish?

"I'm sorry, sir, but I cannot allow you to enter these wards. The women are being treated for venereal diseases and until I am satisfied they are cured I can allow no one—"

"May I ask your name?" Doctor Bennett interrupted smoothly, at the same time holding on to Archie's arm, for it seemed he would be held back no longer from tearing this bloody place apart, *any* bloody place apart to find his beloved wife.

"I cannot see what that has got to do with—"

"It might have if Mrs Goodwin is found to be here. She is a perfectly respectable married woman, the wife of this gentleman and the daughter of Mr Noah Goodwin. I cannot imagine, if she is found here, what will be directed at you." And where else were they to look, for already the men from Edge Bottom House and Lantern Hill and from the glass works were scouring the countryside for, but praying not to find, the body of the wife of the man who employed them. "There will be great trouble," he added quietly.

Mary saw the door of the ward open and through it stride the powerful figures of Mrs Beth's husband and father and she began to weep thankfully, for she really didn't think Mrs Beth would last another night. She had stopped bleeding, she herself had ascertained that, as the women in charge didn't seem to be concerned, but she had also stopped recognising Mary. She stared somewhere over Mary's shoulder, her eyes shrouded with deep shadows, haunted and yet unseeing, unknowing. She obediently sipped the brackish water Mary put to her cracked lips but would eat none of the sloppy food thought fit for the women to survive on.

"They're here, darling," she whispered into Beth's deaf ear. "They've come for you. They've found us. Oh, thank God, thank God."

Archie's roar of appalled disbelief was heard in every corner of every ward in the hospital and beyond, even Clancy, who had been told to wait in the hallway and keep his eye on the disgruntled doctor, made aware that his little mistress had been found.

She did not seem to know him, he kept saying to his father-in-law as they wrapped her up in the filthy blankets which were all that covered her, carrying her out of the foul ward and down the stairs to the cab that had been hastily summoned, Noah brooding on the fact that his lovely girl must be carried in this decrepit vehicle when there were clean and comfortable carriages at home. He wanted to take her from Archie but Archie wouldn't have it, holding her body to him in an agony of fear and tenderness. She was hot and yet clammy and Doctor

Bennett, who feared an infection, though he did not say so, said she must be taken at once to his house in Claughton Street where Laura could tend to her and where everything he needed for . . . well, all his things – instruments – were there. "She doesn't seem to know us, Noah." Archie kept repeating desperately on the short journey into St Helens.

In a second cab Harry solicitously lifted Mary into his strong young arms, shushing her as he might a restless animal in his charge. She wept and wept and he wondered what the bloody hell had been done to these two young women, for Harry Preston, despite living in the same house as the two dedicated women who were both members of the NUWSS, had taken little interest in their aims and had certainly never heard of Mrs Josephine Butler.

They waited in Laura Bennett's narrow hallway, restlessly roaming from the kitchen to the front door, even Harry, while Clancy, leading Plunger and Genette, rode Molly to Lantern Hill to inform Mrs Goodwin that her daughter had been found and would be home soon. He was to drive the carriage over to Doctor Bennett's where she had been taken and bring her home as soon as the doctor said she was fit to travel.

"I've ter tekk the animals back ter Edge Bottom, Mrs Goodwin, and the servants'll want ter hear about the young mistress."

"Where was she, Clancy?" Mrs Goodwin begged, her face all hollowed out, her eyes enormous with fear for her daughter. It had only been a few hours since she and the master had heard Mrs Beth was missing, but the contemplation of what might have happened to her had turned her from a right good-looking female – for her age, Clancy thought – into an old woman.

"She . . . I'm not sure, Mrs Goodwin, but she were at the hospital. An accident, I suppose," he answered vaguely, for it was not up to him to give a report, besides which he didn't rightly know *what* had happened.

Abby Goodwin wanted them, both her daughter and her maid, brought to Lantern Hill, but Archie wouldn't hear of it. He was determined to have his wife – and don't forget she was his wife and it was his decision that counted – in her own bed in her own house where he could keep his eye on her. Morna and Ruth would look after her, but if Mrs Goodwin could part with Harriet Woodruff, who was known for her common sense and unruffled manner in an emergency, he would be very grateful. Just for a few days, he said. And there was Mary to be nursed too, don't forget, for she had suffered the same . . . the same indignities his wife had been put through.

"They've both been examined, Archie. As the husband of a suffragist you will know what that means."

"*Examined!*" Noah bellowed, white-lipped with anger. "In what way? What has been done to my daughter? Because whatever it is and whoever has done it will be made to pay—"

"Noah, let Doctor Bennett finish," Archie told him, his own rage only just held in check.

"She and Mary have both been subjected to an examination by speculum."

"What the devil does that mean?"

"It seems from what Mary tells me – Beth has not spoken yet – that they were taken into the lock hospital under the pretence that a charge of common prostitution had been laid against them."

Archie had to grab his father-in-law by the arms, for it seemed he was about to strike his old friend, Doctor Bennett, but some vague memory came to Noah regarding his wife and daughter who were both ardent fighters in the war for equality among women. They had spoken of such a thing and that girl, that maid of Beth's had had a brush with them, the authorities, some time ago. He had taken little notice, for it had happened when he was having troubles of his own with Milly and that sod of a husband of hers. It had not concerned him but now it did!

"She has been . . . I'm sorry, Archie, Noah, but it must be said. She has been torn about. I have had to stitch her, and the other lass, for they must both have struggled. They were held down and—"

"For God's sake, man, that's enough," Noah Goodwin moaned, but Archie lifted his bowed head and glared at him. His usual good-natured, good-humoured expression was missing. He knew he would never be the same man again, but he had to hear what had been done to his wife in order to deal with it, and with whoever it was who had carried it out. Until yesterday he had been a reasonable man, moderate, fair, self-contained and unhurried, soft-spoken and inclined to laugh at most things. A happy man in love with his wife and without enmity towards any man. He was that no longer.

"I have only what Mary has told me, old chap," the doctor said to him, putting a hand on his shoulder gently. "Mary was taken on Saturday and subjected to the examination, the second time she has suffered it. Had it not been for Beth she would never have recovered the first time, for she was a virgin and had not been touched by any man. She was used to trap Beth, Archie, you know that, for we have Mrs Smith's word that Mary never got to Balaclava Street. Somehow, God knows how they did it, for Beth has been unable to tell us, they took her yesterday and when Mary saw her for the first time she had been . . . had had done to her what Mary had suffered. She bled, lost a lot of blood and is torn about. I'm sorry, Archie."

Noah was twisting and turning, a visible menace to himself and all those about him, savage in his pain and despair and rage, but Archie stood like a stone, a pillar carved from granite, his very face the colour of granite, his eyes, the lovely hue of a delphinium sky, blank and pale, slits of pure ice and Doctor Bennett had it in his mind to pity the man who had done this to Archie Goodwin's wife, for when Archie found him he would kill him, and slowly!

They took them both back to Edge Bottom House. They had been tenderly bathed in Laura Bennett's tin bath before the fire in her own bedroom, helped by Laura's maid, Biddy, then put in a clean nightgown apiece and wrapped in Laura's soft blankets. Mary cried with the pain of it, for she had been stitched too, though Mrs Bennett and her maid were as gentle as they could be, but Beth's face was blank, as were her eyes, and when they washed between her legs, exclaiming at the blood that still seeped from her, she showed no sign that she was hurt. She moved this way and that as they asked her, stood up and was dried on one of Laura's rather worn towels, then wrapped around with a blanket, sitting where they put her waiting for the Goodwin carriage to come. She drank a little warm milk and sat, staring unseeingly into the fire, while Laura held her hands. She didn't cry like Mary, which Laura didn't like, for she was a woman who believed that a good cry often helped some women. Not herself, because she was strong and resolute, always had been, so perhaps that was what held Beth back. But somehow she thought not.

They were all there at the front of the house or in the hallway, even daft Dottie, to welcome back their little mistress, some of them who had known her for many years. Her mother had driven over from Lantern Hill to help with her nursing, should she need it, and to hear from Doctor Bennett exactly what had happened to her. Something to do with Mary Smith, the poor girl who had been subjected to an intimate examination under the Contagious Diseases Act which was, of course, no longer legal. The baby, naturally, would be kept at Lantern Hill for the time being, since it was evident that Beth would not be able to care for her as she had planned.

The servants had no idea what had happened to her; an accident, Clancy had told them and when they pressed him for details he was strangely reluctant to speak, which was strange, for Clancy, being an Irishman, loved a good gossip. Harriet had been brought over and for a moment it was all smiles and a few tears, but one look at Archie Goodwin's face and they melted away, shepherded by Mrs Kyle who had caught the signal Mrs Woodruff had passed to her. This was no warm and happy homecoming, they realised, as they began to shuffle towards the front door and when, picked out of the carriage by Mr Archie, Mrs Beth began to scream shrilly, they were all paralysed with shock, Mrs Goodwin becoming even more gaunt than ever. The women put their hands to their mouths and Morna moaned deep in her throat, for she had had more to do with Mrs Beth than the others. Was Mr Archie hurting her, for God's sake, that she should shriek as she was doing? And she had begun to struggle as though doing her best to escape his loving arms.

"Dear sweet Christ," Mr Archie was heard to whisper, turning frantically for someone to help him, for it seemed he might drop her she was struggling so frantically. After that one shrill scream she was silent as if she must make no noise and it was Harriet, no longer a young woman, who leaped to help him.

"Abby, take her other side," she muttered. "Leave go, for God's sake, Archie. I've got her." And she had. They made a sort of chair for her, her mother and Harriet, and staggered with her towards the arched doorway that led into the house.

"Get out of the way, you men, clear off," she hissed. "Morna, get behind us and Ruth, lead the way up the stairs to Beth's bedroom. Is it ready? Good. Oh, and fetch Mary, will you, Mrs Kyle? I think she might . . ."

Archie looked as though he had been poleaxed. His wife had struggled against him, had fought to get out of his arms, had screamed in terror and it was not until the women had come forward to help her that she had calmed down. Mary, walking as though she had her legs stitched together, which, he supposed, with that part of his brain uninvolved in these horrific events, she had in a way, followed slowly and the women and their burden disappeared from his sight up the stairs.

The rest of them didn't know what to do, including his father-in-law. Males, all of them, except Dottie who was snivelling up the hallway in the direction of the kitchen, and it was then that he began to realise that his lovely, beloved wife was afraid of him, of them, of the men in the house, for it was they who had done this to her.

"She'll recover in time, Archie," a quiet voice at his back said and there was Doctor Bennett climbing down from his ancient carriage. "She's been . . . well, you might say she's been raped and it will take some getting over. She . . ." He drew Archie away to the gate at the side of the house, forcing him to go because Archie wanted nothing more than to get up the stairs to his wife. "You must be patient, Archie. I don't want to tell you this but what she has gone through you must share with her eventually. She was pregnant, you see. Only a few weeks, but they took it from her and she will need time to recover."

Archie Goodwin bowed his head to his chest and wept.

17

The naked woman on the bed laughed, a deep throaty laugh, arching her body and throwing back her head so that the long line of her, broken only by her high breasts, looked magnificent against the long, tangled mass of her rich copper hair which reached her buttocks. The man whom she sat astride moaned and threw back his own head into the crumpled pillow. His hands reached for her breasts which were full and rosy-tipped, fondling and pinching them until the nipples were hard and peaked, then he too sat up until they were face to face, she in his lap, his throbbing penis still buried deep within her. He kissed her, a cruel, savage kiss which forced their teeth together and then he thrust his tongue into her mouth which she immediately bit, drawing blood.

"Dammit, Milly, must you be so bloody ferocious," he growled, the words barely distinguishable around his bitten tongue, but his eyes were slitted with passion. She loved it when he was cruel with her, savage and rough, for it was not really his nature and she knew it was she who provoked it.

"You know you love it, Todd Woodruff," Milly Thornley moaned into his ear and then took the lobe into her mouth and bit that too. They were like two animals fighting instead of a man and woman making love, drawing blood, rolling and scratching and gouging but careful, nevertheless, not to mark each other's face. Milly began to shout, which Todd knew meant that she was coming to her climax, for this was not the first time he had been in her bed. He rammed his mouth against hers, effectively silencing her except for the moaning in her throat and together they exploded into such a frenzy Todd was convinced, though he was but twenty-four years old, that he was about to have a heart attack. They were panting, sweating freely, the sheets beneath them wet and crumpled, but this was how Milly liked it and if Milly wanted it, Todd was happy to oblige. Besides which, he was not averse to it himself. She was like a she-cat in her lust, for he knew that was all it was, lust, and her demands were as violent as any man's. She was quite magnificent in her naked beauty, her skin so white it was translucent, her back smooth and gracefully arched, her breasts full and peaked, her waist, which had recovered months ago from childbirth, sweetly curved, as was her hip and thigh. Her body was long and swaying and it swayed now as she enticed him back to the bed from which he had just arisen.

"Come back here, darling," she ordered, her voice husky. "I haven't finished with you yet. Leave that damned uniform where it is and come and do to me all over again what you have just done."

Milly watched her lover with narrowed eyes and, like him as his eyes devoured her, was ready to admit that Todd Woodruff was a strikingly handsome man. His eyes gleamed in his dark face, the lamp on the bedside table reflected in the deep golden brown, the colour very much like hers. His body had a hard, male beauty which she couldn't help but admire, dark, wide of shoulders, the narrow grace of his hips, his flat, taut stomach, the long shapeliness of his legs. And he was a superb lover!

She could remember when she had first become aware of him, not just as Todd, her childhood playmate, the son of her father's servants, but as a man who was worth a second look. It had been at one of Hugh's wild parties, the gentlemen, most of them officers in his old regiment, engaged in one of those incomprehensible games they seemed to revel in, one carrying another on his back while they beat at each other with cushions in an attempt to unseat the "rider". The noise had been indescribable and Milly, who had become increasingly bored with the whole childish thing, was relieved that old Lady Thornley had at last taken herself off to the dower house where she resided with her cook, Mrs Kendall, and two parlour-maids, her own carriage and Hartley, the groom, to drive it.

The gentlemen had fallen in an inglorious heap on the billiard-room floor and somehow, having drunk himself almost insensible, Hugh had hit his head on the corner of the billiard table and with the help of the giggling, drunken officers had been put to bed unconscious.

"D'you think we ought to send for the doctor, Milly?" Todd had asked, the only one among them to give a damn, it seemed.

"No, let him sleep it off, Todd, and will you please help me to get rid of this lot because all I want is my bed."

After they had gone Todd had felt bound to check on old Hugh who he found snoring peacefully in his dressing-room where a narrow bed was made up. He had shut the door carefully and was about to go down the grand staircase that led to the even grander hall when Milly drifted from what he presumed was the bedroom she shared with Hugh, dressed in nothing but a floating, shimmering, almost transparent bit of nonsense which he believed women called a negligee.

"You still here, darling?" she had whispered, for it was the fashion to call everybody by the endearment, even when you barely knew them.

"I was just making sure old Hugh hadn't fallen out of bed." They had walked towards one another along the wide hallway and without any prearranged plan or even the slightest hint that it could happen, he put his arms about her, his mouth on hers and before he could say, "What about old Hugh?" who was sleeping in the room off the bedroom, they were tearing at each other's clothes and thrashing about on the bed. It had been absolutely glorious, they had told one another breathlessly and who would have thought, after all these years, and so on and before they knew it they had fallen peacefully asleep in one another's arms, which was the most insane thing to do. He had wakened as dawn tinted the sky in the east to the palest pink and with an oath he had struggled into his clothes, kissed Milly who was still sleeping like a child and slipped out down the back stairs. It had been thrilling and, at least to him, strangely moving. They had been lovers ever since.

"Milly darling, I was due back at the barracks ten minutes ago," he argued now. "And if the old man sees me creeping back he'll have me on the carpet and I'll never get my promotion. I don't want to be a lieutenant for the rest of my days. I have ambition, Milly." He grinned the wicked and impudent grin that was so endearing to the ladies. "Rise above my station and all that," referring to his parentage. His mother was a housekeeper, his father a groom, and yet thanks to the Goodwin family he had risen to the dizzying height of an officer in the 3rd Battalion of the King's Regiment (St Helens). But he wanted more. A captaincy to start with and then marriage to a decent woman, a woman who would bring him money and prestige but, by God, he wouldn't find it in Milly Thornley's bed!

"Well, I do think you could spare me another few minutes, Todd. How can you deny that this is worth being hauled over the coals for?" She rose to her feet on the bed and sighed languorously. She lifted her chin and began to move gracefully, thrusting the coppery bush at the base of her belly towards him, then, with a wicked grin, she licked her fingers and thrust them into that soft, warm, moist centre of her which was ready again. Todd could feel his erection immediately respond and Milly smiled, for though he had put on his shirt the lower half of his body was still naked. "I can see you want to, darling. Todd, darling, please, sweetheart." And with a gesture that might have been obscene but was curiously graceful, she flung herself back on the bed and opened her legs wide so that the man could see every pulsing movement of her womanhood.

"Confound it, Milly," he muttered hoarsely, "you're a bloody wanton witch," but he could no more resist her than a dog can resist a bitch on heat.

For another half-hour they played the long but hurried game of seduction, the passionate exchange of sensuality they had found with each other. They both knew exactly what pleased the other, using every nuance and shade of what they called "love" to bring one another to the intense peak of pleasure they had surprisingly found with no one else.

He hurriedly dressed and she watched him, still rather intrigued by how good-looking he was and by how much he pleased her in bed. She had not slept with Hugh since the child was born, afraid that he might still have that appalling disease he had given to her earlier in the year. He said he was cured but until he proved it by consulting with Doctor Bennett, whom she trusted, she had refused him her bed. She had been quite amazed that he had allowed it, for if there was one sure thing that could be said about Hugh, it was that he would have his own way no matter who got hurt in the process. It appeared that at the moment he was happy to leave her alone. She was aware that he had a new mistress, some older woman whose husband was in his seventies and no use to her, but it was said she was the most accomplished enchantress in the art of love and she was certainly keeping Hugh amused.

Todd was the only man she had ever slept with apart from Hugh, since that dread of catching syphilis again had prevented her from entering into any of the dalliances that were readily available to her. They had begun entertaining as soon as she had regained her health and their parties, wild and noisy, were the talk of the town and an invitation to one was prized above all else. Nothing but the best for Lord and Lady Thornley, the most expensive pink champagne, caviar, salmon, lobster, pheasant, oysters, game, scarcely any of the food eaten except by the servants, for the guests, many of them officers from the barracks and their female companions, were too busy drinking vast quantities of champagne and wandering from bedroom to bedroom in search of a change of partner, romps in the newly restored billiard-room and dancing in the newly restored ballroom. Milly had begun to notice, but didn't much care, that the more respectable ladies and gentlemen, those of Hugh's class, were beginning to drop off, but as long as she had a good time, and she did, who was concerned that what she called the *stuffier* element of society stayed away.

She was surprised when Todd came over to the bed where she lay in what she knew was a delightfully provocative pose, and, bending down, kissed her tenderly on the mouth. He smiled and smoothed her tumbled red hair away from her face, then kissed her forehead.

"What was that for?" she asked, smiling.

"Nothing, except to say, be careful, Milly. You and I, we're discreet, but if Hugh was to find out – that is if you took another lover, he might not care for it."

"Damn Hugh, and anyway, why should I take another lover? You suit me admirably, my pet. Besides, Hugh's very wrapped up with Lady what's-her-name and scarcely notices me any more."

"Doesn't he want an heir? Most men in his position do."

"He hasn't mentioned it." She looked slightly apprehensive and Todd felt a surprising surge of tenderness towards her. He knew, as did all Hugh's so-called friends, that Hugh had passed on the clap to his wife and had been damned sorry about it and you couldn't blame her for not wishing to resume relations with him, but she must give him a son very soon. She was still young and he supposed there was plenty of time, but just the same, he would hate to see her hurt again.

Milly moved to the window after Todd had slipped from her

room, going down the back stairs to avoid the servants. His horse was tethered under the trees to the front of the house and she smiled, for did he honestly think that the servants didn't know of their relationship? Servants knew everything that went on in the houses of their employers but it pleased Todd to think he was being discreet and defending her reputation. He really had turned out to be a most satisfactory lover and she would be sorry when it ended, as it was bound to do. She watched him emerge from the trees, as did the grinning gardeners, and gallop off down the long drive. It was turning to dusk and the pines at the edge of the lake had become smoky and the oaks more livid in their watery bronze. Below the wood was a steep, grassy bank, in spring richly decorated with primroses and later, more delicate still with wild strawberries and the dark purple of vetch, stitchwort and scarlet pimpernel. She knew them all because when they were children, she and Beth, Harry, Sally, Todd and Archie had played together in the grounds about Edge Bottom House and had learned the names from Archie who had been older. What a happy childhood they had known, she thought sadly, and before she could stop herself her mind turned to Beth and she wanted to weep. Dear God, what was the matter with her? A few hours spent in Todd Woodruff's company, who was known for his kind heart, and she turned into some sentimental, silly female, sorry for her sister who surely, with a bit of an effort, could easily snap out of this stupid state into which she had fallen. True, she had suffered an ordeal that was enough to send any woman off her head, but then so had she, Milly, and she had got over it.

She sighed and wandered away from the window, sitting down in the low velvet chair before the fire, gazing into its heart with an unfocused gaze. She supposed she should really think of getting over to Edge Bottom House soon, not only to see her sister but to visit her daughter who had lived there for the past five months. It was just the thought of that dreadful leg really did upset her. Thank God it didn't affect the women who looked after her, for they all seemed to adore her but she really didn't think she could cope with a child who was crippled.

She sat in a basket chair under the massive oak tree, her face placid and smiling, a bit of sewing in her hand, watching now and again the antics of the dog, Archie's rough-haired terrier, Boy, who had taken a great fancy for the baby. He tried to play with her, bouncing up and down, pretending to fight, sometimes knocking her over where she sat on the rug but she didn't seem to mind, struggling to sit up again and grabbing a handful of his ruff, whereupon he growled in mock ferocity. She gurgled with laughter, turning to look at Jane, sharing the moment of joy with her nurse, while Jane sat anxiously in her chair, not yet convinced that the great dog might not harm the child. She was a lovely child, six months old now with fat and glossy curls of the darkest brown, the colour of treacle, arranged on her head. Jane brushed them into fat sausages and today she had tied a ribbon of blue satin in them. Her eyes were the blue, the incredibly brilliant blue of Hugh Thornley's, surrounded by thick black lashes and there was no doubt, should he have seen her, which was unlikely, he would have claimed her for his child. Her nose was a still a baby nose, a blob in the middle of her face above a rosy mouth which, when she smiled, revealed a single tooth like a small pearl.

Beside Beth sat Mary, for it seemed Beth Goodwin could not bear to have her maid out of her sight, not for a moment. Although Archie was patience itself, keeping out of his wife's bedroom and sleeping in one of the spare rooms at Edge Bottom House, he had aged considerably in the months since that dreadful day when his wife and her maid had been tortured. There were deep lines scoured from his lean cheeks beside his mouth to his chin and threads of silver in his crisply curling blond hair.

That moment when he had tried to speak to her of her ordeal, to tell her that it made no difference to the way he felt about her, he would remember for the rest of his life. It had been like a nightmare, unreal, the figures of her mother and father, of Harriet and Morna like shadows that wavered and faltered through a slow-moving mist as he realised that his wife was afraid of him. Even her father was pushed away when he tried to put his arms about her and Doctor Bennett had hurried them from the room leaving only Mary, Harriet and Abby to shush and comfort her, to hold her in their soft, female arms, to calm her with the draught Doctor Bennett handed in to the bedroom. They had put her to bed but until Mary was placed in the narrow trundle bed beside her where Beth could see her as she drifted off into the nightmares of the last few days, they could not settle her. She talked only to Mary in those first few days and it was left to Mary and Harriet to check her wounds, the stitches Doctor Bennett had put in and to administer the laudanum which put her to sleep and allowed the doctor to remove the stitches and check the wounds. They were healing, he said, and with good nursing and nourishing food, which she was getting, she would recover.

Mrs Kyle on hearing this began to cook as though her life depended on it, preparing the most nutritious and delicious meals she could contrive to tempt the invalid's appetite, broths with the very best cut of meat, custards with a dozen eggs in them, egg wine made with sherry, beef tea, jellies made from fresh oranges, hot chocolate made with fresh milk and a dash of cinnamon, barley gruel, baked calf's foot, chicken broth, and even went as far as to beg Mrs Goodwin to allow her into the sickroom to ask the invalid what she might fancy.

As long as she had Mary within reach she would respond, clinging to Mary's hand, and in those first few days they accepted that Mary, who knew exactly what Beth had suffered since she had undergone the same ordeal, was her one link to reality, but as the days and then the weeks passed and her husband was still rejected and was unable even to step into her bedroom without hysterics, Doctor Bennett knew that Beth had retreated into some secret shelter where no man was allowed to enter. She was polite with the women who waited on her, with her mother who sat and held her hand and cried when she left the room, though Beth didn't know this, even with Mrs Kyle who wanted nothing more than to "build her up", an expression her own mam had once used, but the only person she wanted with her was Mary.

They had been back at Edge Bottom eight weeks when Doctor Bennett, who found it very difficult to treat Beth from outside her bedroom door, messages passed from him to Mary and from Mary back to him, drew Archie into the conservatory and closed the big double doors behind him.

"Lad, I'm worried about Beth," he said abruptly. "This aversion to the male sex is perhaps understandable after what she has gone through but she should be getting over it by now."

Archie walked slowly to the end of the conservatory where the doors stood open on to the garden. He reached up to a camellia which was tumbling from a hanging basket and put it to his nose, sniffing deeply, then let it spring back. It was a lovely place, this winter garden, as his mother-in-law called it, created many years ago by Abby Goodwin's grandmother and he often came here on his own to ease the dull and aching pain that was constantly with him. He didn't seem able to hope any more and it was slowly killing him. He had tried many times, carefully and calmly approaching his wife as he might some dreadfully wounded and frightened creature, to talk to her, sometimes barely entering the room in the hope that she might allow him to talk to her if he kept his distance, but each time he did so she would go rigid, strain away from him, even at that distance, and begin to shake her head in horror. Dear God, he was her husband. He loved her more than life itself and would do anything to help her to be herself again, but try as he might, every day, since he thought repetition might accustom her to him, she began to scream on a high-pitched shrill, reaching for Mary and sinking her face into her maid's neck, clinging to her desperately.

"Make him go away, Mary," she would moan. "Make him go away." And with Mary's pitying face imploring him to leave he would slip away, closing the door quietly behind him.

"What do you propose to do, Doctor," he asked with what sounded like indifference.

"I have asked a colleague of mine to come and talk to her. She will not like it since he is a man but I am out of my depth here, Archie, and I need the help of someone, a doctor, who is concerned not with the body but with the mind. His name is James Crighton-Browne. He does not believe, as so many doctors do, that there are organic explanations for mental illness."

Archie winced, keeping his back turned to Doctor Bennett.

"I don't know how we are to do it but if Beth isn't dragged back from whatever pit she has fallen into God alone knows what will happen. The loss of her child through what was . . . was rape, as I've said before, even if it was with an instrument, has compounded . . . Well, I will say no more but as her husband I must have your permission to fetch in Doctor Crighton-Browne. He is young and progressive and—"

"Fetch him, for if she doesn't come back to me I will lose my mind. She is . . ." A thin, anguished sound floated into the wrought-iron roof of the conservatory and John Bennett felt his own heart constrict for the pain of this man. They had never discovered who it was who had lured first Mary, and then Beth, into the foul place where they had found them. There had been talk of special police, those who had once arrested known prostitutes, but they were no longer employed since the Contagious Diseases Act had been repealed. Public houses had been scoured by the men Noah Goodwin had hired to find the man who had mentally crippled his daughter but nothing had been found.

"She won't let me into our own bedroom, Doctor, the place where we loved one another and where . . . where our child was conceived. I have loved her since she was born, for I was there when she came into the world. This is clawing my heart to rags and I can do nothing to help her. Perhaps I am looking at it only from my own point of view and what I have lost, but unless she recovers, neither shall I. What in God's name am I to do?" It burst from him like a moan. "All these weeks and none of us can get near her . . . only the women."

"It's understandable, Archie."

"Why is Mary not affected, then?"

"She has, she is healing. She has Beth to care for and so she has something to cling to. They are, in a way, leaning on each other and when Doctor Crighton-Browne comes it might help Beth – and Mary – if they are examined together."

That had been four weeks ago and again it was a memory that pierced Archie to the very core of him, lashing him with the images he could not get out of his mind, nor ever would. Mary had been prepared, warned in advance what was to happen and had tried to tell Beth that there was nothing to be afraid of. That this man was a doctor.

"He was a doctor, Mary, the one who . . . who . . ."

"I know, darling, but this one is coming with Doctor Bennett and you know you trust Doctor Bennett."

"No, Mary, please don't let them. I cannot bear to have their hands, any man's hands on me."

"He is only going to talk to you, Beth. I won't let him touch you. I promise."

"Don't, Mary, please don't let them."

So that even when Doctor Crighton-Browne entered the room, before he crossed the carpet, talking in the soothing voice he used on his damaged patients, she had begun to weep, to cry shrilly like a rabbit in a trap, to throw herself about in her chair and the two doctors had hurriedly retreated to the door.

He came three more times, each time doing his best to get close to her, to win her confidence and trust but it seemed to do more harm than good so, sadly, he had gone away again. It was her husband he felt sorry for, he told Doctor Bennett, because the poor man looked as though he were going the same way as his wife in his despairing anguish. Perhaps if they were to get her into the home – he did not say asylum – he had in York he might be able to help her. But her husband had simply gone mad, saying that if that's all he could bloody well suggest, put her away with the insane, then he could send in his bill and get the hell out of his home!

18

Milly galloped down the drive at Thornley Green, aware that her mother-in-law would be watching her from her drawing-room window with vast disapproval. The dowager Lady Thornley had made it quite clear that it was high time her son's wife was pregnant again and she was convinced that while Milly rode that wild horse she was hardly likely to do so. In her opinion!

The animal Milly rode was Hugh's, an ebony gelding with a white star between his velvety eyes, a strong horse, high-spirited, which the groom had been reluctant to let her take out, saying he was a gentleman's horse and would she not ride Flame, the sorrel she had brought with her when she married his lordship, but she had laughed and tossed back the silken curtain of her hair, which was not even tied up with a bit of ribbon, Jack noticed. But worse than that was what she had on. Ladies, real ladies, rode side-saddle and wore riding habits that accommodated this exercise, a full skirt underneath which they wore tight, kid trousers so that in the event of an accident, or a high wind, should the skirt blow back all was decent beneath. Lady Thornley had discarded her skirt and was preparing to leap into the saddle, not side-saddle, mind, but astride the gelding, in just the trousers! She had on a shirt, surely not her own for it was very mannish, the buttons undone at the neck and halfway down her chest, so that Jack could see the tops of her breasts. Bloody hell, he told Stan later, he could feel himself getting stiff just looking at them, for they were on display for all to see. She set the gelding to a gallop before she had left the stable yard and with her hair streaming out behind her had gone full tilt round the side of the house and off up the bloody drive.

It was almost the end of September but the morning progressed, as warm as a midsummer's day. Though Milly Thornley did not notice, for she was not interested in such things, the summer flowers were dying away, roses, phlox and delphinium becoming seed heads among which Gibson and Tyson, the gardeners, were busy. They watched her headlong dash by with open mouths and much shaking of the head. The oaks in the great park were beginning to bronze and swallows were leaving, but it was still glorious with chrysanthemums and red-hot pokers coming into flower in the crisper air. There had been a hint of frost earlier on, Gibson had remarked to Tyson, glinting on the lawns. Blackbirds stabbed away at the fallen apples in the orchard but none of this concerned Milly as she rode headlong between the opened gates of Thornley Green and turned in the direction of Lantern Hill. She galloped madly across the bridge that divided Higher Dam from Parr Mill Dam, badly startling two labourers who were clearing the ditches alongside the lane to which the bridge led.

"Gerron, yer daft sod," one of them muttered, not so that she could hear, of course, since she was Lord Thornley's wife, but they could not stop staring after her, none the less, for she really was a sight for sore eyes, as one said to the other. Her tits hanging out for all to see and them legs of hers which looked as though they had nothing on them!

She didn't keep to the lanes but jumped a hedge into the woodland that ran alongside them, the early autumn sunshine turning its summer beauty to a soft and mellow gold. Trees, which had carried a great and bountiful burden of leaves of every shade of green from the palest to the deepest emerald, were now transformed to amber, copper, rose and flame.

Leaves drifted on to her head as she dodged between the tree trunks and the animal's hooves crushed wood sorrel and anemone. Rabbits cowered among the fern and woodcock and pheasant hid in their nests, for this was Lord Thornley's land where he and his guests shot in season.

But Milly saw none of this as she dodged between the tree trunks, at great danger, it seemed, not only to herself but the beautiful animal she rode. Milly did not see beauty in nature, despite her upbringing among those who did. She admired a good-looking man, a costly gown, a magnificent jewel, but the loveliness of the autumn day, the woodland, the sky, even the horse she rode and the impeccably bred hound dog which belonged to Hugh and which raced beside her, she discovered, meant nothing to her. She was in her element here, for all her life Milly Goodwin had courted peril, risking her neck from an early age on any horse that was not tame, gentle or easy to handle. Branches hanging low from close-packed trees snatched at her hair, which flew like a banner behind her, but it was not until the trees began to thin out and fields appeared, fields that belonged to her father and in which men were tending the harvest, that she drew the gelding in and slowed to a trot, then a walk. If her father saw her he would create such a fuss at her appearance she would never hear the end of it so she simply walked on past the entrance to Lantern Hill and took the lane that led to Edge Bottom House.

As Jack's had done, Harry's eyes were out on stalks as Miss Milly, on the ebony gelding, which he happened to know belonged to her husband, rode into the yard. She threw her legs – sweet Christ, was she naked? – over the pommel and slid to the ground. The gelding, whom she had ridden hard, was in a lather, his head hanging, subjugated, it seemed, by this woman and could you help but admire her, for she really was a courageous rider.

"They're in the garden, m'lady," he told her, his face ready to stretch into an intimate smile, for he and Milly Goodwin, as she had been then, had got into all sorts of scrapes in their childhood.

"Thanks, Harry." And she grinned at him, for though he was but a groom he was an attractive man and she was always aware of an attractive man.

They were sitting further out on the lawn this day, for beneath the oak tree and out of the sun it was too cool. Beth, her face placid, blank, Milly would have said, was seated in her usual basket chair, her usual bit of sewing in her hands, and Milly wondered what it was she was constantly stitching. Mary sat beside her and in the perambulator, which so far Beth had never touched, lay Milly's daughter, thankfully, Milly noticed, with a light blanket pulled up to her waist. She was asleep, her long lashes resting on her flushed cheeks, her rosy mouth slightly parted, her dark hair, so like Hugh's, tied up with a white ribbon to match the dress she wore. She was a beautiful child, Milly admitted coolly, wondering why it was she felt nothing for her own daughter, but secretly knowing that it was because she could not bear anything that was not perfect and Alexandra was not perfect. Far from it. She had not herself seen the deformed leg her daughter had been born with but just the thought of a foot with no toes on it was enough to make her shudder. A rough-haired dog lay protectively beside the perambulator, raising his head and beginning to growl at the hound which had followed Milly, but with a shout to Harry to come and fetch Hugh's dog, which he did, the terrier subsided, his ears twitching, his nose twitching, his eyes still suspicious.

Beth looked up as she approached and for a moment she began to struggle with something, ready to leap from her chair and run.

"It's all right, darling," Milly heard Mary say. "It's Lady Thornley." Her eyes, as were Jane's, were on Lady Thornley's buff kid trousers and it was apparently the sight of these that had panicked Beth. Mind you, despite the trousers Lady Thornley was eternally female, her flaunting breasts, her hair hanging in a tangled cloud to her waist, her gracefully swaying figure proclaiming her provocative femininity.

"Beth, are you still lolling about in that damn chair?" Milly declared. "And I never thought to see the day when you would be satisfied with a bit of sewing in your hands. I happen to know Mother and Laura are in Manchester attending one of their interminable suffragist things so why aren't you with them? You were very keen once, as I remember." She flung herself down in a spare chair and glanced about her, keeping her eyes from the perambulator, vowing that the moment the child showed signs of waking she'd be off.

But despite her totally self-absorbed nature, Milly was shocked and concerned that her sister was still apparently *wallowing* – yes, that was the word she would use in describing her sister – in the self-pity she herself thought appalling. Dear God, she had gone through it once with Hugh and surely, given a little backbone, her sister could pull herself together and get on with her life. It was said she wouldn't let her husband near her, for God's sake, for servants' gossip travelled and even poor old Doctor Bennett had given up on her after fetching that brain doctor from York and doing little good with it.

"I . . . I didn't feel up to it, Milly. The journey and then . . . well, Mother will tell me all about it. The speaker is Emmeline Pankhurst who lives in Manchester. She is only thirty and comes from a radical political background and is—"

"Yes, yes," Milly interrupted impatiently. "So why haven't you gone with Mother and Laura to hear her speak? Not that I'd be seen dead at one of those affairs but—"

"Please, Milly."

"Oh, all right, have it your own way but I really think you should make some effort to . . . to get over this thing, if not for your own sake then for Archie's. You never entertain, so I've heard, nor are even asked any more to parties and dinners. I know, why don't you come to Thornley Green next week? Hugh's friend Johnny Cassell is coming up from Leicestershire, bringing his bride-to-be and her parents. It will be a bit boring and I'd be glad of a bit—"

Beth stood up abruptly, beginning to shake, her head moving from side to side in horrified denial. Mary rose with her and reached out her hand but Beth seemed to be blind to it and Milly watched in amazement.

"For God's sake, Beth, it's only us and the Cassells. Hardly enough to send you into . . ." Suddenly she softened and she rose to her feet and put her arms about her sister. Milly was often amazed at how different she and Beth were, for after all they were sisters. Twins, even, but whereas Beth was sweet-natured, gentle, serenely lovely, shy sometimes, a good woman who had put her own life in danger to help the maid sitting next to her, Milly Thornley was self-willed, passionate, energetic, loving strong excitement. She was self-assertive with a fierce and undisciplined temper but she was genuinely concerned about her sister. She had heard from her mother of Beth's aversion to anything in trousers, and why it was so, but she had not realised how badly affected her sister was.

"It's all right, darling," she murmured, "but really, you should not let what a man did to you affect you like this. Dear God, I know Archie's a bloody saint but believe me he's the exception to the rule." For a moment the luminous golden brown eyes of Todd Woodruff invaded her vision and she was astonished at the soft feeling of . . . of what? She didn't know what it was that filled her heart. Todd was a man and therefore not to be trusted, which was what she was trying to tell Beth, but somehow she found she could not put him in the same category as Hugh, or Hugh's officer friends since he was not the same at all. Now what had made her think that? she wondered, then became conscious of her sister shivering in her arms and she stepped back, laughing.

"Take no notice of me, darling. I'm not a nice lady at all, you should know that, but I'm fond of you and it really irritates me to see you like this. But never mind, send that maid of yours for some tea and then I must get back."

Beth was reluctant to let Mary out of her sight but, trembling, she sat down and stared rigidly at Tucker and his lad who were at the far end of the garden doing something to the creeping plant that twined about the arched gateway. They knew better than to approach Mrs Beth, but sometimes it was hard with her sitting there to find something to do far enough away so as not to alarm her.

"Won't . . . won't you look at Alex, Milly?" she asked hesitantly, making a determined attempt not to turn her head and search for Mary.

"Perhaps another day, Beth. In fact, I'm not sure I should stay for tea. Hugh will be back from . . . from wherever the hell he gets to and he will expect me to be there." Which was a lie, for Hugh Thornley didn't give a damn where his wife was. As long as her father's money poured into his bank account he was perfectly content with his life. He would want an heir soon, he had told his mistress carelessly, she would understand that, but in the meanwhile life was very pleasant. Alicia was very accommodating and, what was more important, she was free from the venereal disease that had laid him low last year. Soon he would allow that old sod of a doctor to examine him, then he would approach Milly and get another child on her. A son, he hoped, giving not a thought to the lovely little girl who lay in her perambulator in the warm garden at Edge Bottom House.

He crept in through the open doorway which Mary held ajar for him, the candle in his hand protected by a glass sleeve which formed a night-light and diffused the glow. He moved slowly across the deep pile of the carpet of the bedroom he had once shared with his wife and when he reached the bed, looking down at her where she lay sleeping, he knelt beside it. He studied her face, the delicate arch to her coppery eyebrows, the flush on her cheek, the parting of her mouth which was as rosy as Alexandra's and felt something start to thump and shake inside him as though his heart had come loose. The hurt was in him sorely and constantly. Although she lived in his house he felt that he would never see her again. She was no longer there for him to see. She had fallen out of his life, ripping a jagged hole in the fabric of it. The pain inside him was terrible and was going to get worse with every bitter moment of realising that as far as he was concerned she was dead. He and Noah had tried everything, the best doctor recommended by John Bennett, keeping their distance from her as her fear of men showed no sign of abating, but in all these months she was just the same. Moving like a dispossessed ghost about the house, clinging to Mary as the only safe thing in her shattered world. She was polite with her mother and the female servants, with Jane who cared for the child, but though she had longed for it, longed to care for Milly's damaged little daughter, she took only nominal interest in her.

He watched her for five minutes while from the doorway Mary watched him, for she knew if Beth woke up and found him hanging over her God alone knew what place she might be flung into, a place from which she might never come back. This was a ritual they went through every night and it broke her heart, for Mr Goodwin loved this woman with a depth and feeling not often seen between husband and wife. She knew he was slowly dying of that love, which sounded fanciful but somehow they were all more worried about him, strange as it might seem, than they were about Beth.

Archie leaned forward and breathed in the sweet smell of his wife's breath and the scent of some soap she used which always hung about her. Her hair had been brushed but as she lay in sleep it had fanned out about her head and picking up a strand he brought it carefully to his mouth. Then, the first time he had ever done so, and bringing a gasp of horror to Mary's lips, he placed a kiss, a touch lighter than a butterfly's wing, on Beth's cheek. He was amazed when a small smile lifted the corners of her mouth and she murmured something that sounded like his name. Then she turned away and continued in her dreamless sleep.

He crept back to the door and when it was quietly closed he swept the astonished Mary into his arms. "Did you see that?" he asked her exultantly. "She actually smiled and said my name." He took Mary's hands and was ready to dance her up the hallway but she escaped from him and from his rapture, patting his arm. She didn't tell him that Beth often begged her not to allow him to come near her since she knew she couldn't bear it.

That night Hugh Thornley stalked into his wife's bedroom as she was having her hair brushed by her maid, Harry Preston's sister, Sally. They were both so startled Sally dropped the hairbrush and as she bent to pick it up knocked a cut-crystal scent bottle to the floor. As it fell on the carpet it didn't break but the scent spilled and filled the air with the expensive French perfume Milly favoured.

"You can go," he told the maid, and she did, escaping down the stairs, then wondered where she should go *to*, for she was not very friendly with any of the servants at Thornley Green. Because they were in the employ of a baron they thought themselves to be a cut above her whose father and brother were both grooms. And what would she say even if they were interested? she asked herself, so she slipped back upstairs and past her mistress's door, making her way to her own small bedroom at the top of the house. As she passed Lady Thornley's bedroom she heard her beginning to shriek and there was the sound of flesh on flesh as though he had hit her, then it became quiet and because there was nothing else she could do Sally crept up the uncarpeted stairs that led to the maids' quarters and into her own bedroom. There were many rooms for the servants at Thornley Green, for once upon a time, in the days of the present baron's grandfather, she had heard, who had been a good man, a good master, wealthy and influential, there had been plenty of servants. It was the present baron's father who had lost most of his inheritance. Now the money was back again, brought by Milly Goodwin who, Sally thought, was getting the hiding of her life in her pretty bed-room.

He raped her. She had thought she would put up with it since she knew quite well that the day would come when Hugh would want his heir to be conceived and she had also come increasingly to believe that she was already pregnant with Todd's child, so did she have any choice but to give way to Hugh? Of course she didn't, but when he stripped her and pushed her on to her back on the bed, removing the quilted dressing-gown he himself wore, she began to fight. She knew she shouldn't, that she should let him have his way, for how could she bear a child when she had not slept with her husband for many months, but something in her was repulsed by him. She and Todd were savage with one another sometimes when they made love and they both seemed to glory in it but this was different. Hugh was just as startlingly handsome as on the first day she had met him, and wanted him. His lifestyle had not as yet affected his looks though she knew he drank heavily and barely got to his bed before dawn, but she just could not stand him to touch her and she told him so.

"Get off me, you bastard," she screamed, hitting out at him, clawing at his face with her nails, but he was strong and merely laughed, catching both her wrists with one hand and forcing her arms above her head.

"Now then, my pet, stop this nonsense, though I must admit

to rather enjoying a bout of fisticuffs with you. It makes your breasts jiggle in the most enticing way and . . . whoa, whoa, girl, mind where you're putting those knees. We don't want to damage the old cock before it's done its duty, do we? Now lie still, or, if you don't mind being hurt, continue to struggle as you are doing. I find I am enjoying myself enormously."

With his free hand he struck her a cracking blow across her face, whipping her head sideways into the pillow, and for a moment she was stunned. His lips fastened on hers, drawing them cruelly into his mouth, biting, his teeth against hers and her stomach rose and churned but she was helpless in his grasp. His hand reached down to her vagina and fiercely he drove his fingers into it, then, with the full force of his body, his penis followed, going so deep inside her she felt as though it might break through into whatever lay above her womb. He pounded into her, like a hammer driving in stakes, and each time her body shuddered and shook and she felt herself beginning to lose consciousness.

"Now then, my pet, don't you slip away. I want you to enjoy every moment of this and let me tell you it will continue every night until you prove to me that you are pregnant. I shall need that bloody pet doctor of yours to tell me, so just behave yourself and allow me to service you as the bull services the cows in the pasture on Home Farm."

She glared up at him, her hatred so virulent he almost recoiled, then she spat full in his face, leaving a trickle of saliva across his forehead and down his cheek.

"You bloody little hellion," he roared, then punched her so severely on the point of her chin she fell away into a black hole.

She came to some time later, alone, aching, bruised, bloody, she was sure, and with a superhuman effort managed to stagger off the bed to the bell at the side of the fireplace. She pulled it weakly and then crawled like an animal on all fours back to the bed where she pulled the sheet up to her chin.

"Send Sally," she mumbled to Polly who answered the bell and hovered at the door, but her mouth was so swollen it seemed Polly couldn't understand her. She came forward into the room.

"Pardon, m'lady?" she questioned.

"Sally . . . get Sally."

"She's gone ter bed, m'lady." Polly tried to see what was wrong with her ladyship, for something was, but Milly pulled the sheet even higher.

"Get her."

"Very well, m'lady," Polly said, peering in the candlelit gloom in her ladyship's direction, wishing that his lordship would have that there new electric light put in, as he had promised, then she could have got a better look at her mistress. She backed out of the room and drifted down the stairs to the kitchen, not hurrying, for there was no one in this house who bothered whether you hurried or not.

"She wants Sally," she announced, "but she's not here, is she?"

"You'd best look for her, I suppose," their new chef said from the comfort of the armchair he had had installed by the enormous kitchen range.

"Well, I don't know where she gets to, do I?" Polly said peevishly.

"Try her bedroom. She's that stuck up she'd rather be on her own than with us."

When Sally, summoned by the reluctant Polly, knocked on her ladyship's door there was no answer, for Milly Thornley had drifted off again into a semi-conscious state. Sally peeped in cautiously, for she had no wish to be confronted by that mad devil her mistress was married to.

"Miss Milly," she whispered, some instinct telling her there was trouble here and after all she and Miss Milly had known one another for a long time. It seemed the right thing to do to call her by her Christian name. She approached the bed, gasping when she saw the state of her mistress, and without thought for consequences she leaped for the bell and rang it.

"What's up now?" Polly moaned when she entered her ladyship's bedroom and was amazed when Sally Preston took her by the arm and began to tell her exactly what she must do.

"Here, I'm not your servant," she began, but the grip on her arm tightened and she jumped to do what Sally told her. Hot water at once, fresh towels and either Stan or Jack was to ride into St Helens and get Doctor Bennett at once.

"Her ladyship has had an accident," Sally told her smoothly, "so run like hell or I won't be responsible for my actions."

19

"What the bloody hell has he done to you?"

"I shouldn't have come. If he finds us here how are we to explain?"

"It never bothered him before. He was never here."

"He is now. Every night he—"

"Don't, my darling. By God, I've a mind to call him out."

"Don't be silly, Todd. He's my husband and is within the law in exercising . . . conjugal rights. When I resisted he went ahead anyway, hence the face which I daren't show in public. As soon as he has got me pregnant he will leave me alone, he says, since he is still bewitched by Lady Bramhall. I've waited here every day for you to come so that I could warn you. We must not see each other for a while and quite honestly I don't know how I'm to get through it. Without you, I mean. Oh, I know I laugh a lot and pretend that . . . that it's nothing more than . . . than a dalliance, that we both like it as it is but . . ."

"What are you saying, Milly?" Todd Woodruff took Milly's hand between his own, bringing it to his lips and kissing it with a tenderness he had never let her see before. He had begun this dalliance, no more than a flirtatious episode which all the officers indulged in, but it had developed into more than that though neither of them would admit it, not even to themselves. Milly Thornley was exciting, in and out of bed. She was great fun, finding amusement in the smallest thing and Todd had been enchanted with her, scarcely able to believe his luck that she had chosen him as a lover. But this was different. Hugh

Thornley was a brute, a man with a vicious temper, an uncertain temper, charming, of course, as long as no one stood in his way. And he would not countenance his wife taking a lover, not while he was still hoping for a son, an heir to the Thornley name. He must be the only one to lie with his wife. Otherwise how would he know the child was his and not some other man's? It seemed he knew nothing of Todd and Milly's affair and had now decided, with his wife restored to full health, and presumably the disease he had passed on to her last time cleared up, this was to be the time.

The sunlight fell on him and Milly as they lay in a shaft of it, their backs to the gnarled trunk of an enormous hornbeam tree. The roots formed a deep nest rising up on either side of them and mosses created a soft, velvet bed on which to lie and had it not been for the tall roan that was tethered nearby, a passer-by would not have seen them. He had his arm about her shoulders and her head rested on his chest. He put a finger under her chin and lifted her face to his, studying her lovely golden eyes, one of which was set in a fading bruise, yellow and green with a touch of purple at its centre. Her jaw was grazed, but it was healing and about her throat were marks that looked dangerously like those made by fingers.

Milly had slipped out of the side door of Thornley Green, walking rapidly across the park, praying she would meet none of the outside servants, the gardeners and woodsmen who had been employed to restore Thornley Green to its former glory, slipping into Rough Wood which lay beside Higher Dam. If somebody should see her she was ready with a tale of needing a walk, a breath of fresh air and, after all, she was his lordship's wife and could do whatever, and go wherever she pleased. Only Sally knew she had gone and would keep the indoor servants at bay, saying her mistress was having breakfast in bed and should not be disturbed. Sally had been her fervent ally since the night, nearly a fortnight ago now, when Hugh had knocked her about so badly. She had accompanied her to Claughton Street, the pair of them darting across the park to the gates and across two fields until they reached Moss Bank where they had hired a cab to take them to St Helens. They had fortunately found Laura and John Bennett at home, both of them being sworn to secrecy.

"I'll tell Hugh when I'm ready," she had said, watching the doubtful expressions that crossed the faces of her mother's friends. "And Mother and Father, so please, now that I know I am not . . . infected I can rest easy. Please, tell no one." The baby would come early, as the first one had done, she was aware of that, but would be full term, and, she prayed, a healthy son.

"I want to kill him," Todd snarled, his usually good-humoured face twisted into a mask of loathing. "To get a son he is raping you."

"Oh, I've stopped fighting, Todd. There's no point to it. He has his way whatever I do and I am less damaged if I don't resist. Besides which, I am already pregnant. I have confirmed it with Doctor Bennett. I didn't dare have him over to the house and he confirmed it. I wanted to be sure I am not . . . not infected as I was last time and he was able to reassure me, so you see, if I was able to tell Hugh, which I shall in a few weeks, that he has succeeded in getting me with child, he could return to Lady Bramhall and leave me in peace."

Todd had sat up slowly as she spoke, his face ashen as the golden amber drained away. His eyes, the same colour as Milly's, were wide and disbelieving. He stared at her in horror, for how could she possibly have become pregnant in the two weeks since he had last seen her? But gradually, his mouth opening and closing in a comical way, it slowly dawned on him what she was telling him.

Milly began to laugh. "Yes, my pet, it's yours, since I've lain with no one but you for the past three months and—"

"But you cannot possibly stay with him, Milly. Not now. Sweet Christ, who knows what he might do to you?"

"Nothing he has not done before, Todd. I am strong and healthy and though I loathe the very touch of him I must put up with it for the sake of the child."

"*My child!*"

"Hugh's child, my darling, for it must have a name."

Todd stood up and began to fling himself about the small clearing, badly startling the roan which did its best to edge away from him, dragging at the reins which were tied to a branch. Todd was not in his uniform but wore a riding jacket and buff breeches, tall, polished riding boots and a cravat tied carelessly round his neck. His hair was uncovered and in the sunlight it glowed like gold-streaked mahogany, straight and thick. He pushed a hand through it, turning again and again, his other hand on his hip, his boots crackling on the carpet of crisp leaves. It was October and the summer had gone now and the many delightful hours they had spent in this clearing must come to an end, not just because of the circumstances, but because of the weather.

Milly watched him and felt the strangest sensation in her chest, a quite painful sensation that she could put no name to. He was so distressed and his distress hurt her, which was amazing, for never in her life had Milly Thornley considered any one else's feelings. This man had put . . . no, had given some meaning to her life, she wasn't even sure how, she only knew that the past three months had been contented ones and when did Milly Thornley admit to being *content*?

Todd whirled to face her. "Darling, come away with me. You can't stay with him, not now. We could go to . . . to . . ."

"Where?"

"I don't know. Anywhere away from that brute. I won't have a moment's peace knowing—"

"And how will you support me? Us?"

"I'll find work."

"No, darling, no. This baby, our baby could be the next baron, the seventeenth of the line and—"

"Bugger that. Sod that, Milly, this is my child and I shall say so to everybody I know. I will not have—"

Milly got to her feet, shaking out her skirt and smoothing back her hair which had become tangled in the bark of the tree. "I shall deny it, Todd."

"I see, you cannot bear to give up being Lady Thornley, even if it means being brutalised by that bastard. You are to bear my child and pass it off as Hugh Thornley's. I thought better of you, Milly, I really did. Whatever else you were you were always honest."

"Don't talk such blithering rubbish, Todd Woodruff. I am married to Hugh and I am to have a child. What good would it do, to you, or the baby, if I was calmly to tell him that the child is not his, but yours? Do you honestly think he would say, 'Very well, Milly, off you go with Todd Woodruff and I hope you live happily ever after'? He would kill me, and then you, and somehow he would get away with it. He has many dubious friends. Well, not exactly friends but strange men he knows who would be glad to see me off, and you too, for a few bob. Please, Todd, do this thing for me. You know you would be putting me in immense danger if you were to confront Hugh. I wouldn't have told you but . . . well, somehow I wanted you to know that this is your child, our child and not Hugh's. That we had . . . oh, I don't know . . ."

He sat down and pulled her down beside him, taking her into his arms, resting his cheek on her dark, silken hair. He held her for a minute or two then turned her face to his again.

"You do care something about me then, Milly. It's not just . . . a bed thing."

But Milly Thornley was not going to admit to having finer feelings for Todd Woodruff, even if she did. She didn't really know why she had told him that the child was his. Some daft notion she had got into her head that he had a right to know, which really *was* daft, for when all was said and done what difference did it make?

She sat up and grinned at him. "Now then, my darling, don't start getting all romantic on me. It will be winter soon and far too cold to meet out here but until then, let's pretend that this is my bed and do to each other what we do there. Now promise me you won't come to the house again, unless it's with the others and your call is official, so to speak. I'll get word to you should I be able to get out here but in the meanwhile, undo these buttons for me and put your hands on what you find there. And you might be interested in this," lifting her skirt to reveal that she wore no drawers!

It had snowed in the night and the garden was a fairytale delight of dazzling whiteness, unfamiliar and yet well known. The snow was thick and fresh, unmarred except by Boy's footprints, who had gone frolicking across the garden when he was let out first thing. He had nosed the snow and made them laugh as he tried to throw it in the air. Then it had frozen and a hoar frost had turned every twig and blade of grass to sparkle separately, hung with diamonds which, as the sun came up, pink and glorious, overlaid the whiteness with its own colour. The world was so crisp you could almost hear it crackle, and Olly had reported that he had had to go very carefully on the road from Lantern Hill to Edge Bottom House. In fact he was surprised that Mrs Goodwin had turned out on such a day.

It was almost Christmas and Abby Goodwin was taking tea with her daughter at Edge Bottom House when a sweating groom passed in the message that Lady Thornley was unwell and could her mother come at once to Thornley Green. The letter was written by Sally Preston.

For no reason at all, that anyone else could see, Beth began to flutter about the drawing-room, standing up and then sitting down again, cowering back in to the cushions on the sofa, looking round her for Mary, who was quietly sitting at the back of the room by the conservatory door with a bit of sewing in her hands. As though the sight of Mary calmly getting on with whatever she was doing calmed her, she picked up her own scrap of sewing and, like Milly before her, Abby wondered irritably what it was Beth constantly sewed on. Sometimes, though she knew she shouldn't since Beth had gone through a terrible experience, Abby wondered – as they all did at one time or another, and with impatience – why it was her daughter had turned into this pathetic creature who seemed incapable of putting that tragic event behind her, as Mary had done, and getting on with her life. Poor Archie, who had been kindness itself to her, was turning before their eyes into an old man. And could you blame him? Well, they had all done their best as he had done but no good had come of it.

She stood up. "I must go. Ever since she gave us the news that she was pregnant again I have worried in case she should contract that awful disease from Hugh. I couldn't bear to go through that again. Ring the bell, will you, darling, and ask Olly to bring round the carriage and could someone be sent to the works to fetch your father. I need him with me if I'm to enter that house again. Oh, dear, I do hope Hugh won't be there, for I do believe your father might attack him again. It is well known in St Helens where he got that scar on his cheek."

The baby, brought down to see her grandmother, sat on the floor, a bright red wooden brick in her hands on which she had been fiercely chewing but at the sound of the alarm in her grandmother's voice she became still, her eyes enormous in her round and rosy face, her lip ready to tremble. At once Mary swooped down and picked her up, patting her back and resting the baby's cheek against her own. In the flurry of Morna running to fetch Mrs Goodwin's fur wrap and getting her into her carriage with the rugs her husband thought necessary, the frantic sound of galloping hooves as Mr Goodwin came flying up the lane, endangering his horse's legs on the frozen snow, and Olly "giddy-upping" to the horses, the carriage lurching off in the direction of Thornley Green, Beth was overlooked and for several minutes she was all alone in the warm and comfortable drawing-room. She continued to stitch, her smooth head bent over her work, but she suddenly found she could not put in the next minute stitch, for her hands were trembling and she didn't really know why. She was safe in her own drawing-room. There were servants in the hall beyond the open door, she could hear their voices, women's voices, for there were no men in this household except those who worked in the stable yard or the gardens.

Slowly she raised her head and looked fearfully about her but there was nothing there, nothing but the dear, familiar things with which she had grown up. The piano where she and Milly had learned to play, or at least Milly had been persuaded to try to play. The pictures on the wall which her mother had chosen years ago, flowers on the piano top, toys which Alexandra had left scattered about the room and the door to the conservatory which stood open and from which came the fragrance of the exotic flowers that grew there and the sound of the singing birds chirruping their little hearts out. An enormous fire crackled in the grate and she could even hear, with the drawing-room and kitchen doors standing open, Mrs Kyle giving "what for" to Dottie. Boy lay at her feet, his muzzle on his paws, twitching lightly in his sleep as he dreamed of chasing rabbits and there was absolutely nothing to fear. Nothing! But where was Mary? Why hadn't she come back? Perhaps she had taken Alexandra back to the nursery, that was it, and she would be here in a minute and until then she would watch the door . . . the door. And when it was flung violently back, hitting the dainty writing desk that stood behind it, she began to scream. At least she thought she screamed but no sound came from her and she knew quite positively that they had come for her again and there was no way she could call for help, for her voice had gone along with the baby they had torn from her body. If she sat perfectly still, perhaps they would not notice her . . . well, not *they* but the man who had come to an abrupt stop in the doorway. He was a stranger to her. A tall, extremely thin man with a close beard and his hair wild about his head as though he had ridden far without a hat. He wore an enormous cape lined with wool and underneath it was a decent suit. His boots were well polished but encrusted with snow.

"Beth," he said in a voice so low she could barely hear him. "Are you all right? There was a message for your father to come at once and when I heard I followed him. I thought you might need . . . Please, please don't be frightened. You must know I wouldn't hurt you," for she was staring at him with great horror-filled eyes. He took a step into the room and was devastated when she cowered even further back into the depth of the sofa. He put out a hand and she looked at it as though it were a cobra about to strike, like a rabbit caught by a stoat, his beloved wife who had not spoken to him, nor he to her since May.

"Won't you tell me what has happened? Why was your father summoned? If it's not you, who is it? No, don't cringe from me like that. You and I have known one another since the day you were born. I was there when you came into the world and from that day to this I have loved you. I would die to save you a moment's hurt so won't you talk to me, or let me talk to you? There is only you and me here. No, no, darling, don't be frightened. Mary is near and will come and take you to . . . to wherever you want to go if you ring the bell. Look, I shall stand here in the doorway and will come no nearer. Just tell me what has happened. Is it Milly?"

Somehow she managed to nod to this man who had such a

kind voice, such lovely blue eyes which were like the blue of the sky or the forget-me-nots that grew in the garden in the summer. And what he said was true. She had only to reach for the bell and before he could take a step into the room every servant in the house would come running.

"Has she started with her baby? Is that it?"

The man, Archie, smiled such a sweet smile some tiny core of her inside her chest where a big black stone had rested for so long now melted. In the hallway Mary, who had returned Alexandra to the nursery, stood motionless, ready to dart to her mistress's side if she was needed but Mr Archie seemed to be talking to Mrs Beth and what's more Mrs Beth seemed to be listening.

She cleared her throat. "Mother . . . there was a message to say . . . Milly was unwell."

"She has gone to Thornley Green?"

"Yes."

"And your father?"

"She . . . she didn't want to go alone."

"Of course not." His smile deepened and he chanced another small step into the room. "It's very cold out. I wonder if there's a chance I might have a cup of hot chocolate? Would you mind that? Perhaps you might have one with me while we wait for your parents to return. Will you ring the bell?"

Hesitantly she put out her hand and when the man – it was Archie, something inside told her – sat down in the chair nearest the door, she wondered whether to ask him to come closer to the fire, for he looked half frozen. In the hallway Mary put her face into her hands and wept, for surely something momentous had just happened here so that when Morna hurried from the kitchen to the drawing-room in response to the bell she almost knocked her over.

"Mary, love, what's up?" she asked, putting her hand on

Mary's arm but Mary merely nodded in the direction of the drawing-room.

They were agog in the kitchen. Mrs Beth sitting quite calmly by the fire talking to Mr Archie, Morna reported. Two cups of hot chocolate ordered and though nothing much was being said, for it was obvious Mr Archie didn't want to frighten his wife after all this time, Mrs Beth seemed quite calm. The width of the room separated them but at least she was accepting him and, dear God, where might that lead? Not a man in the household had spoken to Mrs Beth since that dreadful day, even Doctor Bennett finding it difficult to help her. That doctor – from what Dottie had unwisely called the loony bin, earning herself a cuff round the ear from Morna – had given her up and now she was sitting, if not exactly calmly but at least without screaming her head off, Morna reported, drinking hot chocolate with her husband.

"What they talkin' about?" Dottie, who would never learn, asked curiously.

"None o' your business, girl. Get on with them pots."

Archie didn't know what to talk about, since he was aware they had reached a crossroads here, perhaps a turning point in their lives together, a new beginning which must be approached cautiously, with great care. He did not even dare stand up to remove his greatcoat in case it should startle her. One thing he did notice was that she did not pick up her sewing which, so he had been told, had become almost a part of her hands. She stared into the fire, her lovely face pensive and the love in him could scarcely be contained. He wanted to fling himself across the room and kneel before her, put his head in her lap and weep, to hold her, to kiss her rosy lips which were so like the baby's, to look into her sweet, innocent face and see something of what had been there eight months ago.

"I wonder how Milly is," she said softly, turning to look at him and his heart turned over at the marvel of it.

"Would you like me to ride over there and find out? I could be there and back in an hour. Or perhaps send Harry."

"Would he have to come in here? Harry, I mean?" Although for some reason she felt reasonably safe with . . . with Archie, she was not sure whether another man might not . . . not, what for God's sake? she asked herself impatiently. She had begun to wonder where she had been for all these months and *why*? Oh, she knew she had suffered at the hands of those monsters, as Mary had done, but she was safe here, wasn't she . . . with Archie.

"No, not if you don't want him to. I can speak to him in the yard."

"Perhaps . . . that would be better."

"Shall I send Mary to you?"

"If you would. And perhaps you could let me know."

"Of course." She was speaking to him in the polite tones one uses with strangers but at least she was speaking. It seemed she couldn't quite face Harry but she appeared to have accepted him, her husband, and he wanted to get down on his knees and thank the God he was not awfully sure he believed in for bringing her back to him. At least part of the way.

As he hurried along the hallway towards the kitchen he found Mary leaning against the wall. "Oh, sir," she whispered, for she knew as well as him that a great stride had been made today in the recovery of Beth Goodwin.

They took Milly Thornley back to Lantern Hill, sending Olly on the swiftest horse in the stable for Doctor Bennett. Hugh had beaten her so severely they all believed she would lose her baby.

"The man's insane," her father raged, as he roamed the hallway and landings of Lantern Hill while Doctor Bennett did his best to put his daughter together again. Her husband had split open her cheek to the bone, a wound that had to be stitched and would leave a scar for the rest of her days. Her right arm was broken where he had twisted it up behind her back and she was bruised and torn in places the good doctor did not dare tell her parents. But there was no sign of the disease that had brought her so low earlier that year. She was a strong, healthy woman and would survive, and so would the child who was kicking furiously inside her.

"It's a miracle, Noah, that she did not lose the baby but she seems determined that this one will live and be healthy."

They were astonished when Todd Woodruff turned up a couple of hours after she had been put to bed at Lantern Hill, begging to know how she was, haunting the place until it was decided she was in no immediate danger. Then he left quietly, asking Mrs Goodwin if she would mind if he called again tomorrow.

20

"I want to go to Lantern Hill, Mary. Will you ask Harry to fetch the carriage to the front of the house? I must find out how Milly is this morning. I know that Doctor Bennett said yesterday that she would be fine when her cheek heals and her broken arm mends but I feel I must go and see for myself. And, then there is the . . . the other thing . . ."

Here she gulped, for what was in her mind was the terrible disease Milly had suffered before Alexandra was born, which brought back the memory of that dreadful day when . . . when . . . she and Mary had been . . . been examined for that same disease. But something had happened to her yesterday, she didn't know what, edging her out of the safe place she had hidden in and though it was very frightening to be so exposed, she didn't want to go back to it. She had been quite surprised to find that she had been disappointed when Archie had returned to tell her that Milly was going to be fine, she was to stay at Lantern Hill for the present and she was not to worry, but he could not stay since he must get back to the works. She had no idea of the struggle Archie had had with himself as to what was the best thing he could do. He wanted desperately to stay and talk to his wife who seemed willing to talk to him for the first time in months, but at the same time he was afraid of alarming her, overdoing it, and sending her back into that terrible state of silent apathy in which she had wandered for the past eight months. So he had smiled at her, yearning to take her in his arms and remove that expression of vulnerability from her face, but had left the house, climbed on to his horse and made his way back to the works.

"Perhaps you would like to dine with Mr Archie this evening?" Mary had asked her hesitantly but Beth had shied away from that idea like a frightened horse and Mary had said no more. Her young mistress had made enormous strides today. She was sorry that it had taken a disaster of such proportions to make it happen, for she had heard Lady Thornley was in an awful mess, especially her face which, it was whispered, would have a scar to match that of her husband.

So Beth had dined as usual in her small sitting-room next to her bedroom, served by Mary, the food brought up by Morna. The excitement in the kitchen was intense because they had been told that their young mistress had actually spoken to her husband, in fact had had quite a long conversation with him, which surely meant that she was recovering from the state she had been in for months. When he came home he had gone at once to the drawing-room, greeting her from the doorway, careful not to alarm her, wishing her good evening and then leaving, and Morna, who had been making up the fire, reported that he had been trembling as though in fear and, they supposed, that fear was that she might have retreated again, but Morna said she had answered him and even managed a smile. They were elated.

She was dressed in her warmest woollen gown in the softest shade of rose pink, wrapped about in the furs her husband had bought her just after they were married: a pale grey chinchilla that covered her from her neck to her ankles and from which her little pointed face peeped out like a pretty kitten from its mother's embrace. She wore no hat and her rich coppery hair had been dressed by Mary into a charming, tumbled topknot tied with rose-pink ribbons from which tendrils curled about her cheeks and over her ears. She was pale and you could tell she was apprehensive, Harry told them later, though she gave him a shy smile and a nod as he stood by the horses' heads. He made no attempt to help her into the carriage, warned by Mary that it might not be a good idea, then when Mary had climbed in beside her, he took his seat and they were off along the frozen, rutted lane. The servants peeped out at her from the kitchen window, for this was a great occasion. She had not been out of the house since the day Mr Archie carried her in, screaming and terrified of anything that moved.

The drive was uneventful. The sun shone from one of those pale blue winter skies that seem to stretch away for ever without a cloud to break its perfection. It was bright and clear. Holly bushes were laden with red berries and the birds, blackbirds, chaffinch and meadow pipits, were busy, even a robin or two swinging on the branches as they ate their fill. Mistletoe thrived in the hedgerows, and twined about the apple tree that grew at the end of the lane, green leaves glossy, white berries like pearls. A missel-thrush, which gave the plant its name, was busy pecking at them and in the ditches willow-herb, not in bloom, of course, looked like a motionless crowd of whiskery ghosts. Across the snowy field a large fox, quite grey in colouring, was trotting purposefully. He stood to have a long look at the carriage as it proceeded carefully along the lane, then promptly disappeared into a wood at the edge of the field.

She was greeted with cries of delight by the housemaids, most of whom had watched her grow up, crowding into the hallway despite Mr Goodwin's grunt of displeasure. They knew he didn't mean it. He was always a man to hide his feelings and the sight of his daughter in the home that had once been hers after all this long and sad time must have filled him with joy. Harriet took her in her arms, saying nothing, her eyes brimming with tears and even Hilda, the kitchen-maid, who still wore the sacking apron she put on to scrub the floors, hovered in the kitchen doorway.

"Come into the drawing-room, darling," her mother said,

turning to Harriet. "Hot chocolate, I think, and perhaps Mary might be glad of something in the kitchen," for after all Mary was a servant. It was really a test to see how Beth would react to being separated from the young woman who had been her faithful shadow all these months and Mary knew it, going gladly with the others. Beth, after anxiously turning her head to watch her go, seemed content to allow it. Abby and Noah Goodwin were exultant, for did this mean their daughter was recovering? They had heard from Harriet who had had it from Ruby, who was Harry Preston's mother, of the excitement at Edge Bottom where, it seemed, Miss Beth and Mr Archie had conversed for several minutes without Miss Beth having one of her "turns". And now, here she was, looking pink and rosy and smiling as she hugged her mother.

"Beth," her father said, unsure whether to touch her, for he had been among the males who had frightened her so badly for the last eight months, and when she moved towards him, her eyes bright with tears, he lifted his arms and sighed thankfully when she moved into them. Nothing was said as neither of her parents wanted to disturb this strange tranquillity that surrounded their daughter.

"How is Milly?"

"Doctor Bennett is with her now. Her face is a sight but John has stitched it."

"That bugger wants locking up," her father growled, "and I'm off to see Henry Curtis as soon as John has attended to Milly. I want a statement from John that I can present to the courts." Henry Curtis was a lawyer and a local magistrate. "This is not the first time that swine has beaten her, and worse, as we all remember, and it should not be allowed—"

"Dearest," Abby interrupted, "you know it will do no good. She is his wife, his property, as I am yours, and if he chooses to beat her then the law says that—"

"Now, Abby, don't you get on that bloody soapbox of yours.

I don't want to hear what should be done according to your suffragist ladies. Haven't I been listening to it for the past twenty years? A lot of it I agree with but I'm not prepared to stand by and see my own daughter abused—"

"Noah, please," putting out a placatory hand, for she was anxious that such outrage, such anger, such masculine fury, which was justified, of course, might send her daughter spinning back into the darkness of the past months, but it seemed Beth was not afraid of her father or what he was saying.

"I agree with Father. That man is a danger not only to Milly but any woman who offends him. I wish there was something that could be done."

"There is and I mean to see that it is, within or without the law."

"Darling, please let's wait until John comes down then Beth can go up and see Milly."

"What if he should come looking for her, Abby, tell me that? Am I calmly to allow this man to take my lass away and beat the living daylights out of her? She is to bear his child, which this time could be a son and he's not likely to allow her or the child to remain with us. The birth—"

"Is not for a while, darling, so let us not cross our bridges until we come to them."

"Hmmph!" Noah said, obviously deeply frustrated that he was not allowed to protect his own daughter.

Doctor Bennett said that Milly was going to be all right. The baby was fine and her face would heal, as would her arm, and that Beth could go up while he talked to her parents.

Beth was shocked when she entered the exquisite bedroom that had been Milly's before she married. The room was warm with the fire's glow, lighting the pale pink silk walls to flickering peach and apricot. The woodwork was white as was the lovely crochet bedspread, while the carpet was the colour of oatmeal. There were flowers everywhere, standing on the pretty dressing-table and reflected in the oval mirror. A peach-coloured velvet sofa stood beside the windows, which were usually shrouded in white net curtains but they had been drawn back so that Milly, who lay on the sofa, could look out of the window. Sally, her maid, was with her, brushing her long copper hair which vibrated down her back and across Sally's arm. A lovely room and a once lovely woman whose face was so battered she might have been in a brawl with a prize-fighter. The scar on her cheek was puckered with stitches, both her eyes were set in deep purple bruises and her lip was split. Her arm was fastened to her chest with a splint and she winced as Sally inadvertently pulled at her hair.

"Oh, I'm sorry, m'lady," Sally moaned, as though it was she who had been hurt, but Milly lifted her good arm and patted her hand. "No, no, it's all right, Sally. See, here is my sister come to see me and if it was the Prince of Wales himself I could not be more pleased. Beth . . . Beth, it's lovely to see you out. I was upset when I saw you last, you were so . . . But never mind that, but how d'you think I look? Bit of a mess, wouldn't you say? If it hadn't been for Sally here I might be dead. D'you know she threatened to hit Hugh with the poker if he didn't stop . . . stop bashing me. Dear God, he might have turned on her he was so incensed. I had refused him . . . his rights, you see, since I am already pregnant but he was drunk and, well, you see the result before you. I have told Father what Sally did and he is going to see she gets a reward."

"No, no, m'lady," said Sally, who had once played with Milly Goodwin as a child and called her by her Christian name.

"Now, Sally, why don't you go and have a gossip with your friends in the kitchen and if you should see Harriet would you ask her to come up to see me. No, no. I can manage and if I need anything I'm sure my sister will give me a hand, won't you, darling?"

How brave she is, Beth thought, how she puts me to shame

with her courage and determination not to let the cruel man she has married drive her out of her mind, as I allowed what happened to me to drive me a little crazy. Well, more than a little, for I have caused much suffering to my family, to my husband and to every male at Edge Bottom House with my foolish fear, since who in my world would hurt me? They all love me or at least hold me in affection and I shall not allow myself to vanish into that black hole where whoever it was who gave my name to the police that day, or at least pointed me out as a known prostitute, flung me. For somebody did! Somebody arranged, paid for, bribed the authorities into taking Mary and then me into the lock hospital and doing what they did and one day I will find out who it is. She smiled at her sister, her previous thoughts regarding Milly's bravery tempered by another which said, brave she might be, but at the same time she was a coward who could not face the fact that she had given birth to a child who was not perfect. She had abandoned her daughter, happy to let anyone have her as long as it was not her. The last time she and Milly had met, three months ago at Edge Bottom House, she had scarcely looked at the beautiful child who lay sleeping in her perambulator. And neither did you, a small voice whispered in her ear, you who was going to treat the child as your own!

But this was not a day for brooding about what had happened to her, not with poor Milly lying here like a broken flower on whom some beast had trampled. She was doing her best to smile but her face did not seem capable of lifting the muscles necessary for such an exercise and her mouth only twitched a little.

Beth knelt down by her sofa. "What will you do?" she asked tenderly. Somehow, though she and Milly had often fought – well, Milly had fought and she had gritted her teeth – as children and young women, somehow they seemed to have formed a common bond in their mutual hurt.

"Stay here until the baby is born and, if it's a boy, who will be the seventeenth baron of the line, go back to Thornley Green but not before I have purchased a gun."

"*A gun!*"

"I'll not have this done to me again, Beth, nor will I bear Hugh another child. I shall learn to defend myself. I wonder if Archie knows of a man who could teach me the art of self-defence? I have heard—"

Beth began to laugh, throwing back her head with such abandon Harriet Woodruff could not believe her eyes as she entered the room. Milly was doing her best to join in but the wounds to her face did not allow it except for some odd snuffling noises which she supposed was laughter.

"Well, it does my eyes the world of good to see you two laughing together. I never thought the day would come when the Goodwin girls would . . . Dear sweet heaven, will you listen to me? You are sisters after all and why should you not share a joke though what you have to joke about, Milly Thornley, is beyond me. You look as though you've done ten rounds with that prize-fighter who travels with the fair. But I'm glad, for both of you. Now then, what can I do for you, m'lady?" she added, the last with deep irony.

"I have heard . . . it was said that Todd had been asking after me and . . ."

At once Harriet looked deeply disapproving, folding her arms over her bosom and frowning at her ladyship. The Goodwin family were her life. She had served them ever since Abby had come, many years ago, to be the wife of Noah Goodwin and even before that in the days of her grandfather, though none of them in the kitchen knew anything about *that*, only her Clem and he wouldn't speak of it, not even to her. Had it not been for the Goodwins none of them, including Todd, would be as they were today. She was friend, companion as well as housekeeper to Abby Goodwin, and Clem, who was getting on a bit, was allowed to work as he pleased, when he pleased, pottering about the stables and the yard and tending to the little plot of a vegetable garden at the back of their cosy cottage. But Todd was her son, an officer in a grand regiment, well thought of and likely to get promotion, so why was Milly Thornley, who was known for being a minx, asking about him? It's true, he had knocked on the front door, and had handed in a beautiful bunch of roses which, she noticed, were in a prominent position next to Milly's bed, asking after her ladyship who he had heard had had an accident, but that was not out of place for he was a friend of Lord Thornley's, often a guest with other officers at Thornley Green where Milly was hostess.

"There have been several people asking after you, Milly, and yes, Todd was one of them, so what has that to do with the price of kippers?"

"Harriet, you know perfectly well that Todd and I . . . and Beth, of course, grew up together and surely it is perfectly proper on his part to ask after me. Perhaps if he comes again you could tell him . . ."

"Tell him what?" Harriet was deeply suspicious.

"That . . . that I was glad of his flowers and . . . oh, never mind. I just thought that you as his mother would . . ."

"Would what?"

"Oh, forget it. I'm sorry I asked," Milly floundered, wondering as Harriet glared at her why indeed she had sent for Harriet. The mother of her lover and the grandmother of the child she carried inside her! What in hell was she thinking of? She could see that even Beth was startled.

"Well, thanks, Harriet, and perhaps you would ask Sally to come. I'm tired and I think I might rest now."

"Would you like me to go, darling?" Beth asked as Harriet left the room. Her mind was filled with confusion, for she somehow had the notion that there was more to Milly's casual reference to Todd Woodruff than met the eye, and that Harriet thought so too. Milly and Todd had, even as children, been close, like brother and sister. They had been the wild ones, the rebels, the dare-devils who had urged the others, Harry and even Archie, who was so much older, into hare-brained schemes that had seemed quite logical at the time. Like the day in the depth of winter when the pair of them had decided to skate on the dam after it had frozen over during the night. They had all taken their skates, she and Milly, Todd and Harry and Sally, who was a year younger than they were, and without telling a soul, slipped out unseen and made their excited way across the fields from Edge Bottom House, skirting the glass works, crossing Sandy Lane until they reached what was known as Little Dam.

"I don't think it's frozen enough," Beth had said doubtfully. She had been seven at the time and even then had been a sensible little girl.

"Oh, don't be such a scaredy-cat," Milly had shouted as she strapped on her skates and, without a thought for danger, slid on to the ice. "Look, the ducks are walking on it," she had laughed and promptly, before any of the others had even got their skates half on, vanished through the ice. For a moment they stood, stunned into horrified silence, then Todd had leaped forward as though released by a spring, waded through the ice which broke up before him and, reaching the place where Milly stood floundering in the fortunately shallow water, had dragged her out.

They had been sent to bed without any supper, with dire threats that if Milly and Todd should contract pneumonia they would all be punished so horribly they would be sorry for the rest of their lives.

Milly and Todd had survived, laughing and giggling the next day on what fun it had been and that was how it seemed to Beth right now. Milly and Todd in some conspiracy which had made Milly ask Todd's mother if he had called again. Some bond, some secret bond that only they were aware of, which was ridiculous, for Milly was Hugh Thornley's wife, the mother of his child with another to come.

Milly lay back on the pillows Sally had heaped behind her, unwilling, it seemed to Beth, to meet her eyes, then suddenly she turned and grasped Beth's hand in hers. She winced as the movement jolted her broken arm but the expression on her face was soft with some emotion Beth could scarcely believe, not in Milly at any rate.

"I love him, Beth," she whispered fiercely, "and he loves me."

"What? Who?" Beth fell back from her kneeling position on the floor beside Milly and almost landed on her back, but recovered her balance, her eyes like great silver pools in the shocked alabaster of her face.

"Oh, I know I shouldn't burden you with this when you have been so ill yourself but I don't know who else to talk to. And I trust you not to tell anyone, not even Archie. Hugh is an absolute . . . well, you know what he is, and what he has done to me, but Todd, though he is a soldier, is so gentle and loving. Dear God, did you ever expect Milly Goodwin to admire such a thing, but since I married Hugh, or rather Hugh married me for my money, I have known nothing but brutality and Todd's sweetness . . . oh, he can be strong, fierce even when . . ." She left the sentence unfinished but there was no doubt what she meant. She turned away and looked out of the window to the pure white beauty of the garden beyond. "I shouldn't be telling you this but I need to see him and I don't know how to do it. I suppose I had some idea that Harriet might . . . Dammit, I must be out of my mind, his own mother. But you could help me, darling, if you . . . if you love me."

Beth stood up or rather staggered to her feet, her head whirling with a swallow flight of thoughts which, though they were thoughts, were not rational ones. Only yesterday, not even twenty-four hours ago, she had been sitting serenely by her fire, her sewing in her hands, safe with Mary and her mother, the baby on the floor, the dog at her feet, and now she was swept away in this maelstrom of feelings that she was not sure she was ready to deal with. An involvement in her sister's life that might, *would* bring only disaster and surely there was enough of that in their lives already.

But she felt alive. She could feel life flowing through her and her mind had begun to clear as she slowly recognised what it was that her sister was telling her. Todd Woodruff was her lover and, more than likely, the father of her unborn child. And Milly wanted Beth to help her in some way. To involve herself in the danger, for it would be dangerous, of deceiving Hugh Thornley.

"What is it you want me to do? Mind you, I'm not promising to do it, Milly, because—"

"Oh, darling, when I am better, my face, I mean, will you let Todd and I meet at Edge Bottom House? It would be perfectly proper for me to visit my sister and even if Hugh should hear of it he would think nothing of it. He wouldn't care, to be honest. He's besotted with Alicia Bramhall at the moment and having . . . having got me pregnant he won't mind if I stay at my parents' house for a while. Dear God, the whole of St Helens will know by now what he has done to me *again* and will not think it strange that I should . . . please, Beth," she said eagerly. "You could write a note to Todd, tell him . . ."

Beth sank down on the low, velvet-covered chair by the fire and a face wavered in the flames into which she stared. It was the face of her husband, the man she had married because she needed to be loved after being discarded by Hugh Thornley. She wasn't even sure now that she had really loved Hugh or perhaps the idea of being in love had enchanted her. And if he had chosen her would she be lying on that sofa as Milly was lying, battered, abused, degraded?

"Beth, I love him. I'm not a child. I suppose I've always loved him even when we were children. I know I'm married to Hugh but that doesn't stop me from loving Todd. How can it? One does not fall in love where . . . Oh, Beth, you should know that."

"Yes," Beth said softly. "I know that."

"I have to come to you, Beth, for there is no one else. If Todd and I could meet at Edge Bottom until the child is born then who knows what will be decided."

"When will that be, Milly?"

"April, I think. I haven't asked Doctor Bennett and it will make no difference to him though Hugh will be made to believe that the child is premature. You see, he and I—"

"Yes, yes, I understand."

"And will you do it?"

"I must ask Archie."

"Archie! But you must not confide in Archie, Beth. This is our secret."

"How can it be? If you are to meet at my house my husband must know the reason."

"I thought you and he were . . . estranged."

A lovely smile lit Beth's face. "We were, but not any more. And it's thanks to you."

"Me?"

"If this hadn't happened I would still be hiding in that sheltered place where I hid from you all, even Archie. But for coming to see you, and this" – indicating Milly's face – "I would probably still be there."

Milly tried to laugh, grimacing horribly. "Well, it's a relief to know some good came of it."

21

She ran up the stairs so swiftly that Morna, who had opened the door to her having heard the carriage in the lane, stared after her in astonishment. It was almost dark despite being just gone four o'clock, the shortest day of the year, and Morna and Ruth had been lighting the lamps and making up the fires in the drawing-room and the dining-room. There was an air of excitement in the house, not just because it was nearly Christmas but because they were all sure that this Christmas was going to be a special one. For a start Mrs Beth had been out for the first time in months, an event that had flabbergasted Mr Archie when he came home for lunch. Well, he *said* he had come home for lunch – anything would do, a sandwich or a bowl of Mrs Kyle's excellent soup – but they all knew it was to check up on Mrs Beth who had actually sat and had a short conversation with him last night. She had still been in bed when he went to work this morning and he had breakfasted alone as he had done for the past eight months and though Morna could see he was absolutely dying to go upstairs and find out if Mrs Beth was still willing to talk to him, even if he had to shout from the hallway, he had not done so.

Beth entered the nursery and was greeted by that endearing smile that reminded her of Milly. The baby sat on the floor, surrounded by toys, all placed within her reach for, with her shortened leg holding her back she was a bit behind normal babies and had not yet tried to crawl. She reached for a soft pink rabbit and held it out to Beth, babbling some interesting thing that had happened in her day and beside the fire Jane smiled fondly. She was surprised to see Mrs Beth up here at all. When the promise of the baby coming to live at Edge Bottom House had been talked about just after she was born, Mrs Beth had been full of plans on what she was to do with the nursery, the colours, the pictures, the curtains, the bright rugs and toys she meant to put in but none of it had come to fruition, for Mrs Beth had been ill and had never seemed to recover. Naturally, when Mrs Goodwin, Alexandra's grandmother visited, Alexandra was brought down to the drawing-room and admired, kissed and nursed, not by Mrs Beth, of course, who merely smiled placidly, but by Mrs Goodwin, but there was no one, at least of the family, who took a great deal of interest in her. The perambulator had been ordered by Mrs Goodwin and Jane pushed the baby about the garden when the weather was fine and the gardeners hung over the contraption, making those strange noises men seemed to think appropriate at such time. Alexandra had studied them gravely, her thumb in her mouth, then beamed at them round it, causing cries of great delight, and the maidservants made much of her, for she really was a lovely, sweet-natured scrap of humanity, not a bit like her mother, they remembered, who had been a real handful, or so they told Jane.

Jane leaped to her feet as Mrs Beth entered the nursery. "Mrs Beth," she faltered, "we weren't expecting you," as though she and the baby were in the habit of discussing who might visit them.

"I have been over to see my sister, Jane. She is expecting another child."

And will she dump the poor little thing on her sister, as she had done with this one? Jane thought but said, "I hope she is well, madam."

"Well, I'm not sure about that. She has had an accident."

Aye, we all heard about her accident, Jane said to herself, for it had got across from Lantern Hill to Edge Bottom House in the usual manner, the servants' grapevine passing on the news that that there swine of a husband of hers had beaten up his wife and she was a bit of a mess.

Mrs Beth was watching the child in the most strange manner, her whole being concentrating on what Alexandra was doing. She sat down and it seemed to Jane that she was seeing the baby for the first time, *really* seeing her, studying her, examining her every movement. The baby was herself scrutinising the pink rabbit with total absorption then, when she was satisfied with what she saw, put the rabbit's right ear in her mouth and chewed vigorously.

"Should she be doing that, Jane? You've cared for many babies so will know whether that is normal, but I'm afraid I'm woefully ignorant."

"Normal, Mrs Beth? Why, bless you, all babies chew things. They don't care what it is. I found her trying to get the dog's ear to her mouth the other day. He didn't seem to mind."

"Really!"

"Oh, aye, my mam had fourteen of us – I was the eldest – and every one of us chewed on an old wooden spoon she kept just fer the purpose. Helps ter fetch their teeth through, see. And Alexandra's got eight. Watch her smile . . . see . . ." as the baby obliged with a wide grin. "She's a love, isn't she?" she added.

She was a love and though as yet she had not held the child Beth found herself kneeling in front of her and offering her a hand, a finger, whatever Alexandra would like. The baby got quite excited, lifting her hands and clapping them both on to Beth's, laughing at this lovely new game. Should she lift her up? she wondered, and when the child grabbed at her hair and pulled it they were both laughing, delighted with one another.

"I shall come up tomorrow, Jane, if I may and perhaps Alexandra and I could . . ." Well, whatever babies did with adults, her shining eyes said.

She wandered down the stairs to her bedroom where Mary was sitting by the fire mending something or other which, to Beth's surprise, turned out to be one of Archie's shirts, for it was not part of her job to take care of the master's wardrobe. She wondered who did it; probably the sewing lady who came in to mend sheets and pillowcases and tablecloths.

Mary sprang to her feet, watching Beth curiously, for there was something very different about her young mistress. Something that had taken place in the last twenty-four hours and Mary found she liked it. Gone was that sweet apathy, that listless indifference, that inclination to recoil at anything out of the ordinary.

"I've just been up to see Alexandra – what a mouthful that is. I think I shall call her Alex. What d'you think, Mary?"

"That seems appropriate. A short name for a small girl." Mary smiled and waited, for it appeared that Mrs Beth must be going to see more of her niece than she had in the past if she was planning a special name for her.

"She's got eight teeth, did you know? Eight teeth and she's only nine months old."

"That's wonderful."

"I thought so. I shall tell Archie tonight." The words were spoken so naturally, without conscious thought that there followed a long and telling silence as though they had sprung from somewhere deep inside Beth Goodwin's heart of their own volition. That was what she would have said and done before the doctor at the lock hospital had raped her with a speculum, when she and Archie were lovers, friends, companions and had saved interesting bits of news or gossip to tell one another at the end of the day.

"Are you to dine with Mr Archie tonight, Beth?" Mary asked quietly, unaware that she had dropped the "Mrs", for were they not friends now, indeed the only friend each had known for the past eight months.

She watched the different expressions flitting across Beth's face. Pleasure at the thought, anxiety, hope, fear, apprehension and all the time her copper eyebrows dipped, then lifted, the frown coming and going as she contemplated the prospect of sitting down to table with a man, a male, one of those who had hurt her so badly that she had run away from them, and from life. But Mary could see that the idea pleased her in some way even while it alarmed her.

"You could wear that new dress you've not yet had on. The one the colour of autumn beech leaves which exactly matches your hair. D'you remember Miss Adela saying that when she showed you the fabric a while ago?"

"I do. Have I not worn it, Mary?" Beth asked anxiously, her mind for a moment spinning away into the past which was often very hazy.

"No, but it would be nice to wear it tonight. I believe Mrs Kyle, who is already well into the preparation for the Christmas festivies, has made a rather special meal for Mr Archie tonight. After all it is the day before Christmas Eve."

"Oh, Mary, and I have not bought any Christmas presents for Archie and Alex, and everybody should have something. What am I to do?" She was childlike in her anguish.

"Nay, Mrs Beth, we shall get the train to Liverpool tomorrow. Harry can take us to the station and you and I will go to George Henry Lee's Department Store where, I believe, there is a wonderful children's department and buy everything we need for Alex. And we could get something for Mr Archie and your parents."

"And you, dear Mary."

Mary flushed with pleasure, as she had longed for this day ever since they had brought Mrs Beth, kicking and screaming, into this house last May. "And we could even take Harry to Liverpool to help us with the parcels."

"Oh yes, but don't tell Archie, will you, or he might try to stop us." As though she, Mary Smith, was likely to whisper to her mistress's husband that not only was she recovering from her dreadful experience but was off to Liverpool in the morning to buy a Christmas present for him.

"No, darling, we will tell no one but Harry and Mrs Kyle. She will keep our secret."

"Mary?"

"Yes?"

"Do you think we could ask Archie if we might have a Christmas tree in the hall like we do every year?"

"I don't see why not. You could ask him this evening. Tucker and Billy could cut one tomorrow and put it up and then tomorrow evening we could decorate it. Alex would love it."

"Perhaps I should go and visit my sister at Lantern Hill, Mary." Beth's face puckered into a worried frown and Mary wondered how long it would be before Mrs Beth was completely her old self again; when this indecision, this inability to make up her mind, to blunder from one worry to the next would disappear. She had never been a forceful person, although the story of how she had accosted Captain Thornley, as he had been then, on his own parade-ground, in front of his own troops had become quite a legend. He had been forced to resign his commission and had sworn revenge on the whole of the Goodwin family and they had certainly had their troubles since that day.

Mary frowned and turned to put Mr Archie's shirt on the side table to be picked up later when she had a moment to spare, and was shocked when a sudden thought darted, snake-like, into her mind. No, not just a thought but a vision of such evil she did her best to expunge it from her mind. But it would not be expunged. Was it possible that . . .? No, he had not the authority; but he had the money, and the influence to distort the law, bribe those men who had taken her, and then Miss

Beth. And he was known for a wicked man, a cruel man, a man who would trample on anyone or anything that stood in the way of his own wishes. You only had to see the way he treated his own wife, who had been a Goodwin. Oh, dear Lord, she must put such thoughts from her mind, she really must, for what could she do about it? She was a servant, a lady's maid, valued to be sure in the Goodwin household but she could not go to Mr Noah or Mr Archie with such wild thoughts. They would laugh at her and tell her not to spread such evil gossip. Or they might not! They might do something, in their rage, that would put the family in even more danger with the law.

She shook herself free of her thoughts, aware that Mrs Beth had said something.

"I beg your pardon, Mrs Beth. I did not quite . . . ."

"I said we could go to Liverpool tomorrow and then on Christmas Day drive over to Lantern Hill and give them their presents."

"That's a good idea, my love," Mary said and the endearment as the first one went unnoticed by both the giver and the recipient.

Archie had not changed. He had longed to knock on Beth's door and see how she was but he was so afraid of upsetting the delicate equilibrium of her mind and the door seemed to him to be so firmly closed against all comers that he had wandered downstairs and into the lamplit, firelit loveliness of the drawing-room and there she was. He was so astonished he simply stood in the doorway with his mouth open, looking half-witted, he was sure, while she smiled shyly at him. She had a glass of sherry in her hand and with great composure she asked him if he would care for one.

"A brandy, I think," he stammered, taking a wary step into the room, not daring to move across the deep pile of the carpet towards her in case she should have "one of her turns" as the servants called her fits of terrified hysteria. Not that there had been many of those when they had realised that it was only men she was afraid of, so they had simply stayed away from her and she had lived in her own safe world all these months.

"Of course. Won't you help yourself?" she asked politely, the perfect hostess, but there was a wary look in her eyes that said she was not quite as composed as she pretended.

"Are you to . . . dine downstairs?" he managed to say, his voice sounding strangled in his throat.

"I think I might, Archie." She sipped her sherry but he noticed she looked often to the door as though measuring the distance from her chair and the possibility of a quick escape should it be needed. He sat down cautiously on a chair near the door then realised that he had chosen the wrong chair, for it cut off her escape so he stood up uncertainly and moved to the sofa against the far wall.

He cleared his throat. "You look very elegant, Beth," he managed to croak. "Is that a new gown?"

"Yes, Miss Adela said it matched my hair."

"Miss Adela?"

"The seamstress."

"Ah, well Miss Adela was right. You look very pretty."

"Thank you."

Dear God, what was he to do or say next? He had known this woman from the moment of her birth and had loved her ever since. First as a child will love another, then as a man will love a woman and yet he was as tongue-tied as a schoolboy. He was so afraid of sending her spinning away from him again should he say the wrong thing and yet she would not be down here, with him, if she had not wanted it. But damn it to hell, it was hard. He wished Morna would come in and tell them that dinner was ready to be served and when she did he leaped to his feet with such force both she and Beth were startled. Beth flinched and he was sorry but she stood up and began to move towards the door. Should he offer her his arm but then might she not recoil from him? Sweet Jesus, he loved her so much he longed to cross the space between them and enclose her in his arms and never let her go again but he sensed that this was not the right time. It was too soon. It must come from her.

They sat, she at one end of the shining table which Ruth had polished to within an inch of its life with fragrant beeswax, she had told those in the kitchen, he at the other. The candlelight from the silver candelabra in the centre of the table shone on the green damask of the dining-room walls, the silver rose bowl in which were arranged the best from Tucker's hothouse, the mahogany sideboard inlaid with satinwood, the silver cutlery, the cut-crystal wine glasses, and the collops of veal in a buttery, peppery sauce that lingered on the tongue and had been especially prepared for Mr Archie by Mrs Kyle, since it was his favourite.

"I believe you went to Lantern Hill today, Beth?" he began. "How is Milly? It is . . ." He had been about to say it was all over the town, the village of Edge Bottom and even the glass works what Lord Thornley had done to his pregnant wife and that her own father had been forced to rescue her from him. They said that Mr Noah had armed his men with pistols and even shotguns with an order to shoot his lordship should he ride on to Mr Noah's land but they would hardly be likely to do that, would they? A hanging offence was not something any of them fancied, even in the defence of Lady Thornley, but how could he tell his vulnerable young wife of what was being said in the parish?

"Yes, she is beaten about the face, Archie." She leaned forward in her distress, not for herself but for her sister. "And has a broken arm." She glanced at Morna who stood by the sideboard, smiled at her, and motioned her to leave them. When she had gone, much to Archie's amazement, she moved her plate, her glass of wine and her cutlery, setting them out in the chair beside him so that they were almost elbow to elbow. "She wants a gun, Archie," she whispered confidentially, "and thought—"

"Bloody hell, Beth, what the devil are you saying?" For the first time that evening Archie spoke naturally without considering his words first. "A gun! And what in hell's name is she to do with it?"

"Learn to shoot and she wants to know if you could recommend someone to teach her how to defend herself. Physically, I mean." There was a steely glint in Beth's eye which astounded her husband. "She says she will never allow him near her again. In bed, I mean. She will bear him no more children and is so afraid of getting that disease again she would kill him first. And I don't blame her, Archie. So, I had better tell you, though I wanted to keep it secret, but Mary and I are to go to Liverpool tomorrow to buy our Christmas presents but do you think we could go over to Lantern Hill on Christmas Day and you could discuss it with her? Not while Father's there, of course, because he believes he can protect her but he can't. Not really. She can only depend on herself."

"Jesus Christ!"

"And there is something else."

"I don't think I can stand any more, darling."

"She wants to meet Todd here. They are in love, you see, and . . . the child is his."

"Todd Woodruff?" he quavered. He fell back in his chair and wiped a trembling hand over his face from which all colour had drained. He began to shake his head and when Morna knocked on the door and popped her head round it he told her quite roughly to get back to the kitchen, which she did.

"I think they're having a row," she whispered to the others who all stood and stared at her. A row! Mrs Beth only just come to her . . . well, they supposed they could only call it "her senses" after creeping about like a little mouse for months and they were to believe that she and Mr Archie were having a row! Never, not Mrs Beth and Mr Archie, for Mr Archie worshipped the ground she walked on and would not raise his voice to her for the world. She didn't know what to do, Morna said tearfully, but Mrs Kyle sent her back and told her not to be so foolish, and when she returned to the dining-room, there was Mrs Beth sitting next to Mr Archie, chatting away about Christmas trees and Christmas presents.

She brought in the charlotte russe, another favourite of Mr Archie's, made with Savoy biscuits, masses of rich, whipped cream and flavoured with maraschino liqueur, and left discreetly. They were talking ten to the dozen, she reported. What would happen next? For really the past couple of days had been so unexpected they didn't know what to think.

The next day was another surprise as it seemed Mrs Beth, Mary and with Harry to accompany them, at Mr Archie's insistence, were to take the train to Liverpool where Mrs Beth was to do her Christmas shopping. Christmas shopping, for goodness sake, and only two days ago she had been sitting mim as a mouse in her chair by the fire. Harry was to put on his best suit and Clancy was to drive them to the railway station in St Helens and be there to meet them when they returned. It seemed that though Mrs Beth was so much better Mr Archie would not let her out without the protection of a manservant and he only wished he could go with her himself, he was heard to say. But with Mr Noah still in a rage about Lord Thornley and what he had done to poor Miss Milly, or Lady Thornley, they supposed they should call her, though he went in sometimes hadn't been seen at the works for days and could you blame him, poor man. So Mr Archie couldn't leave the place to run itself, could he?

The shopping trip had been a tremendous success and it was a good job he had gone along, Harry told them, for he had never seen so many things bought and the money that was spent was more than he and Clancy would have earned in a lifetime. That George Henry Lee was the biggest shop he had ever seen with departments for every blessed thing anyone could think of. Dress departments, where Mrs Beth and Mary pored over scarves and hats and belts, gloves, fans, furs, parasols and lovely lengths of material, whose like and colour he himself had never seen. He hadn't known where to put himself, really he hadn't, but he daren't take his eyes off Mrs Beth, for if anything had happened to her Mr Archie would have had his . . . well, he couldn't bear to think of what might happen to his, well, private parts. Dottie had gaped and Mrs Kyle had looked frosty, but the rest of them giggled and begged Harry to go on, for none of them had even been in the larger shops in St Helens, never mind a big city like Liverpool.

They had gone into the gentlemen's department next, he told them, and bought silk scarves and cravats and gloves, a lovely waistcoat of striped yellow and black which he overheard Mrs Beth tell Mary would be just right for Mr Archie.

But it was the children's department, not just clothing and such, where Mrs Beth had spent a bloody fortune on pretty dresses, bonnets, dainty little shoes, a fur muff, baby clothes such as little jackets and what he was reliably told were "bootees". Yards of lace and silk and satin and other materials with which it seemed a new baby could not do without and he supposed she meant the one that was waiting to be born at Lantern Hill. So many toys he wondered how one child would ever have the time to play with them, meaning Miss Alexandra. Books by the score, clockwork clowns and baby dolls, a teddy bear that growled when you turned it on its back, a tiny perambulator, the exact miniature of the one in which Miss Alexandra was pushed around the garden, and her not even able to walk yet! A rocking horse and a doll's house, balls and crayons and a tiny set of teacups and saucers, plates and a teapot. She was like a child herself, her face rosy, he reported with great satisfaction, and it had been his pleasure to watch over her for the day, becoming bright red himself as he spoke.

Then he became secretive, tapping his nose and grinning and saying that that was not the end of it neither. What did he mean? they asked, crowding round him but he would say no more, telling them it was Christmas Eve and tomorrow was Christmas Day and until then they must all wait and see.

"They're going over to Lantern Hill for Christmas dinner," Mrs Kyle informed them, "and taking Miss Alexandra." At that they all became quiet, for what was Lady Thornley going to make of the lovely child who slept peacefully in her nursery upstairs? Her own daughter, nine months old and on whom she had never clapped eyes.

22

Milly's son was born in April, a perfectly formed, healthy boy who, at the moment of his birth, which is when it is accepted that a child most resembles its father, was the image of Todd Woodruff. Harriet Woodruff who helped at the birth knew that her earlier suspicions were confirmed and that she was looking at her own grandson! She took him in her arms and looked across the bed at Abby. Their eyes met and the knowledge lay between them.

By the time Beth saw him, the Honourable Miles Thornley, as he would be known, had become what all babies are at birth, red-faced, indignant, his mouth open on a wail of displeasure, his little pink tongue quivering in his wide, shining mouth. It was a mere half an hour later that she carried him, a great concession allowed by the nurse Abby had employed to look after him, to the room which, as it had been at Alexandra's birth, was a makeshift nursery; although all the servants who saw him cooed over him and thanked the Lord that he was perfect, not one of them noticed Harriet Woodruff and their mistress go into the mistress's bedroom and shut the door behind them. The master was at the works with Mr Archie, only Miss Beth, as they still called her at Lantern Hill, waiting in the drawing-room for news of the child's birth and she was soon absorbed in the flurry of attention the new baby needed, the bath the nurse gave him, dressing him in his little clothes which seemed too small for him he was such a big boy, or so the nurse said. He was put to the breast at once, not Milly's, of course, but that of the wet nurse who had been waiting since Milly's labour had begun.

Beth knew who he was, whose son he was, since Milly had told her, but he was so beautiful, just like Alex despite the fact that they did not share a father, she was mesmerised and at that moment it did not seem to matter. What was to happen next was put to one side as she watched the handsome little boy being prepared to meet the world. To meet his grandparents, his maternal grandparents, and the fact that his paternal grandparents were also on the premises was not even considered. He was here, safe, healthy, or so Doctor Bennett informed them, as was Milly, which at that moment was all that mattered.

She was not privy to the scene in her mother's bedroom, for somehow it had not occurred to her that Harriet, as the boy's grandmother, would have recognised him as such and so she had not noticed she was not present nor wondered at the absence of her own mother.

They fell into one another's arms, trembling, not speaking, though from Harriet's throat there came a sort of whimpering sound which was more telling than any words. For five minutes they stood clutching each other. They had been friends for over twenty years and through those years, many of which had not been easy for Abby Goodwin, they had stood together, servant and mistress but friends and now, surely, this was the deepest pit of despair they had ever shared.

Harriet started to babble. "I knew. I told myself that I was imagining things that day when Noah brought her home and she asked me about Todd. Had he been and when I said yes and what was it to her she put me off but I knew. He brought flowers and haunted the kitchen door, or was forever at the cottage and there was Clem so pleased to see his son and all the time he was hanging about waiting for news of . . . of his mistress."

"Dear sweet heaven, Harriet."

"And then suddenly he wasn't there any more but something made me suspicious. She was forever driving off in the carriage to Edge Bottom House."

"She went to see Beth."

"Don't insult me, Abby. She and Beth have never been particularly good friends."

"Lately they have."

"Only because Milly needed somewhere to meet . . . to meet my son who is the father of the child who has just been born. Dear God, what is to happen?" she wailed. "Hugh Thornley will be here as soon as he hears he has a son and will take him away to Thornley Green and unless Milly and Todd are to confess . . ." She began to sob so hysterically, ready to fall about and knock into the furniture, that Abby led her to the chair by the fire that glowed in the grate, as a fire glowed in every grate at Lantern Hill. This was a disaster for Harriet, a tragedy for the child. Why, oh why could it not have been a girl then Hugh Thornley would have been indifferent and perhaps left well alone, but the child would be the future Lord Thornley, heir to the name, the title, the estate and there was no way the present Lord Thornley would allow the boy to remain at Lantern Hill as he had done the boy's mother since Christmas.

It had been a peaceful time, these last three and a half months. Beth had come over every day, the first time bringing Alexandra, which had not been a great success. It had been Christmas Day and Harry, resplendent in the smart new cravat his mistress had bought him the day before in Liverpool, drove the carriage up to the front door. There had been great excitement in the kitchen at Edge Bottom House when Mrs Beth, carrying Miss Alex, and Mr Archie, carrying a great armful of beautifully wrapped parcels, had entered as Mrs Kyle was just putting the pork in the oven for the servants' Christmas dinner.

"A happy Christmas," the mistress and master had cried

and the baby had beamed at them with the greatest goodwill. They had all bobbed curtseys, and Harry and Clancy, Tucker and Billy, Alfie and Arthur who worked in the stables and paddock with Mr Archie's handsome horses, were sent for. It had been a crush but such a feeling of happiness nobody minded, even the baby, who was passed from one to another. She grew excited, flinging her arms about and clapping her hands and they had all laughed.

She had bought a present for every one of them. Lengths of material in lovely colours for the women to make up, enough for a dress, handkerchiefs of lace and mittens of muslin which were far from serviceable for the maids, and of wool for the men. There were scarves and cravats and Dottie began to cry since she had never had anything so lovely in her life, she wept. If someone would show her how she would sew herself a dress for the summer and how did Mrs Beth know that pink was her favourite colour? And she had thought the Christmas tree that Mrs Beth had decorated in the hall was a miracle!

There had hardly been room for them all in the carriage, what with Mrs Beth and Mr Archie, Mary and the baby and the dozens of presents that were somehow stuffed round them. They had drawn up at the wide steps to Lantern Hill, its door flung open by Ruby to reveal the Lantern Hill Christmas tree dominating the hall, its branches bearing a load of tinsel and candles, the holly rich with berries, the mistletoe, the leaping fire in the hall grate and Milly, black eye and all, seated in the drawing-room in a kind of frilly peignoir borrowed from her mother which was the only thing that fitted her.

It had not gone well. Milly looked at her lovely daughter for the first time and her face and eyes wore a blank expression that told them nothing. It might have been the child of a perfect stranger, a pretty baby but, since Milly was not fond of babies, nothing to do with her.

"Here is Alexandra," Beth said softly, walking towards her

sister, the baby in her arms and though she had tried to prepare herself for the pleasure, the maternal warmth that surely any woman would show, and also the terrible image of Milly returning to Thornley Green with her first child, since she was bound to love the baby at once, as Beth did, it had not happened. Alex wore a pretty new dress that Beth had bought the day before. It was white muslin, the bodice embroidered with pale yellow daisies, the skirt full and long with a frill about it embroidered with the same delicate flowers. There was a narrow velvet sash round Alex's plump waist and on her feet she wore tiny yellow velvet slippers to match. But she was excited, her eyes a dazzle of blue stars and as she struggled to show off her "clap hands" to the pretty lady in the chair, her dress worked up to reveal her shortened leg. One of the slippers had been cleverly cut and stitched the night before by Mary so that it would fit the foot that had no toes and Milly fastened her eyes on it in horrid fascination.

"Will you hold her, Milly?" Beth offered, but Milly laughed and put her hands to her belly, shaking her head in denial.

"What with this lump kicking inside me" – which shocked them all, for none of them knew that the baby in her womb had already quickened – "there's no room on my lap, Beth, surely you can see that?" She turned to the small table beside her and lifted the cup of hot chocolate she was drinking to her lips, dismissing her daughter as though she were a kitten or a puppy in which she really had no interest.

Beth looked round helplessly as though to ask her mother and father, but really more to Archie, what she should do now. Mary, who hovered at the drawing-room door, moved forward at once and took the child, saying she would show her to the servants in the kitchen, for this was Miss Milly's daughter who none had seen since just after she was born. Archie came to Beth's side and without thinking reached for her hands, ready to comfort her, but she flinched away from him.

He had spent last night, Christmas Eve, when she had seemed to be more inclined to share her pleasure with him, helping her to wrap the presents she had purchased that day and had even had the thought, sadly to no avail, that she might allow him to share her bed that night. Not to make love to her, for he knew it was too soon for that, but perhaps just to hold her in his arms. When the present-wrapping was done she had wished him a pleasant goodnight, just as she did to Morna, or Ruth, and had gone upstairs with Mary behind her. It had smashed his composure and when she had gone he had sat down with a sensation as if he were falling off a cliff. He had berated himself bitterly, for what else had he expected? It was only a day or two since she had come out of the thrall that had held her all these months, but she had been so excited in anticipation of tomorrow. Christmas Day with her family, the presents she was to give them, decorating the tree when she had instructed him what was to be placed where. Now she could not even bear a comforting hand when Milly had upset her. But at least she was not to lose Alex, that was evident from Milly's reaction at the sight of her damaged daughter.

He had not been pleased at Milly's constant visits to Edge Bottom House in the next few weeks nor that Todd met her there despite being warned by his wife.

"I don't care for it," he told his wife at dinner as January moved to February and he had learned from Harry that Lady Thornley and Captain Woodruff had actually walked down to the paddock to look at his horses.

"What if her husband hears of it?" he had continued abruptly when Morna had left the dining-room. His spoon was poised over the fragrant bowl of Chantilly soup the house-maid had placed before him. He had meant to wait until he and Beth were alone in the drawing-room after they had eaten but the moment she sat down at the table he could wait no longer.

He and his wife had continued in the pleasant but sterile condition that had been their marriage since the day when Beth had come out of the shell in which she had been hiding for eight months. He did not dare to approach her on the matter of their resuming their physical relationship, for he was afraid that if he went too fast, or expected too much of her she might retreat from him for ever. After the incident at Lantern Hill when he had moved to comfort her and she had recoiled from him he had made no move to touch her. The trouble was, or so it seemed to him, that his wife had become *sexless*, neither male nor female, which seemed a foolish thing to say, for to look at she was eternally woman. Her breast was high and round, her waist slender and neat, curving into her softly shaped hips and she appeared to be just as she was when he married her. Ready to laugh with him, to talk at the dinner table, to tell him of her day and ask after his but at the end of the evening she would bid him a polite goodnight and go up the stairs to her own room. He wanted her. He desired her as a man desires a woman but she was beyond his reach and he was afraid that if he tried to bridge the yawning gap between them he would widen it even further. She spent most of her time in the nursery with the baby, or, when her sister visited, drinking chocolate in the drawing-room. Milly made no effort to see her daughter and Beth did not press her. He knew that she was fearful that if Milly should become attached to Alexandra she might want her back and that, he knew, would send his wife spinning away into some dark storm from where she might never recover. They walked on a tightrope, he and Beth. One slip by either of them and it would have them both off.

Beth looked startled. She had just been pondering on how attractive Archie's fair hair was in the lamplight. It seemed to have streaks of sunlight in it and though she knew he had brushed it before he came down, as she had seen him do dozens of times in the past, unruly curls fell over his forehead, touching his eyebrows. His eyes snapped a vivid blue, in the lamplight the colour of the bluebells that misted the woods in May.

"Pardon?" she said.

"All this with Milly and Todd. She's always here and, to walk about openly with Todd Woodruff is madness. Confound it, Beth, you know what Hugh Thornley would do if he knew his pregnant wife was consorting with another man."

"Consorting! Archie, she is seven months pregnant so what on earth can they get up to, for goodness sake?" But she seemed evasive and he put his spoon carefully on the plate beneath his soup plate.

"Does she come to see the child? Does she go into the nursery to play with her daughter?"

"Well, no. You saw what she was like at Christmas."

"Yes, I did. Not that I object to your seeing your sister but I cannot think it wise that Todd Woodruff should meet her here. I know Hugh is . . . is a womaniser—"

"He has a mistress."

He had picked up his soup spoon again and was preparing to resume his meal but he glanced up sharply and Beth saw something in him that he had never employed against her in all their lives.

"A mistress, and what has that to do with us?" He was angry. His eyes narrowed and he scowled, and when Morna knocked and entered the room he waved her away shortly.

"Well, nothing, I suppose but Milly told me when she . . ."

"When she what?"

She had begun to squirm and then with a suddenness that took his breath away she went on, "When she told me that Todd was her lover."

"*Her lover!* I know you told me . . . but I cannot believe it." She saw the suspicion flare and grow in his eyes and he leaned back in his chair as though his strength were gone. "And perhaps there is more that you would like to tell me, Beth. Perhaps about the child she carries."

"Archie, please, she has had such a hard time with that man and when he beat her and broke her arm. I was sorry for her, so that when she asked me if she and Todd . . . I told you and you agree—"

"Beth, oh Beth, you must see what danger we are all in should Hugh Thornley take it into his head—"

He stopped speaking abruptly and his face took on an expression that she could not read. It was contemplative, thoughtful, an expression that seemed to say he was on the verge of knowing something, something that eluded him. Like some memory that one can't quite remember but which is there, on the periphery of the mind so that each time you thought you had grasped it, it slipped away like a fish in a stream.

"What is it?" she asked, then, for some reason she herself could not understand, she stood up and moved along the table to him. She put her hand on his shoulder and leaned towards him and, to his astonished delight, kissed him on the cheek.

"Beth?" His voice was hesitant but she moved away from him and resumed her seat and he knew that it was a tiny step she had taken but was not to be drawn about it. He cleared his throat which was clogged with some emotion, then he said gently, "The child is his, isn't it? Todd's?"

"She says so. She had not . . . not been with Hugh for many months but she and Todd had become lovers. She does not say so but I believe she truly loves him."

"Dear God, and he feels the same? Do they not know what danger they are in, and not just them but us? You! Should Hugh find out he will . . . he is a dangerous man, Beth, and I fear not only for their safety, but yours. And when the child comes, should it be a boy he will take it at once, and be within his rights to do so, to Thornley Green and she will have no choice but to go with him. I am truly amazed that he has left her alone all these weeks. The servants talk and, though not knowingly, could put us all in danger. Jesus, I thought your father was mad to arm all the outside men, those who knew guns, but now I can see he might have been right. Will you promise me you will go nowhere on your own? You must have Harry or Clancy with you at all times, even when you go to see the horses. I know you take Alex but if . . . I can't bear to think about it, my darling. And it's no good saying Mary will be with you. Look what happened to Mary, and you, last year and if . . ."

Her face had whitened and she gripped her spoon so tightly when she put it down it had left deep indents on the palms of her hands. She half rose with a strangled sound and at once he leaped from his chair and went to her and without giving her time to elude him drew her into his arms and held her closely.

"No, no, my dearest girl, don't struggle. You know I mean you no harm. I have been so patient, Beth, allowing you to heal at your own pace, but the thought that you might be in danger again crucifies me. I love you, you are my precious . . . there are no words to tell you what you mean to me. There, there, my love, I should not have reminded you, let me hold you."

And amazingly she did, relaxing against him, her face buried in his shirt front so that when Morna chanced another peep round the door, for surely the master and mistress had finished their soup by now, she was "knocked sideways" as she was to tell them later in the kitchen by the sight of the pair of them in one another's arms. She crept out again and swore she wouldn't go near them until they rang the bell!

"It seems I have a son, Mama," Hugh told his mother the next day at breakfast. He had walked over to the dower house especially to inform his mother, since he would need her help in the arrangements for receiving his son. He had accepted her invitation to break his fast with her and though he had not crawled into his bed until five this morning after a hard night's drinking and gambling and certainly did not need anything but a stiff whisky, he nibbled on a piece of toast. It was not often he and his mother ate a meal together but he had been told the news in a brief note from his mother-in-law who felt it her duty to let him know that the doctor had been to Lantern Hill and a healthy boy had been delivered. He had decided to go at once, he told her, the carriage was already waiting at the door, and just let that sod try to stop him, meaning Noah Goodwin, for if he did he'd have him arrested. The law was on his side in this. In fact he could have forced his wife to come home weeks ago but it had not suited him at the time. She was no good to him the way she was. All swollen up and lumbering about the place like one of those enormous beasts he had seen at the zoo as a child. He had Alicia to divert him and he had only been waiting for news of the sex of the child before he made a move. A girl would not have been welcome, even a healthy girl, not like the other deformed creature his wife had presented him with, but he would still have brought her to Thornley Green to be raised in her proper place. And he needed Milly to produce his heir if this one had proved to be the wrong sex, which, thank God, it hadn't. Anyway, another boy would not go amiss in the future.

"We shall need a nurse and nursemaids and . . . well, you will know, Mama, so can I leave it to you to arrange it all for me? I shall go this morning and bring them back here."

"But she will hardly be out of childbed, Hugh," his mother protested, but he brushed her aside impatiently.

"She's a strong girl, Mama. That is one advantage of marrying into a class such as hers. They may not have the right blood but what they have is healthy and it will not hurt her to be moved. See if you can get that nurse . . . what was her name?"

"Corbett, I believe, Hugh, but she may not come on such short notice."

"She will if she's paid enough. Send Jack Fell at once to bring her back, then she can come with me to Lantern Hill and perhaps it might be as well to have Doctor Newland waiting here for their return."

"Will she come, Hugh?" her ladyship asked fearfully. "You know what an obstinate young woman she is."

"Indeed I do, Mama, but she is my wife and the mother of my son. I have allowed her some . . . freedom these last weeks because it suited me and I knew where she was and that she, and the unborn child, would be well looked after, but, of course, in the present circumstances her place is here."

The dowager Lady Thornley knew full well what her son had done to his wife, for her screams had been heard all over the house and had been reported to her by her servants who talked to those in the house. She was afraid of her son and was only too glad to be no longer living there, though she had initially argued that her son's wife had no business giving birth in her father's house instead of her husband's.

She picked at a piece of toast in much the same manner as her son and wished he would go and leave her in peace. She remembered his father whom he resembled so closely, not just in looks but in temperament, and wondered what it was, what devil had been born in the two men. Still, it was really nothing to do with her any more, thank God. She had not wanted to leave the lovely old house to which she had come as a happy bride, not knowing then of her husband's nature, and in which she had lived for thirty years, but she was fiercely glad that she was not to be present when Hugh brought his wife back there. She would walk over with her maid and make the arrangements Hugh had asked for, the nursery would need a good scrubbing and since her daughter-in-law had gone to her father's house she would be surprised if anything had been done in the house in the way of cleaning. Still, this was her grandson who was to come home and she must make the effort.

"So I can rely on you, can I, Mama?" Hugh asked her, rising to his feet. "I might just ride over first to make sure of Nurse Corbett, for I don't think I could manage to sit in the carriage with Milly and our new son without some help. In fact I might ride Star over to Lantern Hill and let Jack Fell drive the carriage with the nurse in it. So, I'll get off then, Mama, and perhaps, later on, you might like to walk up and see your new grandson."

Greatly daring, Lady Thornley asked, "Will you bring the little girl, Hugh?"

"What little girl?"

"Your daughter, my dear. If the nursery is to be opened she could—"

"I have no daughter, Mama, and you would be wise to remember it."

23

The carriage turned in at the wrought-iron gates of Lantern Hill, passing through the gateposts on which large stone acorns had been sculpted, and proceeding to the left on the immaculately raked gravel drive round the lawn and on up to the wide steps to the front door. Beside the carriage rode Hugh, Lord Thornley on his magnificent ebony gelding which Noah Goodwin's money had bought him. He himself was resplendent in a Norfolk jacket worn with a brown bowler hat which was associated with gentlemen who belonged to the upper crust. The jacket was brown tweed and under it was a bright yellow waistcoat with brass buttons. Since he was riding he had on a pair of buff-coloured riding breeches with well-polished brown riding boots. His gloves were of buff kid and he carried a small riding crop.

Frank Jones and Jack Martin, the head gardener and the under-gardener at Lantern Hill, were supervising the clearing of a stretch of the garden which Mrs Goodwin intended to turn into another rose garden with a trellised bower in the centre under which she would place a wrought-iron bench. She fancied a small fountain as well and the men had been discussing the water pipes that would have to be laid to accommodate this design. The two gardening lads, Billy and Nathan, were industriously turning over the soil to which well-rotted compost had been added under the gardeners' watchful eyes but all four looked up, then straightened up to watch the carriage and, more to the point, the rider who stopped at the front door. The man got down from the saddle, waited for the coachman to take his horse along with those pulling the carriage, and looked about him disdainfully before climbing the steps to the front door and rapping on it with his crop.

"Quick, Billy," Frank hissed as he and Jack moved slowly towards the front door, trying their best to appear not to be doing so, "run round the 'ouse an' warn them that he's here."

"Who?" the lad asked, scratching his head.

"His lordship, that's 'oo. Now run like the devil an' tell Olly an' Clem an' Tommy ter be ready fer trouble. An you, Nate, go like wind ter't works an' tell master."

" 'Oo is it, Mr Jones? 'Oo shall I say?"

"Master'll know."

It was Ruby who opened the door, falling back in alarm when she saw who it was. This man seemed to have the ability, his reputation going before him, it appeared, of instilling fear in the most stalwart heart and Ruby was only a housemaid who had been privy to his menacing ways in the past.

"Is Mrs Goodwin about?" he asked, brushing past her so carelessly she fell against the door. "Tell her that her son-in-law is here and while you're at it fetch my wife and son." He strolled back to the doorway and beckoned to someone in the carriage and from it stepped the starched and formidable figure of Nurse Corbett who had indeed succumbed to the enormous amount he was prepared to pay her. She had been due at another confinement this very morning but his lordship had been most insistent, quite alarming really, that she had come at once to look after his recently confined wife. She moved up the steps and stood just inside the doorway and all the while Ruby stood paralysed, frozen to the smooth square of carpet on which her well-polished boots seemed to be fastened.

"Well," his lordship said dangerously. "Are you deaf or just dim-witted, woman? You heard me, I presume, ask for the mistress of the house."

And might, she thought, have landed her one with the little whip he held in his hand, had not the mistress herself run down the stairs at that very moment.

Abby had heard the doorbell and glanced out of her bedroom window to see who might be calling at such an early hour and the sight of the carriage, whose crest she recognised, and the well-bred animal held by the coachman, ebony, with a star between the eyes, caught her a blow in her midriff so that she could hardly breathe. She and Noah had known this would happen. That their son-in-law would be coming to fetch his wife and son home had been accepted, but not even they had imagined that he might be here a mere day after the baby's birth or Noah would not have gone to the works this morning. There had been some trouble at one of the glasshouses and though Archie was almost as experienced as Noah in the blowing of glass they had been trying out a new procedure, for glass-making was always moving forward and Noah had wished to see it. She knew that Archie sometimes resented Noah's continuing interest in the works he had built up into a mighty empire, but while Noah was still the owner there was nothing he could do.

"Good morning, Hugh," she said breathlessly. "Have you come to see your son?"

But he interrupted her rudely since he had no time for these people whom he thought of as low class and vulgar. Money they might have, for which he was glad, but his family were landed aristocrats, going back into the mists of time and it offended his well-bred sensibilities to be forced to deal with them. "No, madam, I have come to fetch them home. I have a carriage outside and a nurse," indicating the large figure of Nurse Corbett standing stiffly by the door. "So if you would show Nurse Corbett to my wife's room she will go up and prepare her for the journey."

Abby was appalled and, seeing her face, Ruby slunk off to

the kitchen to warn them all that they would certainly be needed. Harriet, who seemed already to idolise the new baby, would certainly stand up to his lordship though Ruby didn't envy her the task.

"You cannot mean to take her now, Hugh. The child was only born yesterday and Milly still bears her . . . the birth wounds. Doctor Bennett would be furious if you were to—"

Hugh smiled. "Do you honestly think I give a damn what that old woman might feel? I have come for my wife and son and I demand that Nurse Corbett" – indicating with his head that the nurse should step forward – "be taken to my wife's room. If needs be I will carry her to the carriage. It is not a long journey and my mother is making all the necessary arrangements for Milly's arrival, and that of the boy. Now then, get out of my way or I shall be forced—"

"Put a foot on those stairs and I shall call the men to evict you from these premises where you are trespassing. You heard Mrs Goodwin. Her daughter is not yet fit to travel and it will be many weeks before—"

Hugh Thornley turned slowly, a smile curving his cruel mouth and crinkling the scar he carried on his left cheek. He appeared to be highly amused, and even Harriet, who had come to defend her grandson from this brute's foul intentions and was therefore surging with the strength given to females in defence of their young, stepped back. The two middle-aged women stood bravely side by side, protecting their own, but Hugh Thornley continued to smile as though in wonderment at their foolishness.

The door at the end of the passage that led to the kitchen burst open and two men appeared, both carrying shotguns aimed at him but he continued to smile and to move forward through the wide hallway towards the foot of the stairs. Olly and Clem Woodruff, neither of them young men, one Ruby's husband, the other Harriet's and the father of Todd, waved their weapons threateningly. But they were servants, both having acquired the habit from childhood of giving instant obedience and respect to the upper classes whom they served and they were nervous, out of their depth. Mr Goodwin had given them instructions that Miss Milly's husband was not to be allowed on his land and had issued them with a shotgun with which to defend the womenfolk. That was all very well in theory but when it came to pulling the trigger, where might they end up? At the end of a hangman's rope, that's where!

"I must ask yer ter leave, yer lordship," Clem said bravely.

But Lord Thornley continued to move towards the bottom of the stairs and when he lifted his handsome head and shouted, "Milly, where the devil are you, woman?" they all jumped nervously.

"Please, Hugh, leave her for a few days until she is quite recovered," Abby pleaded and Harriet put her hand on the handsomely carved newel post at the bottom of the stairs with the apparent intention of clinging to it until forcibly removed. She didn't know what was to be done here. She and Abby hadn't had time to prepare a plan which they must discuss with Milly, of course, to prevent the removal of their grandson and her head was whirling round and round in a fog of terror. She could, of course, announce to the rest of them that this child was her son's child and not this bastard's who was grinning at them contemptuously, but what might that unleash on this family, on herself and Clem, on her grandson and on her son, the boy's father? Hugh Thornley was a vindictive and cruel man and would not hesitate to avenge himself on the wife who had betrayed him and on the man, once his brother officer, who had been her lover. He was of the aristocracy and had great influence among his own. Noah Goodwin was also a powerful man and would fight to the death to defend his family, by fair means or foul, but the outcome could be so horrific, destroying so many lives. Harriet knew she must, for the moment, keep her thoughts and her words to herself. Noah would be here soon, she was sure of that, for she was pretty certain he had been sent for and until then, until authority arrived they must do their best to keep this brute from reaching his wife and her new son, the one he believed was his.

"I'd be glad if you'd stand aside, madam," Hugh said silkily. "I have no wish to hurt you but I must be given access to my wife and son. You must know the law is on my side and why the hell I am standing here arguing with you is beyond me."

"And it's beyond me too, Hugh, for it's not like you to be put off even by a loaded shotgun held to your chest. Now come up here and give me your arm to get me down the stairs."

They all looked up in amazement, even Hugh, at the figure who stood at the top of the stairs. Milly Thornley, enveloped in a capacious woollen cloak which covered her from her neck to her ankles, one belonging to her mother and which she had worn during the last weeks of her pregnancy, held herself upright, one hand on the matching newel post at her side. She was like a young queen, smiling, courageous, her spirit shining through her pain, for the child had been big and Doctor Bennett had stitched her. Standing beside her was the wet nurse holding the sleeping baby. The nurse looked terrified, for she had heard of the great Lord Thornley and what had happened to this woman beside her, as who in the district had not. She'd be off back to her cottage as soon as may be but for the moment the poor lady could hardly walk, never mind carry her own newly born babe.

Harriet moaned and turned her face to the newel post to which she clung, while Abby sagged against the wall. Milly had taken it out of their hands and resolved this drama in the only way she knew how and no matter what they said or did, or what Noah might say or do when he arrived, how could they stop their daughter from returning to her husband if she had set her mind to it?

"Well done, darling," Hugh said delightedly, for though he had not been afraid these people could stop him from his course, it made it so much easier if Milly came of her own accord. He pushed past Harriet who had sunk to the bottom step, her head bent to her knees, and ran up the stairs. He did not even glance at the child, for though the boy was just what he wanted he would not concern himself with him, at least not at this early age. He had been told he was healthy and perfect in every way and that was enough for the moment.

"Here, let me help you," he said gaily to his wife as though they were a normal married couple who had affection for one another. "Nurse," he called to the immobile woman by the front door, "get up here and take the child while my wife and I negotiate the stairs. It is all ready for you at home, my pet," he told Milly, putting a strong arm about her and almost carrying her down the stairs, then, as she swayed he called out to the men in the hall who were watching with mouths agape. "Here, one of you, help me to carry my wife to our carriage," and at once Tommy, whose job was to muck out the stables and sweep the yard and was not very bright, sprang across the hall and up the stairs.

"Take her other arm, man," the gentleman ordered and though Tommy was not awfully sure it was correct for a man such as himself to touch a lady like the gentleman's wife, he did as he was told.

"Don't look so worried, Mother," Milly said as they paused for a moment by the front door. "You knew this must happen sooner or later and it happens to be sooner. The boy cannot be kept from his heritage and I from my husband, isn't that so, husband?" She turned a brilliant smile on Hugh Thornley and they all watched, the servants, her mother and Harriet, marvelling at the brave and tragic figure of Milly Thornley who had come through the front door with a broken arm and a battered face only months ago and was going back, they supposed, to more of the same!

Abby and Harriet, leaning on one another for support, watched their grandson being handled into the carriage, held firmly by the nurse whose expression said she was not one to stand any nonsense, from mother or child. She had been told that a wet nurse would be waiting in the nursery at Thornley Green, but she would be in charge of it until the mother was up and about which, if she had her way, would not be for weeks yet, since she was a firm believer in keeping the mother in bed for at least four weeks and then only to move to a chaise-longue beside the bedroom window.

They stood there, the two grandmothers, still staring towards the gateway long after the carriage had gone through it, and when Noah Goodwin came flogging up the drive, his horse all lathered with sweat, he found them still there, frozen, stunned, unable to give him a coherent account of what had happened, or even to speak of their devastation.

He would go after the blackguard, he snarled, when he got the tale from the servants. Take some men and bring his daughter and his grandson back home, for he'd not have her abused for a third time. Who would go with him? he shouted to the men who still hung about, somewhat ashamed of the way they had simply stood there and watched Miss Milly hauled into the carriage by her husband, but that was it. He *was* her husband and she seemed to have gone willingly and so what could they have done? She, along with the child, belonged to him. She was his possession, as was the boy, and could a man take another man's possession and stay on the right side of the law?

. He was about to climb back on his horse, swearing he would go alone and if Clem would hand him that shotgun he'd end this thing for ever. He'd shoot the bastard and if he was hanged for it, well then, at least his precious daughter would be safe.

Abby began to cry in great gulping noisy sobs and her husband hesitated. For the last twenty years he had made this woman his life and he could not bear to see her upset. No matter how small or how large her distress, he instinctively rushed to put it right. And this distress was of the large sort, he knew. His male senses insisted he get on his horse and go after the bastard who was putting his family through so much misery and even danger, but his wife's tears were something he could not withstand. Harriet had put her arms about her and drawn her close, weeping herself, and the servants, even the men, were gathering around them on the top step. Nan, the scullery-maid and only sixteen years old, threw her apron over her head and cried in sympathy and Noah was undone.

He threw the reins of his horse to Olly and ran up the steps, taking his wife from Harriet's arms, stepping back so that Clem could get to Harriet. Both men knew something unusual was happening here, not just the appalling fact that their Milly had been taken, not quite by force but damn near it, and it was causing their womenfolk to fall apart, to cry broken-heartedly.

As they were about to lead the women inside, the servants clustering at their backs, the sound of carriage wheels on the drive made them all turn. For a moment, and he was ashamed of it afterwards, Frank Jones despaired that he would ever get the drive back to its normally pristine condition what with horses' hooves galloping up and down it all the live long day, then the carriage, driven by Harry Preston and with Clancy Morris beside him, came to a slithering stop by the steps. Beth was out of it and up the steps before Harry had fully drawn the animals to a proper halt. Mary was with her, her plain face anxious, for it was very evident that something dreadful was happening at Lantern Hill. Last night when Mrs Beth had told Mr Archie that she intended to drive over to Lantern Hill in the morning to enquire after her sister and the new baby, he had been quite rough with her, and Mary had been there to see it.

"Goodnight, Archie," Mrs Beth had said at the bottom of the stairs, as she did every night, smiling at her husband and he had answered as he usually did, his face sad, Mary had thought, from her position beside the door to the kitchen where she had gone to fetch Mrs Beth's evening chocolate. Doctor Bennett had given instructions months ago that Mrs Beth must drink plenty of milk and this had become a habit.

"Oh, Archie," Mrs Beth had said, turning back to her husband who had seen her to the door. "I shall be driving over to Lantern Hill tomorrow and I shall probably stay for lunch so—"

"Absolutely not, d'you hear me? Not while that bugger's on the loose. You are to stay within the confines of the gardens until—"

"Archie, don't be ridiculous. My sister has just had a baby and I wish to—"

"I don't care what you wish to do, my girl." And he had taken her by the forearms and shaken her so fiercely her hair had begun to flop about her face. "You will not—"

"Let go of me. You are hurting me."

"I'm sorry, but I will have my way about this." The two of them had glared into one another's face and for a moment, no more than a fraction of a second, there had been something between them, an element that Mary might have recognised as sensuality had she known of such a thing. Then he shook her again as though for good measure, turning away abruptly.

"I'm sorry, Beth, of course you must visit your sister. I don't know what came over me except to say I am afraid for you with that man, knowing what you know and with Milly so . . . so flighty. But promise me you will take Harry and Clancy with you. I cannot allow it if you do not." He still had his back to her and again Mary, who was a very reluctant eavesdropper, thought Mrs Beth was going to reach out for him, touch his back, comfort him for his obvious distress but she had drawn back and with a quiet goodnight had continued up the stairs.

"What is it?" she shrieked now. "What has happened? What are you all doing out here on the doorstep? Why is Mother crying, Father, and what is wrong? Oh, sweet Jesus, dear sweet Lord . . . She put her hands to her face, covering her mouth, her eyes filled with horror. "He's been here, hasn't he? He's been to claim what is his, hasn't he? What did he say? Did he see Milly and the baby? I suppose he forced—"

They were all looking at her, an identical expression of such despair on their faces, of hopelessness, she took a step backwards and nearly tumbled down the steps. The gardeners hovered about on the lawn not knowing what the devil to do, to stay or to get on with their work as though it were nothing to do with them, which was not true, for they had known Miss Milly since she was a little tacker. Mrs Ellman, cook to the household, and in the absence of Mrs Woodruff who seemed to have lost her mind, was doing her best to herd her small contingent back to the kitchen, her arm round Nan who was still weeping, though not terribly sure why. Ruby and Nessie, Hilda and Sarah made their sad way through the wide hallway and back to the kitchen where Mrs Ellman ordered a pot of tea, and the men drifted back round the house to the stable yard.

"Come in, lass," Noah said to Beth, "and you too, Mary. Ring the bell for Ruby," he told her when they had all shuffled into the drawing-room. When she did and Ruby came snivelling through the door, he ordered coffee, for it seemed she'd no chance of finding out what they wanted to drink.

"I'll have a brandy," Noah muttered to no one in particular after depositing his wife and Harriet on the sofa, "before I go off to Thornley Green to find out what that—"

"No, Father, you must not do that," Beth told him, her voice clear, sharp.

"Must not! Don't you tell me what I must or must not do, my girl. That sod's taken my girl."

"Did he force her, Father?"

Noah looked at his wife and Harriet, both of whom had stopped crying but were silent, heads bowed in sorrow, then back at his daughter.

"What the devil d'you mean by that?"

"Did she go with him willingly? Mother, you will know."

Abby bowed her head, then shook it so that her renewed tears flew about her, spotting her gown. "Yes. He was shouting for her, saying he had come to take her and his son home. The men came with . . . with their shotguns, Noah, but none dared threaten him. He had a woman with him, the same nurse, and he said she would be looked after. I begged him to leave her for a few more days since the child was scarcely a day old but he took no notice. Then, there she was at the top of the stairs, smiling at him, declaring she was ready to be off. Oh, Noah, she was so brave. I was proud of her but . . ."

Noah was across the room and had her in his arms before she had finished speaking and beside her Harriet sat stiffly, her face like death, and when she spoke her lips were so tightly clenched the words she spoke were barely audible.

"You must tell him, Abby, or I will."

"Tell me what?" Noah growled, looking over his wife's head at Harriet.

"Father, Milly did the only thing she could do to protect us all."

"Oh, and what was that then?"

"She went with him since she knew if she didn't he would never rest until he had destroyed us all. He thinks the baby is his and so he came to claim him."

There was a long silence. In the room were Noah and Abby, Harriet and Beth . . . and Mary.

"I don't . . . you will have to explain that to me, girl.

Something is going on here that is beyond my understanding and I would like someone to tell me what it is."

Beth was aware that she was gambling on nothing more than hope here. Hope that her father would understand, would accept, for the time being, what was happening and would not go rampaging over to Thornley Green, as he longed to do and fight Hugh Thornley for what was his. Her father was not a young man. He had been strong, tall, broad-shouldered, a fighter in his day and his fierce temper was well known. And his obstinacy, his belief that he was in the right. Could she trust him to listen to what she had to say, to realise what Milly had done, and why? Brave, strong, true Milly who had endangered herself to save those she loved. If her father would not listen Milly's actions were for nothing.

"She has gone back to Thornley Green because she believes that is where she belongs, Father. He is her husband—"

"But not the father of her child," a bitter voice said from the sofa where Harriet sat beside Noah and Abby. Noah turned to stare at the speaker, his mouth open, quite comical really had it not been so sad.

"Pardon?" he whispered.

"The father of the boy is my son, Todd Woodruff and I am his grandmother, along with Abby. Beth might spout of the rightness of it but I won't accept it. Not in a hundred years. So, Beth Goodwin" – standing up and shaking out her skirts – "make of that what you will."

24

Todd Woodruff tied his tall grey to the branch of a beech tree, whose leaves were just coming into bud. The leaves were bright and shining, almost translucent, but Todd had no eyes for their beauty as he crept quietly across a clearing, soggy with the wet leaves that had fallen in the autumn. There had been heavy rain and there were pools in which sodden grass grew and he was up to his ankles before he knew it. His shining boots which his batman had polished just this morning soon looked as though he had tramped across an open field, and even his immaculate blue trousers had splashes of mud on them. The rain had stopped and a shaft of April sunlight glinted through the branches of the trees, casting shadows across the carpet of copper-coloured leaves, and caught the brightness of the buttons on his scarlet tunic. He had left his forage cap hanging on the pommel of his saddle. His dark hair, straight and the colour of treacle had copper highlights where the sun caught it as he moved through the wood at the back of Thornley Green and, as everyone who saw it did, he was stilled for a moment by the house's timeless beauty. Since Hugh had married money gardeners had moved in and were busy restoring the surrounding park and gardens to the magnificence of his grandfather's day. There were smooth lawns everywhere, set with clipped privet hedges of every size and shape. Water-lilies floated in a pond, their glossy leaves as polished as once his boots had been, and further on there was a large lake to which swans had been returned. The house itself was a soft and rosy pink, glowing in the spring sunshine, large and square with a dozen round chimneys and a strong guarding tower at each corner. Mullioned windows, oriel windows, deep bays and a steep battlemented roof, for centuries ago an Englishman's home had been his castle and in need of defence. And over it all hung an air of tranquillity, of grace and peace and purpose, which was at serious odds with the man who owned it.

Todd had just come from his parents' home at the back of Lantern Hill and the contrast in their cottage, neat as it was and where he been brought up, to Hugh's house could not have been more striking. Sometimes he wondered if the Goodwins had really done him a favour in educating him as they had; in buying him a commission in the army; in setting him up as a gentleman, mixing with gentlemen when his mother and father were servants. He was betwixt and between, so to speak, in limbo sometimes as he did his best to move from one world to another, and though he knew his parents were inordinately proud of him, especially his mother, they were not always comfortable with him.

"I hear old Hugh's got himself a son and heir," Dicky Bentham had drawled in the mess last night, the first intimation Todd had that Milly had given birth and at once there were glasses raised to old Hugh's son, for though Hugh was no longer in the regiment he was still remembered. Not exactly fondly since he was a man to be treated with some caution but he had been great fun and his exploits were still talked about. "And what with one thing and another I should imagine he's glad he left the regiment when he did."

"Why is that, old chap?" asked Lieutenant Teddy Edwards.

"You must have heard the rumours, Teddy." Dicky took a sip of the brandy that the steward had just poured out for him.

"Well, I did hear something but are they to be believed?"

"I was told, reliably, that the Akas, who are one of the northern hill tribes of Assam, and who, by the way, still use bloody bows and poisoned arrows, are continuing with their border dispute and the Black Mountain tribes along the Indus have become troublesome again. No, it's us for the Indian frontier, chaps, or I'm a Dutchman and my parents did not come from Holland."

There was a general round of laughter and a growing sense of excitement, for the prospect of some action fired the young men to hot blood.

Todd was horrified, and it had taken all his strength to join in the merriment that somehow, though Hugh was no longer one of them, the birth of his son and the probability of going against the hill tribes of India seemed to generate. In the midst of the buffoonery he had managed to slip away without being noticed. He had wanted to bellow that this was *his* son, Todd Woodruff's son, not Hugh Thornley's, to stand up and tell them the truth, but he had been forced to drink and carry on as they were all doing before vanishing. This was an appalling development in the midst of his already horrendous problems and he must, absolutely must, get to see Milly as soon as possible and the only way, as far as he could see, was through her sister. God's teeth, if he should be sent to India what was to become of her and his son? Some plan must be thought out, some place of safety found, some shelter where she could hide, but how was he to protect her if he was on the other side of the bloody world? Oh, God. Oh, dear God.

He had been at Lantern Hill just as day was breaking, knocking quietly on the door of his parents' cottage, for he did not want to disturb the rest of the servants who lived in the row. His mother fell back in amazement when she opened the door and at once she put her hand to her mouth as though to hold back the cry of despair that longed to echo, not just in the cottage but up and down the row and even as far as the house.

"Is it true?" he asked, grasping her upper arms cruelly. "The child is born?" A darkness moved at the back of his eyes.

"Oh, Todd, what are we to do?" she cried hopelessly, and he was aware that his mother knew that the child Milly had given birth to was his.

"You know?"

"Son, how could I not? He is you when you were born. Oh, he's dark and has brown eyes but then so has Milly, so his lordship will know no difference but—"

"I must see her." The expression on his face softened and the darkness in his eyes vanished. "Can you get me in? I must see her, and the child, so that we can . . . you see there is a chance I may have to go abroad with the regiment and I must . . . Mother? Mother, what is it?" The expression that had crept over his mother's face alarmed him and his voice rose as a terrible fear invaded him. It had all seemed so simple as he had galloped over from Longworth. He would take Milly and the child to some . . . well, he was not awfully sure where, but to some small house where she would be safe from that brute, she and the child. He would find the money from somewhere to rent a place until he came home. His mother would help him there. He would need to hire a nurse to look after them, and a maid and . . . what else, what else?

"She's gone, son," his mother whispered as though she were afraid to speak in her normal voice, which, in a way she was, for she had not yet got up the courage to tell Clem that he had a grandson. God knows what he would do, or say.

"Gone? Gone where?"

"Her husband came yesterday and took her and the child back to Thornley Green. Nobody knows, Todd, least of all him, that you are the father. The Goodwins, of course, and I believe Mary was there but she will be discreet."

"Discreet! I don't want discreet, Mother. I want to shout it from the rooftops that Milly's child is my son. Everyone must know, everyone. I won't have her living in that house, with my son and that swine."

"No, no, no. Todd, can't you see you will be putting her and the child in the gravest danger? What d'you think that man will do if he learns the truth? Caring nothing for the consequences, he'll kill them both. We have to go about it secretly, get them away to some safe place." Harriet was becoming hysterical, her voice rising almost to a scream and when Clem, pulling his braces up, entered the kitchen his face was gape-jawed with bewilderment.

"What the bloody hell is going on here? What's up with yer mam and what the devil are you doin' here so early in't mornin'? It's barely six an' . . ."

There was a ghastly silence, a silence so complete they could distinctly hear the stirring of the rooks in the woods across the fields at the back of Lantern Hill. Clem looked from one face to the other, his own beginning to show fear, for there was something dreadfully wrong here. His wife looked as though she might faint she was so stricken, so pale, so haunted, and his son looked no better, though, being young and excited about something, he had more colour in his face.

"Someone had better tell me, lass," he said gently to his wife, laying a hand on her arm and at once she fell against him. "It's summat ter do wi' what happened yesterday, in't it? Summat's goin' on and yer'd best tell me."

Harriet sighed and, leading her husband by the hand, drew him to the small fire that was never allowed to go out, even in the summer. The cottages were well built, for Noah Goodwin never did things by half, but the windows were small and did not allow in much sunshine. Nevertheless it was cosy, well furnished in the old style and had been home to the Woodruffs for the past fifteen years.

Harriet sat him down then placed herself in the rocking-chair opposite him, holding his big, work-scarred hands in hers. Their son watched them.

"Milly's son was not sired by Lord Thornley, Clem. He thinks he was but he's mistaken."

"What?" Clem gabbled, falling back from her as though he knew he was not going to like what she was about to tell him.

"No. Milly had a lover; she loved him, Clem, it was no light thing, was it, Todd?" turning to look at her son and Clem followed her gaze.

"What yer sayin', lass?" he croaked.

"Milly's boy is our grandson, Clem. Todd's son, and we want him back, don't we, Todd?"

And now he was here at the back of Thornley Green with no idea what he was to do or even why he was here. She'd hardly be likely to be out in the park, would she, her only two days from childbed, but something had brought him here in a wild gallop, perhaps to get away from his parents' devastation, for his father had been distraught, angry first, furious even, ready to knock his lad to the ground for his flighty ways, but totally devastated when his mother had calmed him down.

For an hour, perhaps more, as he had lost track of time, he sat on a fallen tree on the edge of the wood, staring unseeingly at the round chimneys and the steep roof, all that was visible of the house from this distance. Several labourers tramped across the lawns and for a moment he thought they were headed in his direction, but they veered off towards the high stone wall that surrounded the property, vanishing from his view. Where was she, his love, he agonised, and not just his love but his son whom he had never seen? A nurse had been with Hugh when he came for Milly and Harriet had told him that Noah Goodwin was sending Doctor Bennett to check on her, which Hugh wouldn't like but he could hardly forbid him entrance. There would be a wet nurse for the child, since the ladies of the aristocracy, like Milly, would not nurse their own offspring, so for the moment perhaps they were safe, Milly and the child, but how was he to get word to her and if—

Suddenly he stood up, cursing himself for his own stupidity in forgetting it in his despair. There was only one person who might get in to see Milly and that was her sister. She knew the truth, his mother had told him, and though she had allowed them to meet at her house before the baby was born, she had not approved and would not approve now. And Archie had been positively hostile. Still, what else could he do? Hugh was a menace to society, to women in particular and what Alicia Bramhall was thinking of, taking him as a lover, was beyond him. But he didn't care about that. He must see Beth. Ask her what she meant to do about her sister. Hugh would not, could not, stand in the way of the sisters meeting. He might, and probably would, forbid his father- and mother-in-law entrance to his home, since he had never forgiven Noah for the scar he had put on his cheek but he would see no harm in Beth visiting Milly.

Turning swiftly and running back through the wet leaves and pools of water, he leaped nimbly into the saddle and guided his grey through the woodland until he came to the small wrought-iron gate let into the wall. Leaning down, he un-latched it then spurred his animal on to the lane that led in the direction of Edge Bottom.

"You are not going alone, and that is that. In fact you're not going at all," Archie said, turning to glare at Todd. "If you imagine I will allow my wife to enter that house and calmly ask to see her sister after all that has happened, then you're off your head."

He and Beth were at breakfast and Todd was mystified as to why, after all he had done this morning, it was still only a little past eight o'clock. He leaned forward in his seat, twiddling with the spoon in the saucer of the cup of coffee he had been offered, gazing imploringly at Beth, for he knew she was the one with the warmer heart. Not that Archie was cold-hearted, Todd had discovered that during his childhood, but he had a cooler head and would not be influenced by Todd's desperate need. Indeed he was deeply disapproving of Todd's relationship, a casual relationship, he deemed it, with a woman married to another man. He knew Milly Thornley's capacity to grasp whatever it was she fancied with no thought for the consequences, for she had been like that since she was a child. But Todd knew this was different. Ask him how he knew and he could not have told you but he steadfastly believed, though it had barely been spoken of, by him or by her, that they loved one another. Milly had never loved a man in her life, even Hugh whom she had married, but she loved him, Todd, and he must talk to her, see his son, work out some plan that would get her away from Thornley Green before he left for India. That is if the rumours Dicky had spoken about were true. She had gone back to Hugh, he was convinced, to protect her family, to protect him and their son, but it could not be borne.

"Will you go, both of you, please. Dear God, I am in purgatory not knowing. He has nothing against you, either of you. You have done him no mischief."

"He hates Noah and that hatred will run over on to Beth— And then there was the scene on the parade-ground."

"Sweet Jesus, Archie, where is your heart, man?" Todd was so obviously harrowed, even Archie, who had no desire to see his beloved young wife insulted, or even worse, felt sympathy move in his breast. It was a Sunday so he was not needed at the works and if there was some emergency Noah could be called upon to deal with it.

"Archie," Beth said quietly, "I would like to see Milly and surely it would not be thought strange for me to call on my sister who has just been confined. I would be glad of your company, for Hugh Thornley can be very frightening. Harry could drive the carriage with Clancy beside him and even Hugh would not be so foolish as to threaten us. He has no reason to.

He has what he wants. He has Milly back home and . . . and his son."

"*My* son," Todd said harshly.

"Yes, yes, man." Archie's voice was irritable and it was evident that he wished Todd Woodruff to the far ends of the earth where he could inflict no more harm on the Goodwin family. Todd saw it in his face but did not tell him his wish might soon be granted!

They were received by the supercilious footman who told them he would see if his lordship was at home. Would they be so good as to wait here. Who was calling? he asked insolently although Archie had already given their name.

Beth put her hand on Archie's arm, leaving it there while the footman moved slowly and importantly through the wide hallway towards a door on which he knocked and then entered.

"Well, well," an amused voice said, as the footman paused in the doorway to allow his master to come out into the hall, "look who's here come to visit her sister and nephew and look who she's brought with her as protector. What's the matter, Goodwin? Afraid I might seduce your charming wife?" Beth felt Archie's arm stiffen and she gripped it tightly. She had listened to Todd's impassioned plea and had felt great sympathy for him, but it was not only for his sake that she was here. Milly was her sister, her twin, and the boy was her nephew. Her mother and father were mad with worry about Milly and it was on their behalf and her own that she was here. So they must not cross this man if she was to come again, which she meant to do. She could not just abandon Milly to her fate and that was what would happen if she allowed him on this first visit to get the better of them.

"May we see Milly, Hugh?" she asked politely. "We will stay only a minute or two but if you say she is not well enough" – even though he had moved her on the day following her confinement, indifferent to how she was – "we will come again tomorrow."

"Will you indeed? Well, I can tell you she is progressing nicely, according to that bloody doctor your family sent, and let me tell you he will not be allowed in here again. He took the servants by surprise and they had shown him upstairs before I had a chance to bar him the house. And the boy is doing nicely. A big boy and healthy, though he came early. Eight months that snivelling doctor said but a true Thornley. Now, will that do you? I have given my report."

"Let me see Milly, please, Hugh," Beth pleaded, while beside her Archie stood like a soldier on a parade-ground, stiff, visibly longing to smash his fist into Hugh Thornley's face.

It so happened that Hugh Thornley was in an unusually good humour that morning. He had won at the gaming tables and then spent the night in his mistress's bed, while at home his wife and newly born son lay safely tucked up and waiting for him. A man well pleased with what he had and, after watching Beth through the curls of smoke from the cigar he was smoking, he nodded. Archie's face was clamped as tight as an oyster straight from the sea.

"Come this way, my dear. I will take you up myself. She is still confined to her bed, naturally, but I'm sure I can prevail upon Nurse Corbett to allow you a moment with her. She is a bit of a martinet but if I ask nicely . . ." He grinned at the very idea of Hugh Thornley asking nicely for *anything* and especially of someone inferior to himself.

Milly was propped up among a heap of pillows and, apart from the small scar on her cheek that Doctor Bennett had stitched after Hugh's attack on her, looked much as usual. Her hair was brushed and lay in a copper swathe across the pillow and there was even a ribbon in it to match her flimsy nightgown. The nurse rose from her chair by the fire and looked disapprovingly at Beth, signalling with her eyebrows to his lordship that she did not think her ladyship was up to visitors yet and it was perhaps this that worked in Beth's favour. No one criticised Hugh Thornley, not even by implication, and when he frowned menacingly the nurse took a step backwards and put her hand on the mantelpiece. Milly said nothing and neither did Beth.

"I imagine there is something you could be doing in the nursery, Nurse Corbett," Hugh said icily.

"Of course, m'lord," the nurse said and scurried from the room. As she opened the door, which Hugh had shut behind him, the footman stood there with his hand raised, evidently about to knock.

"Yes, what is it?" Hugh hissed.

"That gentleman, sir, the one with the lady."

"Yes?"

"Is he supposed to be wandering about, m'lord?"

"Wandering about? What the devil d'you mean, man?" Beth held her breath, doing her best to avoid Milly's eye, giving thanks for Archie's quick thinking. He knew she wanted to speak, even just for a minute or two, to Milly but there was little chance Hugh would leave them alone. Not unless something called him away that would not only enrage him but would give him an excuse to vent his temper on a Goodwin.

"He's in the library, m'lord, halfway up the steps and reading one of your lordship's books. I tried to draw him back to the hall but he—"

"The bastard! How dare he make free with my house. He'll pay for this, by God." And hustling the footman before him he ran from the bedroom and could be heard galloping down the stairs. Beth prayed for Archie's safety but he was strong and well prepared. Like Noah before him, he knew how to fight, in and out of the prize-fighting ring, and in his pocket, as a last resort, he had a small revolver that fired five shots. Not that it would come to that but best be prepared, Archie had said as they left home.

"Beth," Milly whispered, then lifted her arms and Beth ran to the bed, kneeling at the side of it to hug her sister.

"We haven't much time. How are you, really? Mother and Father are out of their minds. Oh, why did you do it, darling?"

"There was no other way. I had to come otherwise he would have . . . God knows what he would have done. I am safe at the moment since even he cannot fancy a woman so soon after childbirth. But tell me about Todd. Does he know?"

"Yes, and he's determined to see you."

"Don't let him, Beth." Milly's voice was urgent. "Tell him I'm well and will get word to him when I can. He mustn't come anywhere near here, not with Hugh hanging about. When some time has passed and the novelty of having a son at last has worn off . . ."

"He's . . . he might be going away, Milly."

Milly's face blanched. She sank back in her pillows and her eyes grew haunted as though Beth had just conveyed some life-threatening news.

"Where?"

"He thinks his regiment is for India. He told me . . ."

They could hear a fracas downstairs and Beth knew that if she didn't get down there, and soon, Archie and Hugh might come to blows, or worse. Archie was teetering on the edge of madness, not of the sort that lunatics know but that known to a man who is provoked beyond his capabilities to restrain himself. A temperate man was Archie, slow to anger, but Hugh Thornley, who cared for no one, who disregarded danger, a man with no conscience, unprincipled and black-hearted, could provoke a saint to murder.

"I must go. I'll come as soon as I can. If Sally could fetch a note saying when Hugh is to be away. Oh, Milly, I hate leaving you. I wanted to see the boy."

"Go, for God's sake, before Hugh kills Archie."

"Yes." Beth kissed her sister's drawn face, which only minutes before had been smiling in welcome, then slipped from the room and ran down the stairs.

"Hugh, old man," Archie was saying, "you really have a wonderful library and it tempted me to enter. Forgive me."

"Well," Hugh said grudgingly. "Never having read a book in my life, I wouldn't know about such things. Now I must go up to—"

"I'm here, Archie. Milly is tired so I left her but, well, thank you for allowing me to see her, Hugh," wondering madly why it was she had to thank Hugh Thornley so obsequiously for his permission to visit her own sister! She took Archie's arm and smiled up into his face and he felt the joy work in him, as her expression was one he had sought for months.

25

It was the longest day of the year and as though the weather knew what was expected of it on this midsummer's day, it was quite glorious. The herbaceous border was at its peak, over-flowing with hollyhock, dahlia, delphinium, wallflower, phlox, aster and stock, the vivid colours a rainbow ribbon edging the perfect symmetry of the emerald-green lawn. Tucker had set Billy to weeding the path and the lad did his best not to be distracted by Alexandra who was, as Jane said, "into every-thing" and seemed to feel it was her right to help him. The trouble was she could not, at fifteen months, distinguish between flower or weed and poor Billy, dearly fond as he was of the delightful little girl, was at his wits' end.

"Alex, do leave poor Billy alone," Beth called from her chair beneath the enormous canopy of the oak tree in front of the house. Morna had just placed a teatray complete with a plate of Mrs Kyle's mouth-watering almond biscuits on the table and, picking one up, Beth held it out to her niece. "See what Auntie Beth has for you, darling."

The baby turned and looked at her, weighing up the delight of "picking" flowers, which was what she believed she was doing, and the prospect of a biscuit. The biscuit won and with a babbled remark to Billy, which seemed to be an apology to the lad for withdrawing her help, she scuttled in that peculiar way she had, like a crab with a broken claw, as Archie privately described it, in the direction of the table. Again she crowed some greeting and waved her arms about in the air, reaching for the biscuit Beth held out to her. Her face creased in a grin of delight and before Beth could say another word, she daintily bit a small piece out of the biscuit. She looked gravely at Beth as she chewed, then grinned again, taking another bite.

"Is that good, sweetheart? You like Mrs Kyle's almond biscuits, don't you? And so does Auntie Beth," she said, helping herself from the plate.

"Good," Alex answered clearly, her rosy mouth covered in crumbs, then she licked her lips and held up her hand for another. "More."

"Say please then."

"Pease."

"Good girl," Beth told her as she handed her another biscuit. She turned to smile at Mary who was mending some small garment belonging to the child, her face placid as she performed her task. She and Beth, who were bringing up the child, were inordinately pleased with any improvement in her progress, which was slow, for not only was the fact that she was a premature baby holding her back, but her infirmity put her behind babies of the same age. She had not sat up until she was eleven months old; did not move in that crab-like way she had developed until she was thirteen months; and now at fifteen months, when most babies had taken their first steps, she had not even attempted to stand up. In all other ways she was perfect. Her disposition was sunny, though now and again Beth thought she saw a streak of wilfulness in her which was not surprising considering who her mother and father were. They had tried keeping her in a large pen when they were outside, for she would go wandering off in any direction that took her fancy, usually where she was not supposed to be, like in the middle of a flowerbed, but she had set up such a screeching and rattling of the bars they had let her out. Beth and Mary were constantly fetching her back to the rug where she was supposed to be, or one of the gardeners would return her, covered in soil, clutching several flowers in her chubby hand and smiling hugely, the men, or more often Billy, holding her out before him beneath her armpits with his scarred, soil-covered hands.

The sound of horse's hooves came from the lane at the side of the house that led to the stables and a voice called out a greeting. The gate opened and Archie Goodwin came through it, closing it carefully behind him, for Alex's one ambition was to discover what was on the other side. The little girl turned and with a great deal of delighted mewing noises began a rapid crawl across the lawn in his direction.

"Aarch," she began to squeal and with a whoop of joy Archie picked her up and threw her into the air, catching her firmly, though both the women who watched winced. "How's my girl, then?" he asked her, kissing her round cheek firmly. "How's my beauty? What have you been up to today?" And as though she understood every word the child began to babble excitedly, turning to point at Billy, at the biscuits on the tea table, at Boy who had long given up trying to capture his master's attention and who lay by the table. Archie walked towards Beth, holding Alex to his shoulder. He put her down on the grass, knowing the futility of placing her on the rug and with a careful hesitancy bent to place a kiss on his wife's cheek.

"I thought I'd come home early since it's such a lovely day. Any chance of a cup of tea?"

Mary immediately rose from her chair and picked up the teatray. Despite Archie's protestations that the tea in the pot would do, she moved towards the house saying she would make a fresh brew. Beth knew that Mary had been glad of the excuse to move away and leave her and Archie alone, for despite their renewed relationship, that of polite friendliness, they were as yet not man and wife as they once had been. Archie still slept in a spare room and their careful tiptoeing around one another caused Archie, at least, a great deal of pain. Mary knew this and was eager to give them as much time alone together, even only a few minutes, which, perhaps with the child, might bring about a complete reconciliation.

"How is Todd getting along?" Beth asked him, picking up the sewing Mary had put down, and he knew it was a small barrier she erected, as she had done for the past year and more, to keep at bay any intimacy that he might attempt.

The incredible affair of Todd Woodruff and his change of career was still a matter of some amazement to them all, and to the town in general, and one of great disappointment to his mother, as she had had enormous hopes for her son who had done so well in the army until he had fallen into the clutches of that witch up at Thornley Green. That was what she called Milly Thornley, even to Milly's mother and father, since had it not been for her he would not have resigned his commission and gone to work in the office of Archie Goodwin at Edge Bottom Glass Works. What a come-down, she had shrieked when he had told her what he was to do and after all they had done for him, Noah and Abby, not to mention the sacrifices she and Clem had made to ensure he could keep up with the other officers in the mess, buy a decent horse, his uniform and all the things necessary to an officer in a good regiment.

"Mother, you know I can't go to India with the regiment and you know why."

"Oh yes, we all know why, son. That woman wouldn't be so easily available to you if you—"

"Stop it, Mother. I won't have you speak of Milly like that. I am as much to blame for the birth of our son as she is. She did not seduce me."

"No, then how did she get you into her bed?"

"Good God, Mother, I went willingly. At first it was nothing, a bit of fun, but we grew to love one another."

His mother flung up her arms and seemed about to spit in the fire before which she, Clem and Todd sat. "She doesn't know the meaning of the word love, and neither do you. Tell him,

Clem. Tell him what it means to love someone. Tell him what we have had and it's not all about bed, my lad," not giving the silent figure of her husband time to answer.

He sat quietly, dignified as he had always been, his head bowed, but he was not as anguished as his wife. He was a simple man and if his son could find a simple job around here, such as he had he would be content. The thought of the lad sailing off to those wild places he himself had only laboriously read about in books was not one he relished, and though he was distraught to think of his grandson being brought up by that sod at Thornley Green, as far as he could see there was nothing to be done about it. Not without making such a brew of trouble none of them would survive it. His lordship would not be satisfied with destroying the child and the child's mother, but would probably kill the man who had sired the boy in the first place. The Goodwins would be the centre of such a destructive scandal they would be crucified. He could understand why his lad didn't want to go to India, leaving the woman he apparently loved and the child she had borne him to the mercies of such a man, and though he couldn't for the life of him see what Todd could do to rectify the damage done, he understood why his son wanted to stay near the boy and his mother.

"Leave it, Harriet," he told her gently.

She turned to him, astonished. Like him she was in agony at the thought of Hugh Thornley bringing up, or having any sort of influence on her grandson, for the man was cruel – look at the way he treated Milly – but as yet she could not, like Clem, think of any way they could bring the child away from what was apparently his birthright, at least in Hugh Thornley's eyes. Perhaps it might be better if Todd was to stay nearby but then supposing he should continue his affair with that madam who was her grandson's mother? Oh, dear God, why could not men keep their cocks in their pants? she thought agonisingly. But then, as Todd had said, it takes two to make a baby and Milly was just as much to blame with her flaunting ways!

So, to the bewilderment of his brother officers, Todd Woodruff resigned his commission and took up a post at Edge Bottom Glass Works. What on earth was the fellow thinking of, they asked one another, to give up a fine career and lower himself to some labouring task in a glass works? But then weren't his parents from the working classes, so maybe that explained it. Perhaps he could not quite bring himself to take up the cloak of a gentleman, a gentleman such as they were. He had always been a bit apart from them, even though old Hugh had seemed to find his company congenial. It was a bloody mystery, it really was.

Todd meant to take the job, any job at the glass works for the time being until he had found something that would be more to his liking. It had not met with the initial approval of Noah or Archie Goodwin, for they knew what was behind it and it could not only cause trouble with Milly and Todd in such close proximity but at the back of Noah's mind was a glimmering of hope that perhaps, with a bit of help, he did not exactly know of what sort at the moment, or even if it could be done, his grandson and his daughter might be, well, parted from that swine who had them. Noah Goodwin was not a man to sit back calmly and let some other man take what was rightfully his – meaning his grandson – and with Todd Woodruff on the other side of the world it would be difficult to bring this about. He hadn't worked it out yet in his clever head, but though he didn't like it, to have Todd working where he, Noah, could keep an eye on him might be to his advantage. After all, Milly seemed to love the fellow!

"Todd's doing his best," Archie answered his wife, diplomatic as always, for though he tried hard Todd was not cut out to sit at a desk all day. He was often to be found in the sheet house watching the glass-blowers at their work, seemingly impervious to the heat and the general atmosphere of what might be described as hellish conditions, taking an extraordinary interest, considering his previous career, in the coal-fired glass furnace. Though fresh air was fed in to the grate from outside the glasshouse by an underground tunnel, the flames from the fire reverberated down from the dome and the temperature put a slick of sweat on his skin beneath his clothes. The figures of the men who moved surely about their work reminded him of some picture he had seen, purporting to be the depths of Hades but the men whistled and called out to one another in such cheerful tones he was fascinated. He watched a half-naked man gathering molten glass on to a blowpipe which was then blown into an open block or mould and this dictated the ultimate diameter of the cylinder. Through five processes the glass was delicately handled until, finally, a sheet of pure glass was placed in the annealing kiln. Archie found him there and wondered, though he said nothing, not even to Noah, whether they had placed Todd Woodruff in the wrong department.

Besides sheet glass Goodwins also had begun to experiment with the making of rolled glass, plate and cathedral glass that yielded profits that balanced the difficulties in the plate market. There was strong competition from the United States and Europe, but with Noah's vast experience and Archie's astute brain, his inclination, being a younger man, to take risks, and his innovative ideas, the glass works surged ahead of all its rivals. It had expanded enormously since Noah Goodwin had married Abby and now employed not only the men involved in glass-making but hundreds of women and children in grinding, smoothing and polishing sheet glass.

"There seems to be something in your tone that says Todd is not doing as well as you and Father hoped," Beth said quietly, her head bent to her stitching.

Her husband felt his spirit sink as he watched her. Were they ever to be as they were before the incident of the lock hospital? Was she ever to be as once she had been to him? Were they ever to be husband and wife, to have a family, children of their own? Beth was a wonderful "mother" to baby Alex. His heart squeezed with the pain of it but he had not totally given up the hope that one day she would turn to him, as she had done a couple of times, in the dreadful circumstance of her sister's marriage, and they would be lovers again, friends, companions, but *lovers*.

"I keep finding him in the glasshouse when he should be at his desk and I wondered whether . . ." He paused reflectively.

Beth lifted her head to look at him. He seemed tired, dejected somehow and though deep down she knew exactly what was wrong with this patient husband of hers and was sorry for it, she could not be any different towards him. He loved her, she knew that, but he wanted more than she could give him and she wondered if she ever would. She too would like a child of her own but the thought of a man's hands, even those of this kindly man, on her body, perhaps invading that intimate part of her that had been so badly damaged, was more than she could bear. Since the birth of Milly's son and the dramatic events that had followed with Todd, which had seemed for a while to bring them closer, he had withdrawn from her, taking great pleasure in Alex's progress and delightfully endearing baby ways. It was as though the love he had poured over herself in great endless waves had transferred itself to the child, for it needed some outlet. She was tempted to put out her hand and place it on his but his gaze was on the crawling baby.

"Yes?" she said encouragingly. "You were wondering . . .?"

"If it would be a good idea to put him – well, not as an apprentice as he's too old – but into the glasshouse. I did it, your father and his father before him did it. It's the only way to learn the business. Not sitting at a desk going over accounts which I'm sure he doesn't understand. He knows Noah put him there to please Milly, perhaps in the long run, to *help* Milly, for who knows what plan your father has in his mind, and I know the idea of being, well, you could only call it a labourer after being an officer in the cavalry must seem to be a bit of a comedown but it seems to me that the fellow has a genuine interest in the process of glass-making." He appeared to be talking to himself and might have gone on doing so had not Alex come trundling across the lawn, clutching in her chubby hand the heads of several daisies. Her speed was quite incredible considering her disability and both Beth and Archie watched her, beginning to smile.

When she reached them she put her hand on Archie's knee, the other offering the daisies to him.

"Thank you, sweetheart. Are those for me? They're lovely." He took the daisy heads and put out his other hand to help her up but she refused it, grabbing at the wicker arm of the chair. She got a good grip on it and as they watched breathlessly she slowly pulled herself to her feet, standing for a fraction of a second on one plump leg. The other, the shorter one, did not quite reach the ground and for a second she tottered, doing her best to keep her balance, then, with a soft cry of disappointment, she fell. Beth was on her feet, ready to pick her up but Archie waved her back.

"Leave her," he said harshly, then with a strong and loving hand he reached out for the child who lay in a crumpled heap of dainty muslin, satin ribbons and bare legs.

"Come, darling, hold Archie's hand." And she reached out, her small rosy face becoming even more flushed with her determined effort to stand.

"Archie, please, she cannot—" Beth began, but Archie waved her away almost angrily.

"She must walk one day, Beth, and to walk she must learn to stand."

The little girl struggled to sit up and as though measuring the distance she looked at Archie's hand which was on a level with his knee. She put hers in it, the tiny one disappearing into his slender but strong hand. She said something in her childish babble then, with a great effort and with no help from Archie, hauled herself to her feet again. She stood, one foot placed firmly on the ground, the other just brushing the grass with the part of her foot where her toes would have been. She was barefoot and the small stump of her foot seemed to dangle, then, still holding Archie's hand, more firmly this time, she placed her crippled foot on the grass and stood, slightly lopsided, her hands in Archie's, smiling broadly. Again she placed her normal foot on the grass and with a bit of a lurch put her full weight on it then moved her damaged leg so that she took a small step. She repeated the performance, moving round the chair, held firmly by Archie, until she came to the table covered with a beautifully embroidered tablecloth and it was here that disaster struck. Leaving go of Archie's hand she grabbed at the tablecloth, determined, or so it seemed, to lurch round the table to Beth. With a crash the contents of the table came tumbling down and might have fallen on the child and, had it not been for Archie's quickness, she might have been seriously hurt.

She did not cry though she was clearly shocked. Archie held her on his lap, cradling her against his chest while Beth hovered over them and even Billy came running, for the crash had been heard all over the garden as cups and saucers and the heavy silver teapot fell in a broken heap on to the grass.

"Let me have her, Archie," Beth begged him, holding out her arms to take the baby.

"She's fine where she is," he said shortly.

"But . . ."

"Beth, will you let me at least have the pleasure of Milly's daughter, as you do. It seems I am not to have a child of my own and so I must make do with another man's. I am perfectly able to comfort her. Besides, she is not hurt, nor even overly concerned with the accident. You and Mary and Jane coddle her and it is hard to believe you will allow her to grow up as a normal child. She must learn to stand, to walk and even, eventually, to run as other children do. I shall teach her to ride and when she is older John Bennett says there—"

Beth's face had turned the colour of bleached calico as every drop of blood ran from her face. She stood paralysed as though he had struck her and Billy, who had heard every word, melted away into the shrubbery, shocked beyond measure, for he had never heard Mr Archie speak to Mrs Beth as he had just done. None of them had. Billy had been weeding the path but he didn't dare return to it even though Mr Tucker would give him what for, since he did not want to overhear another word of what was being said between his master and mistress.

"How could you?" Beth whispered. "How could you say such a thing?"

"Which part do you object to, Beth? You know it's true. I know you and Mary and Jane love the child but you are over-protective."

"Those are not the words that . . . that have stabbed me to the heart."

"What did I say to have so upset you?" He was caught up in a mixture of anger, despair, hopelessness and it seemed with a desperate need to lash out at her for the hurt she inflicted on him day after day, month after month, with her cool politeness, her total indifference, or so it seemed to him, to his feelings. He was a man, dammit. He loved her, not just as a husband, but as a normal, virile male and the past months had been sheer hell. It was, he supposed, none of her doing, what had happened to her, and he was desolate at what that had been but surely, surely, after all these months . . .

"You accuse me of not giving you a child, when you must know that I was . . . that they tore it from me. Oh, God, I can't bear it." She began to weep helplessly, tears washing in a torrent across her face. Alex watched her, her eyes enormous, her own lip beginning to tremble, then she turned her face into Archie's waistcoat and her small body shook in distress, and then, to add to the drama, she began to howl. Within several seconds Jane was there, and Mary, and even Morna, for the child's cries had roused all the servants. Mary took one look at Beth, then glanced at Mr Archie and without a word lifted Alex from his arms and shepherded them all back into the house. Boy shivered and licked his master's hand and Archie fondled his ear before standing up and moving hesitantly towards his wife, who was staring out over the garden, great tears still rolling down her cheeks. He stood behind her and when he put his hands gently on her shoulders she did not, as he had expected, flinch away from him.

"Beth, my Beth, forgive me."

With a convulsive movement she turned and flung herself into his arms which tightened about her. Her head tucked itself beneath his chin and her face pressed itself into the curve of his throat and her body shook so that both of them trembled in unison.

She began to moan deep in her throat. "Oh, how could I? How could I? What have I done to you? Selfish . . . only of myself . . . and then to deny you a child of . . . Say you forgive me . . . my fault," and on and on she babbled, no more than a word or a part of a sentence comprehensible to him. He kissed her hair, her wet eyes which she turned up to him in supplication, her wet cheeks, her ears, her neck and her mouth which seemed to welcome his and he was made aware that something that had been broken inside his wife had been miraculously mended. His words had shattered that terrible rock in her heart. Her outpourings were the draining of a boil, the discharge that comes from a wound that had festered quietly inside her since the lock hospital. He didn't understand why it should happen now, unless it was the declaration of his own pain, his own feelings, not just towards her but for the child, which had liberated her but she was lifting her wet face, eager for his kisses, her mouth opening beneath his, and all under the fascinated, horrified gaze of poor Billy who wished the ground would open beneath his feet and drag him down into it.

That night for the first time in more than a year Archie Goodwin made love to his wife in the soft, candlelit glow of their bedroom, the candles' flames flickering on their entwined bodies, the need in both of them lifting them, to the drifting sea of rapture that had usually eluded Beth. She heard her own voice, and his, through the pulsing of their heartbeats, through the booming of waves that carried them to an unfamiliar shore. She was borne up, lifted, broken in a shimmering light and when the aftermath came she found she was weeping in great heaving sobs, and so was Archie. They clung together like shipwrecked sailors, inert, locked together, the intensity of their love amazing them both.

He held her, kissing her wet cheeks, tasting the saltiness of his own tears and knew that he and his beloved wife had come home.

26

"I have decided to give a garden party in aid of the movement, darling. Do you feel up to helping, perhaps with one of the stalls? I know you are only just . . . well, you have been out of circulation for a while and I wondered if perhaps you might not wish to get back into the thick of it so soon. You have only to say. The weather has been so glorious I'm hoping it will remain that way and that the sun will shine on Saturday. Lydia is to put in an appearance, perhaps help with the raffle, and many of our more prominent members have promised me they will try and come. Your father, of course, is not at all pleased, for I do believe he would like me to sit at home and not stir from the house unless it's with him."

Abby Goodwin smiled and placed a hand on her daughter's silk-clad knee, putting her cup and saucer down on the small table beside her. "Do you think Archie will agree? Since you regained your . . . er, health he has been a different man, he never seems to stop smiling and cannot bear you out of his sight, but he always appeared to be in agreement with our beliefs in the past. Dear God, he should be, for he has been brought up with them but I'm not sure he is ready for you to get back—"

"Mother, Mother," Beth laughed. "Stop worrying about Archie. He knows my unshakeable belief in equality for women and their right to vote as men do. He is of the same conviction, though when it comes to his wife he, like Father, would rather I stayed at home and let others do the fighting. But he also knows after . . . after what happened to me and Mary that there is absolutely nothing that will stop me from doing all I can for the cause. I would rather have his permission, or shall I say approval, but whether he gives it or not I shall go on."

"Well done, then I shall go ahead with the arrangements. The front lawn should be big enough for the stalls and then, if guests want to wander into the park they may do so. I shall have to get extra staff in. Harriet will help there as she appears to know everyone in the district, as I suppose I do, since I was born close by and we will easily find suitable girls."

"Why don't we make it into a sort of a fair, like the one that comes to St Helens every year? You know, merry-go-rounds, coconut shies, hurdy-gurdys, peep shows, nothing vulgar, of course but something not only for substantial families like the Holmes and the Sheens but those from the working classes as well. From the glass works and collieries. Decent folk who work hard and would love a day out. Many of the women are firm believers in what we are doing and are eager to help us in the fight even if their husbands aren't. It might encourage more members."

Beth sat back and beamed at her mother, then sprang up to rescue one of her mother's exotic plants from the enthusiastic attention of Alex who was dragging it, pot and all, across the tiled conservatory floor. The door to the conservatory stood wide open and on the broad step that led down into the garden lay her father's two Labradors, Charlie and Freddy, who had patiently suffered the baby's rough handling. She had climbed on their backs, clung to their smoothly brushed coats, kissed their wet, black noses and begged them, in her childish babble, to play with her. When they seemed inclined to refuse she had turned to the many other exciting objects in her grandmother's conservatory. Beth had held her up to stare wide-eyed into the cages where pretty coloured birds sang their hearts out; to sniff the glorious scents of the bird of paradise flowers in their big terracotta pots, the bleeding heart vine and climbing hibiscus, its frilly-petalled crimson flowers hanging down like Japanese lanterns which Alex patted gently. There was jasmine, a magnificent wax plant, passion flowers with edible fruit and, naturally, tall palms which reached the glass roof. Orchids grew in hanging baskets and water hyacinths in a tiny pool, all very tempting for a small girl whose curiosity was boundless. In the centre sat a cane table with a bottle-green cloth which reached the floor. Across it was thrown a white lace cloth and on the table was the usual paraphernalia of afternoon tea. Pine chairs overflowed with vivid cushions and a black and white cat, the kitchen cat, which often escaped his duties as mouse-catcher sprawled, as was his wont, in the warmth of the sun-filled "winter garden", as an earlier Mrs Goodwin had called it.

The garden party, despite its mixed members of the classes, was a huge success mainly due to the determined women, many of them wives of prominent men, whom they dragged along, reluctantly, it might be said, for would not Noah Goodwin, who had great influence in St Helens, be deeply offended if they did not support his beloved wife. These women had been closely involved in the women's cause, along with Abby Goodwin and Laura Bennett and, more recently, Abby's daughter Beth. They did not normally mix with the lower classes and probably would never have done so but for their association with the suffrage movement, about which most of them were passionate. They had been incensed by the remarks made by Mrs Humphrey Ward, a bestselling novelist, that she believed women would be corrupted by politics and chivalry would die, for heaven's sake, and that if women became involved with politics they would stop marrying and the British race would die out. Did you ever hear such nonsense? they said to one another. She said that women's brains were smaller than men's, making them less intelligent, that women were emotional creatures and incapable of making a sound and reasoned political decision. They might not make a sound and reasoned political decision since they were never given the chance, but some of them helped their husbands in business and ran busy households as well, which was a damned hard job! These women might look askance at the rather unusual amusements that were on show today but they put their hands in their pockets, for the Suffrage Society needed as much support as could be rallied.

And even their hard-headed husbands were impressed by Miss Lydia Ernestine Becker who was a Lancashire lass from her head to her toes, even if her father was of German origin. She was plump, bespectacled and the cartoonists made fun of her, but all who listened to her that day were forced to acknowledge her intellect and her thoroughness in outlining the future for women, even if the men were not quite sure how they would fit into this scheme of things. She had a complete mastery of the intricacies of parliamentary procedure. Her work as a parliamentary agent and editor of the *Women's Suffrage Journal* had made her the backbone of the movement in its early days, but her entreaties to the ladies to hold fund-raising parties such as these, to attend bazaars, rallies and lectures, to go on the organised marches and processions, to campaign peacefully, lobbying for support from MPs, to write to the newspapers, were often not well received by the younger members, who were of the opinion that more could be done to bring their cause to the attention of the public and, more importantly, to Parliament. None of the politicians had, so far, taken their demands seriously, treating the issue with ridicule whenever it was raised in Parliament. Some of the women had listened to Emmeline Pankhurst, whose oratory was so uplifting. And of course there were still seven million men who were not yet enfranchised, working-class men, which included the poorest, servants who lived in the homes of their employers – which meant all Noah Goodwin's male servants – criminals and lunatics. Women thus joined the ranks of criminals and lunatics, a point Miss Becker emphasised and which was repeated in the posters, postcards, leaflets, books and handbills printed by the movement. Nevertheless Miss Becker took the opportunity to beg the ladies to join the union. Any woman could become a member by paying a shilling, which was not at all to the liking of the glass workers, the colliers, the bricklayers and other working men who had come with their old ladies to see the fun and could ill afford a shilling!

They had all gone, including Miss Becker. The maidservants were beginning the daunting task of clearing up the debris the masses had left behind, the men were helping to dismantle stalls, one of which Beth had manned, selling knick-knacks from her home and from Lantern Hill which had gone like the proverbial hot cakes, since there was many a working man's wife who prized an ornament come from the home of one of St Helens' wealthiest families. Her mother lay prostrate on the sofa in the drawing-room, exhausted but exchanging with Laura their delight at the success of the day; the menfolk, Archie, Noah and John Bennett, had retired to Noah's study for a much needed whisky; but Beth, after listening to Miss Becker's inspiring speech, could not quite settle with either party. She wandered across the grass at the back of the house where, an hour ago, men had sprawled with a glass of ale in their hands and women had chided tired children, and where now Frank Jones and Jack Martin surveyed their flowerbeds in dismay.

She had reached the strip of woodland before she realised it, coming to a halt at the fence that divided it from the parkland, her mind flying back to the days when she had climbed it and found Hugh Thornley waiting for her. What a child she had been, an innocent, inexperienced child who had been taken in by the flattery and handsome face of the man who was now her sister's husband. She had believed she was in love. She had been intoxicated by his attention. He had set her pulses and heartbeat racing at every meeting. She had believed that he was beginning to love her as she loved him and she had dawdled through her days with a secret smile in her heart as she waited for the proposal that had never come. Instead he had become engaged to Milly and how poor Milly had suffered for it.

It was as though her thoughts had conjured him up and she felt the shock of it punch her in the chest, expelling the breath from her lungs. She knew she was about to faint even as she leaned for support on the top rung of the fence that divided them, but the thought of falling to the ground in front of this monster, perhaps being touched by him, picked up by him, dragged her back from the brink. Nevertheless the blood drained from her head and her legs turned as soft and boneless as jelly. She began to shake, not just with shock but with fear, for the expression in his eyes was as cold and frozen as the ice-blue waters of the Norwegian fjords that she had seen in a geography book. He was smiling affably, leaning against the broad trunk of the oak tree beneath which he and she had sat, his left leg bent, the sole of one foot against the rough bark. He was smoking a cigar, its fragrance pungent in the still, warm summer air and she had time to wonder why she had not smelled it. His warmly appreciative, boldly appraising eyes ran over her body from the crown of her burnished copper hair to the tip of her ivory kid boots, which matched exactly her ivory gown, lingering insolently at her breast and his smile deepened.

"You look well, Beth," he said. "You seem to have recovered from your ordeal of last year. And I trust your maidservant is equally restored to health." He drew on his cigar, blew the smoke into the air, watching as it drifted up into the leaves of the tree then suddenly turned his head to look at her and in that moment she knew. She knew who it was who had reported to the authorities, or to those who purported to be the authorities, that Mary Smith, who was already on the register of known prostitutes, and Beth Goodwin were selling their services to soldiers at Longworth. A huge bribe must have been offered but then Hugh was a wealthy man and she and Mary had been "raped" in that terrible place and she, Beth, had lost her child. Who else could have, or would have, reason to take revenge on the Goodwin family and in such a terrible way? They had, as a family, expected some drastic outcome when her father whipped Hugh Thornley and humiliated him in front of those he would consider to be his inferiors, but none had come, or so they had thought, but, of course, it had. A revenge that ran in ripples through the whole family though it had been taken out only on herself. Perhaps there was more to come – who knew? – and for a moment she was tempted to look wildly about her for the sight of one of her father's outdoor servants but she knew there was no one about. They were all busy with the stalls and the coconut shies, the gardeners shaking their heads over the destruction of the flowerbeds.

But she could run, and she could scream if he should take a step towards her, but something stiffened inside her, stretching itself along her spine so that she stood upright, fearless, the loathing, which had once been love, and the contempt, which had once been admiration, shining from her silver-grey eyes and holding her firm and steady. She wanted so badly to leap the fence and spring at him, to hurt him, wound him, kill him as he had killed her baby, to avenge what he had done to her, to Mary, to Milly and to his own daughter. She had reason to believe that she was pregnant again, perhaps only a few weeks but she would not jeopardise the child's safety, or her own, for there would come another opportunity to make this devil pay for what he had done to her family. She would make it come. She would tell no one. Not Archie or her father what she knew to be true, for they would rush off in their male eagerness for revenge, their guns and their whips about them, thinking not of her or Mary, which did not mean they did not care, but intent as men are on punishment, on reprisals, on avenging the wrong done their women, one of whom was, of course, Milly.

"So it was you, Hugh Thornley," she said quietly.

He raised one eyebrow in a question and the brilliant blue of his eyes gleamed in that lazy, cynical smile the men in his command had known so well. His arrogance, his well-bred assurance that whatever was to happen he would not be the one who came off worst.

"You have had quite a shindig today, I see, so I thought I would ride over and see how the peasants have their fun. You enjoy entertaining the lower classes, do you not, but then I suppose you are only a generation from being a member yourself. I only wonder that the millocracy, those who are in trade as your father is, condescend to mix with them. But I suppose not long ago their forebears were no more than labourers, like your mother's family still are. I have made it my business to find out what has become of them. Their name, and your mother's name was, I believe, Murphy, and I was not surprised that one of them, your mother's brother, Tommy by name, works on one of my farms. Isn't that a coincidence? I've been informed, by the way, that he's a lazy beggar and I'm thinking of asking my steward to get rid of him. Your mother was a bastard, wasn't she, and your father certainly is one, though not in the same sense. I really must make sure none of my family come into contact with your family again lest the slur of it rubs off on my son. I have impressed upon my wife that should she visit your home, alone or with my son, she will be sorry for it. Tell your father that, will you?"

"No, I don't think I will, Hugh. But thank you for the warning. It seems you are prepared to go to any lengths to threaten every member of my family and my mother's family and it makes me wonder what it is you are afraid of. But now that I am aware of who it was who denounced me to the police I can make up my mind what I am to do about it."

Her mother's mother, Beth's grandmother, had died several years ago after being kept in comfort by her daughter in the same cottage in which Abby had been born. Her brothers and sisters, *half*-brothers and sisters since they had not shared the same father, had married or scattered about Lancashire and her mother had had little communication with them since. But it seemed that Hugh Thornley, in his unbalanced mind, had thought it worth his while to discover their whereabouts and, through them, since Tommy was one of them, hurt the Goodwins. What was wrong with the man that he should spend his days devising ways to avenge himself? She knew her father, Noah, with his whip and herself in the way she had denounced Hugh in front of his men on the parade-ground had enraged him to madness, but surely turning on her mother's family, the innocent men and women who had no part in her parents' life, was beyond believing.

He grinned and shook his head as though at the folly of this woman who had the foolish idea that she was a match for Hugh Thornley, his pride and belief in his own place in life making him boldly careless. Then, taking one last draw on his cigar he threw it into the undergrowth, leaped nimbly on to the back of his ebony horse, tethered nearby, and saluting her with his crop walked the animal away along the narrow path. He turned at the curve of the path, reining in his horse for a moment. "Oh, and don't let me hear that you have been to Thornley Green again. I know you have visited Milly on occasions but do not come again. D'you hear?" He turned and urged his animal into a trot until he was out of sight.

Beth let out her breath on a long, shuddering sigh, still clinging to the fence. The birds, which had been silent as she and Hugh talked, gave voice again, wood pigeons crooning, the early cry of a tawny owl that nested in a hole in the oak tree and the loud clattering alarm of a blackbird.

She stood for perhaps half an hour, her mind still and yet far below its surface was a tumult of thought, which she knew she would study in far more detail when she had got over the shock of meeting Hugh Thornley. And she was aware that she must calm herself before returning to the house where Archie was to pick her up in the carriage. He didn't know yet of her secret joy, that the child that had been torn from her was to be replaced with another and she thought she might tell him tonight. He had promised to bring Alex over with Mary, for they were to dine with her mother and father, and Laura and John Bennett, all eager to see the little girl who was making such remarkable progress. She would be put to bed in the room where Beth had known her childhood, Mary beside her, and later Archie would carry her home in his arms, sleeping trustfully as children should. They loved the child, all of them, and Beth was certain that Alex's lack of parents, of a mother and father which all children have and which soon she would question, had done her no harm.

Archie was understandably overjoyed when, in the candle-glowed privacy of their lovely bedroom she told him she believed she was to have a child.

He threw his arms up to the ceiling, his head back, his body arched, then he sank slowly to his knees and put his face in his hands. Beth sprang from the bed where she had been waiting for him to join her and hurried to his side, putting her arms about him and drawing him to her breast as she did with Alex when the little girl was distressed.

"Archie, dearest, oh, Archie, I don't know whether to cry with you or laugh at your reaction. I know you . . . both of us have waited for this ever since we were married but, darling, there is no need to be quite so overcome."

He mumbled something, his mouth against her throat, then he lifted his face to hers and laid his lips against her cheek. He cupped it reverently and she was ready to shake her head and smile, but she knew somehow that this was, perhaps, the most important moment in Archie's life, even more so than their wedding day.

"Do you know what this means to me?" he said softly.

"Yes, my darling, I do, and to—"

"No, no, you don't. You are pleased that you are to have a child but, my love, you already have family, blood family, all about you and always have had. I have known great affection and care from your family and I am truly grateful for it, but this means I shall have a child, a person in whose veins *my* blood will flow. Can you understand that? When I was told that last year you had had taken from you the child we had made, although it was only just a minuscule entity inside you it was a part of my heritage, wherever that came from. My blood and bone and muscle and it was taken from me, and you, by some beast of a man who . . . Oh, I was well aware that it was you who suffered the horror of it but I felt the loss more than most men would have done. Do you understand, my darling?" he begged her.

She felt her heart loosen and move in her chest with her love for this dear man who had, through Hugh Thornley, suffered as much as she had. It had driven her out of her mind but his had known a mighty buffeting that had nearly sent him over the edge. And she had done nothing to help him. That was what hurt her the most now. Inside her, though her heart was soft with love for him, something twisted and hardened and she felt it course along her veins in a great surge of hatred for the man who was doing his best to destroy, not only her and Archie, but her mother and father and now, it seemed, even her mother's distant brothers and sisters. From what he had told her this afternoon he meant to throw out his net of loathing and draw them all into it until he could sit back and tell himself his revenge was complete. He was a dangerous man, a man whose mind was deranged, distorted with hatred and if something wasn't done, and soon, he would succeed in his ambition. And what of Milly? She was surely the most in danger of them all. She was a Goodwin and vulnerable because of it. His son, or the child he believed was his son, was safe for the moment but if Todd's part in his conception should be discovered Hugh Thornley would slip over the edge of the abyss on which he teetered and his wrath would be terrible.

They crouched in front of the small fire that Beth had ordered lit, for the evening was chilly, their arms about one another and dreamed into the flames, but their dreams were of a very different nature. Archie spoke occasionally and automatically; instinctively she gave him the correct murmured answers over the future of their baby. She agreed to everything he said, even that she was not to go about without Harry or Clancy beside her, smiling a little into his ruffled hair, for what good would Harry or Clancy be against the madness of Hugh Thornley? She was not to go to Thornley Green even to see her sister, for he did not trust that bastard, and again she smiled, for had she not already been forbidden to visit Milly by her unstable husband.

"Keep to the grounds, darling, and when you take Alex walking go where you are in full view of the outdoor men. I think I'll have a telephone installed in the house then you can get in touch with me when I'm at the works and I shall persuade Noah to do the same."

"That's a good idea, Archie, but I shall have to go into St Helens to be fitted with new gowns. I can barely fasten the ones I have and though she hasn't said anything I'm pretty sure Mary has guessed."

"All the more reason to take Harry and Mary with you when you go. Keep out of his way, darling, and though I'm sorry you won't see as much of Milly she will probably be able to get over to Lantern Hill. I must know you're safe, sweetheart, or I shan't be able to work and then when . . ."

He went on and on, making his plans, his thoughts concentrated on her safety and that of the coming child, on Alex's reaction to a new baby, on her parents' joy at the news, not to mention the servants, but his voice dwindled away into the background of her thoughts, which dwelled on how she was to make her family safe from the machinations of Hugh Thornley. Although nothing had been said about today since Archie did not know she had seen her sister's husband, it was as if he sensed some terrible thing creeping up on them and had to make her understand the need for careful precautions against the havoc Hugh Thornley might cause. That was the word that was uppermost in Archie's mind: *might*. But she knew different. There was no might about it. His lordship was bent on a path of destruction and in his arrogance he had boasted of it to Beth who had to stop it. So many people were involved and though it seemed ridiculous to believe she was the only one who could stop it she knew that to be the case. There were men in the two households and, she was sure, relatives of her mother, who would gladly see to the disposal of Hugh Thornley, but they would go at it like bulls at a gate, heads down, guns at the ready, or pitchforks, and the consequences to the family would be catastrophic. It must be done quietly, discreetly, so that no blame could be laid at the feet of the Goodwin family. And there was really only one other person in the world who she could trust to help her!

She held Archie passionately to her, her chest hurting badly with the explosion of her love for him. He turned at the pressure of her arms, smiling, believing her passion was for what they had shared so often in the past weeks, smiling delightedly, then somewhat worried, for should they be doing this, and this, with a baby inside her, but doing it just the same, and as she sank into the depths of rapture with him the cruel and smiling face of Hugh Thornley vanished from her thoughts.

27

They shivered in one another's arms, the intensity of their emotions rendering them unable to do more than cling to one another, both astonished by their feelings. They strained their bodies together as though each were trying to get inside the other, small, incomprehensible sounds coming from them both, whimpers almost, two wounded animals huddling for comfort. There was no sexual urge between them, no urgent desire at that moment to tear at each other's clothing as they had done so often in the past, just a hunger, a desperate need to be close to the only source of love either of them knew.

At last they drew apart, studying each other's face. He was not yet twenty-five but there was a single strand of white in his dark hair and deepening lines scoring his cheeks from nose to mouth. His face had lost all boyishness over the past months, hardened not only by the despairing knowledge that his son, who he had seen only twice since he was born, was believed to be the offspring of another man, but also by the deepening strength of his love for this woman, and by the hard, unremitting labour of the work he did at the glass works.

Since August Todd Woodruff had been training, an apprenticeship if you like, in the sweat-drenching, heat-draining, fire-scorching confines of the sheet house at the Edge Bottom Glass Works. He had been surprised when Archie, with whom he was on first-name terms, since they had been brought up together, had called him into his office, dragging him with little reluctance from the long line of figures he was doing his best to balance in the outer office.

Archie had not wasted words. "I believe you are not in your element in the office, Todd," causing Todd to blink and his heart to drop for he was willing to work at anything that supported him until he could achieve the life he wanted for himself, for Milly and for the boy, who, to his chagrin, had been christened Miles Thornley. He had even been invited to the christening, which seemed ironic. He had, with others of Hugh's acquaintance, some of them officers from regiments that had taken over at Longworth since the 3rd Battalion of the King's Regiment(St Helens) had sailed several weeks ago for India, sat halfway up the church and watched the insolent arrogance of Lord Thornley swaggering about Todd's son, seething at his own impotence but forced to go through the charade for Milly's sake, and for the child's. He had wanted to stand up in the church and bellow that this was *his* son who mewed at the font and that the woman who held him before passing him over to Johnny Cassell's new wife Muriel, whom Hugh had chosen as godmother, was *his* woman and that as soon as he was settled in a new profession he meant to take them far away from Thornley Green and St Helens. He had made a start with the chance Noah and Archie Goodwin had given him and the incentive of the future kept him at it. He only hoped that Hugh's influence would have little effect on the baby but since he was still a baby and of little interest at the moment to Hugh he allowed no thoughts of despair, though he was often close to it, to enter his mind. Milly loved the child, that was obvious, and it was whispered about in St Helens, for she took no interest in her daughter but doted on the boy. He and Beth had discussed it in private and Beth was of the opinion that it was the father of the child, Hugh of Alex, and himself of Miles, that influenced Milly's feelings. She loved Todd Woodruff and so she loved his son. She loathed

Hugh Thornley and though she did not loathe Alex who was his daughter she seemed to have no interest in her. She was happy that the child had loving "parents" in Archie and Beth.

Since a man of his age could not live in the tiny cottage his mother and father occupied, Archie had arranged for Todd to move into a small house in Bamford Street adjacent to the glass works, one that was meant for the manager of the works but, since Archie himself was manager and lived at Edge Bottom House, had been empty for years. It had kept him occupied, painting and repairing, with Clem's help, the neat detached villa, furnishing it with old-fashioned pieces found in the attics of Edge Bottom House which Beth had no use for. His mother, knowing that she must accept Todd and his new life, had brought several of the maids and scrubbed and scoured the place from top to bottom, her only comment being that if she heard of that hussy setting foot in her son's house she would not be responsible for her actions, son or no son!

Now he sat in Archie's office, his heart in his mouth, for if Beth's husband, and his oldest friend should tell him he wasn't suited to his job he didn't know what he would do.

"How would you feel about working on the floor?" Archie asked baldly, meaning the sheet house or the crown furnace. "I've caught you in there several times. You seemed very interested and I wondered if you would care to train as a glass-blower. When you are experienced, if you take to it, and let me tell you it's bloody hard work, you might move on to better things. The men won't know, though I suppose they might guess, that your wage would be that of an experienced glass-blower since I'm fully aware . . . well, it's none of my business but I believe you are hoping to . . . Dear God, Todd, what I'm trying to say, and my father-in-law agrees, is that the sooner Milly and the boy are taken away from Thornley Green the better. A sheet glass-blower from Choisy-le-roi near Paris has just signed a contract, not with us, I might add, but with the

Eccleston Glass Works. He is to work in St Helens for two years at a weekly wage of £6 10s 0d with a house and fuel free. That's a bloody good wage, since a skilled man in bottle-making and flint glass-making takes home between 30s and 40s a week. You have a home and—"

"I'll take it."

"Don't you want to—"

"I'll take it and, thanks, Archie. You must know my plans and how desperate I am to get Milly and the boy away, but how long it will take only God knows. I want just to pack up and take them with me, somewhere, anywhere, but unless I have a trade, a profession, I can offer them nothing. I live in terror that he might harm her, though I suppose he wouldn't hurt his son." He gave a bitter laugh. "*His* son . . . but Milly, I can't sleep at night for fear of what he might be doing to her."

Todd Woodruff bent his head and for a pitying moment Archie felt the need to get up and go to him, put an arm about his shoulders, for what the man suffered was horrendous. He could hardly imagine it. He and Beth were so recently reconciled and their lives were a joy to them both after so much suffering and pain, but Todd was in a worse position, for he had no idea, except through Beth who visited her sister, of the health and progress of his son and the safety of the woman he loved. He had held the child for half an hour when Milly brought him to Lantern Hill, Hugh having gone to Cowes for a weekend, giving Milly the chance to show off her son to her parents. Under no circumstances would she have dared to go to Lantern Hill while Hugh was about. His loathing of his father-in-law was as strong as ever and his determination to keep his son and his wife from seeing her family was as hard as a rock. So far, apparently, Beth told them, he was keeping his distance from his wife, for he was still obsessed with Alicia Bramhall but how long would that last? And when it ended would he turn his sights on his wife, for an "heir and a spare" was customary?

That had been three months ago and now, with Hugh gone to Leicestershire to hunt with the Cassells, a visit to which Alicia Bramhall, who was a good horsewoman, and her elderly husband had been invited, Milly had driven over to Edge Bottom House with her baby son, leaving him there with Beth.

"I've sent him a note. God knows what the men in the sheet house will think, one of their workmen getting a billet-doux in the middle of a shift, but I couldn't think of any other way to let him know that Hugh is away. Young Sidney, he's the boot boy and quite devoted to me, I believe, though I've no idea why unless it's because he seems to destest Hugh so – I can only think Hugh has been cruel to him – ran across to the works this morning after Hugh left. Darling, I'm sorry about this and I'm sure Archie will be furious but I must take the chance to see him. I'd take Miles but a woman carrying a baby is bound to be noticed, and if I could borrow some clothes, perhaps of Mary's, you know, the clothes of a working woman, I could hurry across the fields to Bamford Street and slip into Todd's house unnoticed. I must talk to him, tell him to be careful. One of the gardeners reported a man hanging about in the woods on the other side of the lake last week and I could only think it was Todd. Hugh would be deeply suspicious if he were found, though he's no idea at the moment that Miles isn't his. Will you do this, darling? If my carriage is seen outside your house it will cause no comment though Hugh will be incensed if he hears of it. He hates you all and—"

"Milly, you can't go on like this," Beth interrupted breathlessly. "You know I will do anything for you and Miles, and Todd too, but you are in such danger. I'm terrified that he will turn on you. What I mean, I suppose, is that he will return to your bed and, you know, I suppose you must know how that will affect Todd. He'd be over there with a shotgun, with Father not far behind him and really I can't bear to think . . ." She shuddered and Milly moved to kneel at her feet, taking her hands in her own.

They were in Beth's sitting-room on the first floor, a great fire curling in the fireplace, the flames lighting the walls and the pretty white curtains to gold and amber and orange. The two women were very alike but for the colour of their eyes and both were beautifully dressed in the latest fashion. The simple lines of the Empire dress were in vogue, inspired by Sarah Bernhardt's costumes in Sardou's _La Tosca_. The waist level was disguised by a very broad sash swathed low and sewn into place, the style hiding Beth's thickening waistline, for she was four months pregnant. Her gown was of dove-grey barege, a semi-transparent textile of silk and wool with an open mesh. It was light and yet warm, for the autumn weather had turned cold. Milly, always a woman to love brighter colours, was dressed in what Miss Adela called "crushed strawberry" and though the colour should have clashed with her bright copper hair, somehow it didn't. She looked quite magnificent and Beth wondered anxiously why it was her husband had not resumed his attentions to her. Her figure was somewhat fuller than it had been when she married but she held herself proudly, her head up, her back straight and everything about her was in perfect proportion. She was enough to catch the eye of any man so why didn't Hugh see her? Or was he so besotted with Alicia Bramhall that his wife was invisible to him?

Milly's daughter was lying on her stomach, her small chin cupped in her hands while she studied with great interest the baby who had been brought into Beth's room and which the pretty lady had placed on a rug on the floor. He was doing his determined best to roll over on to his stomach and when he finally managed it and was face to face with her he let out a rapturous shout and did his best to reach her. As yet he could not lever himself with his hands and arms but floundered on his stomach, his arms and legs going ten to the dozen as though he were swimming. Alex glanced at Beth and pulled a face as though to say wasn't he comical, then turned to study him to see what he would do next. She wanted him to come and play with her, like Boy did, but when she indicated that he should follow her he merely crowed and grinned and made further efforts to crawl. She herself was eighteen months old and ever since she had stood up last June had made great progress in the matter of walking, though as yet she still lurched from side to side. John Bennett had recommended a surgeon in Harley Street in London who had a special interest in children, particularly those whose legs were deformed by rickets, and it was hoped that an operation might at least help to balance the way in which Alex walked. The Great Ormond Street Hospital for Children, founded in 1852, had a wonderful reputation and Doctor Mackintosh was closely connected with it. There had been great strides in the last half a century in the nursing of children, some doctors applying themselves solely to children's health. Doctor Mackintosh was one. It made Beth wince to think of the lovely child being operated upon, her baby flesh cut open, but John had explained that it must be done or Alex would lurch and limp her way through life, which he was sure neither she nor Archie wanted. Nobody thought to discuss the matter with Alex's biological parents!

Beth noticed that Milly assiduously averted her eyes from the child, especially when she was walking, which angered her, but then if Milly took a fancy for her daughter what would she, Beth, do? Though she supposed there was no chance that the child would ever live at Thornley Green, not with Hugh so adamantly against her. Despite the fact that she carried Archie's child inside her, son or daughter, it made no difference to either of them, they had both begun to look on Alex as theirs. She wondered if now was the time to divulge to Milly her certainty that it was Hugh who had bribed the authorities to take herself and Mary to the lock hospital and that she believed that only she and Milly could prevent him from harming them further. Even now she hadn't devised any particular plan, discarding this or that or the other, for the only way to stop Hugh was by – oh, dear God – by destroying him and how the devil were she and Milly, two defenceless women, to do that? She was pregnant and terrified that some dreadful thing would happen to this baby as it had with the first but something must be done before Hugh damaged her family any further. It was a risk to keep the knowledge to herself but her fear had kept her silent and she vowed, as she watched Milly whipping about the room in great excitement, that as soon as her child was born she would speak, *whisper* to her sister of how they should go about defending themselves against his viciousness.

Mary had been summoned and willingly allowed Milly to dress in her plain grey dress and cloak, her shining head concealed beneath a close hood. Only her boots gave them trouble, for Mary's were too small.

"Dammit, why didn't I think to bring an old pair with me?" Milly fumed. "Haven't you something to fit me?" turning urgently to Beth. "We're the same size." And after a quick search at the back of Beth's wardrobe, while Milly fretted and dithered, since she was eager to be off, a pair was found.

"Darling, my darling love," Todd kept murmuring, then reached for her again, kicking the door to behind them, crushing her into his arms, raining hungry, demanding kisses on to her face, her hair, her mouth, while she struggled to undo Mary's unfamiliar cloak, then the buttons on his work jacket which he still wore. She found she couldn't speak. Her throat had closed up but she opened her mouth to him, responding to his fierce hunger with a need just as fierce of her own. Both of them tasted the honeyed sweetness of tongue, the inside of their mouths and both of them knew that they would not be satisfied with their tongues exploring but needed the explosion of Todd's body inside hers. They had no time to go up the stairs to the bedroom where Todd, night after night, tossed and turned and longed for her, but threw themselves down on to the hooked rug that lay before the kitchen fire. Naked now, both of them, he kissed her breasts, running his hands down her waist, her hips, her thighs. Roughly he treated her and she gloried in it as he knelt over her. Her own hands could not get enough of touching and fondling and he arched his back in what seemed to be agony before thrusting himself deeply inside her and, though they did not at the time know it, or even care, impregnating her with her second son.

Afterwards, holding her, with despair tingeing their love, they were closer to anguish than to joy. How long before they could have this again? This stolen moment, a love that was set to break their hearts and the added hopelessness that Hugh Thornley had the fate of their son in his hands.

"I don't think I can stand much more, Milly," Todd said, his voice hollow. "Every night I imagine him coming to your room and . . . and raping you as he did before."

She sat up, leaning on his chest, her glorious hair falling across him like a curtain made from the finest silk. She pressed her lips softly to his. "No, darling, not once has he tried."

"But he will. He'll want another child. Dammit, Milly, we must go. We must get Miles – dear God, how I hate that name – and run away. I know Archie and your father would help, though it kills me that I might have to accept money from other men. Why the bloody hell did I go into the army, for it trains a man for nothing but killing? I have no way to earn a living except as a labourer."

"You will be a respected glass-blower when you have—"

"Even that won't bring me what I want to give you and the boy. Would you live in a house like this?" He looked round the working man's kitchen with its plain dresser, the great black range, the pine table and chairs, the old rocker with its worn cushions, the rag rugs, and upstairs it was no better. A bed, a wardrobe, a dressing-table, all cast-offs from Edge Bottom House. Milly had been brought up in great luxury, the comfort of her father's fortune, and to expect her to live as a labouring man's wife, if such a thing was possible, which it was not, was bordering on lunacy. They could not even hope to meet like this, for once Hugh came back from hunting in Leicestershire, Milly would be tied to Thornley Green and her son with her.

"I love you, Todd," she whispered, her voice breaking. "I don't know why, or how it came about, for I was always a fly-by-night with no thought for anyone but myself. I would willingly live in a house like this with you and our son but there seems no chance of that."

She turned away on to her back, throwing her arms across her face, beginning to weep, for she could see no way out of their desperate plight. No matter where they went, she and Todd and Miles, Hugh would find them, come after them, using the money she had brought him, and though she had begged her father to stop supplying Hugh with funds he said it would affect her and the boy if he did and he could not bear to deny her the comforts to which she was accustomed.

They held each other, Todd calming her, for she had become distraught, holding her in his arms, soothing her towards the bitter parting. She clung to his strength, as Todd Woodruff was a strong man now, not just physically but emotionally, and he was set on his course to have this woman and his son in his life. He didn't know how, or even when, but his certainty surrounded him and stopped him from losing his mind. She touched his face and hair and neck with passionate, feverish hands, as though needing to impress the feel of him for ever into her soul. She who had started this affair with the light-hearted selfishness that had been her nature was now being crucified by it, but he kissed her, a deep, tender kiss and against the silkiness of her loosened hair murmured that it was time for her to go.

Together they moved out of the back door of the house, which led into a small, overgrown garden. They embraced again and there was passion and desperation in the way their lips met, a feverish longing in the clinging of their hands at parting, for they did not know when they would see one another again. He realised he had not asked her about his son but that could not be helped now. He moved to the back gate and peered out. When he signalled that it was clear she pulled Mary's hood over her head, held her cloak tightly about her, since the cold was striking, and hurried down the back lane that led beside the works and out into the open fields towards Edge Bottom House.

"How dare she involve you in her sordid affair? Even to come here when Hugh is so dangerously inflexible that she should not see her family is bordering on madness. God knows what he would do if he should find out. Someone will talk, oh, not on purpose, but it's bound to get back to him. His bloody coachman for one. And to bring the child. Is she out of her mind? I won't have you upset, especially now."

"What *is* upsetting me is your tone of voice, Archie Goodwin. I will not be spoken to as though I were a naughty child who has—"

"Sweet Jesus, Beth, you know what he's like. I fear for you, and for the safety not only of our child but of Alex. I wouldn't put it past him to drag her back to Thornley Green just to spite us, which is a stupid word but you know what I mean. He doesn't want her, and neither, so it seems, does Milly. Did she speak to her daughter, by the way, or take the slightest notice of her?"

"Well, no."

"And isn't that typical of Milly. Caring for nothing and nobody in her determination to have her own way in everything. She fancies a" – here he almost used a word that was obscene but his upbringing as a gentleman and his respect for his wife prevented him – "a half-hour with her lover so she gets you involved."

Archie Goodwin strode violently about the drawing-room, dragging his right hand through his already dishevelled fair hair. He had a glass of brandy in his left hand, for the news that his sister-in-law had been to the house, and not only that but she had left her son in his wife's care while she slipped out to meet her lover, had rendered him mindless with rage. He needed a stiffener before he sat down to dinner with his wife, but he just couldn't seem to sit down and when he did he sprang up again at once to surge about the room.

"Master's in a rare old rage," Morna whispered confidentially to the others when she returned to the kitchen. "Madder'n a wet hen and we don't need two guesses as to what caused that, do we?"

"Now then, my girl," Mrs Kyle remonstrated halfheartedly, for like the rest of the servants she was keen to hear how the master would react to the news that Mrs Beth's sister had visited today and left her baby son in their mistress's care. There was bad blood between the Goodwins and Lord Thornley, they were all aware of that, but they couldn't resist whispering about the happenings of the day. They weren't daft, or blind, and the sight of Lady Thornley slipping out of the side door dressed in Mary Smith's plain clothing had not gone unnoticed. Where she had gone was a mystery, but it was their belief she would be up to no good, for they remembered Milly Goodwin, as she had been then, before she married. Most of them had not been employed at Lantern Hill but those who had, perhaps on the occasion of a party or a ball, had seen what she had got up to!

In the drawing-room the storm continued. "And what's to stop Hugh coming over here and causing more trouble if he should find out about today's visit? Darling, you know what you mean to me and especially now with the baby on the way. It's bad enough you and your mother dashing here and there working for the suffragists but I had hoped that now you might give it up for a while, at least until the baby is born. Edgar Holt was doing business in Bolton yesterday and told me he saw you at the gates of Yates's Cotton Mill with that woman—"

"That woman is Emmeline Pankhurst," his wife said coldly, "and happens to be a leading force in the suffragists movement. The Pankhursts have done more work for the movement than any of us. They spend their time talking to working women about the right to vote, which they deserve, you know that, Archie, and I understood you to be in favour."

"My darling girl. My precious love, I am, you know I am, but just at the moment I cannot bear to see you put yourself in danger."

"From what, Archie?"

"From bloody Hugh Thornley! I have only just got you back and now you're involved with Milly and Todd and God knows what he would do if he found out. He's an evil bastard and I live in fear he may do you harm."

For a strange moment he seemed to lose the thread of what he was saying, just as though a stray thought had wandered through his mind, distracting him, a thought that had something, Beth presumed, to do with Hugh Thornley. He gazed at her, or rather through her, and she rose to her feet and moved towards him.

"Archie, what is it?" she asked anxiously.

"Beth . . ." His mind seemed to come back from wherever it had wandered and he took her hands in his, then bent to place a soft and very tender kiss on her lips. "You're my whole world, do you know that?" he said softly. "If I thought you were in any . . ."

"Any what?"

"Well, let's just say I would be glad if you stopped going, for the time being, to these meeting and rallies. And from helping your sister and her lover to meet."

"Archie!"

"I mean it, Beth. I have an awful feeling we have not heard the last of . . ." He smiled suddenly, taking her hand in his and drawing it through his arm. "Let's go in to dinner or we'll have Mrs Kyle threatening us with a rolling pin for being late."

28

It was January and snowing heavily when Todd and Milly met
secretly for the third time at the house on Bamford Street and
by now Milly was aware that she was pregnant again. Hugh had
once more gone south to Leicestershire to do a bit of hunting
with old Johnny, taking Alicia with him, though this time her
elderly husband had elected to stay at home saying the weather
wasn't to his liking. Not that it made any difference to Hugh
Thornley whether the old fool was there or not, for Johnny and
Muriel were very liberally minded, in fact all their set was, and
placing their guests in convenient bedrooms was taken for
granted. Alicia's husband accepted this since he had, in his
time, moved from his first wife's bedroom to that of some other
man's. He was long past that now, of course, and as long as his
beautiful young wife was as discreet as society demanded he
looked the other way.

Beth was well into her seventh month and though she had
made a vow to herself that she would think of something to put
a stop to Hugh Thornley's wicked feud against her family she
had not yet come to any firm conclusion. She supposed it was
because of her pregnancy which made her slow and tranquil,
content to sit at home with Alex, to take no more than peaceful
walks in the autumnal then winter garden, watching the child
scamper through the fallen leaves, collecting shining conkers
which she placed carefully in the pocket of her frilled pinafore,
pine cones, fir cones, nuts, seeds, the changing colour of
hydrangea blooms, leaves and dying flower heads to make

up into the bowls of pot-pourri that Beth placed about the house. Alex helped her, throwing bits of twigs and bark into the basket with a child's enthusiasm.

"This do, Beth?" she would shout, holding up a bit of the hedge clippings Mr Tucker and Billy had overlooked or a scrap of bark from the changing trunks of the trees, a twig, anything that caught her sharp eye.

The seasons changed. Winter had come with sharp blue skies and a hazy opalescent frost, the stark outline of the denuded trees behind which red sunsets slid down to the earth. The air in its windless chill seemed to tinkle like crystal as she and Alex wandered down to the paddock to feed the horses with carrots and apples. Christmas was soon upon them with the enormous tree Tucker and Billy brought in, the laughter of decorating it with Alex's wide-eyed help and then the snow in the New Year, 1890, a new decade. The year in which influenza travelled across Europe, an influenza that was described as "Russian", no one knew why, and which led to pneumonia so that John Bennett was run off his feet and warned Beth that she must not go into town, not in her condition. Nan, the scullery-maid at Lantern Hill, who was "walking out", with Mrs Woodruff's permission, of course, and whose gentleman friend was a worker in the print works of Mr Alfred Hardwick, where several of his workers were struck down, became seriously ill and for several days her life hung in the balance. Harriet Woodruff put the girl in isolation, nursing her herself, keeping the rest of the servants well away, but when Harriet went down with it, it was said in the town that Mrs Abby Goodwin rolled up her sleeves, donned an apron and pulled her through. They were known to be more than employer and employee but what was Noah Goodwin thinking of, allowing his wife to nurse a servant?

Snow fell and was thick and fresh in the garden, frozen by the hoar frost so that each twig and blade sparkled separately as the big red sun, which had gone to earth the night before, came slowly over the horizon, overlaying the whiteness with a tinge of pink. The world was so crisp you could hear it crackle. On every window pane the frost drew patterns and through it all Beth moved slowly, waiting for the spring when her baby would be born. Hugh Thornley was temporarily forgotten since it seemed Milly was safe and well. Sally, her maid, came over to see her brother Harry, reporting to Mrs Beth that all was quiet at Thornley Green and the boy was thriving. The master, she said with a set face and eyes that looked over Beth's shoulder, was away more often than he was at home, hunting with Sir John and his wife in Leicestershire, shooting up in Scotland or deer-stalking, and Lady Thornley sent a message to say she was well and that Mrs Beth was not to worry.

It was a peaceful time and though Beth dwelled on their last meeting when Hugh had threatened all kinds of disasters to her family, nothing had happened. She had made discreet enquiries about Tommy Murphy, her *Uncle* Tommy, she supposed, and it seemed he was still working at the Home Farm on the Thornley estate so Hugh's threat to have him fired had come to nothing. Lord Thornley had left Lady Thornley in peace, though Sally did not say so in as many words, for it was not her place, only coming into his wife's room or the nursery to inspect the progress of his son.

Sally walked over in January, her stout boots and thick woollen cloak hiding her figure, and it was not until she knocked on the kitchen door and threw back her hood that the gape-jawed servants realised it was not Sally at all but Lady Thornley. She laughed at their astonished expressions and shook the mud from her boots before taking them off and throwing her cloak, or rather Sally's cloak, to the settle beside the fire.

"I don't know why I didn't think of it before, Beth. It's a perfect disguise. Everyone knows that Sally comes here on her day off to see Harry and thinks nothing of it. She told the servants that I have a headache and don't wish to be disturbed, then settled herself in my dressing-room until I should return. Now where's that gardener's lad of yours? What's his name, Billy?"

Beth, who had only just recovered from the shock of seeing her sister pop her head round the sitting-room door, gaped, no sound coming from her mouth.

"Don't look like that, Beth darling. You know why I have come. Hugh is away again, as, thank the good Lord, he is quite frequently during the hunting season, and I'm not about to miss the chance of meeting Todd so ring the bell and fetch the lad up here."

"Milly, please, I cannot be involved again in your—"

"My what? You know I love Todd and since his son was born I have seen him only twice. Now, will you ring that bell or must I? Perhaps I'd better do it since you are so big. Dear God, when is the baby due, or is it to be twins? I know I was enormous with Miles but—"

"Stop it, Milly, just stop it. I will not allow my servants to carry notes to Todd. The risk is too great and besides, Archie would have me whipped if I—"

"Oh, poo, you silly woman. Archie have you whipped! He wouldn't harm a hair on your head and you know it, especially since you are carrying his child. Now please, don't let's waste any more time. Send for Billy. I have the note here all ready to be put into his hand and it's but five minutes to the glass works. I'll have a cup of hot chocolate for it's damned cold out there and then I'll slip over to Bamford Street. I have a key and then when—"

"Please, please don't, Milly. You . . . we are all in grave danger. You don't realise. Just because Hugh has left you alone ever since Miles was born doesn't mean he is never going to . . . to want to . . . you know what I mean. He will want another child and if you won't agree he will force you. And he is capable of more than that, Milly. He loathes the whole family; even Mother's brothers and sisters are being menaced by—"

"What the devil are you talking about, Beth?" Milly's voice was low, puzzled, but ready to laugh at Beth's fears. "What in hell's name are you saying? Mother's brothers and sisters! Dear God, we don't even know them, it happened so long ago. I had forgotten all about it and—"

"Tommy Murphy, Mother's brother, works on the Home Farm on the Thornley estate and he said—"

"Who said?"

"Hugh."

"When did you speak to Hugh, Beth?"

Beth gripped the arms of the deep armchair and hauled herself out of it, beginning to prowl about the room, wringing her hands, wondering where that resolution she had known at her last meeting with Hugh had gone. She supposed it must be her condition that was making her back off from the unbending intention she had known then. A feeling that all fecund animals know, that of wishing to protect what is growing inside them. Because of the peace that appeared to have fallen about not just her, but Milly, she had told herself that Hugh had lost interest. He had his mistress, the money to indulge his every whim and fancy, a healthy son in the nursery and a lifestyle which, for the moment, held back the boredom that had often been his undoing in the past. But it would not last and when he looked around him for something else to do his eye would alight on his beautiful young wife. As long as Milly acquiesced all would be well, but Beth knew she never would. Not now. She loved Todd Woodruff and like all women in love the touch of another man would be abhorrent to her. She would fight him. And she would suffer for it and the feud would begin all over again, her father involved and even, God forbid, Todd Woodruff dragged into it.

"Milly, please don't go to Todd. You know nothing can come of it."

"He is the father of my child and the unborn I carry inside me."

Beth fell back into the depths of the chair from which she had just clambered, her face like alabaster, her eyes glazing over in horror. "Dear God," she whispered.

"Aye, dear God indeed, though whether such a being exists is something I doubt. This time I cannot pass it off as Hugh's. Now, tell me when you spoke to him."

"At the garden party. He was in the wood. He threatened us all. He told me I was not to visit you."

Milly stood up and reached for the bell. "I can't understand why you didn't tell me of this at the time, but it makes it all the more imperative that I see Todd."

"But what can you do? What can Todd do? If you run away with him, which I know you wouldn't without Miles, Hugh would raise hell to bring you back. Miles is his son, you must realise that, and no man will part—"

"No, he isn't, he's Todd's."

"In the eyes of the law and in Hugh's he is his son."

"I will tell him the truth."

"Don't be ridiculous." Beth's voice was cold. "You would put us all in the gravest danger. Not just you and Todd and probably Miles would suffer, but he would see to it that Mother and Father, Archie and Alex—"

"Beth, I cannot live like this for ever." Milly's voice was high with pain. "You know what it's like to love a man so could you contemplate getting into bed with another? With one you fear and hate? Could you?"

Beth sank back more deeply into the armchair and cradled her swollen belly with gentle hands. She shouldn't have this to contend with, she agonised, not when she was awaiting the birth of her own child, when she should be happy and content in her husband's love and protection. The scene at Lantern Hill after her mother's fundraising party had created a feeling of determined resolve in her to free her family from the menace of Hugh Thornley for ever which seemed to have slipped away over the intervening months. Though at the time she had come to no conclusion on how she was to do this she remembered she had had some vague idea of discussing it with Milly, which seemed strange since she knew either her father or Archie and certainly Todd would have had no hesitation in taking the necessary steps to immobilise Milly's husband, but lurking in the background of these thoughts had been fear for the three men. What they might be incensed enough to do and what the outcome would be.

So, reunited with Archie, pregnant, believing that Hugh was finding entertainment elsewhere, she had done nothing.

"We must talk, Milly. Just you and me."

Milly rose from her chair, her eyes on Beth, searching for some meaning behind her words. But Beth's expression was unfathomable. Her grey eyes glittered strangely and though her face was still the colour of the white marble fireplace there was a high spot of colour on each cheekbone.

"What about?"

"Dear God, Milly, must you ask that? Surely you can see what clouds are gathering if you continue this . . . these meetings with Todd. Hugh is bound—"

"These meetings! Anyone would think I saw him on a regular basis every week. I snatch at the chance, any chance."

Now Beth got laboriously to her feet and with a savagery that surprised them both, seized her sister by the upper arms. "I will not have my family harmed by your irresponsible actions, d'you hear? Go, go and see Todd today but promise me this will be the last until you and I have made a plan."

"Made a plan! What the devil does that mean?"

"I don't know. Sweet Jesus, I don't know, but I tell you this. I cannot live under the malevolence of his presence in my life, or yours, or that of my family for very much longer. I'm to have a child and I will not have that child growing up with the threat of Hugh Thornley hanging over us. It's not to be borne. Now go, Milly, send Billy with a note and meet Todd, but this is the last time I'll be a party to it. Do you understand? When the baby is here and I can get about, you and I will meet. I suppose he allows you to go to Miss Adela's? Yes, then that is where we shall talk."

They made love, gently, tenderly, with none of the fire and passion that they had known in the past. She did not tell him of the child who was to be born, probably in June, and her curving figure, full and womanly, did not give her condition away. The conversation she had had with Beth still lingered oddly at the back of her mind, but her whole being was concentrated on the wonder of being here in Todd's arms, of smelling his own personal smell, that of smoke from the glasshouse, the lemon-scented soap he still used, for he had been brought up to be fastidious, and a masculine smell of sweat which was not offensive but peculiarly attractive to her. He had not shaved that morning, since he had not expected her and the dark stubble on his chin and cheeks prickled deliciously against her breasts and thighs. His kisses seemed to have a different feel to them and his uncut hair was a thick mass of waving darkness as she sank her hands into it and drew him up to her breasts. She sobbed with the joy of it and at the same time her heart was torn and bleeding, for how could she give this up, how could she give *him* up? He was her love, her man, her soul mate, which sounded foolish but was true. She could not remember a day when he had not been in her life, even when she did not see him, for he had been there, a small boy, waiting for her so long ago when she and Beth and their mother had come home. It was in the far distant past and she couldn't say she remembered it because she had been no more than a baby, but he was a part of her life as much as her heart and pulse, her blood and bone were part of her body.

He was silent so long she thought he had fallen asleep with his head on her full, round breast, but when she stirred so did he, sitting up in his bed and draping his arms about his bent knees.

"Darling," she smiled, enquiringly.

"This can't go on." His voice was abrupt, cold even, and she felt fear pierce her like a splinter of ice.

"You want us to stop seeing each other," she faltered.

"Of course I don't want us to stop bloody seeing each other, woman. Or perhaps that is the correct way of putting it, *seeing each other*. I want us to live together as man and wife, not *see* each other. We must be together even if we're not married. I want you to bring my son here and stop fucking about with Hugh Thornley who you know you loathe. Is it the title, the money, the house? What? I cannot stand the idea. Look at your face." He put up a tender hand and traced the scar which could still be seen faintly on her cheek. John Bennett had made a fine job of sewing it up and it barely showed and certainly did not spoil her beauty, but it was a symbol of what Hugh Thornley was capable of. "What scars will you have when next I see you, Milly? No man, if he is a man, can suffer the knowledge that the woman he loves is being abused by a man he hates, or indeed by any man. Come here to me, Milly. To this house. I'll look after you. I won't let any harm come to you."

To his astonishment she leaped from the bed and stood before him, hands on hips, naked as a newborn babe with a look of damn-all defiance in the lift of her head.

"Am I to leave the boy then?" she hissed. "For let me warn you Hugh will not part with him lightly. Miles is his son, the heir, in his eyes and if I was to remove him we would be forced to leave the country."

"And what's wrong with that?" he asked eagerly, throwing back the covers and leaping to stand beside her. "I could book us a passage on a ship from Liverpool."

"To?"

"Jesus, anywhere! America, Australia, Canada. I've got a bit of money saved, enough to buy us a passage and I'm sure Archie or Noah would loan me a sum to keep us until I get a job. Your father has enormous influence. He knows people, businessmen in many parts of the world, those who have bought his glass and bricks and who, with his recommendation, would employ me. It would be hard at first, my love, but we would be together, the three of us."

"He wouldn't rest until he'd found us, Todd." But it was said hesitantly and he could sense that she was listening to him with increasing interest.

He wondered why in hell he hadn't thought of it before. He supposed he had believed naïvely that everything would come right in the end, that Hugh Thornley would be made to see sense, to understand that the boy was Todd's son and not his, that Milly loved Todd Woodruff, and would leave them alone. That he himself would learn his trade and with Noah Goodwin's help move up the ladder at Edge Bottom Glass Works until he was in a position of some importance. What a joke! He wanted to laugh, to weep, to burst into hysterical peals of uncontrolled mirth, for what could be more ludicrous than the idea that Hugh Thornley would calmly give up what was his, even if he didn't want it? It often surprised him that he hadn't taken the little girl, his child, and shut her up in the nursery at Thornley Green with a nanny to guard her. She was legally his property but, by God, the boy was not. Perhaps in the eyes of the law but certainly not in Todd's.

"Will you give it some thought, my love, will you?" he asked eagerly, taking Milly's hands in his, the incongruity of their naked bodies, both so beautiful in their own male and female way, engaged in such a serious moment striking neither of them as peculiar. These stolen moments were a joy and a hell to both of them and were so dangerous, not to him who could take care of himself, though he knew Hugh was an out-and-out bastard, but to this woman whom he had so unexpectedly come to love.

He gave her a little shake, smiling eagerly into her face. "It could be done if we planned it carefully. We'd tell no one, only your parents and mine, and Archie and Beth."

"That's a lot of people."

"Are you saying they would let it out?" He was shocked.

"No, of course not, not on purpose but there are so many servants, who, unknowingly I'm sure, would pick up a hint and let . . . Oh, Todd, I'm frightened."

"You! Frightened! Come now, Milly Goodwin, you've never been frightened of anything in your life. Darling, my dearest love, say you'll think about it, please."

She pulled away from him and reached for her clothing, which was scattered about the bedroom. Her dress might be the plain servant's garb of Sally Preston but her undergarments were of the finest lawn, lace-trimmed. She pulled on her drawers, her breasts falling forward in a delightful bounce as she leaned down, and for a moment the male in Todd Woodruff was diverted. His body responded and Milly eyed that part of his anatomy that had reacted.

She began to laugh, reaching for her chemise which was draped over the end of the bed. "You can forget that, Todd Woodruff. If I don't get home those bloody footmen will be wondering what I'm doing lolling in my sitting-room, and where the devil Sally has got to. It's a long walk up to Thornley Green so hand me my gown and put some clothes on yourself."

"Milly . . ." His voice was low and throaty, a voice she recognised and responded to and, unable to resist the feel of one hand inside her chemise which was only half buttoned and the other slowly drawing down her drawers, she sighed deep in the back of her throat and gave herself up to the rapture of being loved by Todd Woodruff.

Sally was reading a book that Miss Milly, as she still privately thought of her, had lent her. It was called *Little Women* by Louisa May Alcott and Sally was so engrossed by the bravery and resolution of Jo March that she failed to hear the commotion at the front of the house. It was almost dark and had she not been so absorbed she would have stopped to light the candles and replenish the fire. She was sitting on the window seat, her knees drawn up, struggling to read by the light of the closing winter day and when the door burst open and the tall figure of a man plunged into the room, she felt her heart stop and then bound forward in terror. The book dropped from her flaccid hand and fell with a thud to the floor. She stared, her eyes wide, her mouth the same, and, in the way of those afraid beyond thought, she began to gibber.

"Stand up when you speak to me, girl," her master thundered.

She shot to her feet, her hands held to her breast, doing her best to stop its giddy gallop, for this was the man who terrorised them all, even the men in the stables, the men who worked his land, big, strong men who would normally let no man raise a fist to them. But then Lord Thornley had no need to raise his fist. His voice was enough, and his reputation!

"Where is your mistress?" he asked and the sudden softening of his voice, its quietness, was worse than the first explosion.

"The . . . the mistress, my lord?" Sally quavered, wondering as she spoke how she had managed to get the words beyond her dry mouth.

"The mistress, my wife. Are you dim-witted, daft as well as deaf, because if you are you shall leave my employment at

once. I want no lunatics about my son so speak up. Tell me why
I find you lounging in my wife's sitting-room, reading a book.
I was told by that other idiot downstairs" – referring, Sally
supposed, to Jackson or Barker – "that her ladyship did not
want to be disturbed since she has a headache. So, where is she?
Where is her ladyship hiding?"

"Perhaps she has . . . has gone up to . . . to the nursery, my
lord."

"The nursery, you think? Well, unless she has crawled into a
cupboard, there is no sign of her. Now then, girl." His voice
hardened to visible menace. "*Where is your mistress?*"

He raised his arm and hit her back-handed across the face,
watching with terrible interest as she fell weeping to the floor.

29

It was well into February before anyone missed her. Beth was used to the long absences during which Milly would be unable to visit her, the visits depending, of course, on Hugh's activities. During the winter months he had been frequently away from home, which had enabled her to slip out to Edge Bottom House a couple of times and to meet Todd but since January, the weeks passing by hardly noticed, there had been no sign of her or from her.

Beth was sewing on a tiny scrap of nun's veiling, delicate and fine, which would be a nightgown for the new baby when he or she was born. It was almost finished and, sitting dreamily by her fireside, her thoughts on the day when she would dress her child in the garment, she was embroidering what was known as a chained feather stitch across the bodice, white on white. She meant to decorate each end of the chain with a satin stitch leaf and a tiny rosebud and when it was finished wrap it lovingly in the tissue paper all her child's garments were stored in.

She finished with a neat knot at the back of the material, then held it up, sighing with contentment. She was in her eighth month, heavy, placid, existing as the breeding female does in quite another world from those about her, even her beloved husband. They were all there on the periphery of her life, hovering, waiting, eager to be of assistance, especially Archie, to fetch her something, to give her a hand out of her chair, or up the stairs, but she was looking inward now, which was perhaps why she had not been consciously aware of her sister's non-appearance.

"Is it finished?" Mary said from her chair on the other side of the fireplace, herself involved in a bit of sewing. Hers was more mundane, to do with mending tears and sewing on buttons, for young Alex, since she had started to walk in that neat, lurching way she had, had become something of a tomboy and was forever catching her skirt on a fence that she attempted to climb or the broken branch of a tree she tripped over. Not quite two years old and like quicksilver as she ran, screaming with laughter, from Mary, or Jane, or one of the outdoor men who tried to catch her. They were constantly amazed by what she could accomplish despite her infirmity and John Bennett was to accompany Beth and Archie, after their child was born, to London to consult with the great Doctor Mackintosh in Harley Street.

Beth smiled as she studied the little girl who, after a walk with Jane during which she had covered at least twice the ground her nurse did, had fallen asleep on the floor where she had been playing with Boy. There was a table in the middle of the room draped in a floor-length green chenille cloth, the floor itself littered with dolls and teddy bears and golliwogs and wooden bricks. Alex and Boy, though he was not aware of it, had been playing hide and seek beneath the folds of the cloth, a game she had learned from Archie, and the patient animal had been dragged under the cloth and told to "stay" while Alex looked for him. She had not quite got the concept of the game and though she knew where Boy was, having put him there herself, she searched for him diligently behind the sofa and chairs and in the folds of the curtains.

At last, exhausted, the pair of them had fallen asleep, the child's curly head cushioned on the animal's flank.

Beth turned to stare pensively into the leaping flames of the fire, her hands cradling the swell of her belly and Mary watched her. It was almost three years since she had first seen this woman, this woman who had rescued her from the lock hospital and saved her from a life of degradation, for no decent woman would employ a girl who had been accused of being a prostitute and taken to the lock hospital. There would have been no course open to her but a life on the streets but here she was, a trusted friend despite being a servant, with fine employment, surrounded by affection, and if Beth Goodwin had asked it of her she would have given her life to save her mistress a moment's pain.

"You're quiet, Beth." She smiled, putting her sewing down for a moment as she searched for a match in the tin box containing buttons, on the lid of which was a rather worn picture of Queen Victoria and her consort. Dead now, of course, poor man, but the dear Queen still mourned him. "Is something bothering you?"

"I was just wondering why Milly hasn't been to Edge Bottom for so long. It must be six weeks since she was last here, not to see me, I might add" – her smile deepening – "but I'm surprised she hasn't walked over to . . . to visit Todd." Mary knew all about Milly and Todd, naturally. Apart from Archie, Mary was the only one that Beth would trust with her sister's secret love and the terrible risks she took.

"Didn't Mr Archie say something about Mr Todd enquiring after her last week?"

"Did he? Do you know, Mary, I feel so ashamed of myself, for I seem to think of nobody but myself and the life I carry inside me." She bent over and held her belly even more closely. "The life that is kicking me at this moment. I'm sure it's a boy and that he's going to be an athlete like his father. What did Archie say about Todd?"

"He actually came into the office, apparently, to show Mr Archie the frigger he had made. You know, the decorative one-off piece of glass the apprentices make to show off their

skill. A swan, it was, with a baby swan on its back and Mr
Archie was quite impressed. Anyway he's forever waylaying
Mr Archie and begging for news of her. He threatens to go up
to Thornley Green and face up to Lord Thornley, which
Archie warned him would be disastrous so he promised to
wait, but I don't think he will hold off for much longer. When
Jane and I took Alex and Boy across the field last Sunday we
saw him hurrying along the lane that leads up to Lord Thornley's estate. I suppose he's even more worried with the . . ."
Here Mary paused delicately, for she knew of the coming baby
that Milly carried inside her and that it had not been sired by
Hugh Thornley. What a pickle this family seemed to have got
themselves into ever since Beth's sister had married his lordship. Mind you, his lordship was no ordinary man but a brute
with a mind that was cruel and devious, and cared for nought
but his own pleasure and the revenge he would wreak if any
man, or woman, stood in his way.

Beth frowned. "Her baby is due in June so one would think
Hugh would have realised she is pregnant and if what Milly
told me is true and he's not been near her since Miles was born
. . . Oh, sweet heaven, Mary, what has happened to her?
Really, I don't know what I have been thinking of these last
weeks. So wrapped up in my own pregnancy and the happiness
it's brought I have let time slip by without a thought for my own
sister."

Beth gripped the arms of the chair and did her best to rise
from its soft depths, floundering like a fish just landed, and at
once Mary leaped to her feet and moved swiftly across the
room, stepping over the sleeping dog and child and gently
forcing her young mistress back into the chair.

"Stop it, now just stop it, d'you hear? There's no use getting
yourself all worked up. There's nothing *you* can do."

"Archie could—"

"No, now you know Mr Archie'd have a fit if he knew you

were carrying on like this. The man to see to it is not Mr Archie, but Mr Noah. After all, he's Miss Milly's father and though I know there's bad blood between them he has a perfect right to go over to Thornley Green and ask after his daughter. If your mother was to go with him, surely Lord Thornley would not bar their way."

"But the baby. How is she to explain that to her husband and not only to Hugh but to my mother and father?"

"They will think the child is Lord Thornley's, for remember you are the only one who knows of Miss Milly's meetings with Mr Todd."

"Archie knows."

"Well, he's not likely to say anything, is he?"

"And Hugh will know if he has not been in her bed since Miles was born. Mary, dear God, Mary, what have I been thinking of these last weeks, letting her—"

"You've been thinking of your own babe, which is only as it should be, but I think you are right that something should be done about Miss Milly. Shall I . . . shall I telephone your mother and father and ask them to come over at once?" That was an indication of how troubled Mary was, for she, like all the servants, viewed the instrument with terror and when the thing shrilled out in the hall there was always an argument as to who was to answer it. Fortunately this didn't happen very often, for the only telephones in the district were those belonging to the Goodwins. And even Abby would rather call up her carriage and be driven over to Edge Bottom House to speak to her daughter in person. It was for an emergency, Archie Goodwin told them and, dear heaven, there had been plenty of those during the past few years! If his wife had need of him Mary was to ring the Post Office Exchange and give his number which would somehow be magically relayed down the wires and he would answer and be home within minutes.

Mary calmed Beth, ringing for hot chocolate which Beth was

to drink while she "got through" to Lantern Hill and before Beth had finished her drink Mr and Mrs Goodwin would be over here, she reassured her, and the whole worrying thing would be sorted out. She was not to move. Here was the bell and while Mary struggled with the intricacies of the instrument if Beth needed anything she had only to ring for one of the maidservants.

They came to the kitchen door to watch Mary in awed admiration as she tackled the thing, picking up what Mr Archie called the "handset", putting it to her ear and then timidly turning the handle at the side. When a voice answered her she held it away from her ear for a fearful moment then spoke hesitantly.

"I want to speak to Mr Noah Goodwin at—"

"What number, please, madam?" the voice at the other end asked politely.

"He lives at Lantern Hill."

"But what is his telephone number?"

At last, after a great deal of scrutinising the numbers Mr Archie had written out and pinned to the wall beside the telephone, she finally found herself talking to a voice that proclaimed itself to be Noah Goodwin.

It was actually half an hour before her mother and father arrived from Lantern Hill, urged by the anxiety in Mary's voice to gallop at full stretch from their home to Edge Bottom House, convinced that their daughter was about to give birth.

"Darling, what is it?" her mother asked her, hurrying across the sitting-room to kneel by Beth's knee. The dog woke up and disturbed the child who, on seeing her grandparents, immediately wanted to play at hide and seek and for several confused minutes, while Jane was summoned to carry away the disappointed and by now wailing child, neither Noah nor Abby could make head nor tail of Beth's disjointed story.

"Begin at the beginning, lass," her father said. "We gathered from Mary that it concerns Milly and that you are worried that something might have happened to her. You know that bastard has forbidden her to visit us. We can't go there so we must abide by that for the moment. Let it all blow over and—"

"No, Father, it is not going to blow over. Dear sweet God, why have I kept this to myself and why have I let it get so far?"

"Let what get so far?"

Her father sat down heavily in the chair Mary had occupied while his wife continued to kneel at their daughter's feet. Noah Goodwin was in his fifty-sixth year and was still the straight-backed, powerfully built man he had been when he married Abby. He had grown heavier with age and his hair had streaks of grey in it but he was still a handsome man. His only concession to age was that he was forced to wear spectacles, which he hated. They were perched on the end of his nose now as he anxiously studied his wife and daughter.

Beth shook her head, the expression on her face quite desperate and her mother made a small sound of distress in the back of her throat.

"What is it? For God's sake, you are frightening us."

Beth took a deep breath as though she were about to plunge into deep water, which she was. "Milly is pregnant and the child is not Hugh's. She and Todd have been meeting secretly. The baby is expected in June sometime and if what Milly tells me is true, and I have no reason to believe she would lie, Hugh has not . . . not slept with her since Miles was born."

Abby and Noah Goodwin stared at their daughter, mouths agape, as though she had lost her mind. It was as though they had not really understood what she was saying, or perhaps it was Beth who did not understand the magnitude of her statement. They knew their daughter, their daughter Milly, had always been a wayward, headstrong, incorrigible child, girl and young woman, hard to handle, but with a heart in her as sweet and generous as any parents could wish for, which was why they had forgiven her so much. But deliberately to court danger, not only to herself and her son, but her family, her family's servants and, last but not least, the man she purported to love, was unforgivable. They could not believe what they were hearing and yet it seemed it was not finished.

"There is something else, Beth, which I have kept from you. I didn't want to worry you further."

All three turned to look at Mary who was standing with her back to the window. Her voice was so quiet it was almost a whisper and Noah Goodwin, who was also a little deaf, said irritably, "Speak up, girl."

"Harry . . . Harry Preston whose sister is Miss Milly's maid, says Sally has not been over to see him and her mother, who works for you, of course, says the same. Six weeks and—"

She stopped speaking abruptly and the other three people in the room all sat as though carved from stone. Stunned, shocked, speechless. It was as though the revelation that not only Milly but Sally Preston seemed to have vanished from their lives had spun them into some terrible dread, a dread they already knew, the dread that Hugh Thornley cared so little for anyone's existence but his own he was prepared to go to any lengths to defend it. His arrogance led him to believe he was beyond the law, the law that said he could beat his wife if he chose. But not Sally Preston. Not innocent Sally Preston who, though she might be a woman who could not claim equality with a man, a servant, a woman of the lower classes, was protected by the law, surely?

Beth felt a great breathless terror freeze her veins. Was this the moment to tell her parents that she believed, knew with great certainty that it had been Hugh Thornley's wickedness that had led to herself and Mary being taken to the lock hospital where an outrage had been committed against them? Where they had been physically raped, not by a man's body, but by an instrument of torture. Archie would be involved, and now it seemed Olly and Ruby Preston, Sally's parents, and Harry, her brother, would be dragged into this horror into which Milly's marriage to Hugh Thornley had precipitated them.

Abby Goodwin stood up slowly, putting her hand to her trembling lips then lifting it to push back a strand of curling hair. Her face was as white as the soft material from which the expected child's nightgown was made and for a moment she remained where she was. She put out a hand and rested it on the mantelshelf as though she momentarily needed support, then she whirled to her husband who still sat stunned and speechless.

For the last two years and more, ever since Hugh Thornley had come into their lives, Abby knew her husband had, going totally against his own arrogant nature, kept himself in tight control except for the one occasion when, tried beyond endurance, he had whipped his son-in-law. He had held his tongue and his temper in check, straining at the leash of his own formidable will for fear it might, in the end, cause damage to no one but Milly. Noah Goodwin was a man very like Hugh Thornley in as much as he would let nothing stop him in his determination to do what he considered was best for his family, for the works and for all those who worked for him, and that only his way was the right way. But his heart was sound, generous, all in all fair and though his temper was fierce it was never vicious. He would never deliberately hurt a living soul though he was known to be hard in business.

Suddenly he let out a roar of outrage, struggling to stand to let it escape more easily but not succeeding. The dog jumped to his feet and began to bark in fright and the women shrank back, for his wife and daughter had seen his fury in the past. Not directed at themselves but at some trouble at the works, some trouble that he was convinced could have been avoided. *He* would have avoided it and would become incensed when some fool made a mistake. He knew every job that was performed at Edge Bottom Glass and Brick Works; indeed he had performed each and every one. He would fly into a rage at the incompetence of any man with whom he did business and who, in his opinion, was worse than an idiot, but his fiery temper, now much reduced due to the love of and for his wife, was held in check in his own home.

"Damn the bastard," he snarled, his lip curled over his teeth so that the dog backed off and ran behind the sofa. "And damn that mindless girl of mine. I thought she would have learned to curb her own wilfulness after the last lot but no, here she is, consorting with Todd Woodruff of all men. Not that I blame him, for any man who gets himself in the clutches of that girl doesn't stand a bloody chance, but that being said we can't leave her there in the hands of Lord bloody Thornley. She must be brought home and the child with her. Not to mention her maid who seems to have become embroiled in this brouhaha—"

"*Brouhaha!* Is that what you call it?" his wife shrieked. "Our daughter is having an affair with the son of one of our servants and, in fact, is pregnant by him. Her husband has her locked up, knowing the expected child is not his and you speak of it as though it were some upset in the kitchen. She must be brought home and for good this time. I will not have my child, my grandchild exposed to the wickedness of this beast and if you won't do something, Noah Goodwin, then I will." She began to cry, great broken sobs that shook her like a young, newly planted tree in a sudden storm. Her husband at last jumped to his feet in horror, his face gone as white as both women, then it hardened and the Noah Goodwin of twenty years ago, the man he had been before the softening influence of his lovely wife, showed in his face.

He dragged his wife into his arms and put out a comforting hand to his daughter, then turned to Mary. "You, lass, get on the telephone to my son-in-law and tell him to come here at once. At once. Hurry, girl, don't stand there dithering and then telephone Lantern Hill and tell Olly Preston the same."

The old brown horse, quiet and patient, that was harnessed to the cart in which produce would be taken back to the farm, nosed in the hedgerow edging the field and the lane, which was no more than a few feet from the mangold hale. It was a mild day, spring not far away and over the sky, the colour of a wren's egg, great white clouds were drifting. The field was patched with sunlight and shadows, and aconites raised their golden heads in the ditch.

The man working on the edge of the field widened the opening of the clamp and dragged aside the inner lining of straw which had protected the mangold roots from the frost during the winter, dragging out the mangolds three or four at a time and throwing them into the cart. He never ceased his labour except to eat his midday bread and bacon and take a swig of ale, bending his back into his job, but anyone watching him would have noticed that his eyes were constantly on the wide-open gates of Thornley Green, which were over the hedge on the opposite side of the lane to where he laboured. The man whistled tunelessly as he worked, the rhythm of his whistling accompanying his stoop, grab, straighten, turn, swing and throw, but his attention never wandered from the gates of the great estate, which belonged to Lord Thornley. He had been at the task for the past week, taking the cart of mangold roots back to the farmyard each evening and the farmer who owned them and the field in which they had grown. When he left the field another man quietly took his place in the depth of the hedge, exchanging a quiet word with him before settling down to his watch. Each morning the first man drove the empty cart across the field, applying himself to some task, digging, stone-gathering, always busy should anyone look over the hedge, while the second man slipped away along the hedge line. If anyone noticed the rather good-looking horse that was stabled not far away in the farmer's barn it was not spoken of. Lord Thornley was none of their business, though they were all agreed he was a bad lot.

It was ten days after the man with the cart first appeared that the sound told him that what he had been employed to do was about to take place. First there was the faint peal of a horn, a hunting horn, then borne on the breeze the noise of hounds yelping and of laughter, of voices chatting in that drawl the gentry affected and the gritty sound of horses' hooves on gravel. The man straightened up, making sure he was well hidden behind the hedge, watching as a long procession of riders, male and female, most of the men in pink hunting jackets, streamed between the open gates of Thornley Green. For a moment he thought he had been discovered, for the hounds, with their keen noses, took a great deal of interest in the hedge behind which he was hidden, then the master blew his horn again and the laughing, chattering riders, the noisy dogs turned right and moved off in the direction of Moss Bank to the north of the estate. In the midst of them, whispering to an extremely beautiful woman dressed in an exquisitely cut riding habit, tight-waisted, was Lord Thornley. The woman laughed and smacked him playfully on the arm with her crop, bending her head on which she wore a black top hat to hide her smile.

Letting the hunt, the new Thornley Green Hunt which Hugh had promised himself, disappear round the bend in the leafy lane, the man threw down his spade and ran like the wind, which was pretty fast considering his age, to the farm where the horse, already saddled as it had been for ten days, was waiting. He threw himself on to the horse's back and with a shout to the farmer's wife, who had popped her head out of the kitchen door, he set off at a mad gallop in the direction of Lantern Hill.

There was a carriage standing in the driveway before the steps, the horses' heads held by Harry Preston, as they had been, like the heaving animal on whose back Olly Preston had just galloped from Park Farm, for the past ten days.

Without a word Noah and Archie Goodwin hurtled down the steps and threw themselves into the carriage and with a shout that startled the horses ordered Harry to "get a bloody move on". Olly only just had time to spring up on the coachman's seat beside his son before the carriage set off at a thundering pace down the drive and turned in a great swathe of gravel out of the gate and along the road that led north to Thornley Green.

30

Jackson opened the door as the bell sounded, the usual supercilious expression he affected slipping like butter in the sun when he saw the four men who stood on his master's doorstep. Quiet they were, not at all as he had seen them in the past, blustering and elbowing him aside as the old one had done months ago. Now they were polite as they pushed him to one side. One of them had a shotgun, not the grooms as two of them evidently were, but the younger one who was married to her ladyship's sister.

"I shouldn't call out, my good fellow," old Mr Goodwin told him, "for my son-in-law will not hesitate to use his weapon, not to kill, you understand, but to defend himself, or that is what will be said in court. Now, all you have to do is show me to my daughter's room and we will do the rest. The key? Ah, so she is locked in as we thought, and I presume his lordship has it? There is no need to jabber, lad, we won't hurt you but I'm sure there is another . . . there is, good. Then Harry here will go with you to get it and then when we have my daughter, her child and her maid, we'll be away. His lordship won't be back for a while so we have plenty of time but let's get to it, shall we."

They could hear laughter and the babble of voices in the kitchen and it was an indication of the state of the household that no one came to see where the footman had got to or who was ringing the doorbell. With the dowager Lady Thornley safely ensconced in the dower house and his lordship's wife "confined" to her room, they were more or less allowed to do as they liked.

The two women, barely recognisable as Milly Thornley and Sally Preston, cowered back into the depth of the sofa on which they were huddled. They were reasonably clean and tidily dressed, which Noah Goodwin thought was probably due to Sally Preston, but the room was cold, the fire gone out, it seemed for lack of fuel. They both looked ill and Milly was battered about the face, and her hair, which someone had done their best to dress, hung about her face in greasy swirls.

Sally was the first to recover, though it was obvious she had not yet recognised the men who hesitated in the doorway. She pulled an enormous shawl protectively about the figure of her mistress, peering in the dim light that fell through the grimy windows, her face revealing her terror, though Milly remained in the same mindless, speechless state.

"Dear sweet Jesus," Noah whispered, moving across the carpet towards his daughter, horrified when she shrank back and began to moan deep in her throat.

"Don't, please, not again." She turned into Sally's arms and sank her face into her maid's shoulder.

"Milly, darling, it's me," her father said hoarsely, reaching out for her, his mind frantic with the thought that this was Beth's ordeal all over again. She had flinched from the male sex and turned in abject fear to her maid and here was Milly, his brave, strong Milly, doing the same. She recoiled from him and began to shake.

Sally started to cry weakly, for at last she recognised who the intruder was, her eyes going over her master's shoulder to where her brother hovered, stricken by the sight of her and of the state of the woman who had once been his playmate.

"Look, sweetheart," she whispered, bending her head to Milly. "Your pa has come for you, your pa is here." She put out a hand and grasped Noah's pathetically. "Oh, sir, thank God. Thank God. Help me, help us. No, no, sweetheart, don't be frightened; it's your pa come to take us home. Oh, sir, you have come to take us home haven't you? I do believe Miss Milly will die soon if she is not taken away from this house and the man who has done this to her.''

With an oath of great obscenity Noah Goodwin picked up his daughter and with Sally creeping after him, her brother's arms supporting her, they stumbled down the wide staircase, followed by the jabbering footman. Olly cleared the way, for the second footman had finally decided to come and see what had happened to Jackson. In the kitchen doorway several servants watched in amazement and a certain dread as to what his lordship would do when he found his wife had been spirited away once again by her father, whom they had all recognised, of course. And not only his wife, for one of the men, whom they believed to be Mr Goodwin's son-in-law, thundered up the stairs to where the nurseries were situated and came down again with the Honourable Miles Thornley squalling vociferously in his arms. Behind him was his nurse, arguing fiercely, but he ignored her and before any of them could even gather their senses the two women, the baby and the men who had come for them were in the carriage and hurtling down the drive towards the park gates.

"He'll kill us," one of his lordship's servants was heard to say fearfully.

Doctor Bennett, who, it seemed, was to be a participant in every drama that plagued the Goodwin family, came out of the bedroom where the two women slept under the influence of the sedatives he had administered, Milly in her own bed and Sally in a smaller one placed beside her. Milly had screamed just as they remembered her sister had screamed when they had tried to separate her from her maid and it was thought expedient to keep them together, as it seemed they had been together in whatever horrors Hugh Thornley had inflicted upon them during the last six weeks.

Abby and Noah rose in unison from the splendid velvet sofa placed at the head of the stairs and waited apprehensively for him to speak. John Bennett had thought it wiser not to allow Milly's mother into the bedroom until he had assessed Milly's wounds, for what mother can cope with the suffering body of a beloved daughter, not once but twice. Ruby Preston, Olly and Harry all hung about in the hallway, he could see them over the banister, waiting to hear the news of Sally's injuries and he beckoned them to come upstairs, which they did, Ruby weeping silently, her husband and son with murderous expressions on their weatherbeaten faces. John prayed, without being conscious of it, that none of them would come face to face with Hugh Thornley, for if they did they would tear him to pieces.

Harriet Woodruff and Nessie Moscrop – a sensible young housemaid who was not likely to panic – had helped him to undress the two pathetic women, to bathe them and put them tenderly into clean nightgowns, tucking them into their beds where they had both fallen into a deep and hopefully healing sleep.

"They will need constant nursing, both of them," he said abruptly. "Milly is in the worst state, bruised and torn about . . . internally. I'm sorry, you will know what I mean, but I can get no sense out of either of them at the moment."

"The . . . the baby?"

"Gone. I'm sorry, and had it not been for her maid – Sally, is it? – Milly would have gone too. They must sleep side by side, it seems, for Milly won't allow Sally to be moved, and then, when they are rested, good food and absolutely no visitors. They are not to be questioned except in my presence and if Hugh Thornley should come calling you may tell him I am going from here to the police station in St Helens to lay a serious charge against him. This has gone on long enough, Noah."

"Dear God, John, d'you think I don't know it? I'll come with you, as will Olly and Harry Preston, for Sally has been almost as cruelly treated as Milly. I don't care if his lordship is related to Queen Victoria herself he will not be allowed to continue with—"

"Yes, yes, Noah," John said irritably, for though he could well sympathise with the pain and outrage his friend was feeling his own first thought was for Milly and the need to have her guarded. "But I think it would be best if I went alone. Now I must go and examine the boy . . . Miles, is it? One of the kitchen servants is with him in one of the spare bedrooms, I believe, but he will need . . . oh, I don't know, toys, clothing, things that Alex has and which I'm sure Beth will send over. Oh, and that's another thing. Under no circumstances is Beth to be allowed to come to Lantern Hill. She is near her time and we don't want another tragedy on our hands. That will no doubt be her now," as the telephone shrilled in the downstairs hallway. "I hope that husband of hers is keeping her tied hand and foot until she is safely delivered."

"May we go in, John, at least Ruby and me? We won't disturb them, we promise, don't we, Ruby?" Abby put a gentle hand on Ruby's arm, turning to her solicitously and Sally's mother nodded.

"For a moment only. Harriet will watch over them and the maid, Nessie, will take a turn. When they have rested I may allow you, Abby and Ruby, since you are the most closely involved, to help but there must be no histrionics, d'you hear, or I shall bar you both from the sickroom."

They both nodded wordlessly. Ruby wasn't absolutely sure what "histrionics" meant but she was willing to agree to anything if it would help her girl. The men, Noah, Olly and Harry, strode about the wide hallway like caged animals refused permission to be let out and get about the business of doing what wild animals do, which is to hunt down their prey. John eyed them anxiously, as he well knew what Noah, at least, was capable of, and could you blame him, but this must be done properly, within the law and he, as a doctor, was the one to lay the charge. Milly Thornley was the wife of the baron and it was still believed in many circles that what a man did with his wife was *his* business, but a man was certainly not allowed to ill-treat a decent woman – and ill-treat was putting it mildly – as he had done Sally Preston. She had obviously done her best to defend her mistress and suffered in consequence.

"Guard the house, Noah. Issue shotguns to Harry and Olly here and I will be back as soon as possible with the police. Not just a constable who would be easily intimidated by a member of the aristocracy but with the top man who is a friend of mine. Lord Thornley will come, believe me, if not for his wife, then for his son, but until he is under lock and key be on your guard. The man must be insane to imagine he can get away with this. Now, Abby and Ruby may peep at their daughters but I beg of you not to be too distressed by . . . by what you see, for they are both strong young women and will recover."

John and the police had not yet returned when Hugh Thornley came thundering up the drive on his lathered hunter, still dressed in his hunting pink, his face a grimacing, twisted mask of fury. Throwing himself from his horse, he flew up the steps and was ready to hammer on the door had it not suddenly opened to reveal the strangely quiet figure of Noah Goodwin. He held a shotgun and his finger was on the trigger, an expensive weapon of which, though he didn't care greatly for shooting, he had four in his study above the fireplace. The other three were in the hands of Olly Preston, Harry Preston and Clem Woodruff who appeared from round the corner of the house, standing just as quietly as their master, but the menace in them was a tangible thing. Olly and Harry Preston wanted nothing more than to drop their guns and take to Hugh Thornley with their fists. They needed desperately to feel flesh crunching into flesh, to feel bone breaking, to knock this man to the ground then kick him to death, for had he not abused Harry's sister, Olly's daughter, and even to put a bullet in him was a poor thing besides this. But they had been held back by the need, reiterated by Doctor Bennett, that this thing must be done within the law if it was to be ended once and for all. Clem Woodruff simply needed to protect his grandson who was at this moment seriously distressed by his removal, not from the nurse who cared for him with starched thoroughness at Thornley Green, but from the familiarity of his baby life and the upheaval of the last hour.

The guns the men held were known as breech-loaders and could fire more than one cartridge without reloading. For a moment Hugh Thornley hesitated, then his natural arrogance came to the fore; his total belief that these oafs could not harm him or stand in his way because a man was within his rights to rescue his wife and son. He began to laugh, pressing forward until the muzzle of Noah's gun was hard against his chest.

"Shoot me if you dare but, by God, if you do, you will hang."

"Oh, I shall not kill you, lad, but one of my men, or indeed all three of them, have orders to shoot you, in the leg, or the foot, not to kill, of course, but to maim so that you will never walk again, let alone hunt. We are waiting on the law, you see, and until it arrives you will remain exactly where you are."

"Get out of my way, you bastard," hissed Hugh, "and tell your servants to do the same. I have come for my wife and son and to tell the truth I'm glad the police are to be involved, for I think you will find I have right on my side. My wife—"

"Is at this moment under sedation, along with her maid, both of whom you have abused. I believe Doctor Bennett is to fetch the chief constable from St Helens and though it will shame me and my family I shall show him exactly what you have done to these two women."

"Do you honestly think you can keep me from my wife and

child, you poor sod? There's not a court in the land would go against me. So stand aside and while I fetch them down here order that groom of yours to bring the carriage round."

"Are you insane or just weak-minded, Lord Thornley?" Noah asked, almost conversationally. He was keeping a tight rein on his temper, which had been his undoing in the past though it was evident that Hugh was rapidly losing his and not only his temper but his reason. "Are you feeble-minded that you don't understand what I am saying?" Noah continued. "You will not enter my house and if you should continue to try, I or one of my men will cripple you. Now get off my step, climb on that animal of yours and get off my land. Go back to where you belong. You will never see my daughter, or her child again. Nor will you see another penny of my money. I mean to bring action against you in a court of law."

"Don't be so bloody stupid, man," Hugh began but for some reason a strange expression chased itself across his face and he took a step back. He was silent for a moment and his face became still, blank, although in his eyes some dreadful thing lurked, like a creature from the very depths of a bottomless ocean. It swam across the incredible blue of his eyes then flitted away and he actually smiled.

"I don't think you quite understand, Mr Goodwin," he said. "I am not a man who forgets those who trespass on his property and my wife and child are my property. You will live to regret this day, believe me, you and yours. You will never know a minute's peace from this moment on. We have long been enemies, you and I, and I have threatened you before, but unless my wife and son are back at Thornley Green where they belong by nightfall you will wish you had never crossed Hugh Thornley."

Archie had gone back to Edge Bottom House to comfort his wife, as her telephone call had been frantic. He warned the men in the stables and gardens to be vigilant, for though Hugh

Thornley's malevolence was mainly directed at Milly and Milly's father, while he himself was at the glass works where business must go on, who knew what fiendish thing his lordship might get up to. Mary was to telephone him at the works should anything, anything at all, worry her mistress, and he would be home within five minutes.

At Lantern Hill beside Noah Goodwin were Olly and Clem, Harry, Reuben from the stables who brandished a pitchfork, Tommy the stable boy, the two gardeners and their lads, even old Doddie, the handyman, who stood silently about the house in various poses depending on their nature. The older men were somewhat wary, but the lads, though they knew it was serious and that Miss Milly's husband was a bugger, a dangerous bugger if the master was to be believed, found a certain exhilaration in the diversion.

It was a fine day, the sky a pale gossamer blue laced over with the thinnest of cloud. The sun shone weakly on the snowdrops which had pushed their green spears through the earth, and wild primroses and violets carpeted the grass beneath the trees which Noah Goodwin had planted. Frank and Jack had been busy at "last back end" putting in the bulbs which were now grown into tall, soldier tulips and proud trumpeting daffodils, and the palest of pale green leaves were misting the row of lime trees. It was a day for lifting one's face to the heavens and breathing in the sweet smell of that moment in time poised between spring and summer, but instead it was filled with menace, with snarling hatred and the swelling need of revenge emanating from the man who stood at Noah Goodwin's door.

Hugh Thornley turned and with superb grace vaulted into the saddle of his tired hunter. The animal had covered a lot of ground today, chasing the fox, skirting the Hawthornthwaite estate, for Lady Hawthornthwaite disliked fox-hunting, moving westwards towards Kirkby Moss. The chief whip, the virtual master of the pack, took charge of field operations and at midday they found and dashed off in a northerly direction, across the railway line where Hugh had been in at the kill. They had found again an hour later but the field moved off quickly and Hugh had decided to call it a day. A long and tiring ride and his beautiful ebony hunter was flagging badly but despite this Hugh dug his spurs cruelly into the beast's flanks, drawing a hiss of outrage from Harry.

For several minutes the men stood about, waiting for instructions from their master, but when it seemed Hugh Thornley had gone he ordered Olly and Harry to continue patrolling the house, guns half cocked, while the rest of them could get on with their work. With a last cautious look about his domain, Noah went inside the house to his wife.

He found her sitting quietly by the still sleeping Milly's bedside. Sally was awake and watching, her own face revealing the fading bruises she had received from Hugh Thornley's fists when she had tried to defend her mistress. She did her best to sit up as Noah hesitantly entered the room, just as though she felt she should leap from her bed and bob a curtsey, but the nurse sent over by John Bennett gently pushed her flat again, shushing her, smiling, a starched and yet motherly sort of woman, the sort Doctor Bennett favoured.

"He's gone, lass," Noah whispered to Sally, moving to stand beside his wife who lifted her hand to him. He took it, looking down into the battered face of their daughter who had been given a stronger draught than Sally.

"She'll sleep for hours, sir," the nurse murmured. "Poor lady, but it'll do her the world of good. She'll be as bright as a button in't mornin', you mark my words," which Noah thought was somewhat optimistic, looking at his child.

Two weeks later Beth Goodwin was awakened by a commotion which at first she could not identify. She turned her head on the pillow to look for Archie but he was gone. The room was empty and for a moment she felt the panic that had overshadowed her life but which, with Archie's love and the expected child, had long gone. The room was dim, lit only by the flames flickering in the grate. Someone, probably Mary, had just replenished the fire, for it burned brightly, but the light from the windows was sombre as though the day outside were grey. It was March and the soft spring-like weather that had coloured February had been overtaken by blustery winds and squalls of rain and for two days now she and Alex had been unable to take their usual walk down to the paddock. The child had been restless, for she was active, bright, curious about everything she saw and touched, and books and games had lost their charm.

But what was going on downstairs? She could hear someone shouting and something crashed as though a vase had fallen. There was the sound of feet pounding along the hallway and a door banged. She distinctly heard Jane's voice coming, she thought, from the nursery and there seemed to be fists crashing against a door. The voices, one higher than the others, babbled in the distance and from far away in the kitchen, at least she thought it was the kitchen, one of the maids screamed. Dear God, oh, sweet Jesus . . . Please, please, what was happening? Why didn't someone come to her? Some dreadful thing was taking place in her home and there was no one here to tell her what, or who . . . Archie, where was Archie, who more often than not left the house for the works before she awakened, but where? Oh, dear God in heaven, where was Mary who was always here when she woke?

There was another crash and this time she recognised the voice of Tucker, the gardener, coming from outside the house, shouting something unintelligible, and the high-pitched squeak of Billy, his lad.

"Get the bridle," she heard Tucker bellow, then what sounded like a curse followed by the gathering sound of horses' hooves on the path that led from the lane to the front door.

"Mary, Mary," she shrieked. "Mary . . ." She struggled to free herself from the encompassing grip of the bedclothes which seemed to be wrapped tightly round her, floundering to get her feet to the carpet, her enormous belly pushing her back on to the bed, then at last she managed to get to her feet. She swayed, disorientated, light-headed, and she was frightened by the ferocity of her beating heart. She clutched at the bedpost, then instead of moving to the bell to summon one of the servants she began a slow drag to the bedroom door which was closed. She opened it, turning first towards the staircase from where the sounds of confusion were coming, then towards the stairs that led to the nursery where determined fists were still beating against the door.

"Mary, Ruth, anybody. Oh, Lord, help me. Tell me what's happening. Archie . . ." Undecided which way to turn, for no one seemed to be taking any notice of her cries, she leaned heavily against the door frame, then, pushing herself away from it, began to stumble towards the head of the stairs.

She looked down into utter chaos. Mary was clutching the telephone to her ear, her trembling hand barely able to hold it and next to her Mrs Kyle stood, her face twisted in what appeared to be terror. She was moaning into Mary's ear and Mary pushed her away in her effort to speak coherently to whoever was on the other end of the line. Ruth was there, wringing her hands and crying noisily, Morna adding to the din, and at the bottom of the stairs sat Dottie, her apron over her head. Alfie, the stable lad, twisted and turned, the muck of the stables still on his heavy boots stamping into the carpet.

"What'll us do?" he kept repeating until suddenly Mrs Kyle pulled herself together and, turning, slapped him across the face. From upstairs at the top of the house the hammering at the door grew more desperate. As Cook turned, the almost senseless figure of her mistress hovering at the top of the stairs caught her eye and at once, despite her matronly weight, she flew up the stairs to her, putting her arms about her and doing her best to lead her back to her bedroom.

"Now, don't you worry yourself, my lass," she said soothingly. "They've all gone after him, the men, I mean, those what can ride and they'll have her back in no time. Mary's talking ter Mr Archie on that there machine and he'll be here quick sharp." Turning to peer down the stairs she yelled loudly, "Will one of yer get up them stairs an' let Jane out afore she knocks door down. Now then, my little lass" – turning back to Beth – "let Mrs Kyle help yer back to bed fer there's nowt yer can do. Mr Archie'll see to it so you—"

"Mrs Kyle, Mrs Kyle, please, where's Alex? Has he—"

"Now don't you bother your head—"

"*Not bother my head!*"

"See, chuck . . ." Mrs Kyle went so far as to forget to whom she spoke. "It'll do no good."

"Where is my child? Tell me or I shall run down—"

"No, lass, no." Then to Mrs Kyle's horror Beth Goodwin doubled over and gasped in agony as the first tiger pain clawed at her back.

31

Hugh Thornley had not been put under lock and key as Noah Goodwin and John Bennett had hoped, despite the seriousness of the injuries sustained by his wife and his wife's maid. Doctor Bennett had been most insistent that the chief constable, a gentleman he knew to be of good character, a moral man and absolutely trustworthy, accompany him to Lantern Hill where Noah Goodwin's daughter lay seriously ill. He must see for himself what had been done to her, he begged him, not once but twice by her husband, and for the safety of not only Lady Thornley but her family, Sir Arthur Brown must come with him and examine her.

Sir Arthur had been appalled. Not only was it highly improper for a gentleman who was not a member of her ladyship's family to enter her bedroom and inspect the injuries Doctor Bennett spoke of and, though he had heard, as who had not, of Lord Thornley's wild ways, he could not believe that a gentleman of Lord Thornley's standing would be a party to the cruelty Doctor Bennett described. He was a man of excellent family with a pedigree stretching back into the mists of time. He himself had dined at Thornley Green several times, not recently, true, and could not bring himself to believe that a gentleman such as Lord Thornley would be involved in . . . in such atrocities.

"There is only one way for you to be sure, sir, and that is to come with me now and speak to Noah Goodwin and his daughter. They will tell you a tale that will horrify you. Oh,

I know Lord Thornley still has influence in this community, thanks mainly to his grandfather who was a decent, fair and kindly man, but his son, and his grandson did not take after him. Hugh Thornley has given his wife syphilis—"

"Dear God, Doctor Bennett, I beg you—"

"No, do not beg anything of me. It is for me to beg of you the performance of your duty which is to investigate the savagery of this man."

"Doctor Bennett, I am a busy man with many heavy duties but if you insist I will send a constable to—"

"Lord Thornley is a forceful man, Sir Arthur, and would reduce a constable or any man not of high rank to a nervous wreck. It needs a man who can stand up to him."

"Believe me, sir, no man will reduce me to a nervous wreck but—"

"That is why I have come for you, Sir Arthur. Bring a constable, for it might be wise to have a man of the law on hand. Oh, yes, Lord Thornley would go to any lengths to retrieve his wife and son from the safety of Lady Thornley's father but Hugh Thornley is a man on the brink of madness, and I cannot stand by and see a decent family and a seriously ill woman threatened like this. Noah Goodwin is guarding his home and his family as best he can within the law but I'm afraid he is becoming desperate. Hugh Thornley is a cunning and evil man and I insist that he be put under lock and key for the sake of everyone involved."

"But Doctor Bennett, just suppose I come with you and . . . well, speak to Lady Thornley, where is the proof that whatever has been done to her has been at her husband's hands?"

"You are a policeman, Sir Arthur. It is your job to investigate a crime when a charge has been laid. I am a man respected in this town and I prepared to be a witness to this man's perfidy. Please, sir, you will never forgive yourself if you allow him to return his wife and child to Thornley Green. His temper and lack of control is such that I fear he may do worse than beat her senseless, *rape* her."

An expression of distaste crossed the chief constable's face, for he was of the old school that believed a man could not rape his own wife, but still, Noah Goodwin was an influential, wealthy and respected man in the community, not one who could be ignored. He had been present at a good many functions where Noah Goodwin had been a guest and his generosity to charity was well known. He had heard that Goodwin allowed his wife and daughter to involve themselves with this new feminist and radical school of thinking, which he didn't care for, and they had been seen at several rallies where he had sent a constable or two to keep an eye on them. Not exactly disturbances, but not the sort of thing he would like his own womenfolk to be mixed up in. Still, he had best at least drive out to Lantern Hill with Doctor Bennett and find out what the devil this was all about.

He had been alarmed by the state of Lady Thornley who, though awake, seemed unaware of her own surroundings. Her face was so bruised and swollen it would not have disgraced a prize-fighter and there were marks about her neck that looked suspiciously like the imprints *fingers* might make. Her maid was not much better, though she was more alert, pleading with him, when she was told who he was, not to let Lord Thornley get them again. She wept disconsolately so that a woman he was told was her mother took her in her arms and he was hurried from the room.

Hugh Thornley met him in his wife's drawing-room with a charming smile and a look of slight bewilderment as though he wasn't awfully sure what to make of this call, but whatever help he could give the chief constable he would be only too happy to do so. He offered Sir Arthur a brandy, which he refused saying he was working and didn't drink while on duty, and when he was asked what duty that might be he felt something of a fool when Lord Thornley laughed and shook his head in disbelief, saying he had never heard anything so ridiculous in his life. They talked for an hour, gentleman to gentleman and when Sir Arthur stood up to leave he was in such a state of confusion he didn't know what to think. The fellow was so plausible, but men like Noah Goodwin and Doctor John Bennett, respected citizens of the community, could not be ignored. He advised Lord Thornley that he would make some enquiries regarding the accusations, wondering to himself where to start, and until this complaint against him was cleared up he must ask his lordship to remain in St Helens and to keep away from Noah Goodwin's property. His wife and son were being cared for and until Sir Arthur was convinced one way or the other he would be grateful if Lord Thornley would, well . . . he did not say the words but the inference was that his lordship would be advised to stay out of trouble.

His lordship smiled courteously as he saw him off the premises, watching for a moment as Sir Arthur's carriage began its journey down the long drive of Thornley Green. It was as well that Sir Arthur did not see the beating Sidney, the boot boy, received at Hugh Thornley's hands merely for being in the wrong place at the wrong time. As the front door closed Sidney was fetching in a basket of logs ready to be placed beside the grate in the wide hallway and though, when he saw his master, he stood stock still like a rabbit confronted with a stoat, eyes distended, mouth open on a silent scream, his master was upon him, throwing the thin wisp of a lad across the hall towards the kitchen door where he lay stunned. He was picked up and flung once more, this time into the fireplace where fortunately the fire had not yet been lit, catching his head on the corner of the stone, lying motionless among the remains of last night's fire. His lordship was bellowing now, none of the words comprehensible and the servants cowered in the kitchen, too terrified to venture out and see what had happened to poor

Sidney. There was a crash as though the grandfather clock had been knocked over and the kitchen-maid, Polly, who had never once encountered her master, since he did not care for females in the front of the house, began to weep silently. Footsteps sounded on the stairs and they all looked up towards the ceiling as though trying to pierce the plaster and ascertain in which direction his lordship had gone. Then, when silence reigned, Mrs Newby and Jackson ventured into the hall, peeping round the green baize door to where Sidney lay.

"Oh, dear Lord . . . oh, dear Lord," Mrs Newby whispered, her hand to her mouth. "He's killed the lad."

Between them they carried the boy to the kitchen. He was laid on Mrs Newby's cluttered table where he coughed and whimpered but gained consciousness, opening dazed eyes which seemed to stare through them.

"Happen we'd best send fer't doctor," the cook said fearfully, still whispering, though there was no chance his lordship could hear her.

"Not me, Mrs Newby. I'm having nothing ter do wi' it," Jackson declared. "See, lad's coming round. Give him a sup o' brandy." It was an indication of the footman's anxiety that he gave the boy a sip of his lordship's best brandy which was reserved in the kitchen just for himself.

Will Goodwin was no more than two hours old when his mother struggled with her distraught husband, demanding to be allowed out of bed, for if he didn't go at once to Thornley Green and bring back her child, she'd damn well do it herself. No, she would not lie still. Yes, she had seen her son and he was lovely, but he was safe in the nursery and who knew what that devil would do in his madness to Alex.

Doctor Bennett looked over her head at her husband then nodded at the nurse who passed him a glass in which a sedative was mixed. Beth Goodwin knocked it from his hand.

"Don't you dare try and put me to sleep, Doctor Bennett," she shrieked. "That brute has Alex and God alone knows what he's doing to her and unless she is fetched back at once I will get out of this bed and drive over to Thornley Green, with a pistol and demand she be returned to us. He's out of his mind, deranged, and what that damned policeman is doing, the one who was going to make enquiries, I can't imagine. Two weeks since Milly was brought home and he is still roaming about. Yes, yes, I know he has been told to remain on his own property but do you honestly believe he will obey?"

"Beth, Beth, my darling, calm down, please, lie back and rest." Archie held her tightly to his chest, his face contorted with this nightmare that had come upon them. It was twelve hours since Alex had been snatched away by her father and Beth had gone into labour, and though he had at once telephoned his father-in-law nothing further had been heard. Doctor Bennett had his hands full with Beth who, despite being in the throes of childbirth, was determined to get in her carriage and retrieve the little girl.

Noah had gone at once to St Helens and challenged Sir Arthur Brown, stating that surely this was proof enough that Thornley was out of his mind and demanding to know what the chief constable was doing about it. How were his *enquiries* proceeding, he had asked sarcastically, and when could they expect some sort of report, and, more to the point, the arrest of his son-in-law who had so brutally ill-treated his daughter and her maid? Now he had illegally entered his son-in-law's house and removed the child, with whom he had had no contact since she was born and taken her from the care of her adoptive parents.

"Was the child legally adopted by your daughter and son-in-law, Mr Goodwin?" asked Sir Arthur ponderously.

"Well, no, but he wouldn't have the child, who is slightly crippled, in his house so my daughter took her in and has cared for her ever since. Her mother was not well, the child's mother, I mean, my other daughter, Milly, so Beth has brought Alex up as her own and Lord Thornley has no right to—"

Sir Arthur held up his hand. He was getting somewhat impatient with all these names and was trying his best to sort them out in his mind but one thing was quite clear. Although he had *warned* Lord Thornley to remain on his own estate or at least within the confines of the environs of St Helens, the man had not been restricted by law! Sir Arthur had made several enquiries about his lordship and had not liked what he had heard. He intended driving out to Thornley Green to question the servants, but he was a busy man and was not accustomed to the sort of work an inspector or even a sergeant could be trusted with. Still, with Mr Goodwin and Doctor Bennett pressing him, influential gentlemen who were becoming increasingly impatient, and with this new development regarding the child, he must make it his business to attend to it as soon as possible.

"There is just one thing, Mr Goodwin, that must be taken into account."

"Oh, yes, and what might that be?" Mr Goodwin growled.

"The child is his and the law will be on his side. He has a perfect right to return his daughter to her home."

"Even though he has been proved to be a madman?"

"No one has proved that, sir."

"And no one will if you're not prepared to get off your arse and make these *enquiries* you keep babbling on about."

"Mr Goodwin!"

Noah snorted. "I see I shall have to take matters into my own hands. Good-day to you, sir."

At Edge Bottom House Archie looked despairingly into his wife's tortured face, then his own cleared.

"No one is going to leave Alex at Thornley Green, my

darling. I shall ride over with some of the men at once and bring her back, I promise. Your father is at this moment with Sir Arthur demanding that he goes to Thornley Green and hands over his granddaughter but you see . . . well, Alex *is* Hugh's daughter and he has a perfect right to—"

"No; no, he hasn't. She is ours. She has been *our* daughter for the past two years. Milly has been guarded by men with shotguns and so has her son but no one guarded Alex."

"Hugh discarded her when she was born and we made the mistake of believing she was in no danger since she was of no interest to him. Now he has taken her for only one reason and that reason is revenge. Now, sweetheart, if you will rest, take the draught."

"No, no sedative but I promise to lie still here and wait for you to bring back Alex to me. Until she is safe here in my arms I shall not sleep nor even try to."

"Shall I ask Jane to bring down our son now that he has been bathed?" Archie could not prevent the satisfaction that gleamed in his eyes at the thought of the lovely boy who lay in the nursery. His son, his blood and bone, but Beth turned away obstinately. She was tired, aching with weariness, for though it had not been a long or arduous labour through it all she had fought them, Doctor Bennett, his nurse, Archie and Mary in her frenzy to have Alex returned to her. At the moment Alex was more important to her than her boy, for the very image of the lovely little girl, two years old and undoubtedly terrified by what was happening to her and of the man she did not know who had snatched her away, was driving Beth out of her mind.

The Honourable Alexandra Thornley sat stiffly on the velvet-covered chair where she had been placed by her father. She wore no coat and was shivering. She was dressed in a fine woollen dress the colour of harebells over which she wore a starched white pinafore. In her glossy ebony curls was tied a satin bow to match the colour of her dress and her white stockings ended in grey kid boots. One boot was smaller than the other. Her blue eyes, which normally shone merrily somewhere between sapphire and turquoise in her rosy face, were clouded, tears hanging on the end of her long, dark lashes. As a baby she had sucked her thumb but as she grew the habit had decreased but now, in her fear, it was firmly plugged into her mouth and she hiccuped quietly, each hiccup shaking her small body with its intensity. It was plain she had retreated into some secret world, for her safety, her security, everything that had made up her protected baby days and nights had been torn away from her. She was aware that the lady and gentleman were speaking in high, angry voices but the place she had hidden in did not allow her to understand the words, had she been old enough. She merely sat, her small, booted feet stuck out before her, one hand to her mouth, the other gripping the white fold of her pinafore as though for comfort.

"But what am I supposed to do with her?" the dowager Lady Thornley begged. "I'm not well enough to care for a child, Hugh, surely you know that. And why have you brought her here?" She looked distastefully at the pathetic figure of the small girl who was her own granddaughter, her patrician features cold and dispassionate.

"What does it matter, Mama? I want you to keep her for a few days until my plans are made and then—"

"Plans? What plans?" His mother watched him warily, for in her own mind she had begun to believe that this son of hers was not quite . . . quite right. She wasn't sure what she meant by that but there was something wrong with him. She had heard whispers brought by her own maidservants, whispers come from the big house about the goings-on in which her son was the main perpetrator. Once she had heard screams as she walked in the garden but she had shut her ears and hurried on, as she wished for nothing more than peace in the years remaining to her. Now he had brought this girl-child who was crippled, so it was said, and she could see that one foot was shorter than the other. Hugh's wife and son had been taken by his wife's father to Lantern Hill so what was Hugh up to now?

"What are you planning, Hugh?" she asked him, sitting up straighter in her chair, for she had been taught by her nanny and governess that young ladies never slumped. Hugh was fidgeting about by the window, peering out as though looking for someone. He had left his horse at the back of her small house, thundering through the kitchen into her drawing-room with the child dangling like a broken doll under one arm, thrusting her on to the velvet chair where she sat frozen.

"Mama, that bastard—"

"*Hugh!*" Even in the midst of this high drama Caroline Thornley was still a lady and would not have bad language in her drawing-room.

"Oh, for God's sake, Mama. Can't you see I'm asking you for help? They have taken my wife and son and for some reason, which is a bloody mystery to me, the law will not allow me to 'disturb the peace' as they put it by bringing them back. But they said nothing about this one," nodding contemptuously in the direction of the hiccuping child. "Now I know that curiously the Goodwins have some sort of affection for her, despite her being a cripple, so I am going to make a bargain. I must have my son and they want this . . . this thing, so I am prepared to make an exchange."

"And your wife?"

"Can go to hell for all I care. I might even divorce her since I have ample grounds."

"Grounds?" Lady Thornley's voice was faint and she allowed herself to buckle slightly in her chair.

"Desertion for one and I believe her to have been unfaithful to me."

"With whom?"

"Oh, I don't know," he answered impatiently. "Now, if you would summon one of your maids to see to the child I must get back to the house because I believe my father-in-law or perhaps my brother-in-law will be here soon. And if you should be questioned you know nothing about a child. Do you hear, Mama?" His voice held such menace that Lady Thornley sank back even further into her chair and Alexandra Thornley sat as still as a mouse caught in a corner by the cat, making no sound, no movement.

Hugh strode from the room, pushed past the two open-mouthed servants in the kitchen, climbed on to his horse and galloped wildly off in the direction of the stables. Lady Thornley reached forward with a trembling hand and rang the bell.

"Remove the child," she said faintly to the maidservant who answered the bell, waving her hand distractedly in the direction of the almost comatose little girl. Alex didn't even turn her head to look at the maid, so deep in mindless fear was she, and the maid, who had come with Lady Thornley from the big house, stared in bewilderment, first at Alex, then at Lady Thornley. They had seen the master come thrusting through the kitchen, of course, with the prettiest little girl in his arms, she and the cook watching, gape-jawed, as he made for the door that led into the hall. The child was so dreadfully frightened, anyone could see that, but they presumed, since it was known that his lordship had a daughter being brought up elsewhere that this was her. Now he had gone and the child sat like a small wilting flower, a spring flower caught unexpectedly in a winter frost. No movement, no sound but the dreadful issue of regular hiccuping which came from her throat and shook her small frame.

"Where is she to go, your ladyship?" Margaret asked diffidently. Margaret was a kindly woman who had been in Lady Thornley's service for many years but she had had nothing to do with children and, having never married, had none of her own.

"I'm sure I don't know, Margaret. Take her to the kitchen and give her . . . well, something to eat, perhaps, and then put her to bed."

"To bed, your ladyship! Where is she to sleep?" There were only two bedrooms in the small dower house and her ladyship slept in one while she, Cook and the maids shared the other.

"I'm sure you will manage, Margaret. Now, I'd be glad of a cup of chocolate as soon as you have settled the child."

Lady Thornley turned away and picked up the newspaper she had been reading before her son came, and Margaret had no choice but to lift the stiff little figure of her ladyship's granddaughter into her arms and carry her from the room. The little girl made no protest but the maid didn't care for the blank look in her eyes. She turned back for a moment.

"What is her name, your ladyship?" she asked tentatively.

Her ladyship looked startled, then, "I'm sure I don't know. Now fetch my chocolate at once."

They arrived at the big house together, Sir Arthur in Noah Goodwin's carriage with Noah beside him, Clem Woodruff at the reins, and Archie Goodwin riding Plunger with Harry Preston mounted on Genette. Jackson opened the door to them and told them he would see if his master was at home, but as the three men, Sir Arthur, Noah and Archie strode into the wide hallway of Thornley Green, Lord Thornley himself lounged smilingly from the drawing-room, leaning against the door frame.

"Gentlemen, what can I do for you? I must say—"

"Never mind the pleasantries, Thornley," Noah said harshly. "We're come for my granddaughter who you kidnapped this morning and I've brought Sir Arthur Brown who you know is chief constable to back me up—"

"Where is she, Thornley?" Archie interrupted, in no mood to exchange verbal intercourse with his lordship or even for the politeness which Noah was doing his best to hang on to. The image of his wife struggling to rise from childbed determined to bring back the little girl who was so dear to both of them was still fresh in his mind and all he wanted was to get the child back so that his Beth could relax and have the rest to which she was entitled. He had a son in the nursery but Alex was his daughter, had been for two years, and the idea of this sod playing ducks and drakes with her for his own ends was exploding his brain to madness.

"Just a minute, Mr Goodwin," Sir Arthur interposed smoothly. "First let us ascertain whether Lord Thornley has the child and if so where he is keeping her."

"Never mind that, Sir Arthur," Noah roared. "I have two daughters, both of them brought to a pretty pass by this devil here and I swear that if—"

"Do not threaten me, Mr Goodwin, and let us not forget that the child, the little girl, is Lord Thornley's daughter and he has a perfect right to her. Now if it can be proved that her welfare is in doubt—"

With a bellow of outrage Archie Goodwin, all traces of his amiable, good-humoured gentleness vanished in an explosion of fury, launched himself at Hugh Thornley and brought him crashing to the floor. In a moment they were both up again, snarling their fury.

If he had deliberately devised a plan with the sole purpose of bringing Sir Arthur Brown to a decision he could not have made one more successful. With a sound like that of an enraged tiger the baron took a hold of Archie Goodwin and set about trying to kill him.

32

The men were so much taken by surprise that for several heart-stopping moments they stood paralysed, their mouths foolishly open, for though they knew Hugh Thornley was sharp-witted besides having a violent temper, the attack on Archie was totally unexpected. Although it had been Archie who had begun the set-to it was Hugh who carried it further. They had struggled away from the drawing-room door closer to the enormous fireplace. Archie had merely been driven to the edge of reason by Beth's distress and needed to knock some sense into Hugh Thornley, but before any of the spectators had moved Hugh had gripped the poker, used to stir the logs when the fire was lit, and clubbed Archie across the back of his head. He fell like a stone.

Sir Arthur was the first to come to his senses, although the clatter of feet up the stone steps heralded the arrival of Clem and Harry, brought to the scene by the sound of battle. Hugh had regained his feet and was brandishing the heavy poker and again they all hesitated, Sir Arthur holding out his hands to keep them back, for it was very evident that the baron had totally lost control. His face was the colour of a ripe plum and his eyes were streaked with blood, so great was his fury. He sprayed spittle at them as he spoke.

"Stay back the lot of you or I swear I'll brain this lout. Trespass, that's what it is. Bloody trespass and on top of that I'm attacked in my own hallway by this man who has no right being here. None of you has." He swayed on his feet, brandishing the poker like a club. At his back Jackson dithered, afraid to move lest it draw attention to himself, but the kitchen door opened and a small figure darted out, a boy with a thin face from which half-healed contusions and bruises were just beginning to fade.

" 'E bashed me, knocked me fer six an'—" But before he could say another word Hugh Thornley turned and with an obscene oath hit out at him with the poker. It caught him on the arm which he had thrown up to defend himself and they all heard the crack of bone. He cried out and fell just as the men, taking advantage of the confusion, surged forward in readiness to grasp his lordship.

"Get back," he roared, "or you'll be next."

"Really, this beggars belief. For God's sake, man, stop this at once," Sir Arthur bellowed. "This is barbarous. Stop it before you get in any deeper than you are." He turned to Harry and Clem who hovered at his back. "One of you ride like hell for the doctor. I don't know, the one who usually attends the family."

"Where is my granddaughter?" snarled Noah, moving menacingly towards Hugh who had backed away from the fallen man by the fireside, almost stumbling over the groaning boy, but Sir Arthur put a hand on Noah's arm and, though he was older than Noah, did his best to hold him back as it seemed he might be Hugh Thornley's next victim.

"Where is my son?" Hugh screeched. "Not to mention my wife, both of whom you removed from their home. Bring them back and you shall have the girl." As he moved backwards to the kitchen door, Clem, Noah and Sir Arthur inched forward, eager to get to Archie who lay like one dead on the great stone that formed the base of the fireplace.

"Do you imagine I would let any member of my family live in the same house as you?" Noah roared. "You're insane and should be locked up and the minute this is over I shall see to it that you are. Now where is my granddaughter?"

The sound of horse's hooves thundered from the front of the house and it was evident that Harry had obeyed Sir Arthur and was racing the mare, Genette, in the direction of St Helens and Doctor Bennett. Jackson, petrified for his own life, still stood in the hallway and as Hugh reached him he cowered back against the wooden panelling of the wall. He began to whimper, but with one last contemptuous look, his master brushed past him and fled through the kitchen towards the stable yard.

As one, Clem, Noah and the chief constable moved to kneel beside Archie, watching in horror as a small pool of blood began to form beneath his head.

"Christ Almighty," Noah moaned despairingly, "what will that swine do next?"

Hugh kept to the grass as he rode towards the dower house, for he knew that the sound of a galloping horse on the gravel drive would be heard in the big house and he wanted nobody to know in which direction he had gone. Jack Fell had retreated hastily as his master entered the stable, the poker still held in his hand.

"Saddle Ebony, quickly, man," his lordship barked, then, as though he had forgotten he was still holding it, hastily dropped the poker. Jack let out a sigh of relief as his master swung into the saddle and galloped towards the stable gate which he cleared with ease, for whatever else he was Hugh Thornley was a superb horseman. Jack wanted to run out and see where he had gone but he was too afraid, remaining where he was until Stan, the second groom, crept through the stable door and asked him in a whisper what was up.

"Nay, don't ask me, lad," Jack answered him. "But whatever it is it's bloody trouble."

As he had done an hour since, Hugh tethered his horse at the back of the dower house, racing through the kitchen and bursting into his mama's drawing-room so explosively that she cowered back in her chair, pricking herself quite savagely with her sewing needle.

"Hugh, what—"

"No questions, Mama. Where is the child?" His expression frightened her and she could barely speak.

"Child?" she babbled.

"Yes, for God's sake, the child I brought here an hour since. Where is she?"

"Well, I'm not sure. Margaret took her." But before she could continue he raced back to the kitchen and as the two women recoiled from him, for he was a frightful and frightening sight, he grabbed the first one and began to shake her.

"Where's the bloody child?"

"Oh, m'lord, I put her—"

"Where, woman, speak up?" Her head lolled on her neck and the cook put her hands to her mouth and moaned. His lordship must surely have gone mad, asking for the little girl who lay without movement in the bed she and Margaret shared. Blank-eyed with terror, poor little mite, she was, and could you blame her, being snatched away by this madman. They didn't know what the dickens was going on but they had done their best to comfort her, though she had not responded.

"She were that tired, m'lord," Margaret began but it seemed Lord Thornley was not concerned with that.

"Fetch her here," he snapped.

"But, m'lord, would she not—" Margaret began bravely but the savagery, the *madness* in his lordship's face stopped the words in her mouth and, leaving the kitchen, she ran up the stairs to the room she and Cook shared and picked up the comatose child.

"Where's he takin' yer, yer poor little dear?" she whispered, expecting no answer and getting none. "Wicked, wicked. Well, yer'll not be cold, wherever it is," for the little girl had arrived in only her frock. Slipping along the landing to the linen cupboard she brought out one of her ladyship's best blankets, soft wool bound in satin, and wrapped the child in it. "Dear God, what is ter happen to yer?" she asked despairingly, then ran down the stairs to the drawing-room and hesitantly handed his daughter to his lordship. Without a word, to her, or his mother, he ran back through the kitchen, the child held awkwardly to his chest. Climbing into the saddle, he settled her before him and then raced away towards the woodland that lay thickly at the back of the house.

The manhunt began at once. Every farm-hand, every labourer, every stable lad, every available man for miles around, their mouths hanging open in wonderment, were gathered at Thornley Green where, from the top of the steps, Mr Noah Goodwin, an important man in the community, told them they were looking for a dangerous man carrying a child. A dangerous man and a child! Who the bloody hell could that be? they asked one another and when they were told it was his lordship himself who had kidnapped his daughter, they were struck dumb. They had not been aware that a man could kidnap his own child, but it seemed Lord Thornley, who they all knew or had heard was wild and cruel, had done so.

The hunt began at the dower house, naturally, for his mother might have been persuaded to hide her son and though she had protested icily that she would allow no hobbledehoys to search her home, it was done nevertheless, from attic to cellar. Oh, yes, the weeping maid told them, she had been here, poor little thing, but his lordship had taken her and galloped off towards the dense woodland and with night coming on where would the child end up? At least she had a warm blanket about her, she told them, she had seen to that, throwing a defiant glance at her mistress. Mazed, she had been, the poor wee mite, like a little ghost and if she had—

"Thank you, Margaret," her mistress had said. "That will be

all. You can show these gentlemen to the door and then get back to your duties."

The maid and the gentlemen had no choice but to do as they were told.

It was about ten miles from St Helens to Liverpool as the crow flies. The horse and rider with his strange burden reached Tuebrook some time around midnight and from there the road ran past the Zoological Gardens and directly into the narrow warren of streets that made up the outskirts of the great seaport. The street he was looking for, Preeson's Row, was close to St George's Church, or so Monty had told him, and after several false turnings he found it off Lord Street, which was one of the main thoroughfares of the city. It was narrow, running through to Harrington Street, the houses tall, terraced, once the homes of influential merchants, and indeed it had been named after Alderman Preeson, a worthy of the city. The houses were well built, some slightly run-down but the one he sought was well kept and lamps shone from behind curtained windows. Railings fronted the house and steps ran down to what was evidently the basement. There was no sign of the house's true purpose!

Climbing down stiffly, for it was damned difficult to ride easily with the bundle he carried, he looped the animal's rein over the railings, ran up the steps and rang the bell. The door was opened by a gigantic black man dressed in the discreet outfit of a business gentleman. Black morning coat and trousers, a waistcoat, a stiff white collar and plain necktie. He said nothing, just blocked the doorway and waited.

"Is Mrs Smith available?" the gentleman on the doorstep asked impatiently, for he was eager to get himself and his animal off the street.

"She might be. 'Oo shall ah say's askin'?"

"Never mind my name. Just fetch her and hurry up about

it." He shifted his bundle from his left arm to his right and the black man thought he heard a tiny sound escape from it.

It so happened that the lady in question, Mrs Smith, if that was indeed her name, was just coming down the narrow staircase, herself dressed plainly in a black gown, totally unadorned, her grey hair pulled severely back into a knot at the back of her head, her smile kindly, the very picture of respectability. She might have been someone's grandmother, but the man who stood on her doorstep knew she was not. She had never married and though she might have become pregnant over the years in her profession, she had never given birth to a living child.

"What is it, Lemuel?" she asked the black man, walking slowly towards the door, her head slightly to one side as though wondering who on earth could be knocking at her respectable door at this time of night.

"A man, madam."

"So I see, and what, might I ask, do you want of me, sir? This is a private residence and it is past midnight so if you don't wish me to call a constable I would advise you to get off my doorstep."

"By all means, call the constable, *madam*! And let us see what the law has to say about a house such as yours."

"Sir, I think you have the wrong address and I would be obliged—"

"This is the address I was given by a certain acquaintance of mine who lives in St Helens and whose taste in female flesh, though it does not appeal to me, I believe you supply. He tells me you meet trains coming into Lime Street station and if it seems a young girl is uncertain of her destination – and there are many who come from the country looking for work – you are of enormous help to them. Shall I go on? I am quite happy to continue this conversation on your doorstep but I would prefer to discuss my business in private."

He smiled and Mrs Smith felt something move in her, just below her breastbone, something she had not known since her girlhood, her very *early* girlhood. It was not fear exactly but it was something she did not like. She was a woman who had known the worst kind of life and it had left her hard, cold, merciless, with the boldness needed in her line of work but she had the strangest feeling she had met her match in the man who stood on her doorstep. She had known men of all sorts in her trade but this one, with a scar on his cheek that gave him an even more sinister look, put an icy finger on her spine.

She stepped back. "You had better come in, sir," she said. Striding arrogantly over the threshold in that way the gentry had as though he were in his own home and had a perfect right to act as he liked, he followed her across the hall and into a pleasant room, warm and lit by several lamps. He did not look round. She indicated that he was to sit but before he did so he carelessly placed the bundle he was carrying on to a chair. The bundle appeared to be wrapped in a soft, white blanket edged with satin and, after a small movement, rather like a kitten escaping from a nest a small face emerged.

Mrs Smith showed no sign of interest. "May I offer you a whisky, sir, or perhaps a brandy?"

"A brandy," her visitor said abruptly, "and as quickly as you can. I have a train to catch."

"Of course." She passed him his drink then sat down and waited.

The man, obviously a gentleman by his clothes, his cultured tones and his manner, took a sip then placed his glass on a small table by his chair.

"I believe you run a business . . . well, not to put too fine a point on it, a brothel, and that you are always on the lookout for likely girls. My, er, acquaintance comes here once a week, he tells me, and you supply him with—"

"I can't imagine where your . . . acquaintance got this tale."

"Stop it, woman. I am not a man to be trifled with. His name is Sir Monty Soper and I don't give a damn how much trouble he gets into. I have . . . a child. He likes children, he tells me, not only because he is perverted but because they are virgins and cannot infect him. He had us all enthralled one night with tales of what goes on here. He is a rich man and twenty-five guineas is a mere nothing to him, which is what he pays you for a girl over ten years old, and up to a hundred for a child below that age. He spoke of strait-jackets, children strapped to beds, chloroformed, gagged and all kinds of activities which he seemed to relish. He said that you even have unwanted babies kept until they are old enough to perform . . . certain acts. Four or five years old, he told us. You are a procuress, madam, and if I were to go to the police I could have this place closed down, for this sort of trade causes disgust, horror and fury. Now, I require no payment but I have a child here who is . . . not wanted."

Mrs Smith glanced at the bundle and at the wan face that peeped from it. She was a sensible woman and she knew this man, whoever he was, could do just what he threatened.

"How old?"

"Two."

There was a long silence then Mrs Smith stood up. "Who does she belong to?"

"Me, but before we strike a bargain you should know she has a deformed leg."

"Let me see." The blanket was removed and the Honourable Alexandra Thornley was revealed in her pathetic, anguished state. She was wet, for it was many hours since she had been removed from her nursery and the sour smell of urine rose up. The woman did not seem to mind but the man took a disgusted step back. The woman studied her. She was a pretty little thing, or would be when she was bathed and dressed in one of the many costumes Mrs Smith kept for the titillation of her customers. Her hair was a mass of fluffy dark curls and her eyes enormous, fringed with long silky black lashes. They were as blue as the sapphires Mrs Smith had in her bedroom upstairs and exactly like the ones gleaming in the man's face. She was like a small, pale ghost except for her mouth which was a trembling rosy red. For a moment she was distracted by the thought of how much a certain wealthy and depraved gentleman of this city would pay to— Then she shook her head and moved away to the fire. The little girl began to sob broken-heartedly and uttered the first word she had spoken since being snatched from her home.

"Archie?" she asked anxiously.

"Who is Archie?"

"Dear God, woman, does it matter? Now, do you want this child or not?"

Mrs Smith seemed to consider while the man fidgeted and then drew out a fine watch from his pocket and looked at it pointedly.

"Very well," she answered, and the words were hardly out of her mouth before the man turned and made for the door. The black man opened it and the visitor leaped on to the back of his horse tethered to the railings and disappeared into the night.

Mrs Smith and Lemuel looked at the child in the chair, the black man seeming to take as much interest in her as the woman. Finally she spoke.

"I don't like this, Lemuel."

"No, missis."

"This child comes from a good home. Look at the quality of her clothes. Who is she and where did that bugger get her, and why? I don't like it at all. There could be a hue and cry and I want no coppers sniffing round here. I must have a think about

this, Lemuel. Get Josephine down here to see to her. We'll give
it a day or two and see what happens."

"Yes, missis."

Beth Goodwin fought like a cat in an alley to avoid the sedative
Doctor Bennett tried hard to give her, screaming that she
would be with her husband and if they sent for the chief
constable who happened to be downstairs to arrest her and
take her to gaol she would not be moved.

"Beth, Archie is concussed. He took a severe blow to the
head—"

"Took a severe blow to the head! He was hit with a poker by
that fiend and you make it sound as though it were nothing
more than— Get out of my way, Doctor Bennett. I will be by
my husband."

"Look, Beth, I have stitched his wound and he will recover.
He is a strong man and given a few days will no doubt be up
and about again. It is *you* who should be in bed. You have just
given birth and need to rest and—"

"Then I will rest here beside Archie. There is a truckle bed
somewhere and I promise to use it but how you can expect me
to rest when my husband is sorely wounded and my child in the
hands of that devil. Sweet Jesus, what is he doing to her? Where
is she, Doctor? Ask my father to come to me."

"He is out with the men, Beth, searching for Thornley. Half
the county is out looking for him, and for your daughter." It
seemed to be accepted that Milly and Hugh Thornley's child
was not theirs but belonged to Archie and Beth Goodwin. They
had brought her up for the past two years, ever since her birth,
cared for her and had themselves come to think of her as their
child. "Every barn, every hut and crumbling cottage, every bit
of woodland is being searched." It was feared that Lord Hugh
Thornley, surely needing to be confined to a lunatic asylum,
might well have hidden the child in some dense undergrowth

and left her to perish in his need for revenge. The Goodwins had his son so he had taken the child they loved. It didn't bear thinking about! In a way he was glad that the blow to Archie Goodwin's head had rendered him unconscious, for there was no doubt, stitches or no stitches, he would have been out with the men. It was growing dark and they would be forced to abandon the search soon and if the child was somewhere alone, deserted in an isolated spot, perhaps on the vast stretch of desolate moorland, she would not survive the night. The maidservant at the Thornley dower house had told them she had wrapped the little girl in a warm blanket but this was a baby you were talking about who, in her distress, would not have the sense to keep herself well wrapped up if left alone.

Doctor Bennett nodded to Mary Smith who was hovering at the window ready to jump to anyone's bidding, whatever it might be. There was a nurse, one of his own competent women, and even a midwife upstairs in the nursery, though the Goodwins' nursemaid, Jane, distraught over the loss of Alex, was guarding the new baby fiercely, only allowing the wet nurse near him. She knew her mistress had intended feeding the child herself but her milk had dried up and was it any wonder with all this going on.

Doctor Bennett moved slowly down the stairs and into the drawing-room where his own wife sat with Abby Goodwin. They both stood up as he entered the room. The chief constable had been in Archie Goodwin's study from where he had organised the manhunt but he followed Doctor Bennett into the drawing-room.

"How is Mr Goodwin?" he asked and both the women turned to look at the doctor.

"He'll do but I wish you could persuade Beth to rest, Abby." He sank down wearily into the nearest chair and his wife went across to him and took his hand, seating herself on the arm of the chair, resting her cheek on his white hair.

"I shall return to the station now, Mrs Goodwin," Sir Arthur said, turning to Abby. "I can do no more here but I need to alert every police station in the north to be on the lookout for the man and the child. Who knows where he has gone and I want every constable on the beat in every city and town and even village to be on the alert. My inspector will be here first thing in the morning to keep you up to date."

There was a clatter of horses' hooves at the front of the house and in the twilight several horses came to a halt at the bottom of the steps. Two of the men, Harry Preston and Clem Woodruff, gathered the reins of the tired animals and began to lead them round to the stables while the others, Olly, Reuben, Tommy and Clancy Morris, made their way to the kitchens where Mrs Kyle had ready an enormous pan of pea and ham soup, hot and nourishing for the men who had been out all day searching every covert, every stretch of woodland, under every bush and shrub, even in private gardens, looking for a blanket-wrapped bundle. Noah came tiredly into the drawing-room and at once, as Laura had done, Abby went to her husband, drawing him into her arms.

"You must rest, darling," she murmured. "Eat something, bathe and go to bed. It's too dark to search any more tonight. Tomorrow you can begin again."

It was as though a whirlwind had blown into the room, swirling about the occupants so that it was almost possible to see the movement of their clothing, frantic, frenzied, ready to blow them all this way and that, and for a moment they were stunned, speechless, paralysed by the pain of Beth Goodwin.

"Tomorrow," she shrieked. "Tomorrow may be too late. Who knows what the devil has done to her, or into whose hands he has put her? He is evil and would do anything to any one of us, even his own daughter to seek revenge. It was Hugh Thornley who consigned Mary and myself to the lock hospital. He told me so himself, did you know that? Did you? No, you didn't because I waited. Dear God, waited, hoping, I don't know what for." She sank to her knees and her mother moaned and moved to raise her to her feet but Beth bowed her head and wept desolately. "And now he has done this to us and it's my fault."

33

The constable adjusted his helmet to a somewhat jauntier angle than his sergeant would have liked, made some remark about the bloody weather to the man on duty behind the desk and, pushing the heavy door to behind him, stepped out of the police station into the black, wet night of Dale Street, telling himself that at least the weather would keep the riff-raff in whatever cellar they called home. He pulled his cape closer about his shoulders and was about to move down the steps to the pavement when a small sound alerted him that he was not alone in the tiled porch.

He glared about him, for if some vagrant was taking shelter on the steps of the police station he'd be inside and sharing a cell before you could say "Ducky Sam". The light from the street lamps cast shadows across the pavement and did not reach every corner of the entrance, and Police Constable Percy Lambert drew his truncheon as though expecting somebody to fly at him from the dark, but there was no movement though the tiny sound was repeated. What the bloody hell was it? Something crouching in a shadowed corner perhaps, and as his eyes adjusted to the darkness after the gaslight in the station he could just make out a small bundle in the far corner. So small as to be no danger to himself, he decided, as he took a hesitant step towards it. Was it a sackful of kittens or puppies, an unwanted litter born in a corner of some slum dwelling and chucked out? For the poor could barely feed themselves let alone a bloody pet! But then would a man or woman living in one of the rotting courts that backed on to the river bother to fetch them here to the police station? Hardly! The river was handy, or more likely a bucket of water carried from a standpipe.

The bundle seemed to twitch and a soft mewling sound came from it, frail and pitiful, and the constable took another step forward. So he was correct in his first thinking. It *was* kittens and what the devil was he supposed to do with them just as he was about to set off on his night duty patrolling the streets of Liverpool?

He bent down and with his truncheon drew aside the edge of the cloth that covered the bundle and nearly fell over backwards down the steps when a pale, forlorn little face peeped up at him. Well, he would hardly call it *peeped*, for the eyes in the face looked at nothing, dull, blank, unseeing, harrowed as though their owner had gone through some devastating experience which the child had blanked out as unbearable. The face was clean, though, and so was the mop of curly dark hair that fell over the forehead. It was a little girl, the constable thought, for he could see the edge of a frill at her neck and there was a bit of ribbon dangling from one curl.

"Bloody 'ell," he whispered, afraid to pick up the child lest he worsen the expression, or lack of it, in the child's face. "Bloody 'ell, chuck, what's bin done at yer? What the . . ." He was so agitated he here used an obscenity that he evidently thought totally inappropriate in front of a female, even one as young as this, for he put a hasty hand to his mouth and his young face moved in compassion. If it hadn't been for the fineness of the little dress he could just see in the darkness and the blanket in which the child was wrapped, he might have thought that some overworked mother had abandoned her child. But this was not one of these and, bugger it, he couldn't just leave her here, could he?

Slowly, gently, doing his best not to frighten her he leaned down and gathered the little girl into his arms, settling her gently against his shoulder, wanting to place a kiss on the thin cheek, for he had two children of his own, but he didn't want to alarm her any more than she had obviously already been alarmed. He turned and pushed his shoulder against the swinging door and re-entered the police station. The man behind the desk looked up as he entered, saying cheerfully, "Wha' yer got there, Perc? I thought yer'd be 'alfway up Dale Street by now."

Perc walked across the worn linoleum to the desk and very gently turned back the edge of the blanket, revealing the small face against his shoulder. "She were on't doorstep, Bert, an' where she come from is anybody's guess burr I think—"

Bert gasped. "Yer daft bugger. D'yer never read them notices what come in? All over't country they're looking fer a little lass and bugger me if I don't think yer've found 'er."

"How is she?" Milly asked, looking sympathetically at the little girl on Beth's knee, but her voice was impassive, casual almost, even though the child she spoke of was her own daughter. A stranger in the room might have been forgiven for thinking the child was not hers at all but belonged to the woman on whose lap she sat. She nestled her curly head against Beth's shoulder and when Beth dropped her arm for a moment she at once pulled it round her again, huddling like a fledgling bird against its mother. Her thumb was plugged firmly in her rosy mouth and her eyes stared blindly at something only she could see.

"As you see. It's been four weeks and she still won't be parted from me or Archie. She sleeps in our bed otherwise she'd waken the house with her cries. Even Jane has been abandoned and Alex loved her as much as she loved us. Of course, having Will in the nursery hasn't helped and the poor lamb is sadly neglected by his parents but then at five weeks I don't suppose he notices. Thank goodness he has Jane to cuddle him and that he seems to have an equable nature. As long as somebody holds him and smiles at him he's content. Doctor Bennett says Alex will recover, forget the experience as children do but it will take time and patience. She was apparently well looked after wherever she has been and was not abused . . . well, you will know what I mean considering who took her."

"And nothing has been seen or heard of him?"

"No. As you are aware Archie and Father between them have made Edge Bottom House and Lantern Hill into absolute fortresses. In fact I'm surprised he allowed you to ride over here at all."

"I know, but you should have seen the escort I had. I wouldn't have been surprised if he had ordered up a troop of cavalry to protect me. He insists I carry the pepperbox revolver he gave me at all times, even in bed. Just like the one he gave to you. He makes me practise every day and I must admit it's a lovely little thing, small enough to fit in my purse. But he could see I was losing my mind languishing at Lantern Hill like a prisoner in the tower so with Olly and Reuben armed with shotguns and Clem at the reins here I am. Miles is in the nursery and Todd is with him."

"Don't Mother and Father mind . . . about Todd, I mean? They've accepted him as Miles's father?"

"Oh yes, now that Hugh's been shown for what he is, not just by us but by the law and the community, Father has arranged for a lawyer to come to the house and talk about divorce. I have grounds now, you see, thanks to the changes in the law. I have not admitted that Miles is Todd's son, which would undoubtedly cloud the issue, but one day we will marry and probably leave the district. Todd is keen to go abroad and I must say the idea appeals to me as well."

The two sisters were drinking afternoon tea brought in by Mary and placed beside Lady Thornley, for it seemed Alex would not be moved to allow Beth to pour it. There was a plate of almond macaroons, cherry jam tartlets, coconut biscuits and light fairy cakes, for Mrs Kyle, impressed by their caller's status, always surpassed herself whenever Lady Thornley visited her sister. The child was offered a biscuit, but she turned her face away and pressed it into Beth's soft breast.

"You see how she is," she said worriedly. "She eats hardly anything. As God is my witness, Milly, if I had that swine here I swear I'd kill him with my bare hands, never mind the revolver in my pocket." Her voice took on a harsher note. "You know it was Hugh who lured Mary and then me to Longworth where we were taken to the lock hospital. It nearly killed me, sent me out of my mind."

"I know, sweetheart. Father told me, but don't upset yourself over it. Hugh Thornley isn't worth the breath you use to speak his name. He will be found and punished for what he has done to all of us. When I have my divorce—"

Beth bowed her head over Alex's curls and her voice was almost a snarl.

"I don't think I care about that, Milly. Do you imagine I like living like this, afraid of my own shadow, especially when Archie is out of the house? Every strange noise alarms me and now that spring is here I want to walk in the garden, go down to the paddock but I can't. I want security. I want revenge for myself, for this child, for my family, for you and Todd, for Harriet and Clem and all the people Hugh Thornley has tormented in the past three years, and I shall have it."

Milly leaned forward incredulously. "What are you saying?"

"You know what I mean, Milly." Beth lifted her head and stared challengingly into her sister's eyes. Milly had regained her looks in the two months since her father had brought her back to Lantern Hill, and so had Beth, who had lost more than a stone in weight during the week Alex was missing and Archie ill and confined to bed. But now they looked what they were, two ladies of quality dressed in the latest expensive fashion, Milly in her favourite vivid turquoise, an exquisite silk afternoon tea gown, sheath-like, tight in front, fuller at the back, falling to a short train of ruffles. Her hair, which had been cut short when she was ill after Hugh's last attack on her, had grown into a cap of tawny curls that drifted over her forehead and ears.

Beth wore cream, a gown very much the same style as her sister's but with an enormous bow in the same colour placed halfway down the back of the skirt. Her hair was piled somewhat carelessly on the top of her head, tied up with cream velvet ribbon with tendrils falling to her neck.

Milly sat back and carefully placed her cup and saucer on the table beside her. "Tell me."

The child in Beth's arms had fallen asleep. Beth stood up and with infinite tenderness placed her on the sofa, pulling a light woollen shawl about her while Milly watched, unmoved that her daughter should be cared for by another woman.

When Beth returned to her chair Milly repeated, "Tell me."

If Johnny and Muriel Cassell were surprised when Hugh Thornley arrived at the front door of their luxurious home at the end of March in a hired cab and with no luggage, they did not comment on it, and Hugh thanked God that the pair of them were as simple and good-natured as a couple of cows grazing in a meadow. Well, Muriel was a cow but by no stretch of the imagination could you call Johnny a bull, for there was not a scrap of meanness in him. His round face beamed as he welcomed his old school chum, leaping to his feet as his butler showed Lord Thornley into the great hall where he and several of his guests were lounging, the gentlemen smoking cigars and drinking brandy, the ladies sipping Madeira. Hugh knew them all, as they had been guests in his own home, attractive young ladies, attentive young gentlemen, the sort one found at somebody or other's home on Fridays to Mondays, eternal guests, moving from one stately home to another in their quest for entertainment. They were all wealthy, for only people with money could afford to gamble with the likes of the Cassells, the Thornleys, the Edwards from Northumberland, the Benthams from Cheshire, to move in their pleasure-seeking circle. Hugh, of course, since he married into the manufacturing class, though his wife rarely came with him, was now able to mix with them on the same financial footing.

As soon as he was able, Hugh drew Johnny to one side, a faintly apologetic smile on his face as he admitted to having been a naughty boy and forced to leave Lancashire in something of a hurry without even a change of clothing.

"You know how it is, old boy," he added with a winning smile. "The ladies, bless'em, don't understand the ways of a gentleman and I'm afraid I had a bit of trouble with . . . Well, I will mention no names but as you can see I am without even a dinner suit. I wondered if there was any possibility that your tailor in . . ."

"Lecicester?" interjected Johnny helpfully.

"Mmm, if I was to ride in early tomorrow do you think he would be able to fix me up with a few necessities? Just for a few days, you understand?" It went without saying that a gentleman, as well as a lady, would need to change into a suitable outfit several times a day. Riding, shooting, luncheon, dinner, even afternoon tea which the ladies took. Most tailors, as did many dressmakers, had garments half made up ready to fit to a gentleman.

"Of course, old chap, tell him I sent you and tonight you could perhaps manage with something of mine. We're pretty much the same build." He threw an affectionate arm about his old friend's shoulders. "Now come and greet the ladies. There's one here who I'm sure would like to renew your acquaintance." He grinned slyly.

"You don't mean?"

"I do, indeed." So Hugh Thornley settled down to what

promised to be a most enjoyable week or two when he would then move on to the home of another "old chum". He had so many he could probably spend the next six months without once having to return to Thornley Green when, he presumed, the trouble would all have blown over.

He had been there four weeks, to Johnny's amazement, as well dressed as any of Johnny's other guests who changed places every weekend, in outfits for which he had not paid. A casual lounge suit for day wear with what was known as a "Newmarket vest" in flannel with a plaid pattern and "peg-top" trousers, a more formal morning coat with pinstripe trousers, an evening jacket and trousers, breeches and tweed jacket since the "crowd" were fond of riding, though the hunting season was over. He had ready-made boots, a warm cover coat, which was really a thigh-length Chesterfield, and underwear of the finest wool.

He had been lucky at the card table so he had a few bob to jingle in his pocket and the "old acquaintance", who was replaced every weekend by another, had proved to be a pleasant partner in his bed, or hers, when Lieutenant Dicky Edwards, back from India with his regiment and with a few weeks' leave coming to him, rode up the grand driveway of Johnny and Muriel's home and was greeted with great delight by all and sundry. Dicky was not as wild as Hugh, who could prove a bit of a handful at times, but a likeable fellow and popular with the ladies. He greeted Hugh with astonishment.

"I'm surprised to see you here, old chap," were his first words as the butler took his cape and top hat, for Dicky had not come in his uniform.

"Oh, and why is that, Dicky?" Hugh asked pleasantly, drawing deeply on his cigar, then lifting his glass to the butler to be refilled.

"Well, with all that trouble at home." Dicky knew, of course, that Hugh's wife had returned to her family home, the rumour being that her health had been ruined by her husband and it was common knowledge that Hugh's daughter had been virtually abandoned by him and Milly. Some problem with her leg, it was said, but her sister and brother-in-law had adopted her, which seemed strange to everyone except those who knew Hugh and Milly. But then it was perhaps not so strange considering Hugh Thornley's character.

"What trouble is that, old boy? I have been staying with Johnny for a few weeks now, haven't I, Johnny?" smiling with great charm at his host. "Have I missed something exciting?" he went on, his smile fixed, but Dicky saw something strange move in Hugh's eyes, a sort of shadow and yet it gleamed with a light he was not sure he liked.

"Have the police not been in touch with you?" Dicky frowned. "In view of the fact it concerns your own family."

"The police! Dear God, Dicky, what on earth are you talking about? Everything was quite normal at home when I left and I fail to see—"

"It seems your daughter was kidnapped, Hugh."

"Kidnapped! Good God!"

Dicky was conscious of the sudden hush that had come over the room as everyone stopped talking to listen to this exchange between himself and Hugh. He didn't know what it was but there was a strange atmosphere, a tension, an unexplained and yet definite sense of unease. Why that should be he didn't know, but then Hugh was known for his total lack of morality, his wildness, his contempt for the law and there was an odd expression on his face, which puzzled him.

"Aren't you going to ask what happened, Hugh?" Dicky asked quietly.

"Of course, old man. I'm just baffled as to why I haven't heard of it. But then Johnny is rather cut off here and seems to regard newspapers as—"

"Thankfully she has been found and returned to her family."

"Who has?"

"Your daughter. That is who we are speaking of, isn't it?"

Hugh leaped to his feet and the hush deepened, and for some reason the ladies drew back in their chairs and the men exchanged glances.

"I'd best get home then," Hugh told them, smiling round at the circle of curious faces. "Really, it seems I can go nowhere—"

"When did you leave St Helens, Hugh?" Dicky asked casually, and again the expression on Hugh's face changed and his eyes narrowed with some menace. But he did his best, it seemed, to keep that ferocious temper of his in check, his smile fixed like that of a gargoyle.

"Do you know, Dicky, I'm not sure I like your tone. Are you inferring that I have had something to do with this . . . this escapade?"

"Escapade! What a strange way to describe the kidnapping of your own child, Hugh. It seems to me—"

"I don't give a damn what it seems to you, Dicky, and if you'll step out of my way I'll get packed and be—"

"Perhaps it might be best if—"

With a snarl Hugh raised his fist and smashed it into Dicky's face, knocking him to the ground. One lady screamed and the gentlemen rose as one from their seats, but with an oath Hugh Thornley ran from the room. Dicky was picked up from the carpet where he lay dazed and bloody, and gently led to a chair. Johnny called for a brandy and as they stood round him in a sympathetic circle the sound of a horse galloping madly on the driveway floated in through the window.

"That was Dicky Bentham on the telephone," Noah said, as he came back into Abby's drawing-room. His voice was cold and dangerous, and both his wife and daughter felt a chill slide down their spine. They were sitting before the fire, for though it was officially spring the wind was cold, whistling round the house and flattening the tulips and daffodils Frank and Jack had planted last back end. The curtains were drawn and the lamps lit and they had been enjoying an after-dinner drink, Noah a brandy, the ladies a light Madeira, when Ruby, who had been persuaded to answer the dratted instrument despite feeling it was somehow connected to the devil himself, had called her master to the telephone.

"Dicky Bentham? You mean that friend of . . . of?"

"The same."

"But what did he want, darling? I thought he was in India with his regiment." There was a tremor in Abby's voice, as she knew there was some drama unfolding.

"He was but he has returned and had gone up to see that chap in Leicestershire." He turned to Milly. "You'll know who I mean, lass."

"Johnny Cassell. A friend of Hugh's."

Noah sat down heavily and reached for his wife's hand as he always did when there was trouble. "Aye, that's him. Anyway, Hugh was there—"

Milly sprang to her feet and was already making her way towards the door into the hall, her first thought for her son, Todd's son, because it seemed no deed was too heinous for Hugh Thornley to commit.

"Nay, sit down, girl. That bugger had only just left Cassell's place so he won't be here – that's if he's coming here – for a while yet. Now we know where he got to when he left. Hiding with friends. I'm surprised Sir Arthur didn't check his known associates. Anyway, Bentham said he was in a tearing rage. Hit Dicky and felled him, then galloped off on Cassell's best hunter! So I've telephoned Sir Arthur and Archie to warn them to be on the lookout and the police will be here within the hour to patrol the grounds and those at Edge Bottom House. God knows what's in that bastard's mind but you can be sure it will be something nasty. There'll be no sleep tonight for any of us. Now I must go and check that all the men have their weapons loaded. The windows will need—"

"Dearest, I'm sure they are prepared for anything, the times you and Archie have been over it all. There isn't one who wouldn't gladly kill him after what he did to Alex, not to mention what he inflicted on Milly. I would like to shoot him myself."

"Darling." Noah turned tenderly to his wife. "There is no way that man could get into the grounds, never mind the house but . . . well, I know you don't like it but I'm glad you agreed to keep that revolver handy."

They were looking at each other, managing a smile, both of them doing their best to comfort the other, and neither of them noticed the expression on their daughter's face. They would have been seriously alarmed had they done so.

34

The man rested comfortably in the fork of the enormous hawthorn, his back against one branch, his right foot bracing himself against another. The tree, left to itself in the secluded and protected woodland at the back of Noah Goodwin's property, had grown to forty feet, its canopy smothered in clusters of white. It was May and the blossoms, called May blossoms for obvious reasons, were so densely packed together the man was totally hidden from view even from someone walking the path directly beneath him. He was dressed in a rather worn working man's jacket of nondescript tweed in shades of brown, old trousers, a knitted jersey beneath the jacket, riding boots under the legs of the trousers and a wide-awake hat which was pulled well down over his forehead. In his hand he held a pair of binoculars which he put frequently to his eyes and swept the park, the vegetable gardens, the paddocks and the back of the house. His patience seemed inexhaustible. This was the fifth day he had taken up residence in the tree.

The dwarf elms and beech hedges along the south side of the property were full of nesting thrushes, blackbirds, tits and finches, for after the long winter the land was renewing itself. The sun had warmth in it, capturing the magic of spring. There were drifts of bluebells under the burgeoning canopies of the trees and trailing clusters of primroses nestling in the roots of the ancient oak tree, but the man neither saw them nor heard the song of the birds. The scent of wild flowers and pine sap filled the air but the man did not smell it. His attention barely wavered from the movements of men on the far side of the park. Frank Jones and Jack Martin, gardeners at Lantern Hill, were busy directing a couple of lads loading two wheelbarrows with what, through his binoculars, he thought might be compost but he wasn't sure and, besides, didn't care. He had never been concerned with gardens or the labour put in to keep them immaculate. His own had improved beyond measure in the last couple of years but he took little interest.

In the paddock a groom was exercising a little chestnut mare and he could hear the faint sounds of his encouraging voice floating across the park. A shrivelled little man who was apparently mending a break in the paddock fence stopped to watch the mare, then resumed his work, hammering at something with an enthusiasm that defied his years. There were two dogs lying in the grass outside the paddock fence, both with their muzzles on their paws, well-bred labradors with glossy coats and when one suddenly raised his head and stared across the park in his direction, he hastily lowered his binoculars. The dog stood up and sniffed the air then, satisfied that all was well in the territory he protected, lay down again and dropped his nose to his paws.

As though on cue a police constable in uniform strolled round the corner of the house, his tunic and trousers immaculate, the brass buttons on his tunic and his number on the collar gleaming in the sun, his helmet plate just as well polished. His belt glowed a deep brown against his blue uniform. Like all the constables in Sir Arthur Brown's force he was well turned out, the only difference between this one and those on the beat in the streets of St Helens the revolver strapped to his belt. He sauntered over to the paddock fence, leaning his forearms on the top rung, watching the groom and the mare, then he stooped to fondle the dog's ears. He spoke to the groom and they both laughed.

The man in the tree smiled, for it was as he thought. As the days went by the men set to guard Noah Goodwin's property were becoming careless!

There was no more activity. The constable strolled on, disappearing round the other corner in his circuit of the house, enjoying the warm sunshine and apparently pleased to have such a light duty.

For several hours, until the sun began to lose its warmth and the day its light, the man kept to the hidden branches of the tree. He withdrew a packet from a pouch he had with him and ate the contents, then took a swig from a bottle that appeared to contain wine, but his concentration on the house never wavered.

At last, as the sun set over the roof of the house, he climbed down from the tree, after making absolutely certain that he was alone. He stretched, for he had been hiding for the better part of eight hours, then set off in an easterly direction towards the woodland's edge where a fine horse was tethered. It whinnied a welcome and when the man climbed on its back, would have set off at a rare old pace, glad to be out of the fast darkening wood. The man calmed him, then walked the animal to where a gap had been made in the hedgerow. The gap was not visible until the man tugged at the undergrowth, then, after moving through it, closed it up carefully behind him.

He picked his way along a dusky lane, crossing the railway line, turning to the left where a signpost pointed towards Denton Green. A twisting leafy lane and there was a cottage standing on its own, a cottage with a small vegetable garden to the side, hens softly clucking and a dog that barked ferociously.

"Is that you, Hughie?" a female voice asked anxiously from a lighted doorway to the back of the cottage.

The man winced at the diminutive. "Who else? Now just let me put the horse in the shed and I'll be in. I'm starving, and not just for food."

The female giggled and moved inside the cottage. She

climbed the narrow staircase to the small bedroom and lay down on the bed, first removing her drawers, pulling up her skirt and opening her legs wide. This was what her new lodger liked, she had found that out in the last week or two, and was quite happy to oblige in view of the rent he paid her. Ever since her Benny had been killed in a farm accident last year it had been an uphill struggle to keep body and soul together for her and Natty, the son born to her and Benny before the threshing machine had got him, and thank God they'd only had the one! Farmer Castle had allowed her to stay on at the tied cottage for the time being, since she worked in Mrs Castle's kitchen, but these few bob from the gent who had stopped at her gate and asked her politely if she knew of any lodgings was a bloody Godsend. And he was a right one in bed as she had found out the first night he had moved in. He'd made no bones about what he wanted, lusty and demanding and, as it was a year since she'd lost her Benny, and being a strong lusty lass herself, she'd made no objection. Mind you, he had hurt her a time or two and had even hit her when she'd refused to lie on her front with her arse in the air in order to take him like a bitch takes a dog, but she had acceded and it hadn't hurt that much. For five shillings a week she'd have done anything to satisfy his strange needs. She didn't know where he went all day and had asked only once to her cost. It was best not to question him, she had found out. She knew he was a gent, though he dressed like a farm labourer, but Dorrie Fielding, while intrigued, was very smitten and perhaps, if she played her cards right . . .!

It was almost the end of June when Sir Arthur decided that he could no longer spare the men needed to guard Lantern Hill and Edge Bottom House against possible threat from Lord Thornley. He had not been seen in the vicinity since he had taken his baby daughter three months ago and the chief constable privately decided that his lordship had taken himself off, perhaps even abroad, staying with friends, of whom he had a great many and who would not know of his crime. The kind of people he mixed with were constantly on the move: Henley, Cowes, Newmarket, Biarritz, anywhere there was excitement to fill their pampered lives. Lord Thornley, though he had no money, or so Noah Goodwin told him, since he had given instructions for the account in his daughter's and son-in-law's name to be closed, was an expert card player and would not find it hard to take money from his friends and was probably living the life of old Riley.

"I'm not happy about this, Sir Arthur." Noah frowned. "That man's a tricky bastard and he hates me and my family with an intensity tinged with madness. You know that. What normal man would kidnap his own baby daughter and abandon her as he did?" For they knew nothing of Mrs Smith and Preeson's Row. "And as for what he did to my daughter, his own wife, well, it doesn't bear thinking about. He went to a great deal of trouble to incarcerate my other daughter, Mrs Archie Goodwin, in the lock hospital, which experience nearly drove her out of her mind. If her husband had not been the decent man he is—"

"Yes, Mr Goodwin, I appreciate that, but there is no proof that it was Lord Thornley who had your daughter arrested," Sir Arthur began, but one look at Noah Goodwin's face stopped his words and he merely bowed his head. "Nevertheless, I'm afraid I must withdraw my men. As long as your own menservants keep a keen watch and, though I shouldn't say it, are well armed, your family should be safe. Perhaps if Mrs Goodwin and her children moved from Edge Bottom House into Lantern Hill for a while, just until we are sure Lord Thornley really has quit the district, then there would only be one establishment to keep an eye on. Her menservants could be added to yours, but then I'm pretty sure Lord Thornley has given up his vendetta. In the meanwhile please telephone me in need and if it will make you feel any better I will have one of my constables come out once a day to check on things."

Noah Goodwin had no choice but to agree.

Lantern Hill was a large house and moving in Archie Goodwin's family presented no problem. A suite at the top of the house had been turned into a nursery to accommodate three children and with Jane and a young nursery-maid called Bessie they all settled in, though only for a week or two, Beth proclaimed firmly. She did not for a moment believe that Hugh Thornley had left the district, since his vicious nature would not allow him to forget what he believed had been done to him. The Goodwins had taken his wife, his son, and, more importantly, his source of cash to which he had grown accustomed, forcing him to rely on his friends, if that was what he was doing, for the very bread in his mouth. They had all been questioned, those in the neighbourhood who had crowded the grandeur of Thornley Green at balls and parties and weekend "Friday to Mondays", even Alicia Bramhall who was known to have been his mistress and whose aristocratic husband had done his best to show the police inspector the door.

It had been reported that Hugh Thornley's magnificent ebony gelding had been stolen from the Thornley stables and who else but Hugh would have taken him, Stan Hartley and Jack Fell said to one another. Star was so spirited even they, experienced riders as they were, were scared to get on his back so wherever he was the gelding was with him, they were sure of that.

One benefit the temporary move to Lantern Hill had given them was the growing return to normalcy of the bright little girl who was beginning to be known as Alexandra Goodwin. Beth and Archie were going ahead with plans to adopt her, with Milly's consent, of course, and as the weeks passed she began to cling less and less to Beth and Archie. The cause of this joy was Miles Thornley, or Michael Woodruff as he was to be known, who, at fifteen months had inherited his father's capacity for laughter, for fun, and his cheerful nature and winning ways, his affection for everyone in his baby life enfolded his half-sister in its warmth. She had never played with a child before and though he was a year younger than she was, he led her away from her fear and the terrible ordeal she had experienced and into the untroubled world of the child. He walked early and went everywhere at a tumbling run, expecting her to do the same, delighted to have a playmate. He chattered to her all day long and strangely she seemed to understand him, doing what he did, trusting as he did, even allowing Todd, who came every day now to see his son, to pick her up and swing her round as he did Miles. Archie was quieter with her, reading to her, painting, sitting at the table or the piano until Miles whisked her away to play lions and tigers, which Archie had read about to them. The baby Will at three months old did his best to sit up and watch them in their games, squealing in frustration, laughing when they did though he didn't know why. The noise from the top of the house seemed to lay a balm on the troubled souls of those who guarded them.

But it was summer now, high summer and Frank and Jack's herbaceous borders were at their peak, old cottage peonies with huge blowsy blooms in rich satiny crimson shades, spires of delphinium of blue and purple, larkspur, pinks, cornflowers, Canterbury bells and night-scented stock and the last of the wallflowers which were unequalled in their perfume and their velvet blossoms. The rose garden was Abby's favourite where she sat with Harriet breathing in the scent of Rosa Mundi, both sewing on some little garment, watching their grandchildren, one of whom they shared, darting up and down the crazy paving path with Bessie the young nursery-maid, with one of the men, Olly Preston, his son Harry, Tom or Clancy, in hot pursuit, the men with revolvers handy, for Mr Goodwin would flay them alive if they took their eyes for a moment off his grandchildren. Will would be propped up in his perambulator, Jane ever watchful at his side, doing his best to join in their games with excited arm movements and shouts of joy every time they ran past him.

Milly and Beth stood in the window of the bedroom shared by Beth and Archie and watched the activity. They were dressed in an odd assortment of clothes, men's trousers held up with tightened leather belts, grey collarless shirts with a brightly coloured neckerchief tucked in the throat, and held in their hands a shapeless cap of the sort worn by labourers. They wore jackets made from some rough material, the only flaw in their outfits, boots that might have been seen on a servant girl.

"We're sure to be stopped, Milly. If one of the men sees two unidentified chaps crossing the park don't you think he's going to be suspicious? They all know one another and where each of them is supposed to be."

"If we keep to the wall of the vegetable garden, where it's shadowed, we should manage to get to the woods without being seen. The woods are only a hundred yards away and once we're in there we can't be seen from the house. Besides, the men have become complacent, we've both noticed that. How far did we get yesterday without being challenged? All the way past the greenhouses and we were dressed in our usual clothes. We have planned this for weeks now, Beth, and you know it's the only way. I have lived with Hugh and been . . . well, let's say I know him better than anyone and I can assure you he's not far away. He'll make us pay for what we're doing and he can only carry out his vengeance from the district around here. I would bet on my own life he's hanging around, well hidden, waiting for the chance to do us some mischief. *Mischief!* Ha, that's a laugh."

Milly turned away from the window and her face was shadowed with remembered pain. Her eyes became unfocused, a dull, smoky brown and she put her hand to her mouth as though to hold in a sound that, once out, would frighten them all.

Beth turned with her and put her arms about her sister and Milly reached for her. For a moment they stood in the circle of one another's arms, their foreheads pressed together, then they parted and became businesslike.

"It's the only way, dearest," Beth told her. "Just as we have discussed. We can't continue to live like this, in fear for ourselves, our family, our children."

"We don't even know if he's there . . ."

"Oh yes, *I* do. It's where we both fell under his Machiavellian spell. Besides, we know his horse has been taken and who else would steal him but Hugh? He's watching this house for his chance and to get from wherever he's hiding to Lantern Hill he needs a horse. He's here and I think I know where."

"You're right. Let's go."

He saw the two men approaching the woodland. In fact he had watched them move around the perimeter of the stable yard, the vegetable gardens and the greenhouses and then walk rapidly across the hundred yards from there to the woods. He watched with great interest, even smiling, for his arrogance would not allow him fear. They were not the menservants Noah Goodwin employed to guard the place as those men walked about openly, their guns over their shoulders. One of the men had a two-handled saw, the kind that woodsmen use and the other an axe. He could hear them talking to each other and one of them laughed gruffly.

Although they did not seem to be looking for anyone in particular he thought he had best hide himself in the hawthorn tree until they had finished whatever it was they had come to do.

"Did 'e say just saplin's, Mick?" one asked the other and

though from where he hid the man couldn't see them he could hear them crashing about like the half-witted dolts they were.

"Aye, ses 'e wants undergrowth cleared."

"Nay, can't see sense in it, me."

"Nor me, bu' yer know what gentry's like."

They were moving further and further away from him and he was tempted to climb down and see where they were going, for if they found Star tethered to the oak tree on the edge of the wood they would, despite being clod-pated as the lower classes were, run and raise the alarm. He decided to stay where he was for the moment, convinced that if they did find his animal he could soon talk them out of taking any action. The simple minded were so easy to outmanoeuvre!

Beth and Milly found the beautiful animal at once, tethered to an oak tree just inside the edge of the woodland. Hugh hadn't even tried to hide him in the dense undergrowth, his puffed-up sense of his own invincibility making him careless. He had been coming here almost every day for three months, waiting for he knew not what, but sure that whatever it was he would recognise it at once and know exactly what to do. A chance to hurt, to kill even, to wreak his vengeance on the family who had ruined him, for he was sure by now that all his friends knew what he had done to his own child. Not that he cared, but there would be a chance, if he was patient enough, to put it all to his advantage.

He heard the two men, still yammering in that rough way the lower classes used to converse with one another, coming his way and he leaned out slightly to watch them go by as they would be sure to do as they tried to make up their stupid minds where to start. He put his hand on a small branch to steady himself and when it snapped under his hand, falling a few feet, at once both men stopped and turned towards the tree.

They did not speak but as though one had given a command to the other they both removed their caps and the tawny hair they had inherited from their mother fell richly about their shoulders, lit by the sunlight that slanted through the branches.

They stood stock still and looked up into the tree, their faces expressionless.

He couldn't help but laugh as he swung himself down to the ground. He leaned his back against the trunk of the tree, both hands in his pockets and looked from one face to the other, unafraid, contemptuous, his eyes like blue flames between his narrowed lids, his incredibly long eyelashes ready to tangle together. He was so handsome. So sure of himself, even in the rough working man's clothes once belonging to Benny Fielding that he had taken from the woman.

"Well, well, well, if it isn't the Goodwin girls," he drawled.

They were the last words he ever spoke, for Milly and Beth at once drew their revolvers from their pockets and shot him, one through the heart, the other between the eyes, just as they had practised. They did not speak to him, or to one another, again as they had practised, for what had they to say to the man who had done his best to ruin not only their lives but those of their children.

Returning their revolvers to their pockets, they left him where he lay, walking out of the shadows into the sunlight.

"We had many a fight but I shall miss her."

"She's done the right thing, darling. There are too many appalling memories here for her, besides which the old lady would have caused trouble over the boy. He's Todd's son, not Hugh's and needs to be brought up away from the Thornley influence."

Beth sighed and leaned her head on her husband's shoulder, the firelight casting shades of gold across their pensive faces. She took his hand and, bringing it to her lips, kissed it tenderly.

"I know you're right, but Mother and Father were dreadfully upset at the quayside."

"They can go and visit them as soon as they're settled. Noah was planning a trip as we were coming back on the train."

"Was he?" Beth smiled. "And was Mother agreeing with him?"

"When did you ever know your mother to stand in your father's way?"

"New York! The new world. A new life for them and Michael and the child. She has confessed to me she already has one inside her."

"What!" Archie yelped as he sat up and stared at her, then began to laugh. "Isn't that just like Milly? She never gave a damn for the conventions but I do think she might have waited until after the wedding ceremony."

"I believe it was Todd who . . . I was going to say instigated it, but I'm sure Milly was not unwilling and the child will be born in wedlock though how they managed to get together with Father's men guarding our every move I'll never know."

But then she and Milly had managed to evade her father's men, her wandering mind whispered to her as she pulled Archie back beside her and leaned into his embrace. They had done what needed doing and because of it their future, hers and Milly's and the children's, stretched out before them in a long road of peace and security.

There was silence for a while as they both stared into the flickering flames. They could hear Ruth humming to herself from across the hall as she cleared the dinner table and the dog who lay curled on the rug before the fire raised his head as an owl hooted somewhere in the woods at the back of the house. He listened for a moment and Beth watched him, remembering how not so very long ago she would have wondered what it was he had heard, then he lowered his muzzle to his paws and blinked into the fire. Upstairs her children slept in the nursery and before the nursery fire Jane kept watch. It was a habit they had all acquired and one hard to break, even though the one who had caused their watchfulness was dead, killed by two bullets from an unknown assailant's gun. Hugh Thornley had a number of enemies and it could have been any of them, as Sir Arthur Brown had said at the time, implying that the police were not going to great lengths to find the culprit. Only the family knew the truth!

She sat up and yawned. "And Milly's not the only one," she said casually.

"What does that mean?" Archie asked sleepily.

"To be with child."

"Oh, and who?" He sat up with a jerk and his face was a picture of astonishment.

"Archie, sometimes you can be remarkably obtuse. We have been rather busy in that department since we came home. Now then, come to bed, for we have an early start in the morning if we're to catch the London train. Just think, this time next year we shall have an addition to our family and our girl will be walking properly if Doctor Mackintosh keeps his word. So close your mouth, Archie Goodwin, and take me to bed."

AUDREY HOWARD

REFLECTIONS FROM THE PAST

'No man will ever take what is mine . . .'

When Abby Murphy discovers she's heiress to one of St Helens' largest glass works, her whole life is turned upside down. Torn from her poverty-stricken family and forbidden to see her childhood sweetheart, Roddy Baxter, she is forced by her tyrannical grandfather to become a lady.

Then Roddy disappears and soon, it seems inevitable that Abby will have to marry her grandfather's chosen successor, Noah Goodwin, and bear his children. Trapped in a marriage where she is little more than a possession, Abby is determined that no matter what else might change, nothing will stand in the way of her steadfast passion for Roddy.

But is she prepared to give up everything she has now for a love from the past?

HODDER